ON KEEPING WOMEN

ON KEEPING WOMEN

HORTENSE CALISHER

ARBOR HOUSE
NEW YORK

Second Printing

Copyright © 1977 by Hortense Calisher

All rights reserved, including the right of reproduction
in whole or in part in any form.
Published in the United States by
Arbor House Publishing Company
and in Canada by Clarke, Irwin & Company, Inc.

Library of Congress Catalogue Card Number: 77-79531

ISBN: 0-87795-169-1

Manufactured in the United States of America

JACKET FROM A DRAWING BY HENRI MATISSE

Contents

TOUCHING UPON YOUTH

"Don't never forget you come from a harbor city!" the father would say, walking his brood of brother and sister down to the end of the pier, early of a spring evening, and standing there with his eyes as satisfied and his hands as pat on his stomach as if he'd just fished this out of the water, like a dirty pedigree. The self-congratulation of city-dwellers is endless, they say, and never worse than when the city is New York.

So be it sister. That's how you came to have it. And to be ruined by it. If ruin was to be lying as she was, a nude body in moonlight, on the riverbank just across the road from her own house, in the beautiful zoned village of Grand River, on the Hudson an hour due north of that harbor, on the river's opposite shore. Would it get up, this body, toward morning, to creep whitely across the road again, through the door and back into the last eighteen years? Or would it continue to lie there, breasts rising and falling in the red sun—and for age thirty-seven not uncomely—until the first commuter bus, passing at six-forty daylight saving, reports to itself a woman's body with a face not unknown to it—"My God, isn't that Lexie, *Ray's* wife?" lying at almost eye-level on the dais of the riverbank—"Not their property even . . . They have river rights, though . . ." and no, not dead—"No, it moved . . . What a thing for the children!"—but alive, uncommonly alive?

Hush now; quiet as the body seems, the riverbank it lies on is slipping its moorings, heading downstream like those coal-barges on which a deckhand is never seen, to wash in perhaps just at sunset, twenty-odd miles on and almost as many years back—at the Morton Street pier.

"There you are, boys and girls," her father said. "Cargo always coming in."

There wasn't a spar on the rosy water, but we knew what he meant, James and I. Down under the unused pier, watery light clambered over the cold green fur on the poles that held us. Across the harbor, Jersey—or the rim of it that was really our Palisades, marred by a few factory-stacks and the brokenly gilded windows of what must be Weehawken—looked more content than it could possibly be. Except for the fact that it was looking at us. At that hour, alone for the moment on a dead-end jetty in the part of town that was still called "the Village," and as close to the slabbery Hudson as three seals on a rock, we *were* the city. And felt the responsibility, like any family who'd cut short dessert in order to stroll out there and accept that grandly yellow sky for all the rest of them still in their houses. Which we did for free, as their city-authorized agents. Who else but us knew so well the cycles here?—how, now that the ballplayers and ropeskippers were gone for the day, the boys with the knives would be returning later to be our muggers and cruisers, alongside the heavier clans who'd lasted through spaghetti and more, and would shortly be out, breathing anisette into the dark and walking that dog which deposited the largest

· 4 ·

turds in the neighborhood, while the poncho'ed young couples would be wheeling those grasshopper strollers in which the thin, bargain-cheap babies sat as stiffly awake as racing-car drivers. Next to arrive would be the lovers of any age, sex or duration, either flopping about in the dark or stilled by it, all like fish on the same hook. Followed by the after-midnight vomiters, coughing it up. Who else but us knew the cycles here? Why they did, all of them. And when we three were unable to get here, acted as agents for us.

We three were maybe elite in our persistence, coming on all evenings except rainy ones—although the energies that pushed father, brother and sister to that joint walk were not the same. Father's "Don't never!" was humorous, the kind of double-negative indulged in by a college graduate who, as an exchange-scholar in history, had seen the world—and Aberystwyth, Wales—but had declined into advertising later. He was at this time editor of a "house-organ" (or company newspaper) for a large, second-rate industrial firm with a name which sounded like *Western Electric* but wasn't, and a plant located across the river, in back of those same Palisades.

Even our mother never properly remembered the many companies who successively employed our father, their names always compounded of prefixes and suffixes like *Therm, Aero* and *Dyne,* to signify the elements these outfits were geared for, and always faintly disagreeable to her and us. The current name held our daily destiny, or half of it, in its robot-like palm, yet we and it never met, and there probably wouldn't be time to. My father had solved this for himself by calling each place *The Plant.* He was a faithful worker, usually not too overqualified for the jobs he held in their publicity or promotion departments, but maybe too well-liked by his colleagues ever to be a threat—and so always the first to be let go. His weakness was that he wasn't working at what he would really like to, but never quite found out what that was. The plant found that out, every time. His compensation, over and above salary, was that even when working in New Jersey, or once as far away as Philadelphia, from which he'd sternly commuted without ever mentioning this to family friends— he'd always kept the city and us together.

At this time "the sunset advantages", as he liked to say—or "the sunrise" as the case might be—were available to him "both coming and going", since he at the moment was traveling to the plant via the West Shore Railroad, and the ferries to Manhattan which then connected it. Each evening he described to us how the New York skyline had looked as approached that dusk: "My God, tonight it was like a grail!" Often for my mother's benefit adding hints of what the United Fruit Company, near where the ferry docked, was stocking. "Bananas, like a jungle!" Or "Tangerines, hon, get some, hunh? They must be cheap." Now and again he told us how much wilder a scarlet the ferries had been when he was a boy down here, and how old Italian men, gruff but winsome, had played the violin on them.

The house we then lived in (after a descent from East Eighty-eighth Street during a lapse in funds) was a brownstone much like the one he'd grown up in, the same few blocks from the river, and we had rented a similar ground floor.

"Well, let's go; let's say 'Good Evening' to the evening!" he'd cry, after a spoonful of one of the boxed puddings my mother put to set the minute she came home from work—and we two always went. Once there, he made it clear that the sunset was the least of our advantages. "With this city at your back—" he'd sigh, and never finish. But we knew the end of that sentence: we could do anything, go anywhere.

"Which way is Paris, which way to Hong Kong?" we'd ask when we were younger, and he'd always pointed the same way, down the harbor. And the same hand scooped us back. Oh we wanted to travel; who didn't? But when we got there, wherever it was, we'd always know we'd be its equals.

Our mother never came on these jaunts. A city social worker for eighteen years by then, promoted to supervisor for the last five, she alleged that she could see "old Gotham" and all her advantages just by rocking in her rocker—her feet up on a hassock, her salt-and-pepper hair loosed from its bun onto her shoulders—and by remembering her day. Each Christmas he gave her a new hassock. "Oh, I've adjusted to you, Charlie" she often said, in her lingo. Meaning that she was resigned to what Charlie said he got out of the city and his children's response to it. After all, that was his career.

The last house, this was, the last one in which we were a city family and together; that's how I remember it now. Also because my particular advantage was just then becoming clear to me, though hidden as well as I could hide. For of course our father hadn't merely offered us New York's beauties, but had also schooled us in its million-dollar choices, neighborhood by neighborhood. East Eighty-eighth Street had been the least successful to his mind; because of "too much Hitler," Yorkville's famous German cuisine, or its cranky small-craftsmen's shops—upholstery, stained-glass—never much stirred him beyond a moody "You two'll know Europe everywhere, even before you go." So, just before the end of our tenure there, he'd been forced to stronger methods, seeing nothing wrong in a father of temperate habit and his teen-aged children canvassing the bars, which in those days were usually named for two-initialled Irishmen, and as he shortly concluded, "Provincial dull. And no preparation for Dublin whatsoever. Not that you two'll need it, with your background." We felt that too, very early—as with such a father, who wouldn't? While we didn't quite know what he was preparing us for, we knew that he was looking for it everywhere. And even after a dozen nightly rounds, and as many faces on and off the barroom floor, we hadn't found P. J. Moriarty's or M. L. Mackey's that unrewarding, until our mother put a stop to it. "Your father's an hysteric about this," she'd said, pronouncing the "n" in "an" in her firm, totalitarian way. "When he works right in town, it always happens. Better that he should commute." Shortly after, opportunity struck; he was canned again. We admired the way she not only weathered father's job shifts but made psychological use of them. She'd adjusted damn well to those sunsets. And so of course had we.

Although by this time, brother James' choices, lucky stiff, were well-fixed. Two important years older than me, he'd spent his most formative years near the Planetarium and the Museum of Natural History, when we were living on Central Park West, and during a time when Aerodyne or Thermaflux was so far down in Jersey that father could do little more than arrive home to wheeze, "The ci-tee is a la-*bor*-a-toree," Gilbert & Sullivan-style, and let James probe his advantages for himself. James had yearned first to be a Navaho, and failing that, an astronomer, but by the time of those spring nights on the pier he was seventeen, slated for Columbia pre-med in the fall, and through the kindness of our policeman on the block (father again) had already seen his first corpse, at the morgue.

All that summer long, our pier-conversations were to be dotted with them, giving father many a chance to point out James's special opportunities. But the night when James had just that day seen his first—a drowning—is the night I recall best. For my own reasons as well.

"Palomino it was, the exact color of a palomino," James said. "And swollen. The head was the shape of a sugarloaf. Those mountains they call sugarloaf." He swallowed, and pulled his five fingers in a line from his nose. "Long."

"Shame on you, James," Father said. "Seeing all of those Western movies. Or seeing in terms of them. A boy like you. When you've got the morgue."

A city boy, he meant. Good New Yorkers didn't stoop

to a lot of things. Father had whole lists of them. Increased by what he saw on the outskirts.

"Right," I said. "That's for people who have to go to drive-ins." I was almost fifteen, brat-protective of myself on the outside, but mushy within.

"Never saw a real palomino," James said, thoughtful. "Never had the opportunity. It was the head reminded me. Of a horse." He leaned over the pier-edge, looking at the water, which because of lack of cooperation from the sky that evening was a tobacco-shadowed gray, occasionally rippling in the wind to a sheet of what could have been one of Father's past products—duro-aluminium. With the second "i" put in because the plant making it had been a British Shell subsidiary. Every now and then a brief city wave chopped to a glint; that was the "i."

"Good place for a suicide," James said. "Wonder if they ever get them from here?"

The pier was crowding up with all the regulars.

"I don't see what good the dead do you for medicine," I said. "Until you've dissected them. And until the second year, you can't." I was jealous of him for having more to feed his imagination than I had, at my schlocky dayschool. Where I learned works like "schlocky." A private school, but so full of the kids of social workers, teachers and radical lawyers, and so pre-selected to a "random" scattering around the norm, that it had gone simple on me. I was very much my father's child, if he had only known.

It would seem odd that he hadn't. I've the same large hazel eyes, not glassy, but clear. You could drop a pebble, I've been told, and never find it. Neither would I. The same surprised eyebrows, the nose just as pudgy and inquiring, though on a girl it might be appealing. The mouth maybe more bowed. Looking in the mirror, the mouth was the only part that gave me hope. It looked as if it might yet spit that pebble out.

But water was my sure element. Why else am I lying

here intead of picking myself up and titupping home like a good householder with a bun on, a wee drunkie mother, but one with good family intentions of baking guiltbread all the next day? No intention of sliding down in though, nostrils open and weed-hair dragging. I want to float on, out of the dream-tangle, maybe even rowing hard at the end.

What was bothering me that night—well, watch out here, Lexie. Take care not to re-interpret your old girlish life according to modern intentions. The way biographers will push Freud right through the brain of some poor emperor or poet or mass-murderer—or Sappho or President Taft or P. T. Barnum—born too soon ever to have heard of him.

But it is true that Father was always vaguer about my opportunities. And that night I was feeling it.

"Father. What's the city going to do for *me*?"

That mouth of ours opposite me fell open. At the heresy. "Why, Girlbud!"

I'm sorry to report this, but that is what he said. His mother was a Southerner.

"Why, Girlbud . . . don't you know?"

He meant that if my response to the city wasn't already so granulated into my flesh that it would take one of his industrial processes to part us, then he had failed me. Or I him. Though to be fair, he never thought of himself as failed toward. The companies had taken care of that.

"Yeah, I know," I say sullenly, through hair I'd taken to wearing like a veil. "But what am I going to do with it?" With which I close my eyes, pull my veil further over my nose and lean my head on one palm.

I'd known what New York was to me ever since I was nine or so, when a bus seat had lent a manipulative hand while I was staring up at a skyscraper, and I'd immediately made poetry of the matter. I'd've known even younger if I'd been allowed to ride buses by myself sooner. For such an occasion, one has to be alone. And perhaps it wasn't a skyscraper—or even the Cathedral of St. John the Divine, which in those days my bus from school passed often. Maybe it was only some tenement with the late light on it, or a misty patch of Hudson afternoon, or a square of that violet-glass sidewalk which looked like some semi-precious stone you were going to be able to wear. Or maybe the pier. More likely, it was all of these together, and then some. For I'd known for some time now that the city could melt me physically, to a yearning I had no words for, no comparisons.

But I have now. Oh water, wheel past me, Hudsoning by me and through me to that seat of my sensations. Weeds and rushes, fringe my face, while I lie here and laugh. While the harbor is mo-oaning. The city's a certain kind of zone for me—not the deepest of our lot maybe, but often the truest. New York to me—and maybe Paris and Hong Kong too; the list of world capitals dizzies me if I think too much on it—to me a city itself is an erogenous zone.

One of mine in fact. Father'd done his work too blindly. My body, sleepily arising to whatever objects presented it in the new dark of sensation, had engorged too well. And could Father now tell me what to do with that condition. I found I didn't want him to. Let me hoard it, and hide.

"Why honey," he said. "You'll be like your mother. I hope."

And I saw he really did.

James and I sideglanced each other. James often gave me those brotherly comforts. Without further advice. He was embarrassed just then to be a brother, I think. Being further on with women than we knew. And with women who were further on.

"Like Mother?" I said. "Why's she's a—a parasite."

"A—a what?" Father said. But I could see the idea intrigued. Mother—with her forty-five-hour-week bunions, and those meals—made out of thousands of boxes maybe, but by her. Mother—with her pulled-crepe-paper

· 11 ·

hair, which went to the tongs for help only if a caseworker's convention needed her, along with her gray, socially justified sweaters and skirts.

"Yes, a parasite. Who happens to work."

On the way home, we three were silent. With my usual talent for missing the true target, I was angry at James. For encouraging me to go too far, and leaving me to cope with the results.

Father shared that talent, also. "I don't know—" he sighed. "I don't know what we're going to do with your *mind*."

Late that night, when the others were bedded down, I get up again, and take the body that inhabits my mind back to the Morton Street pier. By then it's late for cruisers, but beginning for lovers, mostly gay. Drizzling a little. And no sign of the whores I'm looking for. I know a few by sight but have never spoken to one. For a while, I can't think of anything except the family anyway. James, on the daybed in the dining room, rolling to a city noise now and then, sometimes onto the floor. Father, dead to the world in his twinbed, wearing the singlet that is cool to his psoriasis. Mother in her twinbed, sleeping the sleep of the just, in pajamas with feet. Because of being a girl, I had a room alone, and the old double-bed they'd been married in. That ought to tell me something.

Until our policeman on the beat comes by—he knows us, but he'll surely chase me—I have so little time. He himself must have the very information I want—not that he'll give it. And I need the female view of it.

Shortly—it's raining by now—Mother comes down the block to give me hers. She slips her arm in mine confidingly, the same as she sometimes does when she sneaks into my bed, a refugee from Father's snore. I turn my back on her, the way I always do. And then turn round again, as usual.

"Anything I can do to help?" she says.

That's kind of her. But I wonder why she thinks any woman with pajamas stuffed in galoshes, and a man's lumberjack covering her dropseat, has advice I can use.

"The city disturbs me." I know that in the end I'll tell her how. But nothing ever got past her language—certainly not her emotions. And that would be that, I thought.

I was wrong.

"Dad told me what you said." She sighs. "He's so vulnerable."

"*He* is." I flip back my hair. "Huh."

That interested her. She studied gesture. "You mean you are? And you're denying that quality in him?"

I flip my hair forward, wetting my nose. "Maybe. I meant—you're the masochist."

"Those puddings!" she says at once. "You're right. Nobody needs dessert."

I put my arms up, and shriek a little.

The cop on the beat passes, eyeing us. Yeah, he knows us; he's the one referred James to the morgue. "Now, girls—" he says, shaking his head. "Now girls." He didn't like fights.

"See—you stopped the rain," Mother says to me, soothing. And giving him the high sign to leave us be. "But you got it twisted about me, lady . . . I'm a worker. Who happens to be a parasite." She stashed her hands on her hips. "Why else do you suppose I'm a radical?"

Lying here in the weeds—there are stars up there now—it's my firm conviction that life teaches everybody to be humorous about at least one thing. If so, it came to her and me late.

"You suppose I could ask Officer Maraglia?" I say. "How to be a prostitute? A streetwalker, I mean." What joy—to walk these streets.

She looks over to where he's disappearing, before she answers me. "Or a callgirl, maybe? Your arches are weak."

But then she feels my forehead, my cheeks. Draws me

to her by the wrists, kisses one of them. And sits down so hard on a wooden piling that I fall into her lap. I can't stay there. She can't stay on the piling. We both stand up.

"Wait a minute—" I say. One side of her dropseat's been snagged open by the piling. I button her up again. "You suppose *they* have little dropseats, sort of out front? Or is that a vulgar thought?"

She stares at the harbor. "I warned Charlie. That you were already over-prepared."

James comes up just then. I know he's fond of me, though he'll never let on. Still won't. "Schizophrenia?" he says. "Often starts at fifteen."

"Seventeen," Mother says, turning on me. "And lay off her. I'm the caseworker here."

My father comes down the pier, scratching. He's wearing my mother's green Loden cape. "Beautiful night, isn't it. I couldn't sleep either." He moons at the river as if he's forgotten he'll be crossing it again, come daylight. But he's heard her. "Come on, Renata, give it a rest. Give Lexie here."

As if it isn't him who always harangues.

James and I sideswipe glances again. We're decently dressed, for us. For the hour, even formally. With parents like ours, we do what we can to restore the balance. Not that it works.

I address them all. "Mother has her clients. And you have the plant. Plants." (I wouldn't pluralize those now; he *was* vulnerable.) "And you both have James and me." (I wouldn't call that an advantage now, either. But for my short hour, I was relentless.) "And James has the morgue. What have *I* got?" I see Father open the mouth I'm already afraid is mine too. "And if you ever call me Girlbud again, I'll positively leave."

"She wants a vocation, Charlie," Mother says. "But she doesn't know what."

I gnaw my lip, betrayed. And betray back, quick as I can. "I do so know. I'm not him."

James's eyes widen. "Do you, Sis. You never said."

I couldn't. There are technical words for sense-confusion; I know that now. And many avenues to it. Music that confuses us with pictures, of a kind the composer never planned. Odors with a little hush to them. Gin that makes Bach smell like flowers. My son, at six, said "Wednesday is pink."

"The city—" I wanted to say to them. "That you have burdened me with. No—trusted me with, too soon. Like jewels I'm to inherit but haven't yet. I want the city, between my thighs."

"Want to study medicine too?" Mother says. "Maybe we could stake you." Her tone's as false as her puddings. "When it comes time."

"Sibling jealousy?" Father shakes his head, doubting; he's the one who spends time with us. "No—I don't think."

How smart they think they are, James signals me. About each other. And never see themselves. Or us.

"No, I don't want," I say violently. "I *hate* horses."

Mother trembles. She feels professionally close to madness in others, but doesn't want it in the family. "Over-stimulated, see? And two years away from college yet. We'll have to organize."

The policeman drifts over. Maybe he's never been sure of us completely. A family who'll stand on a pier at four in the morning, discussing its business . . . *Outré,* yes? And no doubt responsible for the way I can lie up here now, at almost the same hour, calmly discussing my life—with my life . . .

"Organize?" the cop says, addressing James as the most decently clothed. "Who's organizing what?"

"We are," James says, pointing. "Her."

So that's how, as soon as school is out that summer and next, I go to study to be a medical secretary. And never get to college at all. As Mother says, "James'll be bringing plenty of interns home."

· 15 ·

As Father says the day I marry one, "You women never look farther than your nose."

This is in reference to the foreign tour he'd briefly spirited me away on to persuade me otherwise, the minute I'd announced my intentions. He'd aimed for Canada, but the hired car had failed us—and perhaps the money too. "Will you just look at the world!" he'd said to me from a window of the Hotel Oswego in Cooperstown, New York. "Look. Look!"

Let them fade now as parents do, into the ruins but still alive. Mother at sixty still repairing the city volunteer—all the way from the Gulf. Father leaving the city altogether—like people who so love cats, but desert them—to follow his nose into retirement with a richer wife—her nightgowns being especially luxe.

James's imagination, bachelor again after two tries, has proved most durable. Often after he's been up the river for the weekend with us, and is off for the city again, he'll whisper something to me, while brother-in-law Raymond kindly goes to extricate James's car from those others which on Sunday afternoons are often pulled up on the various front lawns of the houses along the road here, like lines of shoats. James's sibling eye is meanwhile casting a small judgment on me—a large woman—like those tiny, flat metal stampings of the Statue of Liberty the class used to be sent home with, after toiling up her inner staircase to look out at her spikes. His wicked diagnosis tickles my ear. "Honorable sister," his voice says. "Float down the river to me any day suits you. Only, not as a corpse." A city judgment.

So here I am—as organized.

When I married Raymond, the tallest, palest (with effort) and most careful of the interns James brought home, the "Dr." had just been attached to him: two perfect initials which swing from him, and sound as he walks. And are never lost. Later on I gave him a matched tiepin and cufflinks of those same initials, which he wears proudly still. Doctors love simple jokes, the grim dears, and in return for the life they lead, a wife whose jokes are not the same may still cooperate. Sometimes when I lay with him, looking deeply into his chest hairs, a few of these would whorl themselves into those same initials, pair upon pair. And until the finalities that brought me here, there was a pattern of moles on his windpipe that my mind's eye was working on.

A blameless man; try as I may, no blame will ever attach to him. Or to his parents. The basement of their house as I first saw it remains the most finished basement in America. With outlines drawn on the floor—garden-shears to roto-cutters, to ladders and floor-sanders—in which all implements are placed. The ladders being alumi*num* without the added "i"; theirs is a household local to the very end. Which end may be those milkcans Ray's mother paints black with bald eagles on them—which no longer hold milk. Around the cellar walls, trunks from another generation stand rigid with non-travel. "A hysterical basement," I report to James, after the engagement visit. "Someday those empty trunks will explode."

And I add how "Since I'll have to pick up my education piecemeal from now on," I've already learned from my father-in-law-to-be that a veterinarian is a man who doesn't kick dogs but doesn't pat them either. Or allow them into the house.

Ray and I've already chosen the shabby Victorian mansion from which he will practice. And in which I will live—needless to say—so I don't.

A lie. (What needed more to be said?) An inversion of the past by the future—which is at least me, lying on the river-bank, chilly but not dead, on grass that gets plushier as my thoughts grow clearer—in front of that same house.

Not angry, really. As my mother used to say in her

lingo: "Concerned." Taken me such a long time to realize I've no lingo of my own. But being in the nude here helps. And there are still some hours to dawn. When I must decide. Whether I'll stay here, and wait to be found, with all my buttons not just buttoned, but off. Or whether I'll get up just in time, and sneak back into the house.

That report to James was the first of many over the years, and in his fraternal eyes I'm accustomed to seeing his verdict, long since fixed. For no matter what's going on in the newspapers or on the battlefields of civilization, while I mouse from stove to village, from planned-parenthood to puddings bidden straight from the natural egg—the word "hysterical" is what's now firmly applied to me. Even by myself.

When did I first look around the hillocky streets of this white river-village to find the trees grimacing against the houses they shelter, the river running away to ask the city: "Su-boo-burbia, is that what her hystery-sterical is"?

The answer's no.

That wasn't lingo, that was prayer.

Why's he have to take you thirty miles upriver?" Father said, just before the wedding.

After the ceremony, he said "*People* don't grow, in places like that. It all goes into the chlorophyll."

After that, he washed his hands of me. It was at the wedding that he met the lady with the nightgowns.

"Ray isn't planning to grow, Father; he's planning to settle." Funny how I knew that, even then. And what was one lost erogenous zone?—at twenty I had them to spare. And had a strong interest in nightwear myself at the moment. Pink satin pajamas, the bridal night, and nile-green, panels blowing, the second day; then the honeymoon ascended by stages to a purple velvet hostess-gown; after the first Sunday, I planned a repeat. So, by easy cycles, to the door of the maternity ward. Four times.

Where we stand before God with a clutch of rubber nipples, or real ones, and can never go back. Nor would I, if one could. Even if in my small way, I intend to change the imagery of the world to conform with what happens there.

In my small way, it's not popular liberty I'm lying here for. Got that back in grade-school, like some of the blacks. Board of Education gave it to thirty thousand of the best pupils in the city—a little enamel flag that James could grow up to wear in his lapel or on his hatband, but which it was understood I could never fly from my grave—and *that's* sibling jealousy . . . After which we were all back in private circumstances again, including the blacks.

So, lying on my riverbank, what do I want from the parliaments of the world? Membership? Sure, that's okay. But come on, what good is it to me, or will it be, in my private practice, which is nothing like Ray's? What profiteth it a woman even if she gain half the token world by genito-urinary contract? What she needs most, is to find her own lingo—and have them publish the Congressional Record in it. At least half of the time. (With automatic translation-boxes on the backs of all theatre-seats, park benches and public conveniences. Including the men's room at Ray's club, which they let the wives use once-a-month on Wednesdays—perhaps just above that little cigar-rest which is screwed to each lav door.)

And alongside the mirrors of all medicine-cabinets in private domiciles.

Meanwhile the world is thrashing toward dawn without much help from me—and what shall I be saying to whoever leans over this patch of ground which is not even our property—"I am your representative from the Nude?"

Since it appears that even to pee, I am not going inside to do it, and perhaps not ever—except to telephone James "I'm sailing southward. Meet me at 4 A.M., at the Morton Street Pier." Friends welcome.

Let us organize me. It's been done before.

Dear Ray:
For you are dear to me, as the customs allow.
You do not kick humans—and have been known to pat them.
I am a woman not entirely zoneless.
And the children have been consecutive. Four times.

Forgive me if I recall their births better than their conceptions. I know I was trained not to.

"You'll forget it in a day," the gynecologist says, with a fifty-dollar smile. "Your abdominal muscles are first-class."

Nothing to it, he said.

"But it's my zone," I say. "I can't be expected to give up all of them."

He laughs, without charging me more for it. "You won't want to stay there long."

So I shut my mouth. His office is in New York, and the women in our village cherish any good excuse for going there. I'm looking forward to nine months of it.

Since it's to be a natural birth, you Ray, the father, are allowed in. I invite James too, as a brother and medical man, but he refuses. On the grounds that he's a doctor of the public health only. I'm disappointed, but of course that is his field.

"The private is not my sphere, Lexie," he says on the telephone. "Thanks a lot."

You're there in a peculiar capacity, Ray, for you. A doctor, with his hands tied. As a father, they're even afraid you might faint. "Some do," Dr. Gyno says, with his cutrate grin. The nurse agrees with him.

So then I ride in, Joan of Arc for a day. Into the stirrups for you, Girlbud—then into the burning bath. At the height, the flames are considerable. But I too have my hands tied. "She's one of those who won't scream," I hear the nurse say scornfully. I thought I had; later she swore not. But perhaps that's how they're trained too.

. . . I remember you though, Ray, leaning over me like a spindle of damp wood which isn't afraid it'll ignite. The lower half of my body is almost totally consumed. I am on the point—the absolute point, of learning my lingo. And then I lost it . . .

"Scream for *me*, Lexie," you said.

So I deliver silently.

A minute after, I'm watching all your antics like at a spectator-sport at which the tables have been suddenly turned.

"Breathe, you little bastard," the doctor says, slapping. And inaccurate to the last.

Above your mask, you're weeping. "A boy, Alexandra. But we'll name him 'Alex,' you bet." On the spot, you're always generous.

"How are *you*, Mother?" the nurse said.

All my insides feel pearly now—the placenta, perhaps. I feel all nacre, the way I do when a man leaves me—mother-of-pearl. But it's blood, I bet. If I choose to look down. I see they don't want me to. Yes, it's blood. My mouth falls open. Though never so wide as the opening down there. I see they want me to close up shop as quickly as decent. Nurse mops. I'm a little heady with what I've done down below. Why, I've given birth to all of you—is what I'm thinking. All of you. In my time. Why can't I speak of it?

The baby does it for me.

"Wah!" —it says "—I'm the only normal one here."

You know how children are.

"*Every*one speaks for me," I said.

I apologize to all of you, for remembering anyway. Such an unnatural act.

James reported that his friend Dr. Gyno thought I took things too hard. "'Very poetical girl, is she, your sister?'" he said.

"And what did you say?"

"I said, 'No. Overqualified.'"

But he never will tell me for what.

So the next time I go to Maternity, I scream like everybody else. And have many more visitors afterward. From our village road especially. People are shy, I begin to notice. too shy to say how living really is—even the loud ones. Mutual screaming helps.

But then I stop going to hospital. "Four times, we agreed upon, Ray—remember? And of course you do. Words which are said—signed, sealed and delivered—are the way you remember your acts. (Between phonecalls which take you gratefully away from them.) Your word is your bond. "Yes," you say thoughtfully. "Perhaps we should rest from our labors for awhile. Having them so close—I warned you. But you were always—"

"Yes," I say. "Hysterical."

So after that, we make love for ourselves entirely. I agree with the Catholics; that's dangerous. That way, you can better scrutinize the sex, and the partner.

So after a while we have rested entirely. Dear Ray.

IN A
FIERY GLADE

"Are you all right?" James says, maybe twelve years later.

Mud in my eye from a bad throw of Charlie my eldest, I scrape cookie-grease off a cushion, feed it to the dog, shunt her off the sofa and sit down haunchily in her warmth. It's Friday, the Saint's Day of the week, domestically. And in June, when the last Parents' Day of the crayola crowd has just snaked its way three times round the school in tributary drawings, and on out into the blue. Soon will be summer, sand on the soles and the heart starred with weenie-roasts. When the first child first plays the piano, one cries. Two others, banished to the tower, breathe together on the Mellophone—which is a trainer for the French horn. In the dark of the landing, I breathe in unison. On hope, my instrument. These days I tremble with selflessness. That candy delight. Stuffed well in, it keeps the language down.

In the dark of the jobs where the men twirl for us, does James, now staring at me, and Ray, now having a cigar in his study, tremble the same?

"Yes, James," I say. "Quite all right. The children are bringing me up."

For the first time in our talks I haven't answered him properly. I've dissatisfied him.

"Why won't you have more help?" he says, veering to look round. "Ray says he could afford a full-time one, easily."

"I am full-time."

"A doctor's wife. It's demeaning."

"Sorry. It's a hobby of mine. That I can't yet spare." But I'm learning, learning. How to satisfy them all.

"You're always—" he says. "Why are you so *always*—?"

Quickly I put a hand on his knee. "I know, I know. But in that case, what help is help?"

Ah, that's better, his eyes tell me. This crazy sister of mine who's not crazy, but just crazy enough. To keep him coming up here. To this house, whose occasional majesty—a river before the door, after all, and a tower to which one can send children—is dimmed by bum tricycles jammed into the privet-hedges, floors soft with the brown family-dirt that's never sinister enough for a big clean-up but ought to be, and rugs reduced to string. And where the food is only reasonable. When he could be at a Saturday night dinnerparty for eight with some of his colleagues, in one of their cool Park Avenue compartments—wine and good linen, conversation like a tollroad for which he has a life-ticket, and an exquisitely clean divorcée, invited just for him. "Why do I keep on coming here—" he's thinking—"because she's my sister? She can't be organized. We tried."

He'd have been sitting in that brownstone of his—next-door to the very one in part of which we last lived as a family. At his desk maybe on the third and office floor—the first two and fifth floors being rented out, just as they were in such houses then. In front of him is his Chinese scroll which he bought in Thailand, his first big job. All the rest is the detritus of two wives. Hard black wallpaper with shiny tearoses in the big party-room above, soft grasspaper whooshed over every other. The topfloor tenants are maybe giving their party, to which they always ask him,

· 26 ·

and to which he always went, until a night his hostess squealed, introducing him, "Our landlord. Don't worry about noise." The groundfloor tenants have children of surprising collegiate beauty whose friends seem chosen for the same; they clatter up the steps and past him with faces that will launch ships. I'll call Lexie, he thinks. Bus from the bridge. No need to take the car, never any girl there to drive back. Sometimes he thinks in time to bring us something, sometimes not.

I know why you come, brother James. But will I ever tell you why?

"Sorry about the potatoes," I say. "I've had a spell of burning them." Once it was puddings. The simple hostilities are the easiest on everybody. "Thanks for the wine."

"The roast was delicious," he says. "What's that noise? Not your neighbor's sunporch again?"

"*We* have a sunporch. Bob's and Betsy's is a conservatory." With one-hundred-seventy-five individual glass panes, some portion of which Betsy regularly smashes in.

Kellihy's is the glamor house of the road, and they the glamor children, aged twenty-eight and twenty-nine. With children of their own, increased by two in the two years since they came. Ever so often, Bob inherits eighty thousand dollars or so, or perhaps the rich Catholic laity to which he belongs on both sides takes up a collection; yet often he and Bets cannot pay the paperboy. In their drawingroom—Betsy's word for it—Bob sits in the center of crawling phone-wires, doing the endless business of a remittance man. He has plug-ins all over the house, dragging them from room to room, chair to chair; a special head-set's forever clamped rosette-like to that groggy, choirboy mug of his, giving him the air of a man in a babycap. He's painfully smart. Painful somewhere to him, I mean. And somehow, to watch. Whenever he does too much business of his own downtown, the family rescues him. No one here's ever seen any of that clan with whom he is in constant communication in his mind.

"Yes, that's Betsy." Betsy's father is a Judge in Connecticut, but she was once in a production at the Pasadena Playhouse. The clash in her consciousness is considerable. But she can't cook, and motherhood is no help to her. "But the rhythm's not bad yet. Maybe only a party. Did you hear cars?"

He hasn't. It's one of those magical nights though, when all the children are asleep or cuddled to themselves and the moon over the river hangs beckoning in the flawless windowpane—I won't break it—and everybody you love is home. Everybody you think you love is home.

"Bob bought her a hundred-dollar nightgown last week, at Saks'. After he gave her the black eye. They had a party in to contemplate both."

The next day, at an autograph-party in the bookshop, for an actress who happens to live up here, Betsy went, in a heavy black veil, and autographed dozens of books on her own before the proprietor caught her at it. She said, "Why shouldn't I? Who else do you know has five children, is going to a psychiatrist, and is only twenty-nine?"

And is a stunner, though this she never says. The veil would be the same one she wears when she walks past us down the road to take instruction from the priest in the next village south.

"Hope it's a party," I say. Otherwise, Ray will have to go over and get her through the night. Get them both through the night.

"I don't hear any cars," James says.

And the smashing's stopped.

The telephone rings. I don't answer it.

Ray comes in. "I'm going over. I may have a drink or two with them. Don't wait up."

Don't blame him. Please don't. Drinking with them cures the moment for them, and Ray never likes to prescribe tranquilizers when there's alcohol in the picture too. He never takes more than one drink himself. But there's such honey over there for the likes of us. Risk and wealth and youth, all slightly rotting—the decadence that brings flies. When the Kellihys give a party, the whole road comes if asked—apple-cheeked matrons and all, big houses or cottages—for a sniff of high living. After a night at the Kellihys, the cottage-mortgage looks great for another week. Or a week of whatever you yourself are. And the stories last even longer. Did you hear that when Holmesie—the Grand River policeman—stopped them on the road for speeding, Betsy leaned out and hit him with her handbag?

James is at the window. "No, not a party." He regrets this. "Lexie—whyn't you go with him?"

I used to. But now I know all the stories.

"Plenty of chaperones," I say. "Violet, the children's nurse, who brought up Master Bob too. She steals Betsy's jewelry, for her Thursday day off to the city. On Saturdays, Betsy goes up to the attic, to Violet's trunk, and steals it back. Black Violet, their kids call her, though she's isn't very. Arthur, the senior Kellihy's former butler, lives there too. Same color, but they're not allowed to call him it."

I like Arthur. His hobby's making silver flatware by hand, which he sells in the village for little sums. With which to pay the paperboy. Arthur brought up Bobby too. "Bob rehires all the old family servants," Betsy once said, proudly. "Can it, Bets," Bob said, that froggy face working. The senior K's pay, I guess. Arthur and Violet are remittanced here too. So if I want to borrow a cup of sugar— why is it always sugar we borrow?—I can watch a retired butler stirring the soup. I used to like to see that; it made me laugh for the resilience of the world. But nowadays I take care to keep plenty of sugar in the house.

They all drink over there, which is their bond. Retiring into their separate corners as their spells of duty cease. Bob'll go upstairs at some point, trailing one of his telephone-cords along. His talent is that he never trips on them. And Ray will be left to get Bets through the night.

"Their eldest son's a pyromaniac," I say. "That's all that worries me." At seven Roddy carries matches in his pockets everywhere. And has been known to light them. "And our trees are so near."

That's all that worries me.

"That another pane of glass?" James's eyes are bright. He knows well enough it's the sound of our back door. Underneath the great river-trees which border all along here, there's a path through the thicket between Kellihys' and us. Which Betsy hopefully dubbed "the martini path" the first year they came. That part of it came to nothing. The martinis, I mean. She has the charm of a child who drinks them. I feel it myself. "Why don't you go, James?" I say. We're siblings, after all.

He smiles, but shakes his head.

Outside, the River Road goes palely wandering. Alongside it and below, the riverline itself blends with the dark of its own water and the opposite shore to a height above all our terraces, making a house-of-cloud above all our houses, with no panes to break. At night, when most are asleep along here, I walk the road, learning it. Two and a half miles to the village north, twenty-seven and a half to the city south, but I have only to walk a few paces. The road is always the same.

"Do you have a lover?" James says suddenly—he knows I don't. "Lexie. Maybe you ought."

"Ought I?" I know I ought; know I ought not. The daisy petals drop.

"In the city," he says. "Why not? It would thin you down."

My laugh breaks in two in the larynx. Like little Royal's cough; maybe he's taught me it. I resisted calling him that—for his paternal grandfather Royal—the veterinarian. Might as well call him Rover and get it over with, I thought but didn't say. And confusing, with a father named Ray. But he resembles neither of them. And nobody is ever confused about Roy.

"Ride the early morning bus in, you mean, to the Elizabeth Arden salon? For an appointment for the hair?

And spend the afternoon in bed?" Or take the car, and park it at the bridge. Taxi to the bridge, and you can be home in time to cook. "Some along the road do. I can't afford it yet."

We have no smashed panes in our house, only loose ones. The wind breathes through them like a learner.

"Can't afford it? Do you know what Ray makes?"

I'm getting to be James's older sister, I think. Not younger. "Guess I'll go up now. If the lecture on public health is over."

He can't bear me to go. He's so vulnerable. With his long, palomino face. He'll spin it out for hours, if I let him.

"Three detective-stories by your bed, James. Winners, every one of them. I read them all, last night."

We stare, head on. I could tell him what he comes here for.

Listening to me is the way he screams.

But until he tells me what I'm qualified for, why should I say?

"Good night."

"Good night."

Upstairs, I stand on my double bed to reach a small, pointed churchwindow. Its upper pane is tight, and kept as clean as any in the house. There is another just like it in the bathroom next door. And in the tower. Through them one can see the whole sweep of downriver, and the road, which now that it's raining hard will still be muddy tomorrow when I walk it, in the four o'clock hour after the chores are done and before they start up again. Chores are comfy, one sinks into them. Better than into tears. Someday I'll exceed my need of chores, but not yet. Strange, how if I did weep, it wouldn't be for a man who's not a bad man (perhaps then I would) but for a wrong turning. Odd, how the wet road steams a different way in winter from what it does in summer. Surely, it's worthwhile, to clock the moods of a road. Sometimes the cat paces me, picket to picket. Soon I'll go down.

My nightgown's thin but not entirely useless. Either for warmth or for love. I lean against the brick wall, shuddering with vitality. Passivity drops from me, chore by chore. I live at the back of other people's days now, drained this way, drained that—and this is likable, which I daren't say. They wouldn't want to hear me say—James or Ray, or other women on the road, either. But I'm learning. Can't afford the torments of the happy, yet. No James, not yet. But I'm learning my lingo, all by myself.

Out there, the house-of-cloud watches me. I'm awake, and all too ready. But the river, for walking out with only, is my lover now. I transliterate well.

Then I see the cat down there, already picket-to-picket on its way. Drop back into bed then, listen for a child to moan. You love the children, you don't recede from them. Serving them with small cookies and hard pats. You live back of other people's days, that's all.

That's all.

But in the night the whole house flowered with her silent Mellophone.

That was the state of affairs around the twelfth year. Now add about five. Six. The house is sleek now, fresh as a prism with the light that comes from gently ringing telephones. And so is she. They have three separate phone lines now: one of course for Ray, one for the three older children's impassioned teen-age conversations, and one for her own activities—the village's word for whatever its women like her (still young and well-favored and perhaps with more energy than is needed) do with themselves. Since she has help, and the accessory services that help demands, the house is now organized. And so is she.

Both the house and she—having arrived with their mutual weight of goods and children at a certain recognizable stage for many such houses along the road and such wives—now spin like tops, singing ones, around an orbit whose central truth hasn't yet been revealed (all are agreed on that) but surely will be, perhaps on retirement, or at the birth of the first grandchild. When it will come too late to be taken advantage of. So meanwhile she goes into the city twice a week. To learn what she can. Parking her car at the bridge.

Once a week is for her real and honest Continued Education, the phrase used to describe the route of women like her, by the college she attends, not in the city actually, but on the opposite shore of the river, halfway down. There she's met women who are in various stages of finding either their professions, themselves, or merely each other—which is not to be despised.

"What a relief," one says to her, "to find so many others who're hysterical." Racked with laughter, the two have to leave the studyhall. "I've never had a fit of adult giggles before," Lexie says. She's begun writing a thesis on Roger Bacon, though not quite able to explain her choice of subject to the instructor. "Because of that sixth-grade-reader story, I think. The one about the clock that said to him 'Time is.' And then 'Time was.' And then wasn't there a last one—'Time will be'? Or not?"

Plaut, the instructor, can't say, but approves the subject. As he's done for all ten of his students, though in admitted bewilderment.

"Not that you aren't as bright as—." He halts. Ten women stare at him, all different, all feral with need. "As butchers," he said. "But the subjects you choose are so in-between. Extraordinary. Not a major subject in the lot of you." Does he hesitate, resting on her? "No. Not one."

They discuss what a truly major subject might be—a ridiculous pastime in which Plaut's blond beard seems to thin itself from being plucked. Perhaps because it discloses a strong chin, even a dimple, those in the class who don't fall for him, tend to confide in him, excluding only the one woman in the class who already has a profession, a second who admits to already having a lover—and herself. At the term-end party, Plaut makes a speech. "I've learned so much," he says. "What strange lives you all lead. Such interior ones."

Their outdoor girl, who, whether she comes in riding-pants or ski-boots, or in bikini on a bicycle, speaks only in monosyllables, squints up at him frostily, but does not condemn.

"Is it abnormal—?" Plaut goes on. "I can't decide. But I think I owe it to you to tell you. That my relations with my own wife have much improved . . . from my chats with you honest ladies. In fact we are going to have another child."

A strange speech. Exactly what Ray might have said, barring the child. And since Ray now teaches a class in birth-control, and their own relations have bettered, perhaps Ray has. What strange lives *they* lead. She herself has neither fallen in love with the instructor nor finished her thesis, for one and the same reason. Her other weekly day in town.

Only her new talent for deceiving others shocks her,

at first so deeply that she wants at once to tell Ray. But even as a younger man Ray used to bumble out everything, and doctorhood has turned any tact he has toward his patients' ill health, leaving him transparent to the rest of life. The three children, now in their divining teens, would know at once. As it is—to come home to family dinner just in time to sit down facing them, with her thighs still ravaged, wet and open from adventure—and to make the usual mother responses: "Charles, will you wash those grubby hands, please"—no.

Or worse, to arrive back before any of them, but so numbed, drugged from sweet excess with a stranger, that after her long soak in the bathroom she can only drag herself to table in her dressing-gown, there to be catered to like an invalid by her own daughters, who are just now in a religious stage, alternated with certain budding sexual vanities and drowning-wild gawks of their own—? No to that too.

There's a pinkening shudder comes over a woman who finds herself mother and lover at once; early in marriage she'd met it first. When she and Ray, on a dark Sunday, and under the shade of her by then bedraggled purple velvet "hostess" gown, had made such slapping suction with their bare breasts that the boy of three and the eighteen-month-old girl, wakened from naps, pattered in to clamber over them and join the game. Under the babies, they finished off.

That was animal-nice but somehow never could be repeated. Except in the breathy nirvana-dreams of lady anthropologists, where mothers gave suck and fuck at the same time. Ending up like the two such on the road here, with each other—two bitch-bellygoddesses, with an appliance between. In the road's only real Colonial house.

Ray, summoned there late one night, had told her about it, entirely without humor—which he can never apply to bodies—but in one of those bursts of confidence which even the best of doctors has to have. Giving her his sex at the same time.

These days, she accepts both more gracefully. The morning after, putting off her second day-in-town until the following week. She's no sexual orgiast in terms of numbers; in fact being with two men concurrently bothers her. Those little friendships which two bodies make, must make, however transient-to-be, those clues of voice and nerve-code so quickly learned; here she doesn't transliterate well. And admit it, there are hazards in these amours. She gets—not so much affectionate as—magnetized. No matter how unsuited her brain tells her a man is—or even how scoundrelly, the rest of the week she tends to brood on him, and to centralize. Casting herself far more importantly in his vision than sense tells her she is. For, because of her home circumstance, it is always she who telephones. And however happily received she is, doesn't that cast a certain light—on these affairs?

They aren't affairs, that's it. Yet how is it then that both the men she's in sequence chosen and been accepted by, both violently different in their attractions—have one resemblance to her. They too aren't in it for sex alone. Though they too mightn't yet know—for what else.

One day, two weeks after Ray's house-call to the two Lesbians (and in effect on her), she drives back from town too late for her ritual bath. No time even to consult with the housekeeper as usual, for the sake of both their dignities. Just in time to sit down to dinner almost like a late guest. In time though to watch Ray come in a minute after.

A doctor-father's always unexpected at meals, always a guest in his own house. Are the children getting used to her being that too, now? As she watches Ray with them, her belly, still electric with warmth, chimes for him in sympathy. Ray's lot with his four children—which is to see them from the distance the time-demands of his life force on him—only exaggerates the lot of every father. Fathers spend their parental lives reestablishing the claims of that one ripple of their own fluid—a moment ever receding from the radials of their other life from the moment it occurs. There's even a tribe, Plaut says, which doesn't know of the nine-month link between conception and birth—hasn't yet made the connection. Fathers, taken together, are merely a tribe who have. Artificially reestablishing that moment long ago. A tribe which has to look like its children too, if possible. Wise of them, the Bible says. Kind of them, rather. Very kind of Ray—who is that generally. Even if his kisses, one each to the two girls and a third on her own forehead, seem always, after his long day, to come from the dispensary. Yet here is she, who has been through that birth-fire which established the children as hers beyond challenge—to say nothing of the hothouse closeness since—trying her very damndest to disestablish herself.

"Ray—" she says, in the soft townvoice that at these times replaces her country one. "You kiss the girls when you come in. Why is it you don't shake hands with the boys?" And for all her intent to help—was it that?—the boys glower at her. All four children stare at her like a jury.

"You were supposed to be at the hairdresser," Chessie, the elder girl says, her eyes lowered over her plate. "Your hair looks terrible."

Oh, there are frictions about her second day-in-town. Everything else about it pleased.

She sat up suddenly in the weeds. Opening her eyes to the blackness that shawled her, moistened now with little playing cusps of cool, windbuds that in a couple of hours will whiten and break into morning. Pleased? A mild statement, unworthy of the past year and a half, year, six months, which roll like an incline up to where she sits bare, on this crest. Alone again, but with adventure just departed. Leaving her with flesh heavy-ripe and a mind as sketchy as a girl's, to await this newest and most fateful one. Outside her own house.

In the dark she laughs to herself like a child at the

top of the highslide, who's just that moment dared it and in the same instant learned its pattern—the zooming down, the climbing up. Before her days in town, her life had been a kind of bodywalk through the daily, in which any triviality of event or object—a chat with a friend in the Grand Union, a boil-over on the stove, even a contretemps with a child, like when Roy the youngest was caught hooking a bicycle lamp from the Speedy Supply—might scribble its shorthand on her faithfully receiving skin.

Now she goes weekly to that tattoo-artist, the city, and is incised.

The world's tattoo. She sees it as a mixed heraldry, of battleflags she's missed marching under, love-affair fashionlace she's still young enough for, and tonic slews of that dirty snow and dark gutter-scum from which the suburbs are so famously free. All each being inked on her as near the bloodstream as possible, until that day when, whorled complete, she will be a truly reddened, purpled, black-and blue citizeness of the world. While all this time, her lovebody remains fair.

Meanwhile the crabgrass crosshatched under her buttocks is hurting; a soft paw of burdock or plantain tickles the small of her back like a domestic animal playing sinister. Lucky no thistles. And that it's not yet fall. Or else the man who had climbed out of the city's Saturday heat—and has just driven off again—mightn't have come at all. And the two sides of her life wouldn't have snapped shut on her. Lucky or not.

Has travel brought me here? Our father's idea of it? Not the man who's now in Sarasota with his new wife in her marina—that frail, recalcitrant old daddy-o whom the wife sends north ever so often—a leaky boat whom the sun has foundered. Of whom dry James says, dining with us after we'd all put father on the return plane again, "We're travel to him, now." Not him, James, but that other mythic tower which every parent is to someone else's youth. "You bought yourself his childhood brownstone," I say to James. "Not even the real one. Not even ours."

"And what did you buy?" my sibling says cruelly, sitting on the porch alone with me after supper. "His idea of Hong Kong? That why you won't go to Monte Carlo with Ray?"

"I've been to two doctors' conventions beginning with M already. Imagine going to Montevideo, when you've never been anyplace else in the world. Not even to Paris, France. And then—to Miami. What secret significance do you suppose the letter M has for internists?"

James doesn't answer—why should he? Whatever he does in that tight project office of his at the Medical Center, it's taken him all over the so-called civilized world—from hospital to hospital. So that he knows everybody's international health, and has never had a patient personally. Not even a horse.

"Montevideo would've been fine," I say, "if I'd known enough to—wander enough. Or if they'd let me." A new air in the throat and a new language. Waiting in *me*, I'd felt—all this time. I took it personally, all that first day. "As it was, I only came back home knowing how to hold my Chivas Regal whisky. And with one of those straw hats—made in Panama."

In spite of all, I'd hired a driver to see the town with. Afterwards at first reporting only that I'd seen the haciendas of the rich. Not that, picking my way in the one foreign language I'd got from being a New York City medical secretary—Puerto Rican Spanish—I'd persuaded the driver to let me visit his home. Where I have coffee and a sweetish pancake, in a courtyard full of hens so scrawny they look like cocks, and four generations of women, all so mushroom-brown in their earth-black that they might be this year's crop of one eternal vegetable—and a little boy in flashy white shorts of the most incredible flax-spun linen—I touch it—who has one bluish-blind eye. Was that trachoma?—I ask Ray afterward, describing it. He supposes so, he says wearily—why? "Is this a medical convention or isn't it?" I say.

So we have a fight.

He's spent the afternoon with some other medicos in a pachinko parlor some enterprising Japanese has set up. It hasn't disturbed him at all that he's done this in Uruguay. But I think travel ought to be separate.

So we have a fight.

Told of the courtyard, he says "Did you touch anything?" And I say "Yes of course. The eye."

"They were all horrified," I tell James. "And funny thing, the other wives were the worst. But it was Miami finished it."

A big hotel shouldn't be pink-and-blue. Or a lagoon either. Both were, with all the guests trying to match. Morning golf—in fake linen, but with 20:20 vision via contact lenses—then a rousing lunch.

"During which I perform the vodka as well as anyone," I inform James. "In case you don't know, the vodka is a local dance. Bloody Mary some call it, but I consider that sacrilege. Done in local costume—a bikini spotted with tomato juice. After which we all retire, to get to know our husbands better."

We hadn't, Ray and I. Perhaps there wasn't that much of us left. So we went down to the lagoon. Swimming wasn't as blue as last year's, people told us, but I liked it anyway. In bather's country, water itself is an emotion.

"And in the cocktail lounge afterwards, you could smell the sexual sweat. All permitted and expected—a general rut." Not too blue, not too pink. But everybody openlegged and lax. "One of the men asks one of the women what perfume she has on. And she says '*Afternoon. At the Royal Esplanada. Bet every gal here smells of it. Or should.*'"

"Some swapping around?" James said. "That's how I lost Linda, praise be. You ever try? No, I suppose not."

James looks butterscotch-pale these days, and his face has lengthened, if that's possible. But he's neither as tidy as he'd had to be with wife Linda, nor as neglected as he'd been by wife Ruth. In between is where James is, and this is unusual.

"Sure, doctors' wives are the worst, Lexie. Don't you know why?"

"No. Though I could write a pamphlet on them." On us. The tough-titty ones who were nurses, and are now half an M.D. by marriage—and have mouths like old urinals. The society Janes who sail, golf, ride and surf, never speaking of the national health, simply being it. The one who's been on the couch for years because of her dead life as an accessory to a brilliant man, and is at last earning a medical degree for her very own. As an anesthetist. The telephone Auntie—swelling with serous love-and-advice on the flattest Sunday. And the sweet-sprung newly married one, who looks forward to bandaging people, by his side. "No, I don't know why. Or which one of the worst I am. Why?"

"Ray practices. What you can only preach."

"Why-ee *sib*—" I say. "Who's your new suffragette?"

Who'll look just a trifle like our mother, probably. With the same censorious smirk. And none of her lifesaving dottiness. I hadn't blamed Linda for switching from my brother to their top-floor tenant, a black playwright who beats her up regularly for being a blond. Copulating with my brother, one would watch that long jaw mobilize itself against its own sadness, above whatever international project was going on down below. Afterwards seeing that long skull relax into its own rigor, the palomino cheeks tanned with travel it never sees, the ponyteeth protruding in happy love-death.

"Poor James—you're like me," she'd said. "Perhaps you *should* have been an astronomer."

The moon comes up over the river to hear his answer. Showing her Ray, who these days has formed the habit of "going down to the dock," as he says, though their strip of river-edge scarcely has one, "to watch." To watch the river, the moon, the season. A habit of coastal people. More and more, after dinner, she saw Ray from the back. The children seem not to notice. Perhaps that's the way they see her.

"Like *you?*" James says. So hard a sound that she sees their two backs as if from behind also, two cats arched facing each other over their pebble of hate.

Yes, I've receded, she thinks. Too far. If I see us all from the rear.

"Yes," she says. "We both have no private practice."

Out there Ray turns slowly, and comes back across the road and up the steps. But not to the two of us. At the last minute, he veers and goes in the side door the patients take. From the beginning, the house has been a convenient one.

"When Ray goes," James says, "I'm giving a party. In town. For both of us. Don't look at me like that. As if I'm a corpse."

It's the way you're looking at me, she thinks.

But training held. "It's the moonlight," she said.

She goes to that party as if it's her first. "What kind of dress, you say—" the salesclerk says, "—a Saturday one?" And the party takes to her as if she's its belle. In white cashmere, with blazing knobs of glitter all down the figure she's fasted to an hourglass curve. James's house has gone comfortable bachelor, in everything except dirt. All the other women guests tend to be nondescript, with hopes of hair well-washed but too young for the face. No match for her—who has been to Arden's. For the first time she feels the belle's contempt for other women. Covering her own longing—for they all work in one or the other niches of the city—governmental, artistic, intellectual—after which they have their own flats to return to, and this dazzling freedom after five. To be with men like the male guests, every one of them attractive in one of the variations of bachelor, a good number separated or divorced, or just not now living with anyone. Many are fathers, with complicated weekend arrangements. The women are similarly divided, but they're not interested in her, when she tries to talk to them. Sexual adventure stalks the fat elbow and knowing giggle of old Markie, the black woman who keeps James's house clean, passes his canapés and pops bed-hints on the side. Most people here are on the loose for bed, but the wind that blows through James's discreetly thick blinds is a tame one, and not mercenary.

A man named Kevin Sheridan dances with her as only Irishmen can, and lowering his handsomely dented face at her as unself-consciously as the cherubs all such types look to her, leads her around the corner to his apartment. His clothes are seedy with what she assumes is life-in-the-raw but turns out to be literature. The place is a box-of-books, with niches for the natural functions. As halfbrother, by different fathers, of a well-known poet, Kevin edits textbooks, researches for dictionaries, translates erotica, all tasks cast his way by his brother. "Crumbs from the lyric table," he calls them—and does the actual writing in his favorite bar.

Where he sat with an air of being in Paris, nursing the first vermouth of the day and paying for his office with wit alone, she thought, until she saw him substitute for Jody the barman, and learned that he had a passion for being a bar's family friend. Extending his patronage only where this was allowed. And where she could find him, anytime.

He's brilliant in bed (always his own, grubby as it is, for she won't use James as pander, being too afraid that James is willing) and gives her many shrewd comments on her life. During the country half of her week, mulling while she performs all the duties of her station, she alas falls in love with him. If subordinating every inch of her days and all her dreams to that one obsessive drive a week and the hours she gets from it—means love.

"You're an intelligent girl," he says, sipping his one luxury, the champagne he likes to have on hand during sex. Before or afterwards he'll drink anything. "Don't let romance get you in the head. What every woman wants is a hard cock. I have one, that's all. Along with some Gaelic charm. It's made a poet of my brother. But not me." The word "cock" sounds tonically—ah, the Village, she thinks—and he seems to be addressing the organ itself, once again pointed at her.

He teaches her to rumple her hair more, also to leave off Ray's pearls, up to now worn in the double row the department stores have taught her—"You've a wondrous neck as God gave it,"—as well as a whole set of the artificial graces a bare body can go in for. And listens to her history as no one else ever has. The books behind and above them inspire her. Although she reads dozens of them because they are his, she must go to the library for them. He will never lend her his own.

"I've been on the road since morning," she'll begin, false-true, arriving breathless in a blue-black dress that makes even the blasé Jody grin, and the real drinkers—a close-knit daily group—turn and buzz. At dawn now, she rises to make her nine o'clock for the hair, at a younger place than Arden's, very expensive, where the young customer-ladies stroll in narrowly in leather, done up in youth even before the hairdresser starts his cutting, the purpose of which is to make them look like gamines who by strength of will only are not wearing the family pearls. Now and then she herself plunks for an entire day of courtesan beauty-care, but Kevin, finding out, laughs her out of it, and indeed she now feels beautiful enough—he has brought her out; whether or not he's what-every-woman-wants, he's a charmer, and kind. So nowadays she spends the early part of the day she's to see him in savoring the city, though usually uptown, going to the Village only for him. Once or twice, she spends it looking for apart-ments for her and him—and looking the impossible straight in its homely face. While for an afternoon the house at home flies out of her head, a gothic moth, de-parted.

"I love this bar," she says, the last night. "It's *where*."

And it is. Where at seven-thirty, just before she and Kevin leave the bar to eat at the booth which is always theirs, his estranged wife, a forty-thousand-dollars-a-year woman's-magazine editor, with a lumpy, farmgirl face which New York has indentured but not made much of, walks in and collects him. Not a bad woman in other circumstances, one of the sad ones, too. Wanting something else, whatever it was. Clearly she wanted more than his cock.

And he had gone, without a backward glance.

Next week, in a dull panic of lassitude, she, Lexie, rose too late for the hair, but went into town anyway. Kevin's flat has folded, just as she'd feared. Nor is he at the bar. She'd known that would be the case too, but where else can obsession go, except round the old track?

"Happens least once a year, kid. She takes him back to Scarsdale. You lasted the longest I ever seen him." Jody slips her this like a chaser. Or a pick-me-up. She knows he won't give her Kevin's address, should he have it. And she knows it isn't Scarscale.

James, who must have known about Kevin and her—the Village always knows—has never spoken of him since the party. But shortly after several weekends of finding his sister disheveled, deadfaced and cooking round the clock—"Springerle cookies," his younger and favorite nephew Royal tells him, "we must have ten thousand of 'em"—James, clever James, dear pimp and brother, gives, not a party but a dinner for sixteen people and their ill-sorted mates. Not one couple of whom appears to be interested in one another. How has he managed it? With the exception of one man farther down the table who seems to be unattached—the tall, rangy dark one who James has cannily not placed next to her—all the men are connected with the public health.

After coffee, she walked out on the terrace James had made of the roof—after re-annexing the top-floor for his own use, once the playwright and James's own wife were gone. The room behind it, where the rest are still having liqueurs, had been the house's ballroom once. Her nostalgia doesn't extend that far back.

Her right-hand dinner partner had been speaking of an eye-surgeon who was diagnosing *myasthenia gravis* from the degree of elasticity in the lid. "Your own are fine," he'd said, testing them. Not *his* field, of course. He himself is just returned from a village in South India where the incidence of multiple-breasted women is remarkable. "Four?" she cries. "Sometimes only three," he says. Giggling when she sparks "You needn't test me for that."

Down the long table which James has had made in Kyoto and shipped home in parts, packed lotus-style, which her own children have helped to put together, the conversation, itself reassembled from so many parts of the world—and of humans—has an eely life of its own, superior to the men who are making it. Composed as their talk is of bread-for-villages and birth-control-for-the-planet, it dignifies their civil-service lips and country-squire cheeks; as they spoke she saw chains of the human colon girdling the globe, foetal armies clashing for stance on it. While down the table, wives chime with assents learned from their husbands, in whose fields, socially speaking, they too specialize. One new young wife, until recently head nurse of a maternity ward, on introduction first-names every woman there, as if they are all due her in hospital the next morning. But others like Lexie are silent, aware now that parties are their only events really, as well as their second-hand way of touching the world professionally. So that their lives, like hers, stalk these parties, and when arrived at them, sit sexually dreaming.

She leans out on James's artfully safe fence, which the children, encouraged by her, have helped to paint. She wants the children to have the taint of city air. Even though it hadn't done for her what it might have, it rings familial still, with the vying parental voices. And for all the dirt, with certain baby-clean hopes. Like the white smoke that sometimes twists from these dark stacks. From the head of his table, James had stared at her in his concentrated way, as if she were a starving village, perhaps. Or that suffering one in whose pipes the visiting epidemiologist from the UN—her lefthand neighbor—had found arsenic.

A woman leaning on a parapet has an animal grace the woman herself can feel. She knows she has a fortyish beauty now, summonable at parties, or suddenly arriving on her at a corner curbstone, as a truckdriver whoops to it. From Kevin, though he hadn't strictly said, she knows its peculiar ingredient. The tigerish attraction, intent from ambush, of the incomplete. She's still wearing the blue-black dress.

"What are you doing out here?"

Smart, this one must be. He senses she's doing something.

"I was streetwalking."

"No, no," he says. "That's not for you. At least—may I telephone?"

Their connection, except when in the bed his first call leads to, has been entirely that way; it's for him that she'd had the third telephone installed. Through all their passages in bed, he remains exactly as seen that first evening. Day Folger, Texan, veteran of women but still single and five years younger than she—in age only—with a fine, mashed-ugly face that reminds one of the movie-star whose name one can never remember, and Indian hair. His folks have a ranch near the King ranch, though not as large; his mother was born on a slice of what was once the Shirley plantation in Virginia—white skin assumable. All his life has been large in gesture, free with money and desperately small in the drama he's hoped from all that output. Only the money has fruited, cleverly on and on. Since the age of nineteen he's backed plays, movies and now records; in his past with women, in and among the many actresses, painters and writers, are a dead rockstar, a live trapeze-artist, a female toreador and a winner of the Pulitzer Prize for biography. For two early years he himself had been an actor, doing so badly that the doomedly shrewder side of himself had caught up with him. Technically he's a "producer," a name he loathes. When challenged however, he stammers it. What he yearns toward, and rains presents on, are those persons—to him enchanted in present heaven—who spin the web of art from their very selves. Since he himself is as male as any drake, such men as encountered he merely options or supports with monthly remittances, meanwhile participating in their stagings on film, disc or in print—and there he has excellent taste. The women he penetrates, probing for the living-doll artiste as for the marble tip of some sphinxly clitoris.

And with the women—by what she can gather from the arsenal of photos at his flat, his artistic taste has been poor, either bedazzled by their looks, or misguided by other ambience. Apparently he has a penchant for the second-rate—particularly for those who can theatricalize it. Probably the prizewinner's been his best so far, artistically, but from her photo, signed in heavy flourish, not nearly stylish enough for the crowd of high-living artists he hangs out with. Real ones, here. Who never eat a meal at home. During her own short tenure, she's met them in those haunts that are Day's also; playwrights at Maude's and Elaine's, actors at Sardi's or Pearl's, or at the Blue Ribbon, just before it closed. And the Lion's Head once, for a trio of Dixieland Jazzers in their eighties—almost as late-in-the-day for her to be there, she thinks, as for them. Lunch, for her, is the most powerful draw erotically. To stroll at noon toward a lover, or with him after, with all its side-implications of secrecy, luxe and time-stop, is European—and a flight. Lunch is also where Day meets the people he's really going to do something with, and where she feels strangely comfortable, almost as if she's not always going to be an amateur. It piques him to have one of his playwrights find out that she reads, and to hear a casting-director say "Why this girl has wit!"—although she's often innocent of her own humor and can never repeat or reuse it knowingly.

Day knows about her poems—since he'll venerate them without reading them. Also—so delicately entrepreneur is he even at lovemaking's height—he's found out about the journal she once kept, and intends to keep again. Though in an access of shame, she bars him from ever mentioning it.

"God, I never saw a girl blush from the hips before. You should be proud." And maybe she is, of the blush.

That evening she has a ride with him in a scenarist's Rolls. And at Michael's Pub, sits at the left ear—the deaf one—of an earl who plays the harmonica. And for the first time, feeling guilt all over, like a bodystocking woven of an allergy-producing polyester, she stays the night. After that, she does this often, without alibi. Spending the morning-after hunting for marvels of dress, tarty ones, which she hangs in Day's closet on East 79th Street, and never takes home. Though she expects he must have other women, she never sees a trace of one.

Day in bed is all confidence, a man-about-town who goes for a woman like a cowboy straight off the range. For their first meeting, she chooses with severe instinct a rustling-rosy underpetticoat, with a bodice like a girl's in a Western, which makes his eyes glisten—though to the end she judges him unconscious of any role. Their alliance thrives only so long as he keeps thinking she must have some talent he is looking for; when she incautiously finds the strength to deny this, his calls begin to fail. Hers to him become unevenly successful. One Thursday, the wrong part of the week for their assignations, she forces it, walking into the restaurant where he lunches with his partner. He doesn't recognize her right off; in a grim rush of bourgeois pride she hasn't dressed for it. He takes her home with him; he's kind. But the minute they enter his apartment she smells another girl, through his awkwardness. That he can after all be gauche in this way wrings her—a little. She wishes for the rose petticoat, but she too has her sentiment; it's the one new garment she'd taken back to her village, as the smallest of links between her two lives.

As they undress, she sees he's uneasy but, as always, able, not a man who needs champagne or carnal chit-chat either; indeed, no sooner had she learned to coarsen her tongue with Kevin, than she's had to clip it back for this Southerner.

Just as they rise, facing each other knee to knee on his many experienced pillows—*his* luxury—the phone rings. With a polite murmur, and yes, lowered lids, he goes into the pantry to answer it. From the bedroom extension-phone, so close under her eye, she turns consciously to the photographs. She likes the bullfighter—who'd gouged him in the pocket and left him—much the best. In this moment, she understands that she too should be gouging him in some way. If, when he comes back, she can say "Yes, you were right: I have a secret volume of poetry *here*"— pointing meanwhile to her throat or her stomach—he'll rise to it at once. Setting out on the double for printer, afterward. Or perhaps: "Carnegie Recital Hall, my concert two weeks from now; remember the date. Well of *course* I haven't told you, Day. I don't wear my harp on my sleeve."

Instead, when he comes back to the bedroom and begins again, too polite not to, she feels even desire fade before her utter urge to have him know she understands his mechanism—to reveal it to him.

As he eases her off the bed to her feet, and standing too, places her arms around his hips, she fixed her eye on the organ of his confidence, as it rose under her. "Producer!" she spat forth, saw him stammer in the flesh, and it was over.

She's proud of having left behind the clothes.

This time, in the aftermath, she's not dulled, but inordinately restless, and ashamed of not having been in love with him. "I am at home, home, home" she says to herself each dusk—"and I need two lives." Spasmodically she still attends the class, which is now in spring-term. One day, outside the college, she meets Plaut, the instructor, walking with his wife. She sees that his wife's baby is well on. He waggles a finger at her. "Going to have to give you an Incomplete."

Her laugh startles him. "But I'm continuing."

All home duties she now performs only adequately, and restraining the cookies; she has heart now neither for excess nor neglect—and has the third telephone taken out. But something from those city afternoons-in-bed has been held over. She knows for sure now that sexually she won't go back again to Ray. Yet she sees to it that her second day in New York now comes only on weekends, when the whole family gets itself together for the Boat Show, or she shops with the two girls. One Saturday, on the way to Olafsdotter's in the Village to buy them clogs, they pass the door of Kevin's old flat on Bleecker. Her haunches shift for a moment, and she says to the girls "Hold my hands." On another, walking toward the Frick, she says suddenly to Ray "Let's walk up a few more, why don't we?" and to the two boys "We'll meet you there"—and so doing, she and Ray walk down Folger's block. Not on the chance of meeting him; he's never in town on weekends. "Why'd you do that?" Ray says. "Oh I dunno," she says, indifferently. Why's he stopped seeing Betsy? But at the Frick, she hesitates. The two boys must have gone in. Her heart skirls—at the discreet way the children are managing. Not confiding, she'd bet, even among themselves. "I think . . . it was to learn more about you and me, Ray." She stands in the street outside the quiet entry. A street—how appropriate. "Ray. Do'ya think—we are almost at the end of it?" He doesn't answer. Even as doctor, he's a man to let things ride; some patients leave him for the highroad to surgery, others praise him for letting nature take its course.

Driving home at his side, the car silent except for the boys, she sees how, after twenty years, he and she are matched—neither interlocked at the head or heels, nor in handfast, but like certain notched wheels which fit each other's serrations: what one or the other cannot confront, the other continues with.

So pass four months. What does Ray do in his study while she watches her house-of-cloud—though no longer from her nightly ledge? Twice that pile of tumulus down-river has opened a window to her however briefly; one day, there may be a door. At four in the afternoon now, never at nine—though she can't say why these changes, she's not really depressed—she still walks the cat.

One day, a Saturday too warm for town, when Ray is off on a trip and the kids are all at picnic, just as the cat and she are returning, the cat leading, she sees a long black coupe drawn up at the door. Even before she recognizes the Jag which for so many evenings—no, so few really—had needled her back and forth between those restaurants, Day Folger gets out, and a girl.

They're looking for a house, it appears, and have found themselves in the region.

He's hangdog, the girl triumphant; in one of the exquisite revenges men are blind to, or prefer to be, she has led him here. "Bonnie's from down home."

She does adaptations for television, Day says. Her first big one is just coming up.

She's pretty in a chalkboned way, but about Day's age, not a girl. A few months more with Day's crowd of sharp-eyed dazzlers and she'll get him to option those upper teeth of hers, and have them crowned. She dresses in the brightly literal way smalltowners do when they begin to make it in New York; down home, Lexie suspects, Bonnie's not quite Day's sort, but up here, it won't show.

Just now she's all after-bed slinks and twitches, aimed at Day. From an excess of secrets, she bursts out laughing. "Dyin' to see the house."

Lexie's breasts feel too big and sloppy in the washed-thin white sweater she's wearing over old, stretched shepherd's-check trousers she always means to throw out.

Though she's only a couple of inches above average height, she walks after them into her house feeling herself its shambly giantess.

Day holds back politely. Bonnie stalks through as if she's buying the place. Or not buying it.

Following after them through parlor—too white-and-red against the river?—library—the best of rooms, dining room, a broad empty swathe at this hour, kitchen (in which the enormous farmhouse plank of a nineteenth-century counter has been kept but its niggling corner sink also), she keeps them from the children's rooms—for the children's sake, especially Chessie's. Watching the house huckster its own views, window-to-window, she's defensive. Yes, it *is* majestic; no, poor tower, we never did enough for it. She'll even defend the suburbs if she can bear to—to Bonnie, clearly one of those girls who'll adopt the city so fast that its born citizens will have to take a step back.

From the top of the house there's a peal of laughter. They've found her ledge. That view of the river will stop their breath. She advances, its smiling custodian.

They've just kissed. A couple househunting for the afternoon, for kicks: "Let's, shall we?" she can hear them saying to the spanking city noon, to the subtle outer noises that lip Day's shaded bed.

She folds her arms, touching her elbows as if they are the points of a heart. They aren't—though she can still see Day's naked chest advancing over her, jackknifing suddenly to put his black head between her thighs. Takes women longer to wrench themselves free of the details. She knows that already.

Though Day has turned red.

He's getting his artiste. Providentially, one from home; maybe that's what's held him back, but he and this girl are the kind of provincials who'll make born New Yorkers look slow. Meanwhile settling a mite slavishly for the brand-names in life, the best of course. How she, Lexie, knows this, is what makes her not a provincial. Has nothing to do with these two. Comes from the piers and the streets.

At the same time, Day's out of this catfight. A little vanity, yes, but his real dramas are elsewhere: commercial, military. The dramas of women are small ones, containable in rooms. What happens to him with this woman will be submerged, whatever it is—years will pass, before he knows. We drag them down, she thinks. And thinking of Ray—do we keep them up?

What Bonnie knows for herself is that Day is the enemy. Who must pay.

Right now, he's uncomfortable. "Lexie. *Is* this house for sale?"

"Not that *I* know of."

"Why Day Folger. You did give the *im*-pression." Quick to the attack, Bonnie addresses Lexie. Not by name of course. Bonnie will leave other women in limbo, if possible. "I do believe I built you up as restless." To Day. "One of my *stoh-ries,* dawlin. You know how they come to me, 'bout people. All I do is ketchum. It's just out of my control."

Down the steps they go, not routed. Routing, Bonnie is. Day's gaze, fast on her as he descends to the car, is holy.

She runs back up the steps to where Lexie is. Whispers "I do believe—it was those clothes."

And trips down again.

Below, the car is hidden by the high hedge. Only river-road people realize how voices float up here. "It was an exp*i*rament, Day honey," hers says. "Y'all know how I have to expirament."

The cloud of dust the couple leaves hanging in the air is unexperimental—exactly the shape and duration for such a car on such a day.

And such people. All three of us.

Gaze at the river. It has no sexual health one way or tother.

Wish for the children, *your* experiment, to come home

and save you, their faces lavender under the beach-streaked hair. Save me—with the work I will do for them. Ray is unwishable.

They are late. She's both inside and outside the children's story anyway. She sees clearly what she is to them. Seeing most clearly what she is not. She checks the time. It's not four o'clock; it's not nine.

She walks the cat.

At the secretarial school where her mother had made her go after high school, the pupils were unlike any of the girls she'd grown up with in the Village. "From the Boroughs, sounds like," her mother said. Working for the masses, she could afford snobbery. "Well—you're traveling."

Instead, she'd chummed briefly, before they all scattered to jobs, with two girls who defer to her city lore: Taylor Crimmins from Carolina, sent to Gibbs because it was still for ladies, even if they must work (and even if named for a General), and Nancy Leighton, brought up by the nuns of Brookline, Mass.—and from the starchy-plump looks of her, on what she called "perdaders" still. Taylor had been reared from birth to know what men could do to her—cast her into the pit of ignored life—if she couldn't first strike one down. Nancy had been cautioned from birth against what a man could do when he struck.

"The Jewish girls are all ready and buttered between the legs for it," Taylor would say in the downright way her daintiness could go when stimulated.

"They've no Christian sense of sin," Nancy would answer. "The Italians, they're more like us, being in the church. But they have to guard against being full-blooded. And after they're married, they like it too much."

"*Worry* is their worry," her own mother said of the Jews, when applied to. "The Italians, they're just close."

She'd been wrapping her gray braid around her head, preparatory to going to an assemblage in one of the asphalt-covered halls she frequented, whose stony echoes and banged-up chairs seemed ready to lapse into a congregation of their own, the minute there was no human need for them. "Going to a meeting," her mother was, to exposit on life—as if there was none of it at home. Perhaps there hadn't been? One thing Renata had never done was ask her children to save her from anything. Knowing better than to ask their father. She'd always known best, and nowadays she and her independence shared a household—an old woman with an untrustworthy companion, arranged for her in earlier days, who no longer solaced her.

"What'll *you* do—?" her mother said back there, to Lexie's question "—oh, I can prognosticate." And never equivocate, her nose says, never shilly-shally like the restfully vague mothers some people had. Even long before then, Lexie had known that she went to her mother to be pierced. "Oh, you, Lexie—your father and I have each done you our particular dirt. Can't be helped. Same with James. James'll be careful—too careful, I think. But you—"

She always gave her diagnosis the way she played her short repertoire at the piano—stolidly, to the end. "You Lexie? You'll flounder." Her gloves are old and loose. She draws them on as hard as if they're new. Renata's own mother ran away when Renata was ten; Renata brought the others up, and herself alongside. "You don't only remind me of granma in the *face*."

Young Lexie sees the guilty face of the runaway being handed on and on, by gypsies maybe, until it reaches her; she herself will probably never even have a pair of really new gloves. From the front door, her mother runs back down the long hall to clutch her, tight. "Flounder strong, hah? For me?" Leaving young Lexie stunned, radiant. Her mother ran all the way down the hall to tell her. (No, to ask.)

Walking the cat now, the river-road is deep in blue air, as if she's wading through hyacinths which part as she breasts them, but the water washing the shore indigo is a river still, brinked from forces beyond the 49th parallel and over the edge of the geography book. She grasps a convenient paling, near the stalking cat; stares out. Is this travel? The cat spurts away, into the dark. Any sudden movement startles them, even a friend's. Are we like that?—am I?

On the opposite shore, the house-of-cloud has followed her. She addresses it: There is no market for my meditation. My language is not admitted. It would be no use for me to write for television.

She opens her mouth wide as a changepurse, and screams for the cat.

When she got back to the house, she went past the kitchen, bright with children fixing their own dinner, as had become the Saturday custom, and waving to them, ran up the backstairs to her ledge. The window was dusty, even cobwebbed, by the spiders that busied themselves in spring. Come autumn, though she knows nothing of their cycle, they'll seem hoarders, nesters, different. In either case, a neglected house. In the webs-and-dirt she writes with a finger: For Sale.

Then she goes down to the kitchen. And for an evening, is saved.

Lying in the grass, where the first white beads of dew are now settling, that night now appears to her like a Breughel hanging unnoticed till then on her wall. Two boys, two girls, two younger, two older, one tall, one small, two of an even height; from moment to moment the alignments shift. The boys are conning a salad—"Keep out the worms!" a girl shrieks in scorn; the two girls have baked a cake. "Yah, remember the first cake she-ee—" the boys jeer back. "For a haffa cup sugar, who put salt?"

Now and then one appeals to her as referee. Although both this habit and her authority are dwindling, tonight she's deep in the human fabric, and honored too. What power she's had over these souls before her! Over there is Charles, the oldest, who could have been named James. Or

Alex, after her, and her grandfather. The power of the name. And of the nose—for in three of these faces her pudgy one, handed down scarcely blended, from the power of her own father, has pushed out Ray's. To be sure, a slender version of Ray's has appeared in Chessie, the older girl, insuring her beauty, what with those large soft eyes which descend—who would believe it?—from Ray's father, the veterinarian.

Chessie's the difficult one. "The talented one," people say, or ask? So many talents, but she's always putting salt for sugar; will she qualify? Charlie is hellbent for aerodynamics, and these days silent as a deposed king— does she think this because he's said to be "pure Ray"? He's made a time-wheel to show them what his father may be doing at this moment in Monte Carlo and Spain, and Ray had given him a detailed itinerary which Charles has hung on the opposite wall. He's jealous, even passionate about his father's position in this house. Perhaps when the males are with themselves, do even their very features veer obediently due-male-center, toward the father and his family? Perhaps heredity's a movable dock, which dips conformably with the weight of whoever's standing on it.

Now dinner's on the table, prepared by children's hands.

"What a lovely sight," she says, "—how magnificent," and means it—she's near tears. The rice steams with a biblical mist. Mustard pot, pepper, water pitcher march naive across table, in caravan. The chili glows. When the candle stumps are lit, she does cry. Finding that she can only make the dry face for it.

"Mother!" This is Maureen, the in-betweener, the sturdy one with the least personal face. She'll nurse me when I'm senile, Lexie thinks; Maureen will settle for a life of devotion if we're not all very careful, but she plays the piano more than serviceably, like her maternal grandmother, always finishing the pieces to the end; perhaps if we push very gently we can at least get her out of that drysink of devotion she's in, if not quite to the Juilliard. Or perhaps she's only in that phase when adolescents crave service, when they go to be monks and nuns. Let her have it then. "Maureen—" Lexie says, smiling, "—my rock."

When little Royal, the youngest, creeps into her lap, though at going-on-ten he's too old for it, she nuzzles him. Nobody jeers. Roy was born with one leg shorter than the other and a wry foot. His infirmity is good for the others; does he know this? It won't sway him; look at the long James-jaw on him, those careful Ray-hands; he's going to be a doctor too. And when asked what kind has already answered: "Like me."

. . . Was that the particular night also the one when Chessie burst out "Salt, salt, salt—what do I care?" and ran from the table, and was brought back by little Royal, the only one who could—because she knew he'd limped up-stairs to do it? Or was it the evening of that day Maureen, the sturdy one, got lost in the city, losing her wallet too and just managing to quaver out the city corner she was phon-ing for Lexie to drive in and pick her up from, before her telephone dime went down? When we drove in here and Maureen saw the three others waiting on the steps, how she bloomed—a flowering. She'd begged the dime, on the corner—would I have been able to do that?

Or was that night the one when, in return for a re-mark about James, I smacked Charles on his cheekbone, seeing in the wide-open second after that my authority with him was forever gone?

Or was it the night. . . ? They parade before her, these nights, their alignments shifted beyond recall.

Does it matter? Like each of those nights, that one is all the nights together.

Though certainly it was the one when Charles, turn-ing his time-wheel for their attention, said "Five hours ahead of us, roughly. Dad'll be in the Casino. Or maybe in bed."

And she thought—by himself? I wouldn't censure him. Thing is, I can't imagine him over there any better than I can at home.

. . . How is it I can imagine any friend at any time, giving them events either wildly devious or hilarious which still seem right for them as they must be, yet my own husband remains secret to me—separate? Is it because he himself is that sort of man, unimaginable by his nearest: Ray? Or because he's Ray the father as well, the father-immediate, stalking battles that I am only wife to, and was only daughter to? The father—thrust into that corner, kicked upstairs to those more objective glories which had to become his, once he saw that first bloody birth emerge from my embattled legs and working crotch: that smeared child, with a dent in his head but smiling curlily, who was my body's issue, glory arrived of my bearing down, who was Charles-to-be, the near-man I smacked—and merely a father's dream. What's fatherhood but a long dream Ray walks in because people do say? Maybe the women ought never let him see our battlefield, but only let him hear dimly, in medicine-man murmurs, of that powerful cave from which he comes in all his pretension. Never let him see birth or be sure of it—are there tribes who've done that? . . .

Certainly it was the night on which, knocking her fists together, ranging the four children with her eyes, she hears herself say "Anyone know a blessing?" And sees she's sent all four of them mute. Her beloved menagerie, against whose hindparts she cracks her whip-tongue. She feels like a cat-trainer, left behind bars empty except for herself. When has her dominion ended?

Yet they see her; tonight they really see her, as happens less and less. More and more these days, they fault her for not seeing them. And she doesn't quite. The image of her parenthood is dying, that's it. On both sides.

"Anybody who knows one—" she quavers "—please say."

Charles sullenly moves his wheel to half-past-one. Yes they're eating late, eight-thirty. But that's never been a sin before.

"Chili that bad, Lexie?" the main cook says. At thirteen, over three years ago, Chessie stopped calling her Ma.

"I know a blessing—" Maureen cries. Her glance falls, before the others. "But it's for meat."

Royal says "Eat a hot pepper, Ma?" in his brightest cherub-tone. Everybody breathing in time with him, he scrambles down and brings her the jar. Like hemlock, she thinks. Or tact. Which from one's own children is tooth-sharp.

The jar holds red and green peppers of the hottest kind—like a vial of Stop and Go. Only she can eat them. Not that she likes them much, but it's her talent, a city one. Nurtured ever since she'd heard Charles, then ten, say, in a boasting match with another boy—whose dad was a champ jogger—"My ma can eat hot peppers straight down."

She chews a green one, and lets the tears sprout. Waving her hands helplessly to show them it isn't just the vegetable. "This is how I feel." She closes her eyes.

The *kitchen* is the blessing. Bedrooms go by ones and twos; the downstairs and halls of a house are by turns a crossing, a layabout land, a divide. But in the kitchen they clambered round me, still my parts, close with me between the ovenheat and the pores of the floor. The body of our bread we were, all together and love-buttered, or what passed for it—all reeky and not quite sour at the edges, like raw milk. That was a menagerie, then. Charles the serious giraffe, Maureen the faithful griffon, Royal the nipping marmoset—were the roles. And Chessie self-styled, whose mind even then burned on her mouth like a feversore—"I'll be the snake."

Clamber on all fours, dirty pantaloons—under my skirt and over my shoulder; I am the mother-animal of you all. And the only person of the afternoon, after school. I didn't need to touch you, to feel it. The umbilical cord, winding up and downstairs and even into the garden, knotted us belly to elbow to ear. Father was for evenings. And Sundays—half.

These are my images. How can I make this known? Now that they leave me. What is the language?

She opens her eyes. Palms together. Is it a blessing? She bows her head, clenches, hoping. "To the closeness of flesh."

Then events come fast, maybe to help her—who knows? When she puts forth this idea in class—that life shapes itself to aid or teach—the other women laugh. "Help you with what?" one says. She doesn't know. Maybe she feels so only because she's so poorly educated; while all the others in class are finishing college, she's only starting it.

Yet—here on the one hand is Ray being taken with hepatitis in Europe. Refusing to let her come over, although neighbors here would have coped. Refusing to allow James. Who however reports "After all, he's never in his life been sick before. He wants to hide. The medical care is apparently adequate."

"Wants to hide? From what?"

James is getting into his car to drive back to the city, to Morton Street. He lets the car door slam on his answer. "You should know."

She watches the dust spurt from behind the rear wheels of James's long-jawed, heavy-assed coupe. "From me?" she calls after it. "He's hiding from me?" In the middle of the driveway, she stands perplexed. Ray in Europe. Which to her is a house-of-cloud which is real. Was it somehow characteristic of him to think of that continent, whose medical practices he faintly despises, as a place to hide?

The line between what they expect her to sense, but not to act on, is a bewildering one.

But the day's such a spanking spring one that she stands there laughing, like a peasant who knows the almanac and how to live by it. James's car so resembles James. Do you know that already, brother James? Then what is it we're both unconscious of?

Yes events are helping. On the one hand as noted, there's Ray in Europe. On the other hand, that same night is the one when she wakes to find Chessie standing over her in the four A.M. light.

"Kellihy's is burning," Chessie says. *"Ma!"*

She leaps out of bed, a maréchal of France. In a nylon shortie. "Wake the others. Put on boots, sweaters, coats. Get to the front door."

Outside the door, they peer north through the great trees, here since the Revolution some say, which so far have breasted two twentieth-century hurricanes. They are pine and hemlock, but in the dead orange glare behind them their fronds hang tropical. Kellihy's garage is on fire—a three-car carriagehouse once, with a turreted servants' quarters above. She hopes Violet and Arthur are out of it, then recalls that they too sleep in the main house.

Hastily she counts again the faces clustered toward her, yes four. Have I only four of these mine-pure diamonds?—how frivolous of me not to lay up more. Of this treasure. She's amazed at the power she's had—to make. These four complex footsoldiers, with the right armament of eyes and hearts—even counting Royal's one little flaw, and all standing here booted and jacketed just as she's asked—her regiment. Later she'll feel greedy again to know their interiors, forever closed to her—but not now. "We're three hundred yards from them," she says. "I remember the house deed. And the wind is blowing away from us. Not toward."

Charlie's face is open with admiration. Ha, you've forgotten your father-wheel, Charlie, I can't help observe—though this is no time for rivalry.

Royal pipes "Is it blowing toward them?" His face is bright with interest. What a doctor he'll make.

Chessie's hanging back. Oh girl, you worry me. "Chess—you were wonderful. Absolutely wonderful."

Chessie weighs this—which she can never believe. Weighs her alter ego, Lexie. "What about the fire department. Shouldn't we have called?"

"I did." She says it lightly. Ego—avaunt. But her smile smiles.

Maureen's face crumples. "Gabriel." The cat.

"Oh darling. In or out?"

"In."

"Ah, good. Good, darling; don't you see?" She looks up at her house, theirs. All intact. "All right then; go back for him. Come right out."

The others are restless. She knows her troops. "Charlie, you have your watch?" He nods alertly; he even swims with it.

"All right, then. You may all go back in. For five minutes only." They groan. "Six. Charles, you're responsible. You may each bring out what you want. Only what you can carry easily. Not too much." They're spraying from her like buckshot. "Mau-re--en. Bring Gabe out on a lead."

She's almost grateful that Kirsten, their old boxer, is recently dead. Of age. She's almost grateful for everything. She is qualified, her tight throat tells her. You are qualified, maréchal, for this. Now advance.

And bim-bam, the fire-engine arrives.

Royal's still at her side. Although his spritely limp is twice the pace of most kids his size. "Royal. Don't you want to get your stamp collection? No? There isn't anything you want to rescue? I mean—the house is safe, I think. But just in case." She quirks at him. "Isn't it kind of fun—to choose?"

This is why the others went inside. She knows them well enough for that. Dreadful, how Royal is the one she always probes.

Royal quirks up at her, in exact imitation. Dreadful, how this is the one she doesn't trust. "Uh-uh. I *got* that."

In spite of herself. "What?"

He shrugs, evasive. But he can't bear not to tell her. "Me." He measures her. His mind's like a small gold whistle, ever quick to his lips. "*You* and me."

Ah chilling, to know one's own child. Once she'd heard a psychiatrist say thoughtfully, to the back of an insulter just then limping away, "Never trust a cripple." Horrible. For a psychiatrist to say that. Yet she'd never forgotten. What the soft, muffling valves of motherhood should have shut out at once. She must be overqualified.

Holding onto Royal, she watches the trees over at Kellihy's. Through the thick trunks thin arcs of water fall gracefully. The fire leaping from the garage looks joyous. They're wetting down the roof of the Kellihy house. Nothing flames there yet, except what all the neighbors already know. Several from the nearest houses cluster on the road in front of it, at a safe distance from the engines, three now, parked up the driveway. It's the great house of the district; it can accommodate three. And has garages to burn. She won't join the group down there; she knows their scratchy, Methodist whispers: *Rich, careless, youth, immoderate, booze, adultery, reckless, improvident—rich.* All these things being bright and beautiful as fire to them. She has a whisper of her own. It was the Kellihys' Roddy with the matches of course, redheaded gleeful pyromaniac, son of poor Bob, the wired frog. Their roof is gleaming: shall she ask the firemen to spray hers? How powerful neighbors are with each others' lives—is that what she's learning?

"Where are the Kellihys?" Charles' voice says. The three are back, Gabriel spitting and arching in Maureen's arms.

"Watch out, he'll scratch," she says. "Even you." Has Maureen brought nothing else for herself? Yes, her metronome.

Charles is carrying one of the machines he makes, on principles constantly changing, never explained. This is no doubt the latest one, bulbous at the core, but fraily pennanted. Under it, acting as its base, are the two green volumes of his book on parrots, in which the illustrative plates are made with actual feathers. He's smug with choice.

Fearfully almost, she turns to Chess. Tall, elongated to more than willowy five-foot-ten, she's dressed now in the old velvet opera-cloak she bought at a fair for its amber highlights—and brown depths. She has topped it with the vintage crushy hat she wears constantly, flipped up now a la Watteau. She stands ready to be mocked. Courting it, daring it; all her aggression is there. She has sad hands, and enormous style. The long fingers turn up at the tips; they're trembling.

The children accept her. No adult ever knows what to say to her. She is mad with such fluency. And does so well at her books. From such brown depths.

Safer not to speak. Lexie salutes, then stays her hand, puzzled. Her daughter, in that hat and cloak, is an intended charade. A linedrawing, meant to—"The Picasso!" she cries, "The Picasso." Bought by her and Ray early on. After the house, their most important purchase—barring her tenth-anniversary pearls. And the most revered object in it. A figure anomalous, in a hat and cloak.

Chess brings it out from under her arm. Unsmiling. But pleased. *She'll be an artist, or a martyr* James had said of her. *She enjoys redress, after being mocked.*

How can I leave them, Lexie thinks—these four personae so subtly risen up from the flesh given them, into tangles that only I know?

Chess holds the print out to the three others. Their heads hang over it like an Adoration. Bearing gifts.

In the grass, she stirs, clasps her knees, plucks a green spear, and lies down with it. The river is whitening, like her life. One can't see a house on its mist anywhere. But yes, that was the moment, back there; that was it.

Back there, the children turn on her. Sometimes, without warning, they act as one. "What about you? You haven't brought anything." Nothing from our house, to save. They've ferreted her out. Her tigerish "I've *got* it!", hugging their four heads to her, doesn't please them. They dislike parental sentiment. "No, no," they say. "Go back in like us. And choose."

"Six minutes," Charlie says, grinning.

They were right, she thinks now, chewing her blade of

grass. When I hugged them, I was telling the truth un-
adorned. But children know early that truth-adorned is
more likely the parental one. I've had to lie down here to
remember that.

So she ran back to the house. From Chessie's window,
which faces north upriver, she can see the whole plan of
the Kellihy fire, a siege already receding and on its way to
be filed in village recollection. With certain embellish-
ments.

Is that Betsy, emerging on the front balcony? The
garage and its turrets are a dead loss, down to the ugly
stone foundation, which remains. Two of the engines are
backing down the driveway. The crowd of neighbors
out in the roadway moves calm and sated in the dawn.
Bob, without his telephones but gesticulating, is among
them.

In the back garden, Arthur the butler comes out with
a flashlight which he plays over the ruins and shuts off
again, musing like the real householder here. And out
front, on the balcony, yes, that's Betsy. She's making gestures of thanks, large ones, from the Pasadena Playhouse.
Wide-in-the-sleeve, and appropriating to herself the still-
smoky heavens, she's like that girl in the old high school
joke—who every time the thunder claps, goes to the window and bows. She knows who she is, better than some
people do. She is the embellishment. She's wearing the
nightgown from Saks'.

In Lexie's own house, safe under its dry roof among
its hundred corners, she runs to Ray's and her common
bedroom. There's a dressingroom off it, and another
smaller room, where she sleeps these days, but no matter;
from here, turning on a heel, she can survey it all, the
whole arrangement—in a thunderclap. She has no time
for her ledge. When she comes out of the house again, her
absurd, precise Charlie says "Four minutes." She is carrying her thesis on Roger Bacon.

She'll never know what they thought of that, whether
they approved. Only Maureen spoke up, with her devo-

tional gaze. "I thought—maybe the peppers. But you can buy those."

Yes, that was the moment. With the house rescued, the children gathered, and the wind blowing away from them. When she knew she would eventually leave.

Afterwards, they'd gone inside and make pancakes, hilarious as a houseful of allnight drunks.

After which, like a nun's veil floated invisibly down on her, what may be the reigning meditation of her life begins. Or its suspension? Every seventh day, Ray's weekly bulletin gives her one more week to muse. Since marriage she hasn't been so alone with her ego, or so taken aback at its narrow, grim persistence. Yet instinct tells her she must be serious; if she lets in humor now—she had it once— she'll fail. At what?

She doesn't allow herself to brood on concrete matters. Ray's weekly letter, three sheets of thin European paper that would melt in a teacup, is full of those. "Pay the insurance; remember the tires on the Volvo. Have them cut the bamboo between Kellihy's and us before it gains headway." As it does every year, despite. "This is the year we were going to train the wisteria into a tree, and clear away the rotting pilings that were once a dock. What of Charles' college applications?" Ray's wooing her from afar, she thinks. He is rebuilding their house—from cloud.

She constructs her days like yoga exercises which come upon her one by one. For a morning, she'll sit at the kitchen table examining like an actress what it will be to be old, rehearsing it. By noon she has it down pat—the mumbling lip, rocking jaw, blinking eye, and shake of head. And tentative hands. Is this depression? Probably. But shouldn't one practice age? When one has so much time for it?

On another morning she'll go into the city, wandering there the whole day to test what the city is to her without lovers.

From a window in the Cloisters, where faith is

museumed in fake rock, she saw through its arch the dead-real Palisades. On South Street she boarded the sailing-ships, which were standing still. She felt the tourist panic—who in the world hereabouts knows who and where I am? A sandwich place unlocked her tongue. Outside it again, a man in a green wool tam, knocked sideways for Ireland's sake, hobbled by her at a clip, not drunk, not crazy, merely stating to the air and whomever he's on the way to "—and oy am the best dommed dogtrainer in *this* town." Right. That's better; this is a street she knows. Her foot treads a small newssheet, still clean, on which, bending without picking it up, she reads: Boston Auto Torpedoes Racist Banner. A broadside for some faction? She visualizes a parade-size banner, upheld by two people, and the small, pointed car; a Volks wouldn't be sharp enough. But she walks on without picking the newssheet up. The essence of her city is in that nonchalance.

Yet when two men from a truckload of Hasidic Jews offer her a flyer she takes it and carefully reads the proper procedure for kindling the Shabat candles. "First light the candles, then cover your eyes with your hands to hide the flame." Yes, the city is still hers. And she needn't call James. Whose role in her life so teases her. Yet I have a life in which people have roles. She goes home.

On still another day, she asks herself "Why do women like me think that being in the world is being *outside* the house?" And goes to the nearby State Hospital, to volunteer. For two weeks she teaches typing as therapy. A schizophrenic boy of seventeen—yes, seventeen is the age—falls in a kind of love of her. Though he's physically sound, his fears and angers are going through the senses one by one, negating them. In music-hall he's gone deaf; in painting-workshop his fingers can't feel though he hears perfectly. In her class, he professes to be blind. She guides his fingers on the keyboard, meanwhile passing a hand between his eyes and hers. He *is* blind.

"I can smell," he says. "You have perfume on. May we kiss?"

When she does so, he vomits on her hand.

The rest of the week there was uneventful. She had other patients who had cycles too, but less overt ones. She noted how they went from talk-talk to silence, from sleep to hard wake. A doctor said "It drears the pain."

At the end of the second week, she quits. "No, I'm not a volunteer," she says, when pleaded with. "No, I'm not your material. I'm looking for a job." So she's found that out. But it's also true that witnessing these cyclic patterns has scared her. Do they resemble hers?—she thinks, walking away from the gray hospital yard whose grass pleads with her for help. What is her central pain? Why's she asking that?

Home, when she pulls up in its driveway, greets her with the sanity of tasks waiting. She tries to visualize the house, dappled now in the noon sunlight, without the penumbra of tasks that shadow it in her consciousness, in the worst early days a snail's smear, dragging her from behind. Yet she's always concealed from others that she enjoys household craft itself. Concealing it from other women especially. But the children know, and tease her; when she polishes furniture they condescend, like slummers in a land they'll never live in, not them. "Ma's polishing furniture again." How bewildered Charles was, when, leaning in humiliation on her oily rag, still half-circling it on the table's oval, she spat out "It's my meditation!" and stalked up the stairs.

Did he know how she lay on her bed, a creature circling in her meditation, trying to weep like a girl? Why has she been given all this time for philosophy, if it shall not bear fruit, or even be credited? Yet the children love to come home and find her tethered to the house, like an animal of which they're fond. Which feels guilty when it slips their leash and runs. What does her chastity or unchastity mean to them? That she's slipped the lines of family, contaminated their mother's-milk? Or only that at three o'clock homecoming time, she's deserted them?

Upstairs, she hauls out Ray's letters and reads between

the lines. Yes, he's homesick in a way—but can it be for this? No, we're both homesick, but not for each other. What would a man like Ray be homesick for? Almost she knows, but won't admit.

For a life, knitted with hers, in which he will be spared homesickness for anything else.

Not like her for a land of condors—if only to see whether the condor flies as pitiless as said. Not for a flotilla of ships, receptive off a shore one strides down to naturally. She sees that armada, that odyssey toward which—whenever it creaks at anchor—the woman may only go filleted, bearing gifts. As in the poem her class is studying. While on board, on the high seas, the sure, sandaled feet raft the rocking waves, tread the great poem, traveling.

"Ah," she said, running up the stairs to her ledge and standing there, as of old. "So that's it." So that's what I'm homesick for.

Standing there, she saw herself in the vague pane—arms winged out for victory, but the head not damaged enough yet to be classical. So these are my images. So it's not you after all, house-of-cloud. No matter how many fiery windows burn through your gray. So my images don't include a house—did they ever?

Next morning, sitting on at the breakfast-table after the kids leave, in her mind she writes a letter to Ray, maybe on that old yellow scratch-pad paper which used to have bits of wood in it. "Dear Ray: I would not use travel to hide."

For an hour, going about her duties in silence, she wore that sentence like a plume on her head. But once out on the parkway, driving citywards, at the first sight in the distance of those silver harbor-needles which rim its coast, her plume collapses. Will all her language-search end in letters to Ray?

Warned in time, she walked into class still hopeful. The group, now well into its second semester, has been through cycles too. At first, they are each other's dear familiars, met passionately. In skittish lunches after class, they laugh immoderately, playing hookey from home. While the confidences flow—stall to stall in the ladies-room—of women who have held their water too long. Couples or threesomes spin off into friendships where they suddenly want to show each other their homes, and the people there. Ending up embarrassed afterward (too much has been said beforehand) when they see their home-treasures in the fierce, cold neon of the class. A schism develops between those who still lunch—watched by the local hotshots—in the plushy bar-restaurant in town, and those purist younger ones, still with the grub-smell and crayony clothes of baby-minders, who have settled for the school cafeteria, where they huddle like a vanguard, away from the older women, whom they see as having settled for good.

In the class outright a few personalities have emerged at once.

Elaine, who slams down from the Bronx once a week in her round black curé's hat, writes food-news for a Bronx weekly, brings them *Hamentasch* cakes for Easter, has had two husbands "Both of them gingerbread gentlemen; one hard, one soft," and once brings her current lover to class with an air of having baked him for the occasion—"I wanted to show him you girls." She's aiming for pre-law, and is obviously a woman who's had her own language from the beginning.

Jean Fackenthal, who lives in the town where the college is, had early on invited them for "tea in my home." Which they tour in silence down to the very dresser-drawers, proudly opened "for a peep," in whose quilted care a disaster-supply of silk bras, panties and nightgowns lie separate. Jean's husband has Parkinson's disease. The children, now in far places, have done well. She's the class renegade; they can only wish she were also the class dope.

"You blame *everything* on being women," she says, rising turkey-red from their first general lunch together. "Half the things you gripe about happen to people from *life.*" She sits in class now and then turning that same color as if it's her obligation to, spitting into their discussions an "*Age,* you fools!" or "What's your sexual liberty going to do about sickness, my hearties?", or "Get yourselves the jobs, the medals; can't you see that's all that's needed?" Or once, approvingly, when a portion of Lexie's thesis is read out: "Time, girlie, that's it; don't you worry, ladies; death will respect us sexually"—while throughout she worked the needlepoint square on which was appearing the heraldic seal of Barnard College (attended for two years only), her shaky hands tremoring intelligences into the wool.

Outside her house after the tour, Elaine said, "Gee, I always wanted to do my drawers like that," and then "Maybe she catches that palsy from him." One of the crayony girls burst into tears. "Tears," the horsey girl said—"Shit." She still never spoke except in monosyllables, but always tagged along, bringing with her like an accusation the ozone of early-morning rides.

By now they are all each others' enemies as well as friends. From too much similarity and too much shredding of the situation, they depress each other, both because some of them will not make out well—and some will. When she herself is with the group, a fish flowing with her kind, she so loves the sensation, the comfort, that a blessed myopia of acquiescence comes over her; she never knows what they think of her.

This morning, there are grumbles because Tom Plaut, the instructor, is late again.

"He takes advantage of us because this happens to be a three-hour class." This is Cee-Cee, the youngest of the vanguarders. "I was told this is a crash course, so I could start my major; we're not even getting through the syllabus."

At the outset, when Cee-Cee brought her two buttery-beautiful children to class, and Plaut told her "This is a college. You'll have to solve your problems outside the class," she'd replied "I want to solve them here."

She's a troublesome girl, always trying to solve things practically. The two children, aged three and four, disrupt the class just by being there. "Why should I pay a sitter— what do I care if they hear about D. H. Lawrence's dirt?" their mother says, but the rest reluctantly side against her, although the word "sitter" is attached to their own hearts like an extra valve. The line of liberty is hard to take. For Cee-Cee is also their proletarian. Her husband's a police-man; both have two years' college, but she's studying on, in order to write a book about his experiences. Which he is all for. And better be, she makes clear. As if this isn't all, she's also Chinese, and therefore one-half the class's ethnic triumph.

The other half is Mrs. Bidwell, a calm, older black woman who has never extended her first name to them. Unlike them, she is a real matriculated student, doing her Master's thesis under the instructor because he is a Renais-sance scholar and that is her field. She wears the white-collar-and-cuffs sets of the upwardly mobile, and is sus-pected of Uncle Tomism. As the vanguard's main talker says, "What the hell's a dentist's wife from White Plains, New York, doing writing on the *Faerie Queene*—when she is *black*?"

This is Billie La Barbara, a worker for the welfare department, who as yet has no children but is majoring in child psychology, for the inevitable. "It's my job makes me sterile," she tells them bitterly. "All that fulfilling of other people. It has to go."

"Yeah, saw him on campus the other day," she says now. "With that wife of his. She gets any more pregnant, he'll have to put her on wheels. He looks terrible."

Odd, how they all automatically hate the wife because she's his, and hold her responsible for his decline. Sagging weight that she must be, and irritable, while he's outside on a pearly day trying to teach us the objective correlative— don't we all know how those months go? But now we're outside, with him. Lexie herself has seen Plaut walking alone, faded and disheveled from already feeding two.

"He looks like one of those Russians," she hears herself say.

They all turn to stare at her. With reason. From being too much alone, her thoughts often elide, or express themselves truncatedly in her own code. In the lunch-sessions, she's discovered that this has now and then happened to all of them. Except to Mrs. Bidwell, who commented "*We* are never alone"—they didn't know whether from religious impulse or anti-white contempt—and never lunched with them again. But Lexie feels herself to be the worst. "Ray's away" she mutters, immediately flushing. Why should she need to excuse herself via him? "I meant like in those novels Plaut has us reading. There's always one man who's going down, down, down. He looks like one of those. Like something dreadful is going on in him."

"Haha," Cee-Cee says. "He liked Lexie's poem; that's what."

Cee-Cee's jealous. So far, Plaut has kept her work in the dark of the conferences she's always nagging for. Where, by her own report he stolidly corrects the grammar and won't be chivied on doctrine.

Yet ever since he read aloud Lexie's poem, even the others haven't been quite the same to her. Maybe she's let down their side.

"Leave Lexie alone," Jean says. "Maybe she's talented."

Jean's still against them, but today she scarcely has time for it. She's showing off her daughter, a tall rose-and-amber girl in full bloom, who is visiting from Hawaii where she has a state job—and a husband who is a professor. The girl looks somewhat like Chessie. But will Chessie ever have the assurance to look like her?

"No I'm not. Not yet," Lexie hears herself, hotly. "I was born in the Village, where artists live. I know the difference."

"So what's wrong with the Boroughs? Edgar Allen Poe lived in the Bronx." Elaine adjusts her hat at them, in the spirit-of-fairplay manner which makes candidates. "Gee, but I saw them too, Plaut and his wife. Even for eight months, that girl he married is a slop."

"Not a girl, a woman," one of the timider vanguarders says. They are of varying tint, after all. Or beginning to be. This one giggles. "She's older than him, by about eight years. She was his last year's student, *this* class."

"So she has to wear shorts, with the front end sticking out like a canoe, and gold mules—to show the under-grads?" Elaine beams at them. "Do I or do I not know my psychology, girls? And I tell you, I never saw a less connected couple dragging around." Family Court, Elaine's going to try for—she's told them—and she'll make it. A Judge. "Why these days, they didn't abort. He's working his doctorate, poor guy; here he's only part-time. Plus one course at City College. In his real subject."

La Barbara sits up. "He's an aborter all right, I bet. Like all of them. But don't you remember what he said? *We* changed their relationship."

Nobody answers her sneer. The three younger ones she's been bossing hang their heads. Is it that they're beginning to understand her? Or to understand that they too are various?

The girl, Jean's daughter, watches them all, open-mouthed.

Billie looks at her watch. "Part-time, what do you know. What a raw deal we got. From the college that has Arthur Ocker the sociologist; he even gives advice to Washington; why couldn't they give us him? Or Chickie Whatshername—the poet. Continued Education, blah. I move we petition to have him removed. Chickie Marcella, that's it—the black poet. She sings too; she's a gas. Let them give us somebody worth*wild*." She leans toward their scholar. Who sits apart from them, they now know, not because they're white but because she's matriculated, and so of finer grain. "How 'bout that, Mrs. Bidwell?"

"He's my subject. I'm satisfied."

Plaut appears in the doorway. Billie's conjured him up.

Even more battered than before. His eyes are circled red, his sweatshirt spotted; his pants, always a sign of a man's spirit or competence, decline around his shoes. Incredibly, a rope threaded through the waist-loops, holds them up. Clothesline, knotted in front. Perhaps he's saving it for his neck. Where's his belt? Has his wife beaten him with it? Some fury has raked his hair into horns. In this quiet court-of-brains, the campus, he sways in the eye of elements. In Westchester County, how can this happen to a man?

She sees Jean and her daughter thinking that. Afterwards, her own shame will be that she's merely thought in a circle, with each of them.

"Got your papers, girls." Plaut's voice, surprisingly firm out of such a joblot creature. Saying "girls" of course helps. "I'll hand them out." Plaut does so. As usual to each with a terse comment. Where briefly, he shines.

Cee-Cee is first.

"You're supposed to be writing *about* a policeman, Mrs. Morland. Not *like* one."

To Billie La Barbara: "'The World of Welfare,' eh? A large title, Miss La Barbara. Unfortunately, alliteration alone is not a summing-up. Also, you seem to think that your job makes you automatically generous. How wrong you are, Miss La Barbara. How wrong."

One by one, the vanguarders get theirs.

"Ah yes," he snarls, shuffling and dealing like a cardsharp. "'Lady Murisaki: Novelist with Bound Feet,' eh? . . . 'Florence Nightingale: Nursing as Slavery' . . . 'Eleanor Roosevelt, The Voice Behind The Power' . . . 'Whale Chauvinism in Moby Dick.'"

His smile is pulling him together, even lifting the pants. "How dainty your humor is, girls. Humor takes weight. See you found your subject, though. Whether it's a major one is still arguable."

Four of the vanguarders have written a collective journal. He parts his teeth. "When your whole struggle, my dears, should be—to try to be separate."

As he picks out Jean's, she nervously introduces her daughter, on whose account, she adds, they have to leave early. For the daughter's plane.

"You look like your mother must have. When she—er—came out." He twiddled Jean's scrupulously typed paper. They all know what's in it. Jean's youth, from which she has surgically removed the entire era, except for the Court of St. James's at which she was presented to the world, and the Paris Beaux-Arts Ball at which she embraced it—meeting the man who now has Parkinson's.

"'An American Girl Abroad—'" he reads "'—In Nineteen-Thirty-Nine.'" He smiles with the daughter, over that golden snob back there in her featherheaded dressingroom, under her Arc de Triomphe of rainbow events. "Nineteen-Thirty-*Nine*" he says then, stiffening. As if somebody'd turned on a lightbulb inside him. A rib of brainlight runs down his very nose.

Lexie shudders, knowing what he'll be saying. He's going to kill Jean's youth, swamp it—with a slice of their objective reality. Does it belong only to them?

"Nineteen-thirty-nine," he says again; yes, this repetition belongs to him, is bred in him like a horizon, Lexie thinks.

"Hitler entered the *Sudetenland* that year," he says, hushed. "Freud died." Plaut wasn't even born then. But yes, it belongs to him.

Because of that, he can even be kind. When it suits him. "Mrs. Fackenthal . . . the English—is excellent."

"Osmosis." What a funny word to blush on. "My husband was—is a journalist."

Is that virtue of her, or poise?—not even to know she's being swamped? Or is it the faintest touch of what in Plaut would be called political? What a bridgegame Jean must play with herself. With much practice in company, at the country club. For she and the daughter aren't really going to the plane. She'll display her achievement where she can. And the class, watching the two of them go off, is now almost fondly on Jean's side.

Women's enmity had so little lasting weight—why? And what is an era—that we don't wholly belong to it?

He's now handing her back her poem. This is the moment I hate, she thinks, screwing up her eyes for the dive into it. The moment when what I exuded in pure longing must come under judgment. There's something dirty about that, they all really think—to exude. And I myself can now barely remember the little birth it was. Then why've I handed it in? Why didn't I stay on my ledge? Eyes lowered, she pretends to be there, safe against the window-frame. She can smell its comforting soot.

"'My Children'—" he reads out. "It's only two lines. Here they are:

"You are the branches I stretch toward poetry.
Then why do I toss you these small bouquests or rage?"

She opened her eyes. A dignity recalled, urged back by the poem, allows it. He's staring at her. The rest of them hang their heads, unsure of the wind to come.

"Know what a pseudopodium is, Mrs. . . er . . . ?" He can never remember her name. "I looked it up especially for this poem of yours." He pulls out a slip of paper. "'In certain protozoa' it says here. 'Each of a number of process-es tem-po-ra-rily formed by protrusion of any part of the protoplasm of the body.'" He clears his throat meaning-fully. "'And serving for locomotion, prehension or inges-tion of food.'"

He folded the slip and handed it to her. "Only that first sentence applies here. Though I suppose the second could, at times. Because—look at those lines of yours, will you, godammit? Anybody ever see a more mixed metaphor? The children are your *arms*. Yet the next min-ute your *hands* are tossing them something. From where? Where's the distance? Branches to bouquets? . . . And yet I did think . . . it does make me think—." His voice sinks, for

the shameful. "—Maybe that's the way motherhood feels?"
He's sidling a look at her, her face, her belly even; is she
supposed to answer? "Well. Hah, Nemmind. Maybe
motherhood is an art, hmmm?—and that's something
I'm—hmm. But anyway, Miss. Madam. The best
metaphors, the good ones that last, are so firmly locked
that you CAN'T disentangle their parts. Can't chop them
up, eh. Like I did yours . . . If I did, that is."

He's almost back to being their kindly, hardworking
prof of last term, sweating to make them see what he
liquidly calls "l-*lit*-ratyooah," poking it toward them like a
diamond they blindly won't pick up, or can't see. "Reason I
develop this; it's because you all think like that, seems to
me. No chain of logic that I can recognize. A sort of
plasma-budding, more like. Really strange. To me, that is.
A sort of amoebic process; that's the nearest. In *all* of you.
And we can surely see it alright alright, in that poem." He
hands it back to her. "Not that it isn't even sort of good,
you know. And yet it's only good—because of the way it's
bad. I tell you what—" He rubs his teeth at the enigma of
her. "It's a poem by an invertebrate."

The class sat up in outrage. Oh stop being so collective, she felt like telling them. He's right.

"I know maybe there's something dirty about it," she
mutters. "You don't have to say."

He jumps, as if she'd skinned a pea at him. "About
motherhood, you mean?"

A hopeless conversation. Between transliterates. She
shrugs.

He brings his shoulders forward as if he's never
glimpsed them before. "Well. Girls. Mothers. Gotta go.
Sorry. Had to come by the office, you know." A hay-
seed laugh blurts from him. He tightens his rope. "So I
dropped those papers off—whyn't you roundtable on
them, spend the rest of the hour on that?"

"Hour?" Billie half-rose. "This is a three-hour class."

"I'm aware of that. Unfortunately, I have to go." He nods at his colleague-for-the-Renaissance. "See you next week instead, huh, Gloriana. Usual conference time."

She wondered if the rest of the class thought Gloriana was Mrs. Bidwell's own fancy name.

"Come by to pick up your check, huh, Plaut? Don't you think we want our money's worth?"

"Look for it intangibly, Miss La Barbara. That's the only way you'll get it."

Ah poor boy. Spouting his schooltalk as if it'll hold him up. Yet that's just how I found out who Gloriana was. Intangibly. Nosing in Spenser because I'm curious. Oh, what issues there are here. And why do I feel sorry for him?

"Looky here." Cee-Cee's voice, a daub of bright American mustard on those porcelain cheeks. "There are crumbs in your beard, Mr. Plaut. That's tangible enough."

"My wife's ill. Sorry."

"Oh-h, too bad. You have Major Medical?" Elaine. Her hat is wonderful. A sympathetic umbrella, a matriarch's portico—and she is only forty-five.

"No," the wretch has to say. "I don't have the plan yet."

"Ah-ah—" Elaine moaned, "—what a world. Because you're only part-time."

"They're fixing to petition you off, Plaut." Mrs. Bidwell. Uncle Tom or not, she's immobile. One will never know just how her motives are mixed. "They have a yen to try Chickie Casella. She sings."

He and she laugh, scholars together.

"Let them. Let her continue her education with *them*." Turning to go, his pants, hitching along with him, have a kind of spirit after all. Or are regaining it.

When just then she, Lexie, is foolish enough to speak. Meditatively. "Ill? Do you mean—your wife's in labor?"

He gives them a sheepish—salute.

Their own howling burst deafens them. Running him out of the room. Shrill waves of it rise and renew. "Ay-yah—*ill* for Chrissake," somebody says, exhausted—and they are off again.

Some one recalls to Cee-Cee—"Sitters!" Sardonic shouts ring from all corners, all ages.

Are they various at all, really? Oh never think that, never doubt that we are, she thinks piously; that's to go back to hell-bottom, the low road of the former slave. Former until the end? She's puzzled. This laughter, this group-tone with its grunty *ayee*—it is certainly inter-changeable.

Silence.

"I shouldn't have said it to him. Or about dirt—why did I say that? I always transliterate." But at least she hasn't blamed it on the absence of Ray.

"No, you were wonderful; trans-what? —you do, huh?; whatever that means, yes you were Lexie; honey, who knows better about dirt than us; yes, she must be talented; haha, is labor illness yet; is motherhood dirt."

Brows knitted, mouths with watermelon grins, they rock her on a solidarity that rests her like an old lap. Early approval, feminine penny-candy-approval which smells lineny too—the whole calyx of a household opening to a child at the bottom of it—of mothers, though I had only one, of sisters, though I had none, and from everybody's gaggle of aunts.

She looks at the class. Singly, I don't much like any of them, except Jean who is gone. Together, they've almost made me cry. And feel basking-strong. Deceptively strong.

Across the ocean Ray floats, a three-letter ripple, or one of the tiny, bobbing buoys we kids used to tie on our fishing-lines when we left them at the pier; taught my river-kids to do the same. When a man like Ray feels male approval, or any of them do, what do they smell nostalgically—a baseball cigar?

He'll be coming home, a cipher, but the relationship still large. To be dealt with. As we deal.

Staring at her classmates, her treacherous mind moves further. Our days-in-town, yours and mine; oh yes, we transliterate bloody well. From female to personal, what's the difference? My other day in town, did I assert the personal, or the female? What *is* the difference? Oh yes, we Glorianas transliterate well. And is this treason: All her relationships with men, with a man—have they been with herself?

Elaine shifts the silence. A generous sigh. "So we can't huh. Ask for his dismissal. Not with a baby coming on. And no medical plan."

From the rear, their horsegirl spoke up, eyes narrowed at all of them, or beyond.

"Siccum!" she said.

Driving home, the winding parkway perspectives send Lexie past the college. Though she'll miss it, she knows she's not going back. To that class where all the women are trying on life like a new hat. Except for Elaine, who already has one.

I, Lexie, won't go anywhere cloistered for women only. There must be an even deeper strength than that to strike out for. I don't need to be a nun to know what the cloister is like. Though cloisters of women are warming and I've spent many heartfelt hours there, what is there about such cloisters that sends us back to the niggling detail? Or keeps us circling there. Along with a consciousness—submerged as the kind of background music only musicians can't tolerate—of gently closed doors.

And I won't go back to the city as if to a man. Nor even as if I were one. The erogenous zone, and that freedom-valve which opens hungrily in the flesh and closes again—I must disentangle them; they're not the same.

Since Day, she hasn't had a man, or a man hasn't had her. She has resolved not to masturbate—that deadbeat flogging which leaves her doubly alone. Even when the monthly butterfly pulses jump in all her veins, when her dreams are wet with orgasmic pools and her thighs wake, open enough to receive one of the stele from Stonehenge, the resolve has been kept.

She smiled, leaning away lightly from the steering-wheel. The air had that first poached clarity before the lion-must of summer coarsened it; the breezes were finicky but no longer serious. And I have my jokes back.

At the same moment, she's thrust back into those adolescent days of similar weather when, stalking the parks and museums, lone and exalted, there had beat in her a pulse almost of knighthood—toward the possibilities of life. Under the downy veil of womansweat that is her body now, she still hears it, beating light. Happiness is androgynous then?—what a surprise.

When she got home, she stared longer than usual at her house. Strictly, it had two towers, one a sort of leftover gambrel somebody gave up on, to the rear of the real one. Any way you look at it, architecturally or not, an ambivalent house. On a narrow road, but the view all river. Small frontally, but with wings added for its second century. The rear kitchen looked directly into the base of the hill, which hid all sunsets; above it, the jutting back-bedrooms attach to the hill itself.

After supper that night, she walked up the back hill. From the houses here—all facing the east, at the bottom of a ridge which hides the west from them—you could see only dawns, which required either gumption or agony. To see the end-of-day colors, as in the vases of that name, you had to climb up here through what once had been a formal garden, gone now to briar but sparking here and there with old bulbs, iris and daffodil, even whose blooms were stunted antique.

Tonight there's a sunset like a centrifuge, sucking the world into a golden pantheon.

Down in the real garden, Charles, with golddust on his face, is training the wisteria up. In the bedroom that juts north with a small bay, she can see Chess sitting like a figurehead, against a background of the lilac-brown wallpaper, patterned like calico, which Chess herself had spent a month pasting on so accurately into the room's gabled crannies, all help refused. The same paper to which—the minute she saw their proud admiring faces—she'd taken a marking-pencil to, in gravenings of red scrawled everywhere. Behind which barrier she'd then drawn a rear rank of line-figures, outlandishly tall—as she considers herself to be—with black blotheads.

It has unsettling power, that frieze, and a certain mad taste. What'll happen though, when we don't have a house where Chess can scrawl like that, can sit like that, where we can check on her? When we don't have a house?

Maureen'll be in the kitchen now; there are kitchens everywhere. Royal, still smug after the dentist's, is out here, watching Charles. With his jaw swollen, how much Royal resembles his Uncle James.

Who is presently in—Kabul, is it? Or Passawatomie, New Jersey? James enjoys returning from the former as if he's been no farther or foreigner than to the latter. And he can return from some local township he's been dissecting as if he'd found it to be the tundra, the veldt, the bush, with habits to suit. "Double-breasted chickens, they eat—" James's supermarket shopping is done for him "—and pizza-to-go, in which every square inch or so you can find a human hair." While Kabul will of course have a hospital to make his own medical center blush.

There's a well-known freedom in not having one's males alongside. Does she think differently then? Like eating a meal, absently, which hasn't been cooked for anyone else. Who'll set down the housewife's true anthropology? Human hair by the yard, brother, and all our turds piled high as copra.

Now why must she think that, when the night air is lensing in like a benediction, and the children's voices haunt in and out of it, her chorale? They're calling her.

They think she is inside the house. A sense of herself, the dark figure without, terrorizes her. She's terrified of her power, that's it. But like any tyrant, uses it. What if all her relationship with the children—has it been for herself?

Later that night before going to bed, she doesn't stand as usual looking out from her ledge. Never again; all ego is there. Instead, she goes down the hall to a little backporch off an unused bedroom, and stands looking out into the black hill. "What do you think—" she breathes, "—am I talented?"

No poems come. But she sleeps well.

All that next week, she roamed her own patterns, mentally marking them for scrutiny in study-reverie where she's both the anthropologist's subject, and the anthropologist. Soon finding that all these conscious observations had long since been recorded, in that umber part of herself which had had nothing verbal to serve it.

For how many years has she been alternately amused, depressed, startled?—to find herself between breakfast and lunch moved from attic to basement, from object to intention, from water to fire to food and to washingstarch, on an assemblyline scarcely willed, but moving as gravely as one's blood-rhythm, beneath all complaint, beneath even a vow. Suspended between past meals, present dirt and the moment's stop-go, she gathers the leftovers of day and twines them for tomorrow's stockpot. Greasing the seasons, she's opening the attic vent to let the wasps blunt their way to spring; she's down in the laundry gently pairing the mittens for snow. Outside the windows of her small centrist system, the arterial world can only lap; meaning brims here, but must wait. She is in the great architectonic of the task; her movements make a drapery through the house. A fugue invisible. Clotted strong with necessity.

What is it, though, to move through the lives of children? Under their helplessly imperial gaze setting out her store of trash fact. Whisking the soiled napkin of somebody's puberty from the bathroom bin, is she redeemed?

To drift toward the creation of cake? For suppers which are never the last. At home parties, like all the other day-long preparers, she serves up her own flesh—in the salmon's skeleton already dissected plain by her own daydreaming, long before the guests get to it.

I the anthropologist saw this with my own eyes. When the woman served us broth, it was cups of reverie she was serving. This webby stuff exudes from them day and night, tripping their conversation, wrapping the mind. The headmen are aware of its force but consider it an inert one, best dealt with privately, but not in their own daydreams. Which are all of the public street, the council-hall and the granary. One of the women, shyly letting me examine a bit of her web, told me that some of the more rebellious or daring or "lost ones" made poems of it. 'But we know these are not the real poems, even for us. The real ones are outside.' When we asked where was outside, she smiled and indicated the window. It is considered among them that when they themselves cross that barrier, which they do endlessly in their own way, they are however entirely different people compared to the men, who in so doing remain whole. She would not tell us what was meant by 'lost.'
And all this I saw myself, in the village of Ys.

"Ma. The telephone."
And how come she's here, bending over the garbage-pail on the morning backsteps, with Royal, the last to leave because his school is nearer, calling that out to her? When only a moment ago she was standing on the evening hillside?

Addenda: After the night, the women say—which is spent lying with the mouth shaped for kisses sometimes received, sometimes not—and after the

· 87

family is packed off in the various chutes which transport them to the outside—the women find it their duty to "weave the village together again" as they say. Which is done by means of holes poked through from housewall to housewall, with wires then inserted. It is an affecting sight, as one wanders from house to house, to see them, each one alone, but joined to another by means of this telephonic thread, and dutifully weaving, each with her mouth still pursed or pouting, the eyes here wistful, here gossip-greedy, but always sororal, the mouth always pressed close to the hole for its obligatory music, trilling its birdsong. When I asked one of them if they consider this done from duty or from necessity she shrank from me, as some natives do when first they see the photograph. It is possible that just as birds gulp air with song, this matutinal urge is a physical one; perhaps the shape of their mouths, still puckered from the night, requires it.

And all this I myself saw, in the village of Ys. Where lives the lost tribe.

And all this time she performs her household duties well.

And the village hadn't forgotten her. Lexie. Would she like to substitute, a voice asks, for the editor's assistant on the county newspaper, which since time out of mind has been published in the next town north? "Dorothy Haber, his girl Friday—you've seen her around, grizzled blond about sixty—she's going in for a hysterectomy. Insists she'll be back at her desk in three weeks. Afraid of her job with old Nutcracker, I guess. But it would help spell you until Ray comes back, wouldn't it?"

It would. Should she be surprised that the voice knew this, and all its implications, probably? Not as an anthropologist. As herself, she was out of her mind—the webbed part of it—with excitement over what a newspaper implied. Although she knows the County News' fussy cubicles and faded staff, from taking an item there now and then—it may be a ship in disguise.

Nutcracker's face is an indented old-man-in-the-moon's, with wens to complete the crescent at forehead and chin. His newspaper, inherited from his father twenty years ago when he was perhaps not yet thirty himself, still services roughly the same half-dozen towns, some in the center-county already gone from farm sprawl to industry during his tenure, others half-obliterated by state roads. One town, on the river below hers, had been a mill-town since the eighteen-twenties, and lustily remains so. To the north, a few hilly parcels bordering the state parkland are still privately owned, and like her own village-strip are suburban in scale but resisting in temperament. The county takes for granted that in its own hilly outland and riverbank, where artists secrete and professionals follow after, is where its true exoticisms lie. Its terrain still makes its visions. And she'll learn that this man, who pulls his short, bony length up from his desk to greet her with a curious effusion, almost a bow, is as intent on preserving these as if they too are part of his inheritence.

"Ah yes—" he says, "—Mrs. Doctor." Giving a courtly sweep to the syllables, and to herself a character. In her brief stay, she'll learn that he does this for all women. Of him she knows only that he has a wife, a homebody in the old style, who makes rag-dolls, prettily sewn of bright patches, which are sold in the local shops; Maureen and Chessie had them once.

"So here you are." He has the sharp, chiding newsroom voice she expected. In the cubicles behind him, whose occupants she can't see, there's a sudden, owlish silence. Paperclips stop rattling. The smell of mucilage is rank.

"Ah yes," he says. "From Grand River. The village of *un*natural acts. On which you and I, Mrs., will be in confidence."

He must do this with each newcomer. Rating them as he does her—person, geography and news possibility—in a glance. His regular staff correspondents, she'll find, bring in items like eggs to market, brown or white, or bloodspotted. He nicknames their territories as if these were landed estates complete with nobles and serfs, instead of towns ten miles from one another, and the farthest of them no more than forty miles from New York. "That's *Orthodoxtown*. Dutch, once. Patroons, and 'mine hosts.' After that, petty shops. Now it's those graveyard shopping-malls. Retired police detectives live there now, and city firemen. Still the same politics." Or— "Torporsville. Inbred from mental retards who were planted in couples and given the ground, in the eighteeneighties. Still use outhouse manure, win all the flowershows—but don't eat their cabbages 'less you wash them with permanganate. Nary a murder there, Missus. But sometimes a dear little *bébé* with one eye." His language is contrary, mixed—sometimes even with Latin, or with a country accent hanging among other cultivations like a scarecrow in a conservatory.

Each morning, standing at the door of his own cubicle, or uprooting her from hers, he shames her, with his special knowledge of her small riverstrip, into giving back what she knows of it. She rises for these addresses the way Jean had told her students were said to honor their professors at the Sorbonne. She saw her village, all villages, shrinking calcified in the high wind of a voice which held its decibel while picking its way through the rubbed gore of any human defilement—while the stunned typewriters stopped behind him, and Applecheeks, the current reporter, halted his chewing-gum. Hoppe's voice is what is nutcracker, at the business of splitting open a life. She learns nothing more of its own, even whether or not it has children—or whether it considers it has a life. Probably— since it so conserves its own facts—no. Or nothing worthy of its own pincer, which goes deeper than gossip, and is more precise than legend. Sex looms no larger in his prob- ings than ritual; he's as interested in the rich hermit who erodes time in winding car batteries of matchless strength made to give away but not sell, as in the local rapesters— and the latter only if they're remarkable. What Hoppe broods over is the human fabric, and the monsters to be made of it. Monsters of fidelity even, or virtue—to him it's all the same.

While journalism makes what comic connection it can. "Chained his lactating wife in the barn, he did. For general use. When the Well-Baby clinic preaches mother's milk in Torporsville, what else can you expect?"

He's half a foot shorter than she and the wens repel her, as does his chalky, missionary breath. He's vegetarian perhaps, or maybe eats only nocturnally. Never is seen to, and his name on the masthead—J. J. Hoppe—is never used, replaced either by "Sir," or "Him." Yet if he put a hand on her, she'd let him have her, even as she's sure it would have to happen for him—in full sight of the cubi- cles. Which wouldn't make a sound. In the light of what they've learned from him. Nor would she.

For she's recognized him. Moving behind his day, which goes from telephone to print and back again, he walks to some other referential tune. He has meditation, which moves *him*. He too must believe there is a shape to what is lived. A shape to be made. Or sought.

Oh yes, she knows him. He's like one of those faceless narrators she's met in print only. A figure maybe standing in a ditch in Byelorussia and recording for no reason except that such things must be—whose pangs one after- ward remembers as one's own. Or standing in the orange boudoir-garden in Algiers, or in the clerk's office in antique Palermo. Wherever suffering that alien life which we know to be ours. Hoppe's what she is. He's the *other* anthropologist.

When he called Grand River "the village of unnatural acts" she'd known he meant all villages really.

"Natural and unnatural," she'd answered him that first time. "And hysterical."

For three weeks, they have an affair of the mind.

In field-knowledge, of course, they're in no way equilateral. He unlocks her village for her, in all its underground moaning. What can she give such an authority in return?

The Kellihys.

"Two days after the fire," she tells him, "Betsy comes doodling down the martini-path. Politely deploring its lack of use. She means—by Ray." Yes, she's told Hoppe that. Or half of it, and he can guess the rest.

"She's wearing black satin, at ten in the morning, and carrying a beer. She waves the can at me, very excited. 'Lexie, how do you get the best swimming pool foundation ever?—When the garage apartment burns down on you! Best he ever saw, the architect says. And Mummy is giving us the ten thousand to pay for it.'"

Hoppe never laughs at anything. His mind is searching its middens, ever analogizing. "'Lamb's Essay on Roast Pig.'"

She doesn't know it.

"Haven't read it myself in years. A hut burns down, as I recall, with a pig inside. Poking the ruins and charred bones, the savages burn their fingers, put them in their mouths—and taste chitlings. Next time they want a taste of the same—natch, burn down the hut again. And that's how you get a swimming pool."

She does the laughing. Though it stops short. "'Mummy' is Bob's you know. The Kellihys have the money. Betsy only has the pretensions. Longings, really. They do doodle, you know. All they know how to. Bob looks older, but they're the same. At twenty-eight, the two of them. Two poor crocks."

"What did you answer," Hoppe asks, "—about the path?"

How did he know? That she'd have said something? "I said 'Betsy. Didn't you think *I'd* give you a beer?' . . . Stinking of me, wasn't it. Because you know, I really envied her. Dragging her silk, drinking from a can. The style of it. Maybe *I* want to be a crock."

"Watch that pity. People like you and me."

She doesn't dare ask—where's that pity rooted? In tears for myself—is that it, Hoppe?

He doesn't answer what she doesn't ask. Their communion is not that sort. But one evening, they're sitting late at the office, doing the Saturday ads. Everything on that paper is still unmechanized, including the view. Below them, the whole dusky valley of the county is spreading its footlights. Downstairs and off the front steps prance the two gay men who run the bookshop, who have just left their ad. Their cotton teeshirts bob on the provincial dusk like striped flares from Paris. They always enter on a fast joke and leave on a slow—both belied by too vivid and double a gesture, their anxiously formalized chat lingering on the air like the frou-frou of soubrettes. Everyone in town knows their house—fluffy as a bride's, when there are two of them. Has Hoppe seen it?

"Mmm." Into that face-curve of his, so pulled at both ends, a pipe fits well. The leaf he smokes spreads an odor palatable. Behind that rough tan shirt he hasn't much chest. But the arm extended her is good; the brown marrowbone knuckles holding the pipe have a polish like ivory. Why is she scrutinizing what has no physical charge for her? Because he's doing the same to her. What charges him is not merely her body. This makes her bridle with pride.

"Homos, they're like women in more ways than one. Both sexes of them." He always made his points in an extra-heavy voice. "People might laugh at them. So they have to live with more style."

"Found a couple more words you wouldn't know," she said, flushing with pleasure. He didn't believe there was any special language among women, or for them. She was beginning not to believe it herself, but she loved the haggling. "This one I frankly never heard before, myself. 'To biggen.'"

"What's that mean?"

"Look it up."

He loved to. His forefinger pored down the big dictionary. "Ha. 'To recover strength after confinement. 1674.' What do you know. Ever since then." His eyes crinkled. "Whatever did they do before?"

"Ah I know—" she sighed, making all one word of it. "—you think I need words to confirm my actions." He's said it. "But words are still so new to me—their powers, I mean. And you've dealt with them most of your life."

And where's it got me?—another man might say. Not Hoppe. He's like a crab, both scuttling the sea-bottom and niched. Who if asked in some Aesop-tale to consider why it is itself, would reply "Because I am Crab." To him, his backwater's no boundary, but part of the sea. He's convincing because he's convinced.

To have a small station in life, she thought—and yet know it to be an outpost. That's it. That would be enough.

"And what's your other word?"

"Oh, that one's just from the female glossary. Not even a word that every one of us would know. Just the kind we would. This one's from something my mother and I happened to look at quite often, that's all. And my daughters could. None of us really noticing."

She stared at her hands as sewing-women do, down at those shuttles weaving of their own volition, separate. "Like a man would get used to seeing the manufacturer's name on the barrel of his gun. Equipment words. But there're others. Clothing words. Product ones. *You* know.

A man and wife might live together their whole lives and never really know—the other's glossary."

"You know, Lexie, you're like some—no, not a child—some pre-girl. Who hasn't been told about the differences between the sexes yet. After four children. Maybe that's your charm."

"And that's your language. Not ours."

"So maybe we do have differing ones. Accept it. It's interesting."

"I do. I just want the world to accept mine."

They've never before flashed and quivered at each other like this. She sits tight. Not wanting any other part of him but the words.

"What is it with you girls and the world?" He got up to scrabble at his desk—a camouflage, since everything there was neat as an artillery range—or as she imagined one to be. A thousand items ready on their pins. He handed her one. "Goes in next Monday, in the social column. Between St. Peter's Sodality benefit and the Veterans of Foreign Wars picnic at Bear Mountain."

She reads it. The Woman's Center committee on rape is establishing a telephone number, to be manned by trained advisers, where rape victims may call between the hours of ten to twelve, mornings, and evenings six to ten. "Jesus. What if you get raped after hours? Or in the afternoon?"

It's grown dark in the room. The two streets parallel to this one, each of which leads down to the river, shine ghostly, as streets of white houses do, before the houses are lit. These were closed for business and would not light, except for here.

"Afternoons?" His voice is small. "No, that's for the city."

He knows about hers, he means. Her afternoons.

"We have rapes here, Lexie. Not in your town, maybe. Come to think of it, I've never heard of one there. You're our aristocrats, too refined. Down there it goes by consent."

· 95 ·

She got up and turned on a dim lamp. "But you'll print that notice. Nice of you."

"I go with the times. And the subscription list."

She leaned back in her chair, an oldfashioned one which revolves if you pedal it, and picked up yesterday's paper. "Especially nice of you. In a paper which also prints this." She reads from a syndicated column called Idolene's Ideas: *"Dear Idolene: I recently found myself without a large piece of nylon-net and with a bowl of soup-broth to clear. I put it in the freezer to partially congeal, then thought of a freshly laundered sleep-cap, complete with flowers and a chinstrap. It was made of three layers of the net and fit over the bowl perfectly. Result: I lost a sleep-cap, but have the prettiest, most efficient strainer in town."*

"Okay, okay. *To partially congeal.* But we get a lot of mail on that column."

"That all you see in it—a split infinitive?"

"Maybe not." Against the waning windowlight, his silhouette waits. The head in penumbra, with the wens half-invisible, is rather fine.

"Listen, Hoppe. That letter's from all of us."

He pedals his chair.

"Oh yes it is. It's from me. Look at me."

He's looking.

"Okay, I've never been raped." She swallows. "There're a lot of us who'll never be murdered, only married. Or not. Never commit a crime of passion." She grins at him. "And we don't want to murder the men; we're too late for it. On the other hand—I've never used a sleep-cap in my life. Don't know anyone who does. But all of us any age—even the ones who can't cook, the rich ones who won't need to . . . There isn't a woman in the country who wouldn't understand about that woman's soup." She chokes. "And why she wrote you—about her accomplishment."

She leans forward. Is it our talent or our curse, she wants to ask him—that we transliterate? But she's afraid to ask. He may be the enemy. Why does she herself feel enmity, for the first time openly? To him of all people—who might have been her friend?

"So you've never seen a sleep-cap." The wen on his chin twists to one side.

"You have?"

No answer.

On his mother? Or the wife? She leans back. These chairs could become a ballet in time, she thinks. If I stay. "What do your initials stand for, J. J.?"

He's relighting his pipe. "My parents were radical dreamers. Before they came here. Swiss irredentists from Locarno, if you can imagine anything more unreal. I was named for Rousseau."

She can't imagine any of it. Except Locarno. "So? But what's J. J., then?"

"*Rousseau.*" Hoppe can't believe she has never heard of him. Convinced, he even takes her hands, drops them quickly. The two chairs remain near. "But it's unbelievable. You're so smart."

"I'm self-read. There are gaps." She grinds back her chair. "College guides you, that's all. I'm not all that sure I want that trip." Lowering her eyes, she hears those excusing "alls" fall like rain. She can smell his breath. "Were your parents—vegetarians too?"

"No. My father had a passion for dried fruit, though. Which I inherit. Though he never shared any of his fruit with us. A real passion. My mother took to carrying a tray after him. For the pips."

"My father did the same with his travel," she said. "He only gave us the talk . . . So I know about Locarno."

"Travel? You want that? . . . What do you want?"

Her eyes half-close. What does she want to extract out of this shuttered red-dark? "I want to voyage into the interior. Mine. Like an anthropologist. And someday, J. J.—maybe I can spell it out."

"Lexie. Open your eyes."

I'll see the wens. She opened them. While she was intent upon her dark, he'd turned down the light. So he knows that about her, and his wens. He's come no nearer.

"Come on, what's your second word? That *we* wouldn't know."

"Belding's Corticelli." She says it slyly.

For he knows so much. About her village, for instance. She can imagine how the whole county's underside looks to him by now, rough and ugly, pink with coarse, blocked feeling, like a sow's sore tits. All ending up in his newsprint morgue. But he shan't get this dainty detail of hers that easily. This foolish necessary. Of our ten-thousand-and-one.

"Sounds like an ointment . . . No? Pretty, though. Too pretty. Like those words people are always saying are the most musical in the language . . . Halcyon . . . Anemone— I could never go for them."

"What do you go for?"

"Old or Middle English ones. Grit. Moil. Bast. All the four-letter monosyllables aren't obscene. Cull. Airt."

"Nice. What's it mean—airt?"

"As a noun—a height or a direction. One-quarter of the compass. As a verb—'to guide.'"

"How come you know so much about them?"

"Did my thesis on them."

"I did a paper once. On Roger Bacon."

"Oh yes, the alchemist . . . You seem to go for whatever begins with A, Lexie. Anthropologist."

"My brother, he wanted to be an astronomer." She bent to scan the column she'd been dummying, trying to peer at her watch. From the sky, the hour must be after eight. Every night a little later. This conversation's like lovemaking. That last exhausted rollover when one's not making it.

"Belding's Corticelli." He's followed her gaze. "That's it of course. From astronomy, isn't it."

She felt heavy, ashamed, knowing why she chose this out of all her treasury of detail. For that sewing wife of his, coolly never mentioned. For the *other* wife. What strange unities are forced upon us. For his face is brighter, relieved to think that this secret word which she sets such store by, comes to her after all via a brother. From them.

"That's it, Lex, isn't it. It's the name of a star."

And in the end they're always more romantic than us.

"No. Not a star." From her tone, she might be speaking to Charlie. Or little Royal.

"What, then?"

She saw into her sewing-box, inherited like his newspapers, like his dried fruit. Stared into absently by one, two, three successive women, each in her turn on her spindle like the spools down there in the box, each spool identified by its circle of faded black print. Maybe they don't even make that brand anymore. From how far back do the spools, the spindled women come?

"Thread," she says. "Thread."

"Thread? Ordinary sewing-thread?" He's aghast. And yes, he knows what the county knows about him. He sees her thrust.

"Maybe not ordinary, J. J. Silk."

How smart he is. And yes, he's the enemy.

"Not J. J.," he says, with a smile so deep that chin-wen and forehead-wen move toward each other. Cracking her life like a nut. "Jean-Jacques. Jean-Jacques."

Driving home, the faintly lit river-road hangs like a bridge through the black. Always like this before the full moon, during which cycle the trees will be drugged with mauve light—halcyon. Yes, he's the enemy, all the more because one can talk to him. And yes, we were making love.

A patch of fog hides the curve of her driveway. The tall house above glows through shakily, like a chandelier, seen by a glaucoma'ed eye. As pictured in the opthalmologist's office of her first job. The old river below creaks like the joists of a floor. Old veteran, old floor—we still have our pact. But Christ, what jobs I get.

Out there, far beyond this water, is there still an incoming ripple—Ray?

The three older children are in the kitchen, at the long table centered under the hanging lamp. "Must do something about that oldfashioned globe," she says walking in on them. Really must. When it can make the youngest face look drear. "Hi."

"We didn't save supper." Charles. "It's after nine."

The table's oddly bare. Of the usual ransackings. They can't have had much.

"That's all right; I'll get myself something . . . Not a neon light though, that would be worse. And not with that ceiling."

Of cherished patterned tin, from one corner of which the paint keeps flaking. She smiles, for the year Charles was tall enough to help Ray repaint. For the year he said, in a newly deep voice: *I'm afraid we have rust.* "When we have to repaint, we'll shop for a light." Lightly running off at the mouth, she has taken up her pattern with them.

"We were selfish." Maureen, quivering. Under that straining middy there are breasts.

"No, I should've called. We were dummying Saturday's paper. That place is run like nineteen-forty, not a thing is mechanized."

Chess' long fingers move as if she's tatting. But she's not. Or not anything except silence. When she speaks it'll be from silence, and silence will follow after. That's her difference, which we've learned to accept. And that's what frightens me—not Chess. *Our* difference. That we accept.

"That Hoppe—he has a face like a witch." Chess tucks her head in quickly, in her usual shame over being herself, with her kind of images. "We thought maybe you were having dinner with him." Her face is mild. She'll say the sharpest, most inconvenient thing, always: you can depend on her. The other kind of silence, the willed one, she doesn't have. There are people who don't understand the ordinary. It's as if Chess had never heard of it.

"No . . . Where's Roy?"

"Upstairs. Asleep." Charles won't add that it's time enough for the youngest to be asleep. He's imperially gaunt, even aging, with the strain of stretching into a man. Behind him are the back stairs, up which, from the age of seven, he used to trot if scolded, so as not to be seen to cry.

"Yes, we are, we are." Maureen, screaming it. Under the blouse, the body strains with revolution. "Selfish!" She bursts into tears. "But why'd you have to take a job?"

"Maureen, Maureen." Lexie cradles her. Yes, yes, people don't enough. "You're selfish, I'm selfish." She makes a rocking song of it. "Everybody, sometimes." And people don't cradle you enough.

The two others look on, peculiarly satisfied.

"No, you fool. She *has* to. I want to, too. Lexie—if you go to the city for a job, will you take me for one too?"

No, Chess never addresses her as Ma anymore; she's always called her father "Ray." The psychiatrist to whom Chess went all last year—and quite suddenly wouldn't go to—had asked her whether she was afraid of her father. At just about that time.

She's never liked Ray to touch her—that's true. Nor anyone, possibly. How I would love to have her in my lap.

"Yah, what kind of job could *you* do." Royal's coming down the back stairs at his hopalong jog, while they all hold their breath; the steps are narrow triangles thinning to nothing, and have no banister. Usually he only goes up them.

But not to cry. When has anyone last seen Royal cry?

"I wasn't neither asleep. I heard everything you said."

"I could be a model," Chess says. "I could show them those pics Charles took." And so she could be, with those glassy bones striking the lens in all their fine catalepsy, that swoon-of-mind which is so bizarrely chic in the right clothing. When Chess dares, she can do anything, and in the craziest hat. When she droops, the pimples come, the down in her nostrils obtrudes its black fur; she swells

· 101 ·

hand-in-hand with her own ugliness—its twin. While the outer world shivers her. "I'm seventeen!"

What, what has given her this confidence?

"Well looka you!" Royal elbows Maureen, there on his mother's lap. His lap. "Off!"

Obediently Maureen slides down. Lexie stays her with a hand, wards Royal from her lap, eyes the two older ones. "What's happened here? Somebody been?"

Or not been? Ray's letter's late.

Charles speaks for them. "Uncle James is back. He stopped by."

"Oh? Wouldn't he wait?"

The other three speak as one.

"He says—call him."

"He says the black community where he's been is a totally—" Maureen.

"Matri . . . matri—" Royal.

"—archal, dope." Chess.

"Ci-vi-za tion."

They crowd her, a bevy, the last being Royal. Usually she adores this choral style of theirs, moving her arms to conduct, applauding the end result like a song. And if Chess joins in, all's right with the world.

Charles hasn't. Joined in. "James says—"

"Yes, Charles? What did James say?" Once, not two years ago, she'd smacked in the face this faithful father-defending boy of hers, this hoarder of itineraries, for flinging an obscenity after his uncle. Her fist, shooting out in allegiance to a pre-family long gone, had hit her own boy in the face; she hasn't forgiven it yet.

"He says—" A grimace seizes him, like a claw from behind. "He says—Dad isn't coming back."

"He said we must prepare ourselves." Maureen middy swelling, is ready to.

And Chess? Is smiling inward. Tatting strength. "We can get along without him. Can't we, Lexie."

Chess said her father tried to molest her sexually once,

Mrs.—the psychiatrist said. *Could that be true?* The man could never remember the family name. A natural alienation. *No, doctor, impossible. But her father's clumsy at showing affection. I've seen him make an awkward try* . . . Afterwards, scrutinizing Ray, mild Ray; they say, the mild ones. No. Impossible.

Royal, subdued, has managed to slide into her lap.

Three pairs of eyes approve of him there. He speaks for them.

"Come here. All of you." She gathers them in. "Chessie, come. Charlie, you too." He comes, reluctantly. He has to kneel, his head close to Royal's. Chess, even in the circle is fastidious, only coolly there.

"*Listen* to me." How collective eyes can be. When they're yearning to be. "Your father's coming back."

And it's true, she can feel he is. Though not how he'll come. In what—shape.

"Just before one comes back, the last days, one doesn't bother to write, that's all. Because one *is* coming back. Remember when we went to Uruguay?" She falters. They telephoned, though, just before leaving. "Hepatitis is a depressing disease." And marriage can be—should she tell them that? "Don't blame him." Ray loves you his way; I love you mine. Though my arms too are slipping from your circle; they aren't really long enough. She tightens them. "Marriages change, sometimes. But families remain. They only grow."

Now she should tell them. That they won't be deserted. Her lips stick to her teeth. "Look. Look—" Her voice comes out a rough grumble. Her real voice. Even though she's never heard it before. "Birth. Giving birth, or getting born from somebody. You have to learn about it yourself." How sacred are the eyes of young persons—is that from a psalm? "Keep asking me things. Just keep asking me. I need you to. But I'm not going to tell you any more trash fact."

Exhausted, she thinks to herself—But are these eyes

young? Chess' mocking ones, Maureen's obedient. Royal's head is under her neck; she can't see his eyes. But Charles' are so needy—why he might be the youngest, not the oldest. She puts her clenched fist on his cheek. Then on his Adam's apple, that he's always swallowing. "But I can tell you one thing, Charlie-boy. That teaser uncle of yours; you were right about him." She swallows hard. "Your Uncle James sucks."

Under her chin, Royal's soft crown turns. His eyes are veiled. What a pang, that she can't quite believe in him.

"Are we still a *healthy* family, Ma?"

She glooms down at that fist of hers. "Families never die." And tumbles him from her lap. "An orgy, an orgy!" she cries. "Everything out of the cupboards. Aren't you starved? *R-rout!*"

And that was ritual, she thinks now. We were always a healthy family about food. Charles made a smashing Parmesan omelet. Everybody did something. And the precious tortoni kept for stray guests—and for James because he always brought the Bajan rum for it—came out of the deep-freeze. It wasn't orgy I was teaching them, but change—of mood, of pace. Of heart. That it is a way. That it can be light.

Maureen played the piano—Gilbert and Sullivan. Evree boy and girl a-live, is either a little rad-i-cal, or *else* a little conser-va-*tive*. Everybodee is selfish—we sang to each other silently—some of the-ee time. And Royal danced.

Next day—Saturday—she went into the city, taking them all. To avoid James. And her own anger at him, a dark weight. Or a fist she can't yet heft.

The children are to distribute themselves around the city: Charles to a rock concert at Carnegie, the girls to walk Fifth Avenue and windowshop the stores.

"Nothing much there in summer," she mutters, ashamed of wanting to be alone, but needy.

They don't mind, they say; they'll have tea in the Village afterwards, but won't call James.

They are *sisters*, she thinks; I never really saw it before.

Royal has cribbed an invitation sent to his father—to the Academy of Medicine, where there'll be a lecture on autopsies, with a speaker from Scotland Yard. James took him to the Academy once; he knows his way round. He organizes them—yes, he's that one. "You can all meet me there," he says, princely. "At six o'clock."

They understand my flight, she thought tenderly, sitting at the Fifty-Ninth Street pond, reading the weekend *Post* which it will please her to leave on the bench for the next incoming settler. From anonym to anonym, lazily—a city gift. How they acquiesced, in a unity of four, understanding too how I want to give the city to them. Suddenly her nail gored the drift of papers on her lap . . . Or else, they are terrified.

When she got up to leave, she took the paper with her. Glad that she had someone real to take it to. Maybe James won't call until late, won't come 'til after supper—which he'll of course expect anyway. Their family-style larder— the questionable luxe of those who buy in case-lots, and some of it peanut-butter—gives him a dowdy sense of clan, easily expendable. On these weekends when James spirals in from the health patroons and their world councils—not all of these spiritually guided, not all of it for the populace—he'll sleep loggily the livelong day in his monotone household, unruffled by other egos, or crumbs not his own. Rising only after all the stalls are closed.

Paper under arm, she's even hurrying to get the car. Maybe it's not possible to lead the logical life.

At the Academy of Medicine, smiling at her children so ably met, she draws them into a cluster round a telephone booth, and nodding at them with motherhood's pearly conviction, dials their uncle, intending to give him for an evening the gift of them. At the last minute, shy of all her brother and she still have to settle between them, she hands the receiver to Royal. "Here, *you* take it. You've been listening to autopsies."

They understand her too, except perhaps Maureen. An enormous warmth oozes in her, surprised. Not pride. Self-esteem, which with their half-formed slips of hands, from their bony young hearts, they are giving back to her.

"It's old Markie. Here, Ma. That hee-hee way she talks."

Old Markie in to do her chores in the night-cool, as is her habit because of her huge fat, is glad to tell her tale. "Yeh, he been. Flew in from the Islands last Tuesday. Bring some beautiful brown people with him. Party last for two days, looks like. Shrimp jambalaya all over the kitchen." From the sound of her, she's eating up the left-overs, more than food included. "Hee-yah, one of them long-legged coffee-beans, I say to her, 'You make me look like Italian roast.' I come in, they just leaving. That girl, she say to your brother 'I fly home with you all the way from Bridgetown. Now you fly me back.' And you know, honey, he done just that. Hee-yah."

"Bridgetown," she said, hanging up. "Can't be Long Island."

"No, Ma," her eldest said. "Barbados."

"He told us about the rain-forests," Royal said. "I want to go."

"Bet you do. Bet you will." She reached out a finger to smooth Royal's jawline. "Have to hand it to your Uncle James. He leads the logical life."

They stare, stolidly.

"Do we have to believe him then? About Daddy?"

A pious girl, my Maureen. Obeying all instruction, even mine. What more can be done?

"Not on your life, kids," she said, too trashy-loud for this muted medical hall. "He's just organizing. You don't have to believe a word he says."

On the Monday, she went in to quit her job.

"Kids need me until their father comes home," she tells Hoppe, who has come out himself to give her the paycheck due. "And Dorothy can come back soon anyway—you'll get along."

"I'm sure I will. But I was figuring on offering you the job permanently."

"Me? But I couldn't do that to Dorothy."

He shrugs. "She'll get along. You write better prose."

"Excuse me—but is that the professional way of looking at things? Or yours? I really want to know."

"Why?"

"Because it numbs me, sort of." From this humanist.

"Why are you so ally-pally with Dorothy all of a sudden? You scarcely know her."

"I—"

"I can tell you." His voice has risen. She can hear the cubicles listening. "Because she had a hysterectomy."

"I—well—yes it is a bond." She can see the male flare in his eye. "Even though I haven't had one yet. But like Kotex, you mean. And breast cancer. And the pill."

What a strange bond that must be, she thought, half-dreaming. That other cloister, that I never really got into, that way. Of women chained in lockstep against birth. Has he children by the sewing-woman—wouldn't he have said? I don't feel them—the loosening breadth that comes of them—in that narrow psyche of his. Or is it only we women whom the children make helpless to life? But why do I let him take for granted what *I* do, may have done? Why don't I crow it at him—Cockadoodle keroo, boys—*birth*. Why do I never?

"Hoppe." She heard her voice, silky. "Hoppe. Do I write good prose?"

"Better than we need." He wears custom shirts, the white stripe-on-stripe expanding with the breath. "But we'd make use of it. The way we did of Dorothy's social connections. Old county ones. You don't have those. But you could write a column say, called Woman's Word." He points the pipestem at her. "And yes, before you ask, that's my viewpoint. And the professional one. And the male one. 'Swhat you want me to say, isn't it."

When he smirks, the wens don't go along with it. Answer *them*.

"I couldn't. That's junk."

"Journalism. It's what I do."

She ignores that. In her way she's persistent, and knows it. "If I could do—like I said the other night. The real business. Underneath the words. All those feverish details we're all so ashamed of. The tiny knife-moves we make in the dark." Which never strike.

"That interior of yours? Unilateral nonsense—without the rest of us. All right, I'll go further. Only nonsense. Without the men."

"Being unilateral can be a strength. It is for you and Ray."

The name checks her, him too.

"But it's true—" she mutters, squinting at him as if he is both of them "—you don't like our voyaging." And draws a long, shuddering relieved breath. Surprised by the power that comes of speaking from one's own symbols. Even when unsure of what they are.

All this time she's been holding the boxed gift she has for him. Why does she always do this to people? A placation? Or a wild slap?

"I—I do want to be a humanist, like you . . . I can't afford it yet." She's fumbled it out low, to the box. Maybe he can't hear her. "I'm going to read him though. I looked him up in the Encyclopedia last night. Rousseau."

Hoppe shakes his head with an "Ach." Throws up his hands. "I'll say this for you. You don't whine."

Oh, poor Lexie. You almost dropped the box you'd hung onto so daintily, the way we do with presents too much mulled, too earnestly shopped for, too prettily wrapped. He'd taken away the mirror you looked into endlessly—spotty and chapped, imperfectly silvered with the past, but honestly yours, you'd thought. And had turned you to that other one, cool and fresh from the glazier, which most people patronize.

"Why—I'm always whining," you said. "I whine all the time. Inside."

You stepped forward so aggressively you knocked poor Hoppe's pipe from his grasp. "I screamed bloody murder, when I had the kids."

And it's true, then. Nobody hears.

She picked up the pipe then. Handing him the package along with it. "Here. A present. For teaching me a lot."

"Did I?" Yes, he looks like Punch, when he's pleased. Or Pinocchio, grown literate. "What's this? Dried fruit!"

An assortment of the finest icy pineapple wheels, copper apricots, and apple-quarters newly come from Russia according to the shopkeeper, rosy little cheek-slices from some Siberian tot. He picked up the cheap black, tin tray she'd added from the dime-store. What's this?"

"For the pips."

For the wife to carry it, the way his mother did. But why do we all elaborate so?—she wants to ask him.

"Lexie. You really are something. Too bad you did have kids."

Deep in her, the lioness roar begins stretching. Unable, of course, to reach the tinkle from her lips. "Th-think so?"

"Sure. You could have been somebody."

She takes a long bet. Humanism like this has to come from somewhere.

"Too bad you didn't, Hoppe? Then so could you?"

Somebody in a cubicle cracks his gum.

She drives home with her paycheck on the seat beside her. Thinking of whether she's learned anything useful about acts.

And all this time, she performs her household duties well.

On the night of the Kellihy party, James comes up his brother-in-law's front steps. Huddled as his sister is, in the wicker chair back of the pingpong table on the porch's side wing, he doesn't see her. So he's back.

She lets him walk unchallenged into the house, which is lit up like an ark behind her, hears him call for the children and not find them; now he must be settling down, to wait. James isn't one to imagine himself on a ship whose hands have murdered one another, leaving every hatch stuffed with a staring head—or have vanished, leaving one fly drowned in a glass of milk. Should he come to one or the other conclusion, he'll write it down for the monthly meeting. Still, she'll let him simmer in there. Until her anger has shrunk merely to him. Or is manageable. Or is gone.

Which is still a matter of getting back her own jokes, of feeling the power to make them fully reposed in her, as the flashy side of that inmost treasure, the strength to honor her own seriousness. In the past weeks, what's she been doing but poking about in her own ash-heaps, so that like a neophyte yoga recruit she may fold her limbs on the embers. Like a kind of daily housework it is, psychological. She'll be ever-grateful to the real housework for protecting her efforts, masking them. She's begun to understand what a nun is, or a monk-philosopher of the absolute— whose every act must reflect what is believed. I am the fieldworker, not in the house of the Lord, but of the family. Not that she's got it right—that fullness. Or ever will. But when she has settled in her mind and fingertips what the balance should be, should have been, but in this household never will be—then she can go.

Reaching out to the housewall, she turns the porchlight on, off, on, off, like a signal at sea.

James comes out, without a word. It seems to her that he is stepping through wave after wave of that other family-at-sea which has floated her here. And him.

"So you're back. From Barbados." And without the girl. That game must have stopped. "Didn't hear you drive up."

"Drove up with a friend."

Because he knows he's in her bad graces, instead of sprawling brotherlike on the only chaise, as usual, and idly chastening her, as family does, from there, he disposes himself on the porch steps, leaning up to her like a stage lover. "Solid with cars here already. Had to park down the road."

"The swimming-pool's being consecrated."

"For the ages, apparently. Yeah, I heard."

He's driven up for the party, then. Not merely for a party's complex of people, which will always draw her, but for his exhausting instalment-plan pursuit of girls. Who will never stay with him until they're fully paid for.

For as long as she can remember, the minute she sees James with a girl, she's inside the girl, in bed with that freckly-white long muzzle and tawn of hair—and staring up. And not liking it, thank God. But then I do that with most men, don't I, even older ones. I'm always the girl in bed, staring up. Waiting for them to say what.

"Going to be a moon," he says. "Funny how you can see its luster on the water, long before it comes."

The trees bulge over the road, heat-monsters come to lap at the waterhole.

"Oh yes, it's going to be a night. There's always one hot night when—it hits." And the moths know, and the birds, and all the other August-stretching animals—why shouldn't we? This is *tonight*.

Next door, no panes of glass are being smashed, tonight. Yards away as Kellihys' is, the vanilla wind of a party—even one where there'll be only whisky—is blowing out of all its doors. One can almost hear the crepe-paper rustle of the skirts the girls won't be wearing, the sweet soak of all the old party-sounds that confetti the mind.

She glances over there—no colors yet. This isn't to be a party where spongecake sopped in maraschino juice is the height. The children have been sent away from it. All down the road.

Drum-drum, skit-skat and blurt of voices now; those must be the caterers. Hard voices, caterers' men have, with the caretaking quality of male nurses. When she went over this afternoon they were just standing about, three men and a boy, in this one-night stand of a zoo they've found themselves in. Tough customers, down to the boy, with the smirk of late-hours hired help. Yet the disc-swish now starting up from over there is pure movie-tone, that old-fashioned ocean-sound they make with airbrushes. And even the silence bits—cornstarch snow. Smash no panes, tonight.

"Charles hung up on me yesterday. When I phoned."

The children have declared for her. That's been squeezing her. Maureen, offering her lunch on a tray. Charles without a word washing the car. When that rain came, Royal closed every window in the house. And Chessie, looking like any other girl in pink lipstick and a sailordress—she knows how they look, well enough—went into the city yesterday, to hunt a job. Calling back brightly, as she ran for the bus "If I get it, I'll commute." They've declared for her, Lexie—who is the house.

"Lexie. Have you heard from him?"

"The usual. It was just late. But I'd already had the furnace checked, and paid the insurance premiums ... The Spanish nuns who run the place he's in continue to be kind. Sister Isaac Jogues, the one who trained in France, has had shingles, but little can be done for her; she's seventy-eight." And that disease, like his, must run its course. "Love to you and to the children." Whom he takes care to mention specifically. And a drawing for Royal. Of what he sees from his window. "Once he wrote 'Regards' instead of 'Love,' but crossed it out."

"Lexie. Don't you see? He's ciphering himself out."

Can a cipher do that?

"I had to warn the kids," James said. "Somebody has to. You just dream on."

"Somebody has to."

He sighs. "You don't change."

An odd, whinnying sound comes from the Kellihys, a high-speed motor, from inside the house. They're sawing wood in there, maybe, for the biggest bonfire of all, stripping the window-ledges, piling on the attic-trunks—the one with the hidden jewelry even—as they go. Or they're whipping up one enormous whiskey-sour to spout from all seven chimneys and fill the pool with such a tincture that we may drink as we swim.

"Dreaming big over there," he says.

"Mmm. If news of the party reached Barbados."

"No. Bob's brother, the one who lives in the Village. The philosophy professor. We have a mutual friend. Who drove up with me."

Some woman they share? Is he grinning? She can't quite see. "*You* don't change."

A burst of laughter, from the brother-sister fount. Briefly, they grip hands.

He slides gratefully up and onto the chaise. "May marry that Bajun girl. Markie approves. For me, that is. But she told the girl on the sly 'You stay black, better. Everybody already want to be: lookit they hair.' . . . Yes, I may fly back."

"After the party."

Yes, he's grinning.

"Well 'ray for Markie, anyway. Maybe all women are anthropologists."

"Huh?"

Everything she says to James is awkward, pedantic, but part of her. "Been studying it."

"At that college?"

"No. Recording privately. In the house. Oh James— this house. Sometimes it's an igloo, with everybody learning how not to freeze the nose. From ordinary human contact. Other times it's Tierra del Fuego—everybody warm as French toast . . . It is hot there, isn't it?"

"Never been."

"To me, you've been everywhere." Scarcely showing it.

"I stopped off to see Mother."

"How is she?"

"Worried about you."

"I gather. She phoned. Maureen didn't hang up." She rose. "Think I'll get us a drink . . . Hope you told Mother all about the matriarchs in Passawatomie—or wherever. I know she'll be gratified."

When she got back with the drinks, he said "How are the kids?"

"As usual. In hiding, from us."

"How's your job?"

"I quit."

He clicks his tongue. Whenever she quit a job in the early days, changing from office to office, thinking she was hunting the perfect job like all the receptionists, he used to say "Shah."

"I learned something."

"How can you learn from a job unless you keep it?" Yet his face in the moonlight looks oddly satisfied. She's seen that look before. Always urging, yet glad.

"J. J.'s an interesting man."

"Who's he?"

"The editor."

"Ah. Hah."

"No. But interesting. Know what he calls this town?"

He waited. She drinks from her glass. Across from them, the water is a field, with an everbearing crop of ripples.

"The village of unnatural acts."

Any town is, Hoppe said. But the topography of yours, Lexie, a single straggle of houses between water and hill, is almost a moral presentation.

In the moonlight her brother stared at her uneasily. Yet he's always done that; he's only her brother. "Yes?"

"Know that handsome girl who plays the piano; you made a pass at her once?"

He smiled. "Nothing unnatural about that."

"No. She's always having affairs. She has twin girls of sixteen, prettier than her; she's only thirty-three. The girls do a lot of baby-sitting. And the father works late in the city. Underpaid. A guidance counselor. Last week he was brought up on charges of molesting a girl, on the late bus coming up here. You know, under his overcoat. She got him off, on grounds of overwork; seems he's been brought up before."

"Spartan she. But nothing to what goes on in Passawatomie."

"But listen. Maureen tells me—the mother takes the twins' sitting-money away from them, to spend on herself."

"That shocks you?"

"Yes!" Because I understand it.

"Why?"

"The peculiar—pettiness of the crime." She won't say—femaleness. Not to him. "And then there's the stealer on the road. Only at parties." We never knew who. "Hoppe—that's J.J.—told me who she is. She looks into other women's bags. Nothing rifled except an address-book maybe, or a grocery-list." She did that to me once, I realize now, in her own house. "As if she just wants to know. And wants us to know that."

"Clever of you. To catch on."

No. Frightening. That I'm able to. "And our Lesbian pair? No one knew they each left kids behind them. Who are not allowed to visit them, Hoppe says. Ray went on call to them once; he says they scarcely know how to have sex with each other." But can't she understand that flight too? "And even that woman over there." Just across from Kellihy's on the bankside, the woman who keeps that backward son of hers on the porch in all weathers. "He must be

· 115 ·

in his twenties now. But she brings him home girls from Letchworth, Hoppe says—morons, you can hire them out for daywork. And feeds them the pill."

James always laughs silently, shoulders heaving. "The man's a creep though, Lexie."

"No, most of those items are phoned into the paper. J. J. keeps them out."

She has her face in her palms, nodding slowly. Ordinary backchat would be beyond those phoners. Ordinary gossip, too. "They're doing their field work. The only way they know how. Through the walls. They want to know what really goes on. If it all . . . really does go on."

"What, for Chrissake?"

She dreams, scientifically.

In the middle of the desert, of the forest, on the edge of Tical in Central Peten, or on the edge of the Ruwenzori that is the Congo, the traveler comes upon the hut. According to anthropology, always the hut of the other tribe. To whom his own is unknown as yet, or has been lost. Or in the Yellow River valley in Outer Mongolia. Or in Grand River, the Hudson, which is in outer America. In a village not Ys. Where daily, to that other tribe, you are lost.

He's watching her. "Whether *what* goes on?"

"Acts." By which she means to ask, as anthropologists do among themselves: What, brother, *is* natural?

But James averts his face and says into the shadows, "Lexie. I did hear from Ray."

So.

"Lexie? Don't you want to hear?"

"I do hear." That you are still our go-between. And that things end as they begin.

She got up, trembling with her own wisdom, which she mustn't waste. "But I'd rather hear it from him."

Over James's head, above the chaise, a branch of rhododendron had thrust itself through the wooden arch between porch roof and balustrade. He sat up, tugging viciously, trying to break the branch, or thrust it back. "Shah. *Shah.*" The old auntie expression their mother had scolded puddings with when they wouldn't jell—does her brother recall that? Probably not. In the midst of a world which had mostly junked Freudian connections between people for less verbal ones, their mother's "adjustments," like some oldfashioned corset, hold them firm.

He thrusts the branch back through the balustrade, where it wavers high. The moon is now above it.

She laughs. "It wouldn't have broken. You don't know a damn about rhododendron."

He got up, slapping the chaise. "Is it any wonder I told the kids what I did? You're not really all that irresponsible. Then why the hell do you go on playing it?"

"Do I?" Yes, I do. "Training, I expect." From being talked to by your profile. And others. It makes you turn round. And is a waste.

"Where are the kids, by the way? Isn't this late for them?"

"Sent away, the whole pack. They're better out of this fracas."

"Sent—all four of them?"

"Chess did balk." She makes herself shrug. "But she finally went. In such a costume, even for her. With Maureen bawling at her 'Oh it's all right for you, you're seventeen. But I'm at the age where I need to be very conventional!' ... You suppose our Maureen has humor after all?"

She smiles to herself. Leaf by leaf, in spite of all blight, they unfold for her.

"So Chess balked did she. Are you surprised? That girl's dependency on you is like a babe's for the womb. And she went?"

Before she can answer—that sudden, hard medical tone scares her so—he's looming over her chair.

"So you've done it. You've really done it."

"Done what?"

"You've got rid of them. Mother always said you really wanted to."

Behind him, a kind of fire-bomb soars from a Kellihy chimney, pushing upward without noise, holding the moment over the trees, and falling—pray God—behind them. The party's beginning.

"So—where'd you send them, huh. To Dad? And to that chickie-whore wife of his, who's always sighing she has no kids of her own to put her money on, nobody to be a chickie-grandmother to? 'They could go to winter school here; I could outfit those girls'—she's always nagging him. 'Thought I was marrying me a family, Chawlie—and lookit us.'"

More signals flower behind him. A whole sky's golden sprouts, but he ignores them. "So that's why you don't want to hear about Ray."

Against that funhouse shower of lights, all his own angles clown him—the swelling jacket, sharp pants and long-tongued shoe. Under them, where's the solemn boy who until this second her family-blunted eye still saw?

Walking with either of his two exotic wives, he still seemed merely the square medical man, a little guyed by their tastes. But this country air will have none of him. He belongs now to a carnival apart. Those gassy caverns are really his eyesockets, in each of which a coal is burning. That jaw gapes just a trifle now; it never used to. What does it want to swallow, even more than girls? And on the crown of the head, where, so much saucier than James himself, Father's coxcomb used to be, is a faded little cockette. What's made her long James of the grasshopper legs and the scholar-soft eyes into this fake-fussy little man, yes, even little, who appears to be prying his way, or buying it, into the crowd in a Toulouse-Lautrec? Only one touch needed—at the lips, the tottering cigarette.

Blue flame spurts as he lights it. "If you really had to, why didn't you—." The hand is shaking. He tosses his head with the first puff, a smoker's bravado. "I have what they need. Everything."

· 118 ·

He means she has what he needs. Or the kids have. He belongs in the ranks of those who can't be personal. I see his shadow thin. The private is not his sphere. *Verily.* As they'd said in that freak church he took her to when he was fourteen and she eleven, where they danced round the ark on Sunday. And he watched me watch. Verily, James. And James, can I ever be angry with you again?

"Funny—James. Mother must have wanted to get rid of us. I never thought of it before. All those puddings out of the same box." When a boxworth didn't jell, or burned, her mother always said to the box "Positively malevolent, you are." "We thought she couldn't cook, the poor clever woman. Maybe she even thought so herself. And remember those anti-male nightgowns she wore? Women in middle age—I know half a dozen like that around here." Dumb flirts, who've turned slattern. Or onetime college-girls, who shear their napes, flatten their arches and address volunteer committees, with executive cool. "Dad's pajamas. Remember the night she came down to the pier in them?" When she must have been just about my age. "And the men proudly take the sexual blame for it." Vaunting their own neglect, or even their impotence. "And the doctors prescribe hormones."

"Never knew you to take the anti-male route." James is pale.

And I am reddening, a goddamn sororal rose.

"It's either that or go toward them, isn't it?" While the fabric weaves on, down below. "Listen, Jimmy. Women don't understand their own malevolences. But I want to. I must."

"Cut the fancy excuses. Just tell me where are the kids. Or I'll smack you, I swear."

"Will you." In spite of herself, the old sibling-sass. She looks down; she's even stuck her chest out. But there are breasts on it, now. "And what'll you do then?"

"Cable Ray. To come for his rights."

"Which are?" Suddenly her teeth chatter at her. "Why'd you say that about Chess? You talk to her doctor?"

"No. Why?"

"You talk to all our doctors. After recommending them. You talked to mine."

"You didn't have a doctor at the time."

What time does he mean?

"I mean the one we called 'Dr. Gyno,'" she said, staring.

"Oh that. Yes, you gave birth to them, your claim to fame. As if you were riding in on a chariot, he said."

"So you did talk . . . What about Chess?"

"Nobody has to talk about Chess. Surely you know that."

Behind her hand she makes a masked grimace. Oh good brother, you are surgical. Over at Kellihys', the sparks have stopped.

"She was already the image of you, at that same age. But already worse off, if you want it plain."

"What age?"

He's surprised. "Fifteen."

That night on the pier. When Mother snapped at you *I'm the caseworker here.* "James. Did you and mother have talks about me even *before* you went to medical school?"

"You were pretty far out. And father wouldn't."

She can see them, the two social workers, diagnostic close—with cocoa afterwards.

And when I was seventeen, the danger-age, you brought home Ray.

"You and she boxed me in for fair, didn't you. I'll break my guts, not to box in Chess."

"You haven't sent them to Mother—in that tiny flat?"

"Don't worry about them; they're safe." She needs to laugh, shriek, plant both her thumbs in his eyes like a pair of phalluses—figure out that last one when I've time.

Better to bargain. Like them.

"Listen, James. If Chess gets a job in town—*can* she go live with you? She likes Markie, gets along fine with her." And with all blacks. Just like you, James. Their distance woos you, makes her feel comfortable. "And she could go

to a doctor you recommend—she's bounced this one."
Under cover of her robe, her hands grip each other. He's
certainly considering. That silence when tribes bargain,
that's what this is. "And perhaps ... Royal. James—?"
She's never weighed her words so carefully for him. Or
her children. "He'll have to go to the Hospital for Joint
Diseases twice a week in the fall. Perhaps *he* could bunk
with you too. For the winter."

And Charles and Maureen—to their father. Charles
to college, anyway. While Maureen keeps house. And she
herself slips through the knothole. To the netherworld, or
feather-world, of her choice. *Tra la.* Like mother, like
child. Not quite. But there was a grandmother, the tribe-
men will say. Who really did it. Who left the children and
ran.

"It's true," he said. "Royal's altogether outgrown the
school here."

This horrible half-medical fantasy she's concocted
stuns her. What comes upon us, once we're bargaining?
Maybe it's the logical life. Will she have to pass through
that prism, whatever she's dreaming? If you know what
you dream.

"I've not been trained to plan," she says, "—and that's
God's truth. I've been vagued out."

He turns on the porchlight. Down at the steps which
lead from the lawn to the road, a light in the knobbed
stone gateway switches on also.

"Hey, don't, I'm not dressed." And down below, the
line of glinting party-cars creeps, doubles back and inches
on, as each driver sees that the available parking has
stretched to farther north. In spite of herself, she leaned
into the shaft of light to watch. "Like a snake molting, ever
see one? We found them up the back, last year. In the old
quarry. They still scrawl these hills ... Okay, let's turn off
the light."

"Wait a minute. Lex ... what do you mean—vagued
out?"

· 121 ·

"Oh—." She's pleased to be asked. Her eyes unfocus on it. "Like there's—too much empty space inside me." She smiled at the precision of that. "That I can't get rid of. The problem is—how to fill it. I've made a start."

"Have you."

"Stop staring so." She reaches for the switch.

He bars her. "When people have too private a language . . . other people stare."

She withdraws her hand. It trembles. "Oh James, that's beautiful . . . if it's friendly." Better not to look at him, to see if it is. Slowly she presses her shaky hand with the firm one. "With Chess it's hats, costumes. A kind of self-protection. Being freaky before they can say you are." Saying: This is what I am. What my family, those fakirs, will not admit. "Poor Maureen, when they went off. It's hard on her . . . Not on me so much." She does look at him. "Well it really isn't . . . but it's a relief to talk about it. I never do, you know. Not even to—her father." No, especially not to Ray. "James, I apologize. For teasing you. They're just down the road, all of them. All the children on the road. It's going to be a real brawl, across the way. Not that the whole road doesn't want to go to it; they're mad to. So the Village Hall's been set up for a kids' party. With a couple of nice old committee-women to play piper. The kids can even sleep over there, if they want. But I doubt if ours will."

"Like Hamlin. A whole village would do that?"

She laughs. "A resourceful one . . . Well for God's sake. Don't you believe me? One would think—what do you think? That I've put them in the pond?"

Is it the light makes him blink, several times? "One never can be sure. How far passivity will go."

She stands up, then. Drawing the deepest breath. Glad she has the space for it. "Can you be so sure—of Ray's?"

And covers her mouth. Against what has come from it.

"Right. If it ever comes into court, on whose side would I flop?" He laughs. Swinging himself up onto the balustrade, where he leans against the porchpost, facing toward the river, clasping his knees, nonchalantly false-young.

She touches his shoulder. "Marry the Bajan girl. Get some kids of your own. If she'll have you."

No answer. Maybe she won't.

"I meant that, then," she says. "About the winter."

"If I can bear Chess, you mean. That I can have Royal."

"Not if you put it that way."

"Hadn't you better? Begin to?"

There is a tiny, bitter pill still given girls for menstrual cramps—a school nurse had first given it to her. She'd given it to Chess once. Feeling the link. Though she herself hasn't used it in years, she tastes it now, a spark of gunpowder on the tongue. *Tastes blue,* Chess said.

"You do grapple them," he's saying.

"Ah, you've been with mother, all right. She phones that, twice a week. Ever since Ray's been away. 'Oh Lex, don't wait like I did. To see it all clear.' I tell her 'That's *your* destiny. What else do you think old age is?' I've been thinking about old age. Oughtn't one? . . ."

"Oh?"

"Don't sound so—doctorly."

"No wonder Mother's worried. I meant what I said you know. About court."

"What court?"

"She wants Ray to be made to come home and take custody. I'm to insist."

"Has *Ray* ever—?"

"No," he says quickly. "Nothing about that. Or about you. Ever."

She sat down, stunned. "I don't know whether to cry. Or to laugh."

"There you go."

· 123 ·

"Eh?"

"People usually say that the other way round."

"Last time I saw her, I didn't know which. She's still wearing those gray do-gooder clothes. Even in Florida." I must use my head, she thinks. For the kids, I always can. "James . . . remember those custody cases she had? And the child-abuse ones? Remember how angry she used to get because mothers in the State are inviolate. 'Because they're made to be—' she used to say '—not because they should.' That's it, James. She wants me to have all the advantages she didn't have." She lets herself laugh.

"Maybe . . . She said to me 'You and I did your sister a real bad turn. Even if this looks like another bad turn, we have to put it right.'"

They laugh until they choke.

"All women're mad," he says, backslapping her.

"All women—have always been mad." She says dutifully. Like a proverb. Or a quote.

"Ayuh," he clowns, in his old Maine accent, carried over the college winter from summers as a camp-counselor. "Ayuh. But now they know."

"I hope. You and Ray could, you know. Two medical men. In court."

"It's possible."

"And who would *I* cable? For my rights?"

"Look, Lex—it wasn't my idea."

"You listened," she said. "Just like—then." She clasped the purple robe about her. Not casually. Seeing it. As she had all these years. "Ah, I don't blame her, really; she was scared for me. Now I've reached the age where she can sympathize a little . . . Or she would like *me* to. Mutually. Her independence is maybe bitterer than she—calculated. Maybe she wouldn't mind the sight of somebody else tasting some of the same. Even if it's me. Or—especially me." She threw up her hands.

"Sis. You're remarkable. You really are."

"Don't say it like a disclaimer. Or an elegy."

He's stripping the rhododendron branch. It won't

break. "Either you mutter or you flash. One never knows how to take you."

"I'm just learning, myself. James—I know why you and mother got together on me. I don't even blame you anymore. I just wish—I hadn't had to learn it."

"Why? I mean—why wish?"

"You and Mother were afraid of me, that's why. The way—I'm afraid of . . . Chess. Oh—James."

She is in his arms. Not bothering to look up.

They break apart.

"Let's go to the party."

In duo.

But he said it first.

"I'm ready."

"Not in that, Lex."

She looks down at herself. "I've had this robe since I married. It reminds me—of me."

He shrugs, "So many things do."

"Right. Just give me time; I'll run out and change . . . Up, I mean." She flashes that, brilliantly. "And when I come down—you can tell me about Ray."

Upstairs, she does what's she's never done before, but often half-meant to. One night perhaps, as a joke. Entering the bedroom of each child, she turns the bedclothes carefully down. Thinking in turn of each child.

To dress takes her less time than she spent in any of the rooms.

"That's nice," James says, when she comes back.

"Yes." The dress has chosen itself. Its dim, auroral flowers, pressed on sheer black, resemble the blotted garden of her mind. "Now. About Ray?"

"He wrote me two months ago. Asking if I could get him a job in public health."

He's watching her, the length of the porch between them. The whole river's glistening now. "Well for God's sake, Lexie. An internist. You can't jump from private to public like that. Giving up your whole life's work."

The hell you can't. But she says nothing.

"I wrote him—'Ray, come home and we'll talk about it. Don't make a decision from sickness.' He never answered back."

From sickness. From internal sickness. But those are the decisions you *must.*

"Sis. Aren't you going to say anything?"

How separate Ray and I have been, then. On both sides. Two sea-bottom creatures fumbling up opposite walls, and forever dropping down again. Back to back . . . All this while Ray has had this relationship with himself.

"I'll tell *you* then. He'd better resign himself. He hasn't the ghost of a chance. And he has this town in the palm of his hand."

The water in front of them sheets golden, back and forth, back and forth, a hippodrome whose arrangements are made far below. The Tappan Zee's the widest part of the Hudson—they like to say here. A salt river even up here, twenty-seven miles from the harbor. And navigable to its source. All along it, northward, there are villages which can be held in the palm of the hand.

Southward is the harbor, and the shifty piers from which one can go anywhere. Traveler beware—of not being the traveler.

"I give you up," James says, passing a hand in front of her immobile eyes. "Let's go . . . Oh wait. My trunks are in the car."

"They're providing the swimsuits." Under her dress, she already has her own bikini on. *The tribe is sensitive to clothing; it must be theirs, and both original and appropriate. Helps cure being lost.*

"Shall we go down the steps and around the front way?" He's diffident. "Or around back?"

"Why—you've never been over there, have you. In all these years." Of sitting on our porch, hearing the smashing. Or brother-in-law-watching Ray. "Let's take the martini-path, huh?" Tonight is tonight.

The path's become a bamboo thicket again. End of

April, after Ray left, she and Charles took scythes to the soft, pushing cane-sprouts; a month later, it was back. Now in August, it's man-high.

She can't remember Ray's face past ten years ago. Not the later face. But the one he might bring home—from nuns, and a sickness of his own—interests her.

"We can't get through here, Sis."

"Yes we can." Taking his hand, she shows him how to sidle this way, that, always advancing, and without tearing his sportshirt. There must be dozens of such talents she's had without noticing them. All of them to do with sidling, with the adjusting of objects to people, and vice versa, from day to day.

On the Kellihy edge, the bamboo is charred; against village rules, have they been burning off again? Yet she admires. Some people simply will not adjust.

Out in the clearing, great trees still half-hide the Kellihys', a square white house, too big for its clapboard lines. Standing on the rise of hill between, turning, she can see her own winged and turreted house through other people's eyes. Never hers, really, and for more than a century not the house of the people who built it, bought by Ray from the Morrises, who had it only nine years, it is still "the Appletons'," who had it for twenty-five. Nobody in a village owns a house. Forget houses. Golden water's floating through the trees.

"Yes, you were wise to buy it," James is saying. "A fine property!"

If I can just sidle through, and past it. Property is murder.

"And for the kids," he says.

On this side you can see the office-wing jutting back. In Britain—according to Ray who'd had a student's tour of Edinburgh—a doctor's office is called "the surgery." He'd actually had a plaque made up, saying that. One foolish glimpse of it from the road, and he'd had it taken down again; she remembers that face of his. Perhaps if she'd had the plaque to see all day, would it have joined them closer? Or if she'd hung one alongside, saying, as she had joked at the time—"Wivery." What's the public health, against the private one? If you live in one, do you die from not having lived in the other?

"Cat got your tongue?" her brother says. "Why Lex . . . what a face."

She must have lost the habit. The last time she wept was when Royal was born. For his foot. Mothers didn't cry much, for themselves. Girlhood was a passion of tears, flung on a bed—and gratefully departed from. During the first year of marriage, that first hard swallow of the strange double solitude, she was now and then flung back. To be absolved by the first child. And to relapse only that once—with the last. She's never wanted to weep for his father before.

All that time, this other solitude, hobbling along beside her.

Are Ray and I a tragedy? For I want to bawl, bawl. But it's too deep for that, too deep. It belongs to the tragic rhythm of the fathers. I can feel it, but not transliterate.

James is urging her along, out of the thicket. Locking her knees, she withstands him. He is frightened of her. She grips him.

"Ray *dreams*," she says, shaking. "*Ray* dreams." And I must tell the children, at once.

"Mind your face," James says after a minute. Wiping it for her with a handkerchief that smells of Bay Rum. He's gawking over the hedge. "Everybody's there."

Or everybody will be, in the peacock way of parties, with a feather on the village curls, or hat. Can't come to Kellihys' as yourself; that's why their parties are so popular. Come as you're not. That's why the kids have been sent off. They already know what that is.

She's already smiling. James, whose shirt has been torn after all, is already swaggering.

They creep through the trees, whispering the last gossip before plunging in.

"Betsy's invited the priest to come bless the pool."

"He coming?"

"He doesn't, he'll be the only one on the road."

"Betsy started by borrowing everybody's glasses. When the acceptances went over two hundred, she brought them all back. 'We're having a New York caterer; Alfie's getting them for us,' she said. 'Isn't that *live!*'"

"Only one cabana I can see. Maybe the whole two hundred're inside it. Who's Alfie?"

"A restaurant in New York that's their hangout. Where she and Bob go when they want to have an affair with one another. Alfie lends them the room at the back."

The hillside rumpling behind these houses that line the river has as many niches as a conservatory. Music is letting out from one or the other of these. There's a sharp-fingered look to the shrubbery. The moon is riding high.

"Must be having one at the moment," her brother's saying. "Isn't that a string trio?" They're at the crest of a rise. Dark shadows, moving over the lawn to the glitter ahead, can't be identified yet. One of these lights its pipe, then goes dark again. Was that Hoppe?

"Come meet the mutual friend." James stretches out his hands, a smiling partner.

This deflates her. For just a second. For the girl in Barbados. For all other girls. "Sure. Love to meet her."

Grabbing her hand, he skims her into the party, over the lawn and through the Hades-ranks, past greetings, past friends who merely wave. A striped cabana billows out at them, tawnily. Empty, no sheiks. The swimming-pool is black but gaudy, ready for the high mass. Silvering meanwhile with a few people, none of them bare yet, unless the bodies of those bobbing heads are, below. Or down at the bottom, is there that bogey of nighttime waterplay, the drowned body bare for always? Somebody slipped below, and ignored? As she and James run, saunter, skim, stopped by no one—how deft he is, really—that image flicks past her. Below the waterlilies brought by the nurserymen last Sunday, a body cooled past lotuses, lulling now and then to the splashing above, its nose scraping the concrete.

Last year's parties—what's happened to her confidence? Town-parties. They skim by her. Would the face in the water be a woman's or a man's?

There's Bob. Up on the columned front porch, which is lit like a stage. Or a cafe. Without his headphones, he looks less like a frog. Having work makes him look younger. Bob has respectable work tonight; Bob's a host. Bob's receiving, at the top of the porch steps. In black tie. No sign of Bets.

"There," James says, winded. A crowd is massed between them and the steps.

Up there in the spotlight, Bob has an arm flung around a shorter man in black-tie also—from the outline of both heads, a brother. As intros are made, the two men rock slightly, side by side. Bob makes everything an act; it occupies. All the while his rueful, molasses-brown stare admits to you, like a prep-school boy treading the boards in a varsity show, "*I'm* no professional."

"Where do you suppose Bets is?" she murmurs. She'll be the attraction. Once we greet Bob.

The man of a pair coming back down from the steps answers her. "The rival faction is at the pool." He and his partner are clearly on their way.

Up on the porch, there's a girl with Bob and the brother, half turned from the crowd below. Is she the one James has come with? Long brown hair, not a good figure, which is odd for James, though her dress is backless. She's talking to several men, as James's girls usually are. She's not black.

"Press on, Sis."

Politely, everybody is. Her foot gets on the first rung. "I was over here this afternoon. Bob was in the kitchen in a smoking-jacket, stirring a huge pot of soup." The caterer's men were working around him, stony-faced. Arthur the butler had gone to have his hair dyed. "Party or no party," Bob'd said, ladling a fine stream on the air "—my kids get their soup." When the men went out of the room, he said "Those apes."

Everybody knows Bob's politics. All hirelings—the whole conspiratorial class—are the enemy. Except for the ones who live in his house to give it character. And love him like relatives. When he meets any of the others he's butter in their hands, and ferociously glaring, slips them large tips.

At her elbow, a woman says "What they've done here. Isn't it unbelievable?"

"Unbelievable," she murmurs back. Glad that she's at last in the swing of it . . . What have they done?

James's nose is up, sniffing.

"Why do all parties smell the same?"

He shrugs. "Human sweat. And bear grease. You should smell them in the Orient."

He thinks she never will. Unless Ray does get into public health. She wishes—that she were wishing for Ray. And recognizes that part of the party feeling. What's it like to go with the wished-for one, to have that girlish conception fulfilled, at your side? Probably, then you stay at home.

Down below the steps, the crowd is moving freely.

People stammer in and out of the dark, ready for antics already anticipated in the dressingroom. Knowing that for the next six hours or more they'll stand so, chat thus, do that, in the framework that is part social confirmation—what a going concern we humans are!—part social surprise. In a unisex cabana. A party was all recognition. If it worked.

What if one could know all the artificial frameworks and rituals well beforehand, of a party, of a country even—and then move? Were societies where this was admitted more enjoyable? The exhaustion of rebellion, the waste of it, she thinks, is that so much energy is spent against the rituals, the framework—while the vital energies and justices escape. Was this why so many people of good will couldn't be bothered? Passivity had its points.

Perhaps she'll write an essay on parties. And send it to Plaut. Labeled "For My Incomplete."

They go up another step, the next-to-last. "Is that her, James?"

"Who?"

The girl's facing their way now. If she were pretty, her skin would be called "porcelain." But as she's plain, her eyes, nostrils and gums are merely outlined in thin, animal-pink.

"Your friend."

"Her? No, I suspect that's the Kellihy sister." James says this through his teeth; they're very near. One couple ahead of them now. Step lively. The last rung.

"Not a her, anyway, dope—" James says in his normal voice. "A him." And they are up. "Ah, how do you do. How do you do, Mr. Kellihy."

Her heart pounds. Can it be Ray—whom James has brought back here? And they are going to take her to court.

Bob never introduces. Present people are present friends. But he cases her pridefully; he likes his neighbors to shine when there are town-guests; she'll do. And gets on to his usual eager burble. "Have you seen Bets?"

No worry in it; somebody always knows where Bets is. The wonder starts when you see her.

Bob leans close. He's pink with sweat. "Bets and Violet were in the attic all afternoon; you shoulda joined them. Trying on each other's jewelry. Drunk as coots." He's gleeful. A dirty story is what he's telling them. Of history before it happens. "I finally hadda go up there, to break it up. 'Steal what you want, Bets,' I said. 'And get the hell downstairs.'"

"Violet does better here. Than when she worked for us," the one who must be the brother says, smiling. "Mother doesn't like jewelry." He has an endearing gap between his two upper front teeth. "Hallo. I'm brother Sean."

"Yah, he's my Irish one." Bob's proud.

"Come on, Sean," the longhaired girl says, "—Violet never worked. When I was a kid, she used to pay a neighbor's boy—remember Slouchy Fitzgerald?—to give me my bath . . . Excuse me. I'm Bob's sister."

"But that's why I came over, Bob," Lexie says. "This afternoon. I forgot to tell you. She's been paying my Royal. To bathe your Dodo. Fifty-cent pieces. He has a cupboard-ful."

"So that's where my Kennedy collection goes." Bob goggles at James. "Smart boy, your nephew. I better watch my Dodo. She's only three."

Somebody buttonholes Bob. He turns aside.

"And a ringer for Bets," his sister says, glancing at the brother. "Slouch only got dimes."

"I told mother she ought to pension off Arthur and Violet, instead of passing them along," Sean says. "She tried to give me Arthur. In a three-room flat."

He seems proud that his flat is modest. And is that philosophy for you? Or for a Kellihy?

"Sean, I'm ashamed of you," his sister says. "Arthur brought you up."

The two Kellihys laugh. So this is the clan never seen. Or part of it.

"Bob reveres you," Lexie bursts out to Sean. "You're his archangel."

He shrugs. "Because I'm a philosopher."

"No. Because you work."

The sister turns, stares.

They see her now. They hadn't yet.

Bob returns.

"Where *is* Arthur?" The sister's wistful, almost.

"You'll catch him, Sis. When you change into a suit."

"The pool's beautiful, Bob," Sean says. "But that huge high-slide thing into the middle of it . . . and all that other, er—equipment. Almost a gymnasium."

"Not to worry. Rented." Bob's hands grope at his sides. For the telephones that wire him to the world, or release him from it. Working is hard work.

"A gym in Gomorrah," his sister says.

Lexie stares at her. She may be an intellectual.

"And Sodom." A man ambles out the central doorway of the house, his blond head bent to examine the front of his black swimming-trunks. On which a snarling tiger is printed, jaws wide. "Jesus. We don't get these in Westchester." He straightens. "Oh there you are, James. See you've met them all, eh?" He hitches the trunks. "I disown these, though. I'm just the family friend."

And the mutual one. Her dress is draining to her feet.

Westchester hasn't been that good for Kevin Sheridan. He's put on the uneasy, whitish weight of the man who gives up drink for food. And that double-amber barroom tongue of his—for home truth? "We-ell, Lexie-love. James said you lived up here . . . And very becoming to you, too."

The Kellihys have turned to other customers.

She wheels around to smack James across his face. But James, backing in, waving benignantly, escapes through the door.

She smooths her hair, instead. "It's always a farce, over here."

"Tolerably. But you—my God, Lexie."

"A woman can never be thin enough."

"Rats. You've waked up, haven't you."

The corners of his mouth always drew her. Firmer than the rest of him—except for that cock. It's still good to have exchanged sexual pleasure with a partner who had given you confidence. Would it please Kevin though, to learn that his understanding is still the tiger she recalls best?

She peers into the house-doorway, down the long center-hall which opens out onto the back.

"No, he'll keep off now. I made him bring me, you know."

"He tell you I was alone? Etcetera?"

"I've known that for the past three months. He comes in the bar, you know. Always did. That's where I met him. During the time you and I were on, he—"

Stayed away. Tactfully. Yes, that would be James.

"So you know the Kellihys. You never said."

"Went to school with Sean. Sometimes run into him. When I'm in town." His eyebrows lift. The pock beneath one is from a dogbite as a boy. Other marks are new—natural. "So I never said."

"Anything." She doesn't even know the names of his kids.

They stare.

And then you—stayed away. She won't say it, because she no longer feels it—that whole scenario. Desertions on street-corners, in houses, lovenests—the whole psychic-dependence story of the woman who's left. To plead publicly, or mourn secretly—her scenario.

"I won't offer excuses," he says. "There were some. Homely ones."

"How you use words. I learned a lot."

"Not from me, baby. You had it before."

"You squander words. I—hang onto them."

"Irish cadence, that's all. My brother makes poetry of it."

"And you—." She will say it. For the sake of all the scenarios that bar must have been witness to. "Made love with it."

"We're using the past tense," he said. "Aren't we. Both of us."

But the breath of the party, that childish vanilla, is still blowing. The string trio is terrible. People are wandering toward it anyway.

"Why'd you come?"

"James keeps talking about you, you know. Talking you up. With a sort of pride. Noticed that even before I met you. He had me wanting to. And I wasn't disappointed."

"Pride? *James?*"

"You seem to be totally unaware. That you're one of those persons . . . whom people keep in view."

"Me? Whatever for?"

"I think it's because you're waiting," he said. "With an energy we can all feel. And watching. Not only us."

That part of it's not strange. She knows he's right. In adolescence how scared she had been of it. And never told. Never yet. Say it to him. You can say it to him.

"I watch the double spectacle of myself, that's all."

"There you go."

"You didn't come up here for that, surely."

"Oh I was fond of you . . . Though my fondness doesn't reach far."

His sense of his own limitations is as acute as a woman's; can this be what he seeks us out for, one after the other, searching for that tenderest sexual spot as other men go for our mounds? An overnight Don Juan, next morning nursing his maleness to size again, in the veiny morning of the hangover bar?

"Oh I explained it to myself fine—why you left, Kevin."

"Tell me."

This is called flirting. When you interest a man with himself. He had done the same for her, hadn't he— interested her in herself? "I told myself the landlord had served you a writ, for taking women in adultery. Or you'd found your eldest and most teenage son kneeling outside the door, blubbering 'Poppa, come home to us.' Or best of all, your wife had the clap. And you didn't want to give me it."

He takes her left hand with his left one. "And you don't really want to know why?"

"Oh I know that. Your only reason was—you do it all the time." And go home to Westchester, which is the boon place, the safe one. Where you keep your "old lady." That canny, despairing, blond old neophyte—I saw her. Who pretends she's asserting herself with you. Every time.

She takes his right hand with hers, so that their joined hands form the box with which old folk-dances begin—"People use sex like money, don't they?"—and they start to dance, to the terrible string band.

He tightens his arm around her waist, drawing her to him, closing the square of space between them. "You don't ask a dollar-bill where it comes from, do you? Maybe you should."

We're not going to. Across the blended, musical grass, James waves at them—still alone, but moving briskly.

"My brother, the pimp." And I'm drunk already. With money in my pocket for more drink.

"No, you're wrong."

"Okay, the *guilty* pimp."

"Never trust what you say at a party." Kevin grips her lightly. "Or what you hear. That band's going to have dreadful guilts, tomorrow morning."

They begin to waltz, as other couples are. It's the only thing to do.

Beyond them, still others are shaking themselves rag-time, out of the fringe of the dancers, toward the pool.

His naked chest must find her dress scratchy. A woman's thoughts texture always toward kindness. Toward the putative child. I want to jump out of that skin. Like a female slave, jumping out of the chariot taking her where she herself wants to go?

At the thought of the tiger on his shorts, she begins to laugh. With her head on his chest, in direct radial with her own tiger further down, his head bent to hers, they begin circling toward the pit of themselves. Behind them, faint, faint, she hears the squelchy clop-clop that beach sandals make against the heel—a pair of these, following them for a time. Not James. Many people must be wearing them.

From the porch above the dancers Bob calls out. "*Have* you seen Bets?"

When the searchlights go on, Bob's the only one not at the pool, though nobody says. The two beams rove the horizon from a setup among some trees at the top of a ridge, their rays intersecting heavenwards and flanging down, one into the river, one into the hill—only to reappear. All faces strain upward to watch the moving fingers write—and say nothing. She sees dozens she knows. She strains toward them, and with them.

"That's right," Kevin says. "Nobody up there."

Held in the searchlight beams each time, there in the streaky shadows of the vines at the back door, is Violet, a dowager out of Ebony magazine—massive cocoa-brown shoulders in black decolleté, a Roman-striped bandeau around a tiara of curls, and her mistress's three-strand corals. Behind her a punchbowl glitters, and a three-tier bar, but Violet typically stands in front. Beyond the bar is the cabana. In front of its orange-and-black howdah-fringed stripes, Arthur stands, shining with gladiator oil, in silver trunks, and barechested except for a huge orange bow-tie. His hair is silver too, lustrous as the bands which clip his wrists. He bows, beckoning.

"Yuck." Kevin's arms circle her from behind. "Ever see anything more minstrel-racist? Than the two of them?"

"Oh no, they do it to themselves." There's no time to explain who bosses the color-charts at the Kellihys'. The searchlights cross, and stop—fixed. On Bets, who's sitting guru-fashion in black mid-air. In a white bikini, Violet's diamond dog-collar, and on her turbaned head, Violet's canary-feather aigrette.

On the far side of the pool beneath her, lower-class trapezes, swing-bars, see-saws and pulley-weights crouch like the servitors in a throne room, before the soaring mastermodel in their midst.

Bets is on top of the very high slide.

"She wanted everybody to enter the party that way," a woman behind them says. "By having to climb up the slide, and splash down. Only the pool was in the wrong place."

"Chut!" a man answered. "They'll change it around in

the morning . . . My God, is that the three-year-old she's got with her—Dum-dum?"

"Dodo." The women always know the facts.

The little girl climbing to the platform has on silvery net panties. And a head-feather like Bets'. Her chub little butt backs shyly against her mother.

"Can the kid swim?" voices say.

"Nothing kills a Kellihy," one answers. "They all float."

"Oh Kev."

"Why Lex. What a face."

"It's the Pasadena party, down to a T—the famous one Bets went to, once. The slide, the gym machines—everything. Bets is always yearning over it." Glass in hand. "Oh Kevin, is that sad? Or not?"

"Wait—."

Bets is urging a slim bottle into the child's fists. Dodo waves it; she isn't shy.

"A split of champagne," the voices say.

"Wouldn't you know."

"Hooray for Bets."

Out of the cheers and catcalls, a cool, penetrating call. "Betsy? What about the broken glass? If it falls in?"

"That's the sister," Kevin says. "Always the little helper. And always right. She went to school with mine. I even dated her—one of my sister's good works. We're not in their money-class though." He squeezes her. "And Sister ain't mine."

Upperclass Catholic. So that's his milieu. Everything she knows about him—his assumed coarseness, the bedeviled drinking, his firm sense of his own style through all of it—shifts slightly to the right. And of course a Jesuit school.

"What you laughing at?"

And the encyclopedias. It also dovetails.

"Oh, look."

Bets, expertly juggling child, bottle and herself, is taking off Dodo's net panties, and slipping the champagne-bottle inside them. More cheers, when the crowd sees what she's getting at. She bows, up there in the Pasadena dream-sky. Bottle and baby in hand, she's never looked more maternal.

A wonderful mother of a sort, Lexie thinks. The slap-dash kind I can never be.

The bottle smashes smartly against the slide. Naked Dodo chortles. Her mother holds up the panties with the shards dripping inside, and flings it safely to shore.

"A clean break," someone says. "The Kellihy luck. What's she doing now? Oh no."

"Gather she didn't get the Monsignor." Kevin ear-kisses her. "Don't tell nobody she makes the sign of the cross wrong."

Bets is poising herself on the slide. Dodo's in her lap. A fine splash. They're down.

A silence, while they're under. The little girl appears first, held aloft by a pair of arms, whose head is emerging slowly.

It's Bob, in a King Cole crown. Hauling himself and Dodo on the raft, he sits her on his shoulders and shakes his clasped hands at the crowd. The raft is large, and stacked with bottles. Behind it, Betsy's feather rises like a periscope. Then she surfaces too, stage-bowing, arms spread like Titania, the little finger of each hand sticking up.

"Safe," the man behind them said. "The kid's even laughing. They must have practiced it. Ah, look at poor Bob." The big crown has slid down around his neck.

"Betsy yelled something," the woman said. "On the way down."

"'Tonight in Hollywood!'—what else. Come on. There's champagne on that raft."

Couple after couple are diving over the side to it. She sees the woman who also steals at parties, playing a passionate and excellent piano in the intervals. Tonight she has flowers in her hair, a hormonal signal to all. The man with her isn't her lover, nor her husband either.

And Kevin isn't Ray.

Other neighbors surround her, Hoppe's anecdotes. Over there's a redheaded man with a smile of gentle concupiscence on his face, who takes care of this as he can. If he seems uneasy, it's not because of his wife, who's at his side, but because of his mistress, who's not. The two are watching her.

The wife has a neat, unmemorable face and eyes slyly loose from it; sometimes she buttonholes other women with the suggestion that they sleep with him—"With my bad luck, I'm not enough for him"—doing this however only during the ordinary wifely day, at the supermarket perhaps or the butchershop, where this procuring may be seen as part of other duties. At parties she is always circumspect.

Her husband keeps the mistress in a large white house down the road; he and his family live ten miles inland. Half the week he stops on the river road first on his way from the city, but sleeps home; the other half he dines at home like any householder, but sleeps away from it— where one may meet him and the mistress out for a morning constitutional. Regularity is what oppresses him sexually, but he hasn't known how to get rid of it.

Here comes the mistress. An Englishwoman, she dresses always in black jumper, and jersey tights of the same, stuck in leather gym shoes—a style which makes stylish women crumble—and has an air of meeting no one. Rumor gives her five children, so competently disposed of in the continental way that no American can cavil. She has short blackberry hair, a steely air of capability, and a set of teeth so perfectly white, plumb and forthcoming that despite her few darts of speech the upper jaw seems movable as well. One imagines her and the husband's congress as a set of teeth slowly ingesting a smile.

But at parties, when the irregular in people tends to show up, the husband's smile grows again. When this happens, the mistress comes and stands at the wife's side.

As has happened now—Lexie sees why. The husband, who to date has never troubled over her, has seen that Kevin isn't Ray.

"H'are you, Lexie?" His smile is a shy throe.

"Hi. Hi." She hesitates, eyeing the wife. But loyal neighbors are expected to ask it. "How's the back?"

The wife's eyes tiny themselves. "Ray better come home soon. That therapist Dr. Bly got me to is great."

Her husband's head comes out at Lexie like a turtle's. From under his womanshell. "Have you met Mrs. Tork?" Yes, he's offering his Mrs. Tork as a sign: as you see, I'm available. When another woman interests him, he introduces Mrs. Tork.

"'Ja do." Even when met, Mrs. Tork doesn't meet. But an animal shudder ripples her jersey.

"Kevin Sheridan here." He's grinning out and out. "Mind if I ask what's the joke?"

Tork measures him. "The card *she* got, from the therapist. 'Happy August. And be sure to keep your hamstrings stretched.'"

Kevin's measuring her. Is there some bond? There appears to be. "Marvelous get-up, Mrs. Tork. Black Mass in the pool, maybe? Though your eyes are parson-blue."

The jaws open. She speaks as if from a rear twiddle of the tongue, or air-passage through the mandibles. "Know your brother, don't I? The poet."

Kevin studies his trunks. "That's my drinking brother." Vaguest voice she's ever heard from him. "Which reminds me . . ." He links arms with Lexie. "'Bye." A ring to it like a wooden nickel's. "'Bye."

As he and Lexie skim off, she looks back. Where are the five children, so competently cared for, of Mrs. Tork? Where are her own? We here are all twined in each others' acts.

"Don't tell me the plot of those three," Kevin's saying. "It's as clear as day."

"The way you are." She's careful to smile.

"Do you mind?"

"Wish I did."

"You need a drink."

She's still looking back. *"Didn't* her upper jaw move, when she stretched her mouth? Didn't it?"

"Like a hamstring. More moving parts at a party, better it is." He waves at the moon, which is now sailing. "Moons, jaws, violins. And a good assortment of lower limbs . . . I need a drink."

The punchbowl's surrounded by neighbors bouncing talk off Violet, who when high speaks a perfect stage-English, which she palms off as wit. She's seventy, and bone-tired from rambling after her adored little pyromaniac and his sister, but vanity is her chiropractor, any day. And she has a prisoner's sense of due north—the Kellihys don't pay her anything at all. Tonight though, she won't look at Lexie, and her enunciation's dropped off. "What the name of this stuff?" she grumps, ladling. "Dunno. *They* made it." Her elbow waggles at the caterer's men who are manning the other and proper bar. "If it make you randy, that why we built the pool."

Kevin has two glassfuls, then another. "Sidecar, I think." He squints diagnostically. "Fortified."

She'd forgotten he'll drink anything.

"You look like the Second Mrs. Tanqueray in that outfit," he tells Violet.

"Gimme back twenty years, and a good lottery ticket, I be the black Mrs. First."

They move to the regular bar, where Kevin has the bourbon-and-bitters she remembers as his drink. "What's Violet got against you, Lex?"

"Poor old thing. She's been paying my youngest boy on the sly. To give Dodo her daily bath."

"Hah. Well, Sister's been made guardian. For when the time comes."

"What time?"

But now he's urging her toward the house. No, I won't

go upstairs, she thinks. In the way of such parties. I won't steal a bedroom.

"Bathroom's all I want, honey."

"You read me," she says, happy.

"Like the Britannica."

They mount the porch easily this time, passing between the deserted columns. The house, erected by a name now lost in the jangles of the 1929 Stock Exchange, is late Greek Revival, very late, and built to a scale nobly ruinous from the first. The thick columns face the river commodiously. From the many added loggias of its facade, the river is viewed ideally through flowers, all of them luckily perennial, as if the founding gardener had so foreseen. A house requiring service, but able with the weight of years to run on half servantless—the perfect house to be inhabited by cracked wealth.

Bob, dressed again, is sitting on the floor in the smaller living-room, the wired one, drinking what he always terms "Whisky-water, Sahib" and gobbling the lumps of table sugar which he claims "keep the liver straight." He has receivers clamped to both ears and is phoning the commodity markets round the world, according to the list of opening and closing times kept always beside him. "Nobody's answering," he says in his soft, wise-to-everything voice. "Nowhere on the goddam flinty planet. Commerce is stopped . . . Hey, not that bathroom, Kevin; one of the kids left a poddle there . . . Violet can't be everywhere. Try the next one down the hall . . . H'are you, Lexie? Have a drink."

She accepts a whisky. Rendering exchange before he has to ask. "I saw Bets. Wow."

"Seen Arthur? Seen Violet?" He downs a lump, insatiable.

"Yes, I saw them. They're a gas."

He and she sit neighborly calm. He's given up pressing drink or sugar on her, knowing she hasn't much taste for either. But he breeds his own slang in her, and she loves that, feeling its do-nothing spirit fed to her, eye-dropper slow.

The room itself is sweetish with the stink of old euphorias. What can be wrong with a man so gaspingly proud of anyone who lives with him? An entourage is work, is that it? Is pride.

"You were great," she says. "In the pool. Positively great."

"A-a, that's the sugar. I can still hold my breath down there maybe a minute and a half. A quarter." He's always showily exact on anything numerical. "Having a good time, Lex?" He nods slyly toward where Kevin went.

"Marvelous. Except—that I can't stop thinking . . . about the kids." Funny, how she can tell him, rather than a woman.

He froggies at her. "Neither can I. Why I came in here. Arthur and I're spelling each other. Giving the dames a night off."

Arthur and Violet brought him up. He is their work.

"Somebody should give you a night off, Lex."

"Me?" She holds tight, not wanting to give the martyr's shrug. She doesn't.

"*We* were supposed to have the twins sit for us. But they finked out. One time after another. Somebody must be paying them more."

Should she tell him? She weighs it.

He mugs at her. "We always pay the sitters, don't worry. Cash on demand."

"Bob—their mother's been taking the money from them, that's why. For herself."

"Why—that's larceny. From her own kids? Jesus. Jesus. That calls for a drink." And for the head-set to go on again. Any mention of money sends him to his telephones. He listens; shakes the headband off. No answers yet. "Jesus. And the twins were so good with the baby, too."

"The baby? . . . You know—I forgot there was one. A new one."

"Bets pops 'em like pups . . . We aim for ten, you know."

"But how could I forget? I must be spaced out."

"You? The least freaked-out woman on the road. Bets is afraid of your intellect. I say you're just shy."

"My—what? You're all nuts. Him too." She gestures.

"Kevin knows a powerhouse when he sees one." He hands her a refill. "We all know you'll do something. When you find out what."

She shakes her head, angrily. "What time is it?"

He shakes his head at her, mocking. "Kids getting out of the village-hall you mean, don't you. Quarter of twelve . . . Oh, Jesus." His watch is soaking wet.

"Get it to a jeweler, quick as you can." The whisky in her dislikes the female authoritative. It's all I have, dear whisky. That why I don't drink more of you?

"Yeah, to Tiffany's. Tonight." He dangles the watch tenderly. "Damn. A birthday. From Bets."

The two-thousand-dollar one. Now she remembers it. And the new baby is a boy. "Arthur! Now I remember. You named the baby for him." We got a card.

"Didn't we though. And wasn't that a party. Bets got smashed. And my parents refused to come. Never admitted to themselves Arthur's gay, you know. Or to us. The party was to be a confrontation. All Arthur's boyfriends dancing the kasotz with each other. But Ma got wise. Sister put her onto it . . . A-a-a, so what? Poor little baby Arthur wasn't worth that much auction-wise."

"Auction?"

"Sure . . . Dodo? Named for dead Aunt Doris—sixty thou. Ma refused the honor, herself. Roddie—ah, Roddie was Dad. One hundred fifty-thou—and this house. And Charline—what a name for the poor kid—but with Uncle Chuck right up front, sitting on his crap-pile, what could *we* do? . . . The balance of the river-frontage. But Bets says

· 146 ·

we must never again lower our taste for anyone." He's watching her. "Charline—that's Lina, catch?" He yawns. "Come on, Lex, don't look so shocked. Where'd you think the money came from?"

"I'm not. Just putting it together."

"We want a Sean. But we want to do that one for free. So a Sean comes later. Maybe last. But we're working up. Except for the pool, little Arthur is pure sentiment."

"I thought the pool—"

"Yeah, Ma and Pa guv it. But Ma made him offer only on condition we change our minds on little Arthur's name. We agreed to it, in good faith." Bob chuckles. "But Bets says she'd been thinking either Arthur or Violet for so many months that when she got to the font, the name just flies out of her mouth; little Arthur is even lucky he ain't Violet."

When Kevin comes in they're laughing fit to kill. Bob is pounding her back.

"Hiccups," she chokes out. "Give me some of your sugar."

"Here you are. And a thimbleful of gin's good, I hear tell. Suck it through the cube."

"Not gin. Urp. Some of your whisky-water—urp— Sahib."

"Me too." Kevin slides to the floor, alongside them. Carefully he separates wires from pillows, tosses a coil of tension-wire-and-plugs over a shoulder, and sprawls back.

Bob's face is calm, unfrogged. A man's. They are with him, three sahibs together. Idling. "What took you so long, Kev?"

"There was a poddle in the other bathroom too. Thought I'd try upstairs. All the bathrooms. Your kids are talented."

"He and Bets plan to have ten of them, he says."

"Why not. Only five bathrooms, though. I counted."

Bob clears his throat. "Maybe I can push Bets to a dozen kids. It's a living."

"Maybe you can." Kevin grins into his glass. "Your sister told me about the arrangement." He squints through a lump of sugar. "They've got Bets to agree—no affairs until the childbearing's over. So that Kellihys can be sure that any property to be left goes to Kellihys."

"Bets is a sport, Kev."

"Sure, Bob. A true sport."

"She's even turning Catholic. Long as the kids are being brought up in the church, nobody asked her to. In fact the church tells Ma—why push it? Snobs. But Bets says—under that kind of contract, being Catholic helps. And after number ten, she'll turn back. She'll only be thirty-five."

Kevin's silent. His wife has the money.

At least a woman doesn't need to exact that, she's thinking. All her children will be hers.

"Course I had to agree to same." Bob casts up his eyes, with a pie-smile. "No go, otherwise. Says Bets."

"Sure, Bob. You're a sport."

Both men break into laughs, and refill glasses. "How about you, Lex?"

"Urp. No thanks."

"Slap your back again?"

"Uh-uh. They're stopping. Hiccups from laughing stop sooner. Ever notice?"

"Do they?" Kevin slides over onto her pillow. "Truly?"

"I may have made that up."

"Let me look down your throat."

As Kevin grasps her chin, she laughs. The tones of sexual interest are limited, after all. Only so many—openings.

Bob's saying "You may be right. Always wondered about those hiccups of Pope John's. That terrible attack he had. Three days, or something . . . No, wait folks." He holds up a finger. "Know what? It was that sourfaced one; did he come before or after? Couldn't have been John."

· 148 ·

Kevin stands up. "I will go now. When Kellihys begin to talk about Popes. They've met all of them. Ma and Pa especially. That's why I don't come to your parties anymore, Bob. Specially the christenings."

"Ma and Pa don't either. They send Sis. Like royalty. A princess, doing the honors of the bazaar."

"I saw her."

"Sis can't have kids, you know. Wants mine."

"Everybody likes property." Lexie stands up, sliding on pillows. "I better go over, check on mine."

"It's dark out there. I'll go with you."

"Thanks, Kevin, there's a path. No, you stay. They wouldn't—"

"Right." A torsion in his face, a breadth, reminds her that he's a parent too.

"Poor old martini-path, hah Lexie?" Bob's fiddling with his phones. "Bets is off the hard stuff, is it two years now? Thanks to Ray. Ray's a sport."

He watches her let the name go by. "Came to our christening party, know that Lexie? Night before he left. Got smashed. Imagine. Old Ray."

"Did he? Well, this is the place for it."

"He still with those nuns? Don't let that last too long."

"He's—traveling."

Both men stare, at the word coming out of a wife like that. Like a defense, a three-note song.

"Lex. Bets and I—the whole road—we're rooting for you two."

"Are they. To what end?" How grudging, she thinks at once. Yet she must part the web, mustn't she?

"Ha, come on. Be a sport. Listen." Bob sets down his drink. "When Ray comes back—a doc with a practice like his is coming back, don't you worry—my advice to you two is—have an affair."

"Thanks. I'll leave that to Bets."

Kevin puts a warning hand on her.

Bob peers at them. Heavy brows for that boyish face;

only see that when he knits them. "Bets' idea, baby. She said 'All those nights ole Doc came over at the drop of a hat, Bobbie . . . Bobbie, love, whyn't we lend them our room at Alfie's?' . . . Betsy's a sport."

No, don't part the web where Bobbie's concerned. His face tells them so. Dangerous "All 'ose nights when I'm getting smashed worse than Bets. Ole Doc getting us through the night. Getting Bets through the night. Never sends us a bill. Never sent us a bill for anything." Raw breaths, like the stertor of the sedated. His mouth, suddenly gone frog. He covers it. "Amsterdam. Gotta phone Amsterdam." He turns his back to them. Filliping the tangle of wires, his other hand scuffles out the handset, puts it on his head. He sits clenched, with the clump of wire on his belly, head bent.

"Do I hear a baby crying up there?" Kevin's pale.

When Bob finally turns round his face is the frog's they know. "A Kellihy yammers, he's alive."

All three of them know Kevin lies.

"Did you say—dark?" Bob rushes to a window. "Dammit, it is. Where've those goons with the lights goofed off to? Where's Arthur? . . . Excuse me . . . gotta—." As he runs out the door they hear him through the window. "What the hell is a party like this doing dark?"

"*Did* you hear a baby?"

"No."

"Neither did I."

She crouches over the telephones. Always wanted to examine these wonderful coils looping out over the floor—a clot of countries, bourses, walking where you walk, yards of it following Bob like a talkie-walkie courier, or a nurse. Upstairs, the white phone set-ups trail like spilt milk from bedroom to bedroom, linking the babies to Bets wherever, on her bed, in her bath, on her chaise, she smoking while she talks to you, while the snub receiver whispers in her ear, or buzzes please-please at her wrist.

The head-set clamps tight on her own hair. Another

receiver bangles her wrist. Sensuously she winds the wires around neck and chest, under thigh, until she's circled.

"What the devil you up to?"

"Traveling. Hello—Amsterdam?" She dials, reading from Bob's list. "If no answer, Switzerland's available. Or Hong Kong . . . The Dutch speak English, don't they?"

"If they answer, what'll you say?"

"I'll ask." Whether the world's steadfast. Whether it's at six or nine o'clock. "Ought to be able to ask a bank anything." From so far away. "Kevin—." Suddenly she's frantic to uncoil herself, to stand aside from these rubberized lassoos which one has to cast like an angler. Holding bonestill meanwhile. Or folded in the lotus position, around a drink. Or stirring soup. "These phones are dead!" She throws them from her like the coils of a snake.

He helps her to her feet, his fingers spanning her waist, her breasts. Reminding her of her own warmth, and his. "Maybe he didn't pay the bill." Turning her away from those wilted wires. The kiss jolts. But she's still watching them.

"Maybe." Or maybe the phones—Bob's office, poor Bob's den where the kids can find him busy, nested behind the cataract of other people's business—were never alive.

Kevin's quiet, holding her in his arms.

The wind, dark as velvet through the open window, isn't telling her anything she doesn't already know. When the wind blows from front to back of her own house, built in three parts and three generations, there's a creak of riggings. This bland beauty here, columned up all at once from a last killing in the market, makes no sound. Married early to an old banker, this house isn't sympathetic to people yet, or may never be. Like those young wives one wonders about—sweet and compliant to the old man, capable to the world, and to themselves graciously false— maybe it still lies marble-faced under the old man's weight.

She raises her head from Kevin's shoulder. Oh I know about houses. It's said that women do. What we conceal

· 151 ·

even from ourselves is that a house isn't permanent. A house is a boat. Living on the river only makes it easier to see. But even the tight old inland farms breasting the wind's mountains, or those hunched, slumside barriers that rim the city with roofs like collapsed foreskins—they're all windjammers to the sky. Monsooned or becalmed. With sails high and handsome, or softly pouching, or slack.

She stares into his keen-eyed face. What my own tribe knows, mutely trancing its trained little hearts, is the fragility of the world. What could we not teach you? Yet we've the innocence that belongs to all the governed. We tend to believe in the permanence—no, the power—of acts. We have the faith of all the acted upon. Yet if that faith goes—as somewhere in these last weeks she knows hers has—what then?

Her head sinks to its own breast.

Outside, the party grumbles its way toward parable. In that process coiling continuous around the planet. Along wires electric or dead. The whole noble, fretful stream of human gossip that goes scalding along the glory-road, parroting the normal or murdering by proxy, or only sweet-talking with youth-sugar which'll drown in the morning—or seeing-dog blind. Tomorrow the whistlers will be blowing bits of the parable through the porous walls, asking for further news of it. Listen! They say last night the parable was *here*. At the Kellihys'!

Listen to the story, rubber-dead or alive. That's what is left.

At the grocery this morning, Mrs. Capostrelli, the owner's wife, bluntnailed sacklifter smeared with the world's eats, knotted whelper of eight and Friday evening bowling-alley cat, says shyly "Me and my women's group; we're going to Italy." Voyaging to witness the canonization of Mother Seton—who lived when, and dies for some now, and draws Mrs. Cap inch by spiritual inch across the sea.

But, I must do more than listen, than observe. It's drawing me out of myself—what a feeling. Behind our houses, our acts, what's this ethical shimmering? It is the story of what we do.

Kevin's been watching. Suddenly she catches wind of herself, nostrils wide, eyes sleeked back, slumped in front of him, listening, one-hand hara-kiri on her belly.

As she comes out of it, he smiles. Snaps his fingers under her nose, presses the joint of his thumb against it. "You're right. Everything at the Kellihys' turns to farce. Let's swim."

Now that he's leading her into the dark charivari outside she rejoices—as if the scene exists for her alone to trail her small revelations through. This is what people must mean when they say they accept the world.

Strange adolescence that I had, this must be what it was urging me toward. Between the body-sweat of acts, and the first tin-flute moral ideas, when I thought I must choose between life-by-drowning and life-under-the-whip—that there was no need to choose.

And no possibility. Any adulthood teaches that. Maybe a locked one like mine teaches it best.

Oddly light, it felt, not to rebel against the great obvious.

"Hey. You all right?"

He's so kind as to ask. As if the state of her mind is a worthy state. A fact. Not a worry.

"Kevin?"

"Yes?"

She smiles at this man whose pose, tightening him to the moment like a drumskin, is that he's in this for sex alone. "I can watch the double spectacle of myself. I can. I can. And not feel ashamed."

"Good girl. But let's have a bottle with it."

Motioning her to wait, he walks off toward the long bar.

From the spot he's left her in, a blank, unshrubbed bit

of service-yard where the earth is worn bald, she can see printed in black cut-out and lamp-glow, her own house. Creep through the hedge and gaze up. Three. Yes the children are home. They're guarding it.

In the corner room at the back, Royal's nightlight is on. He got used to it in the hospital long ago. Sometimes he can be heard conversing with himself as doctors do to patients, in that quasi-medical dark.

Next to his room, on the farther side of the house, Maureen's room can't be seen, dear girl, but she'll be there.

Charles' room, between his and Chess's, can't be seen either, but there's a light in the library downstairs. Reading there late sometimes as she goes up the stairs alongside to bed, he doesn't lift his head but buries deeper in his lone carrel, the only adult left in the house.

And Chess—now we come to Chess. We have to. Her room at the north front corner, facing here, is dark. Maybe she's making cocoa for them all in the kitchen. Too bad the children's party interrupted the lipsticked gaiety she's been bringing from town. But even if I hadn't come over here, Chess would have had to go to the party, or not go to it.

The familiar dread and anger comes over her, a tocsin sounding between past and future, warning her that she can't control events for this child; that this child will have a life whose events must be controlled. Maybe Chess is already asleep in that drugged way she sometimes has, right after dinner, going up the stairs, somnambulist—I did that once; didn't I do that once?—adolescence is the time of heavy sleep. Though did I ever alternate like Chess? Those times when she stays up all through the night, immobile, even immune to cold, as if warmed by a burning fright. When only Charles, gently exasperated, clumsily kidding, tonically sane, can bring her down, out of it. While I wait, wracked, outside the door—oh I hope we're not back to that.

There. The kitchen light, barely to be seen from here. Creep nearer, almost halfway. There, dimly—thank God.

The front door that faces the river is opened. Charles, calling to Maureen. Maureen, coming up the front steps—"I've got him." She means poor Gabriel, the cat. So the Kellihys can hear us too from over here; somehow we've never thought of it. "Come in, will you? We're having cocoa." She hears the door close. There. Royal always takes his cup upstairs. All safe at home; she can trust Charles. She's shaken with love for him. And I've got them all placed right . . . Funny, how she still uses her fingers to count them, as if in her heart she's given birth to a horde.

Then, in that upstairs room, the north corner one with the bay—a light's snapped on. That room is the prow of the house. At first, nobody's there. That wallpaper pattern's clear if you know it. Behind the scrawlings. A figure comes to the window then, and sits. Long-necked—a girl's. With a blot-head. It will sit for hours yet. The people over there have long since given up asking it to come to bed. It is the figurehead of the house. Ask the waves of the river to ask what it is looking at. No one else dares.

All are at home. If not safe.

When Kevin comes back, laughing and burbling of his encounter with the barman, and toting two bottles, she's crept back through the hedge. Humbled.

"Here. A split of champagne for you—darling little bottle." He presses it. The cork soars. He has her glass ready. "And Jack Daniels for me." He drinks. "Let's find a niche."

"Let's swim first." It looms like a cure.

"These baroque delays. Ah women. I warn you." He swigs.

"My pearls are baroque. You taught me not to wear them, remember?"

He doesn't of course. While in her fidelity, as if in a gel, every move he made on her flesh is preserved. Even his talk has been an oratory, faithfully echoing, often visited. Staring at the real man, she rebuilds his robot; reinvests it with his sounds, but her sensations. Finding his familiar mystery still strong. That butch face, frail only at the eyes. The well-cut, word-kissing mouth. Thoughtfully she adds a bit of ruddy to those maritally pale lips. Men are what you make them. Or hers are.

Then she's in his arms, has his tongue, each of them with their bottle dangling from a hand.

As they start up the hill to the pool she stashes her glass in a thick bush, but he catches her at it. "All the more for me."

"I like leaving it there. For someone to see, maybe weeks after. And say 'Must've been a party here.'"

"As if they wouldn't know. For years yet. A legend."

"No—for time itself, I mean. All the while spinning on—don't you secretly applaud?"

"God no." He drains the glass and tosses it over his shoulder. "Had my way, it would leave me where I am. Or better still—where I was." He reaches for her. And for her bottle.

"Ah, Kevin." In the dark she feels for the pock over his eye, smoothes it. "Time's the one thrill the chemicals can't destroy, can't duplicate—I saw that on a Nova show. It's why we'll never evolve a mouse in a test-tube."

"Or a woman. So let's make hay instead." He doesn't move. The bottles held in his one hand clink cool against her thigh.

She moves her mouth back and forth across his throat, where the words are. Why must she sound like a freshman pedant when she's most serious—is it that she has to express the basic, which is all she knows, while he has whole backgrounds of expressed argument? And why must she pick these times for it?

She kisses deeper, grazing her teeth on his chest. It's because I've never really been in the drawingroom of ideas. Of black-tie discussion. I've no status there. I still have to fight for the power to ideate. At any time. At just this time.

"I'm gauche," she says. At once, she feels its strength.

His forefinger traces her lips in a circle, round and

round. "You people. *You*—people." He grasps her chin, turning it in his vise. "I don't mind *being* with a woman for life. It's when she starts connecting me to it. You people pick up a matchfolder on a curb in Kansas City, you have to find out who dropped it, from maybe Paris, France."

In the dark, her face is burning. Toward nightfall a woman's thoughts ought tend only toward the dangling slipper, the midnight roweling. "Travel."

"Tidying up. Tidying up."

"Okay. So where *did* you come from? You never say."

"See?" He tilts her leftover bottle, draining it. "I just—flew in. And the whore at the Encyclopedia Motel said 'You look a lot like your brother.'"

"I meant, where were you born?"

"I know what you meant ... I was brought up in Riverdale. But my folks came from the South Bronx. From when people still hung their heads out to dry—in church. Until Freud came along and hung up their underpants alongside. Tidying up."

How Irish he is, yes—every prickle shows. And we who have so many prickles of our own—we're won by that in him. We people.

"Freud wasn't a woman."

"All Jews are women. Being in the true church." He flashes his teeth at her, breathing close. The sexual underlies everything he says. Or he pretends it does. It's his whisky, more than the whisky itself.

"You should meet a friend of mine, named Plaut." She grits her teeth. "Between you and him—I'm defined."

From the top of the hill, an exultant shouting. A white glare blanks them. The bushes jump. He pulls her up the crest, into the shaft of light.

Black-on-black, under huge accessory lights which the caterer's men and a few vainglorious guests are holding chest-high like halberds, the swimming pool, bobbing with pale-gold oval faces legioned among lilies, looks like a

Japanese Satsuma plate. No one's even splashing. A solitary, up on the high slide. Under the surface are they all hand-in-hand? The string trio's stopped.

"Yah—all these people want to *dis*connect," Kevin said. "But look at them."

And the lights go out again. By design?

"That friend of yours—." He tongues her ear. "You sleep with him?"

"His wife's having a baby."

Kevin let out a sign. "All the more."

"You're just pretending. That nothing counts."

Another sign. "Why would I do that?"

"Because you're afraid of getting rooked."

"Not at all."

"Why then?"

"Maybe I haven't the price for it. For whatever I used to think I should have."

"And what's that?"

"Shut up, will you. Let's swim."

And now she wants him. He excites her. Because he's admitted that he wants more than her, more than this. They may even be paired off together because of it. She could drop her dress right here, but she'll use the cabana for luxury's sake: she's never been in one.

At the cabana door, Arthur's gone. He'll be watching the baby, tender homosexual father, grandfather now. He's always very courteous to her too, in a particular way. Not to her herself, or to Mrs. Doctor. Certainly not to Mrs. White Next-door. And least of all to what the men are after. For which Arthur will perhaps find a boy. No, there are certain gays—there was an orderly in the maternity ward once, with whom she had long nocturnal talks—who make her feel deeply and peculiarly a woman. They bow—curtsying almost—to her woman-parts. Nothing personal. Tribe to tribe.

Inside the darkish tent she delays, stretching the dress slowly over her head, hunting a towel. One wall is all shelves of suits and towels, in a corner there's a chemical

commode. She makes use of it, luxuriously. The striped-
duck walls smell rented, flirty patio-stuff, a party accom-
modation migrating from poolside to poolside to shelter
tanned daytime-torsos, or palely fumbling evening bodies,
whose hopes stripe up as they enter here. It doesn't smell
of the sea, like those wooden, salty bath-houses of her
public-beach childhood did—privies where one couldn't
pee, but elemental still with kindly whiffs of fundament
washed clean or about to be, toenails out of hiding, socks
crumpled, and the sea riffing outside, lackadaisical.

Absently she's taken off her bikini and trunks.

Someone's here. Someone's followed her in, squelch
squelch. Belatedly her ears record it. Across the cabana,
breathing hard. Hoppe. Walks toward her. Stands gleaming. Her eyes are adjusting to the dark. Hoppe is naked
too. Erected. Head hanging as he breathes in the rented
dark.

Not humbly. His organ speaks for him.

A silent pleader he is, shorter than she. Hand on his
penis, knuckled in ivory. Her nipple fills his mouth. Between the wens.

She rushes from the tent. Feeling at her pulled breast.
Kevin's waiting, just outside. She presses the scraped
nipple against his bare chest. Some nakednesses you're
naked with. Others make you naked against. Behind
them, a word is said at them. At her. The sandals recede.
Squelch.

"Who's your friend?" Kevin's eyes, bent to hers, are
clear. They clear with drink. There's not a dirty word in
them.

"He's a—specialist in Anglo-Saxon."

"'t's what I thought."

Over Kevin's shoulder a searchlight picked up the receding Hoppe, ribboning him.

"Not all four-letter words are obscene." She was shivering. A spastic boy, jerking along, had first said it at her,
when she must have been well into her teens. She hadn't
learned what it meant for years; there'd been a kind of

· 159 ·

undercurrent she shouldn't. These days, they asked. Maureen being taken by the hand. "Let's go ask that baby brother of yours what he said." Royal telling them, with a not so medical glint. "It means a female opening." Maureen and she turning their backs on him.

She rubbed at her scraped breast. There was no mark on it yet. A breast bruise sometimes appeared later. After four strong sucklers, hers wasn't even uddered, the way some women get—the way maybe a mother's breast should be. Though Maureen came to her anyway.

"Kevin—" Pressed against his chest, her mouth, open in soundless cry, hunts the nipple there. Finds it. Almost at once, she straightened up, hard-voiced. "Cripples should be slapped when they deserve it."

"Was he. I didn't see."

No, it's my own boy, she should say. Who's one of those. But the more Kevin knows of her circumstance the less likely he is to sleep with her. Or she with him. They depend on each other's anonymity, that blinder tenderness. And had she meant only Roy?

She stared into the darkness that was Hoppe. "Neither did I."

He wraps his bathtowel around her like a husband, tying it under her armpit.

She's still shaking. "Don't know why I took off that suit."

"You don't really need it."

"No I don't, do I. I'm practically home."

"Home—?" he says.

"Uh-uh, Kevin. No."

"Then—they must have a dock here. If we must swim."

"I want to swim in the pool." In that black glue up there. With the village. She makes a run for it.

The pool, maybe sixty feet or so long but narrow for its length, is an odd one. Most pools are at their best when relieved of people—a rejecting glass, happiest with sky.

But at noon this one looked like nothing—a misplaced inlet, leaked from better times.

Approaching it now from the narrow end she can see that habitation still dictates here; it's built on the foundations of a house. Craves people. Bodies are thrashing there; now an arm lifts gilded, now a head. The arc-lights are working again, sentinel. On the high-dive, a man is poised, pretty with biceps, foreshortened in the neckless way of men in comic books. A wet mushroom-cap of blond hides his features, but she knows him; it's the youngest caterer, the tough. He's crossed the party line. But that's okay, the village prides itself on being egalitarian. When he dives—"Perfect!"—at least fifty bodies applaud.

On the steps at the shallow end she receives their wave, flinging aside her towel. All the benches around the pool-rim are loaded with discards. Treading water, she sees everyone she knows, no one she need greet specifically—and sees what the pool is. This is a flooded room. Some in it appear to be naked, others not. By an odd courtesy, no one's touching. Each body, pedaling its territory, has the same incline. Though here and there a couple, bridging arms, floats serene. Water, the secret tickler, is the only licentious one here. Pedaling softly herself, she passes by smilers she could name if it mattered. A large man, said to be a gambler, said to be Mafia, and recent purchaser of a house here, glides past her in lazy rapture. No more music; the trio's in the water too. She doesn't see Hoppe. Along with all the others, she too is now an anecdote. And at least it's safe here. With so many careful, ritual feet trundling the water heel to heel, how could there be a drowned face down below? Her face tilts oval like the rest. The gilding lights pass over it. She is in the Satsuma plate.

Kevin, seeing her head go under with eyes closed, jumps in and pulls her out.

"Laid out straight on the bottom," he says, wrapping her. "You're no drinker."

Streaming water clutters her mouth. "Were no children there. Had to investigate."

Kevin, peeling the soaked towel from her, rewraps her in a fresh one, clasping her to him from behind. Swaying her into warmth, like a nurse.

On the long concrete lip of the pool, Violet, lumpy dowager Cleopatra dancing alone, strips off her necklace, tossing it arc-high. To the tough, just emerged. They play catch with it.

"Caterer team's staying the night," Kevin says into her nape. "Bob's fixed up the basement for them."

"Good." Water's still draining from her. "Maybe that one'll give Dodo her bath."

"Or Violet'll give *him* one."

The boy's stopped the game of toss. Strutting over, lifeguard style, he fastens the corals around Violet's neck. The strong-man muscles in his upper arms move of themselves.

Behind in the water, no one applauds.

At the shallow end of the pool, couples start slipping up the steps and out into the dark. One anecdote doesn't like the sight of another.

She and Kevin sit on a bench, watching them. Kevin has a bottle again. Cognac. "Here, this is good for you. Not champagne."

She laughs. "Where do you keep those bottles? You have no pockets in that suit."

When they made love, he used to reach behind him for one. Sometimes even in the midst of things. Always just afterward. A silhouette with a bottle, that's how she best remembers love with him. "You used to pull them out of your hair, I thought. Or your ear."

"Always a bottle under my bed. You know that."

The water's washed away her reserve. "Mmm. But why'd that give *me* confidence."

"Come on. I kept showing you the mirror, that's all."

"You were always nice about my looks."

He takes the towel from her. She's dry. And feels foolish. Nudity scanned, not for nudity alone.

"Jesus. Don't you women ever separate from your looks? You're a worldbeater, is what I was trying to tell you. Worldbeater. Living in the back woods." He tipped up the bottle. "I scrammed because of it. I'm too good a hotwalker for horses like you. Done it once too often. I was afraid I'd ask you to live with me."

She took the bottle from him, remembering those dreamy apartment-hunting afternoons. But that the fantasy can be double—I never dared that. "What's a hotwalker?"

"Never been to the track? They walk the horses after the race. And sometimes before. Long before."

And sometimes, do they marry them? She remembers the wife, that last evening at the bar. Coming in from her job, desperate. Keeping her desperations for the evening. A competent business-woman, humbled only by fatality. But scarcely outsize. Scarcely a worldbeater. His symbols are too cheap and easy, aren't they? She can imagine saying that to the wife.

"You didn't scram, Kevin. You were come for."

"Arrangeable. I know what works."

He took the bottle back. "No more for you. You can have a fresh towel . . . And no more for me, after this one. Or I'll spend the night here."

"You are spending it."

"Right. I meant the day."

"No Kevin. That won't work."

"See. You know that too. Ah Lexie, someday there'll come a man for you. I'd like to be there when you meet."

Someday. The jukebox prescription that all the Judys sing. She got up, clutching the towel. "To hell with that. I want to meet myself."

"You're going to. Anybody can see that a mile off."

"I can't."

"How do you? See yourself?"

Can she tell him? The brandy can. "Like a member of a tribe that's—everywhere. And that nobody much but us sees."

So she's said it. Aloud. And the minute she has, hears herself graduate from that stance. Oh no, Lex—there's more.

"Like at Popocatapetl?" Kevin's nuzzling her breast. "Or Zocha—what's that other Mexican volcano sounds like 'milkshake'? Can't say it . . . But your secret's safe with me."

"It is with everybody. That's the trouble." She looks down at him. And now we're going to mumble onto each other's flesh what the soul can't keep to itself. She stiffens. "Who's that over there?"

A couple, stealing into the bamboo, toward her house.

He sees them too. He won't answer.

"James—wasn't it?" The family knows the family anywhere. "And that girl—the sister."

"Not her. Home hours ago. Totting up the Kellihy estate. No—that was Tork."

"Taking her to my house?" That's the end. But what difference to the children? If *I'm* out *here*.

"No. Listen. They're going up the hill."

From the crashing up above, they are.

"What's at the top up there?"

"An old railroad track."

"That's for Tork."

"I thought all along you knew her."

"Never met her, actually. My brother's mistress once. Specializes in poets. Used to get into their poems quite regularly. Know his 'In glades, in fiery glades—'? Doesn't once rhyme with 'shades'—though you're always expecting it."

When she speaks of her own brother, does her nose fine to a white ridge like that? But Kevin also whitens when he drinks. He reddens only when he dances, like the night they met. "I drink for my brother," he said later. "I'm his antibuse."

· 164 ·

All's quiet, up there on the old track. My brother—the horse.

"Anyway-y" Kevin's saying—"far as one knows, Tork has yet to copulate inside a house."

And I never have, outside one. "Kev—I never heard of your brother, until I met you. I have these gaps."

"Bless them," Kevin said. "D'ya know—we're quite alone."

The pool is still quivering. But yes, they are. Behind them downhill, the house is still brightly lit. The vanilla's gone from the air.

"Your village seems to've gone, Lexie. To tuck the children in?"

The rented high-slide glitters crazily; it has a wired red-and-chrome crown jutting above it, so does the high-dive. Maybe Bob's crown was rented too. Like all human apparatus deserted, the diving-boards look obsessive, forlorn. She walks toward them.

"We could be Adam and Eve," he says, following her. "Except for my belly. And all those apple cores."

Strewn at the pool's edges are bathing-trunks, bras, pairs of huaraches, bottles, glasses—a few with lemonpeel in them. Real apples would have a strange innocence here. Imbedded in the fresh cream paint of the poolside are the small flies that were falling in clouds the day the contractor finished up—a small plague commemorated. And bemoaned by Bets—who daily picks her way through her raddled emotions in a floral state of physical cleanliness. Even delivering her babies, Bob says, "Like an envelope." With hands clasped on her most recent crucifix.

Not like me.

The necklace that Violet and the boy were playing toss with is lying on the ground.

"Bets' corals. That's not like Violet." She picks them up.

"Tidying. Tidying. Thow 'em in the pool, why don't you? Bet it's already full of diamond wedding-bands."

"I can't." The beads hold a story; it clings to her hand. "They belong in Violet's trunk. For Bets to steal back."

"Violet was smashed. So'm I." But he stands tall in his borrowed trunks, and shaped by games of toss toward targets not hung onto, able to let women go and perhaps even children; even his bookishness hangs at ease for him, in the libraries; all those books he owns are only the necessary few. He's not linked forever to the dreaming world of objects, as she is. There are men who are, but none of them has come to it along the path she has. Under the silent, hope-chest instruction that twines early in girlhood. In order to stop the traveling.

As always she feels humiliated by the process, but can't stop it. "I ought to put these beads somewhere. Maybe in the house."

"The house?" With careful tiptoe he's at her side. "I wouldn't, I were you. The servant's ball won't be to your taste. And you won't find the Kellihys."

"Where are they then? Skipped?" Stealing out with a suitcase full of nightgowns, walkie-talkie headphones wired to one of the best brokerage-houses, and a clutch of credit-cards the bills haven't caught up with yet? To catch the cruise-ship they had their wedding-night on? That they've forgotten doesn't run any more.

"The Kellihys?" He squints at them. "Bets'll be gone down to steerage, for a spot of near-rape. Keeping it to eye-level, until Master Bob arrives to carry her off. Just in time for both of them. Leaving behind large tips. And then—the Kellihys will be having an affair. Not in the matrimonial bed of course. Maybe in the one spare room that doesn't have television. Or has never been fixed up. There must be one."

Sure there are, in most of the houses on this road. Or it can be done on the linen-closet floor, in the smaller ones. Or in the family-room at three o'clock in the morning, in the developments. The tension between marriage and tidiness, sex and children, life and television, goes on all the time.

If that's what he means. How long will it take me to learn how lone and single my interpretations are?

"So that the world can hear their cries," he said. "Aaa—deliver me from married people's parties. Couples who have bashes all the time, so that the ree-lay-shun-ship may have an audience."

"I've done that. It's often the wife." Ray had his outside audience; I was never part of it. And he was never mine. "When Sunday gloms in, a line of cars pointed at your house can be quite a cheery thing." And the kids were cheered because I was. "I sometimes think the mother-moods spiraling out of all the exhaust-fans will choke the nation." Fuming up from the damp spot on the bathroom tiles, glassily regarded. Or from when you hear your heart beat in the cellar laundryroom, alone with the gray board-and-batten walls and the spiders' polka-dots. Dirt isn't what angers a woman; it's our solace.

He wasn't hearing this undervoice of course; how can they. And half goes unsaid anyway, in the deadhead head.

"Not a chimney toppled," she said.

Is he asleep? No, for he's grasped her again. Oh, they can recognize us, coming upon us in the confessive dark. And nurture us. But not hear us. "But you never set fire to the house, Lexie. You'd never do that."

"Oh wouldn't I?" she says dreamily. "Maybe not quite. Anyway it was little Rod, over there. He carries matches in his jeans as if they were money." Later he'll switch like everybody. To sex. "Kev. It *was* Roddy?"

He shrugs, not taking his arms from her.

She goes over the whole entourage. Arthur? Violet? Bob? Bets? Careless yes—except for Arthur. Indecently. "No shit—you have to tell me. We saw a newly charred place over there. In the bamboo. Tonight."

"When I went to take a leak, Sean and Sister were just leaving. Sean said, 'That's some girl, Kev—the one from next door.'" He squeezes her. Bracing her, like a coach. "And Sister said 'Next door? Well I just hope they've doubled their insurance coverage.'"

"We have . . . Kevin. It couldn't be—Bob?" I won't say it could be Bets. Will he?

He isn't answering.

"But this place is their life," she says. "They—"

"Have babies for it." He strains her against him. She leans back, wishing she could see her own house. Her breasts are in his hands.

"My son goes ice-fishing," he says. "Every winter holiday. Mad for it. Just because once, when drunk and loving I took him with me. Never done it again myself." He's smiling, the eyes discs, the voice chill. Objectivity grows on him like lust. "The kids play our music that's all. When they do it louder than us—should we be surprised? Sure, Roddy did it. But he gets the idea from both sides."

"And the sister—wants to be guardian."

"Ah—Sister." He sits on a bench, pulling her down with him, cradling her between his legs. "Doesn't even like the kids. Thinks they're brats. Worse. Decadent."

So they are, poor babies. Children of a not too bright bacchante, and a frog not quite allowed to be a prince.

"But she wants them." His legs tighten, squeezing her.

"Will she take Bob and Bets to court?"

"Court? She'll only have to wait." He cocks his head. "Listen."

It's the regular sound of it that's so riveting. A waste so methodical. The sunporch is being smashed in again.

"It's a true marriage," Kevin says. "They both want the same thing. And you know?—they're going to get it. Maybe the gods don't love the young Kellihys quite enough yet. But they'll acquire a taste for them."

"We all have."

A taste blent almost with love—for the legend they prepare for us. A silly, gauzy extravaganza, of a girl flinging babies into the air like mortgages to be burned. Of a young man with a butler in the house, stirring his own job of soup. They're our rogues, she thinks, who we hang on the kitchen hook for all to see in the evening—are the

Kellihys. Our spotted darlings, ever so slightly cracked. They're a legend tailored just for couples. The whole village's acquired a taste for them. We can see far worse things on the telly, but somehow it's not the same. The Kellihys smash our glass for us.

Then there's quiet. It must have been about a quarter of three. Out the Kellihys' kitchen door comes a pell-mell, a hullabaloo. A truck in the driveway coughs, put-put, swings into full whine and grinds down their lane, spitting gravel backward. The black-top was worn out long ago; costs the earth, nowadays. Or a pair of twins. The truck soughs south, south.

"The caterers are leaving," she says. "Like rats."

"I hope—" he says.

At first she takes it for an answer. Or a portent.

"Hope I'm not too drunk to move." He turns the most lucid eyes on her. "I only do it this bad in the country, you know. In the city I'm reasonably safe. Didn't know that about me, did you."

And the wife comes and gets him up there—anyway. Because she knows it won't work. I can understand that fatality. I might do the same. Seeing to it that the children play their father's music. Saying to him, weddingband hollow, and with a cast in the eye that sheers childward "Won't you go icefishing once again—anymore?"

When he puts a hand on her, love drains her toward him. He sees me, that's it. Or I see him.

"There's a dock," she whispers. "The Kellihys have only frontage. But we have a sort of dock."

As she gets him to his feet, the weight he bears down on her with staggers her . . . It's her need . . . A pot of roses flowers between her legs, thorns and all. Far above it, eight feet taller and in another climate, floats that simpleton coconut, her head. From behind her, the animal of herself jumps her, and clamps her waist, simian. A woman in rut evolves the history of primates, every time—with appropriate flora added. Yet the theory of evolution had to

· 169 ·

wait to be phrased by a long-celibate don. And the word "rut" comes from the stag. If there's no word direct for a woman in this state must I invent one? A word takes its own time. Best to brood on it—on the state of me moving with my burden, into dock.

Four legs she has, at least ten arms and an indeterminate number of leaf-fingers—and still growing. Yet she is thinking, all this time. A woman in sex—in *brood*—is in her highest state of intellection. Vanity's gone from the head, into the trunk. The body ripples with humor arboreal.

And the best destiny of a coconut is to fall.

We're across the road on the riverbank on this dais of lawn, and will never get to the dock. Why should we? Kevin is propped against a large stone. I am propped against him. From our toes, the river below flows south. And against all logic, the night is getting deeper.

"Are you well and sacred?" he says with a laugh, looking down at himself. His tongue sounds sleepy. "Used to say that to us, at Collegiate."

"Am now." I'm sleepy too. "Glad to get out of there. I don't like that pool. Too many faces in the water." Including her own. All staring with marble-eyed fright into underwater living. Saying to their lack of image "This is not my true life."

North of them, on the great ugly causeway the village fought against and yearned for, the cars one after the other go bombing into town. It's a sound not unlike smashing. Leaving quiet air behind.

Just beyond their heads is the cottage where the defective boy-man sits all day on the porch, making true sounds. We all live with his criticism. Never making reply. At night, when bidden to come in, he tosses his toy—a pair of shoes, a woman's—over the side. The shoes remain on the landfall off the basement porch below until morning. Does the legend of the girls his mother hires really happen? Maybe it's happening now. Everybody's secret is safe with somebody.

Kevin's on his elbow. "Vital signs not good, Lexie. Guess I can't. We left it too long."

Lying on her elbow alongside him, her own need half-leaked away, she turns up her other palm, to the dark. No, it's not the liquor. It's the past; we've had too much, yet not enough of it. If we'd just met, we'd've clapped together. Or if we'd lived together once—there's profundity in that.

Her mouth's against his chest. "No it's the past. It's between us. Like a limp cock."

"Lucky me—I have two of them." He pats the top of his swimming trunks. Under the elastic she feels a bottle, stashed there like a holster. He hauls it out.

"No Kevin. Don't."

But he's already leaning into the bottle gripped between his knees, his bent thumb-knuckle pressing like the expert campaigner he is.

Prying it. As he should be prying me.

The cork pops.

"There I go," she said.

Drinking first, he chokes. "You're a comic."

He always drinks first. As if at the back of his mind there's a wine-waiter, totting him up.

With eyes opening to the dark, she can do that for him. A flint-white broad forehead, Sheridan's—a fine nose. A mouth never vulgar, even when a bottle's in it. But what's there about this handsomeness that makes you feel nostalgic for it even while you're face to face with it?

When he offers the bottle this time, she accepts. So they drink, by turns into his mouth, into hers.

So this is sex.

She sees it—for him. For her. Those times, in his flat. The moment when with loins still locked, not breathless but absolved from breathing, when they should have been floating in the holy nimbus won for them by their own contractions—and he'd reached sideways for the bottle, pulling at it deep. Saw her shock; laughed. And she saw what he maybe wanted her to see: "I repudiate." The

· 171 ·

shock went beyond any insult to her, or to women generally. It was always for him she felt it.

But now she feels—bottle passing over to him—that he doesn't drink against what life does to him—bottle passing over to her—but against what life could do for him.

He's asleep? Not asleep. A man in profile's what Sheridan is. His belly shines at her, full-face. She puts her face on it, nuzzling. Sliding down. When she takes him in her mouth like a bottle, he groans assent. The warm-raspberry aura of the drinker is in his flesh. No taste. As she moves, learns to move, her mouth's not her mouth but another opening, linking slowly to her own core. Never done more than kissing before, never asked to. Never urged down, the face blotting faster, teeth shivering like a thoughtful animal's. I was once serviced by mouth by Day, but at the end with him, always loins. Now my face is my loins. Obliterating slow. I become my lovers. I—am not. This I do, not even knowing the correct name for it. In the imaginary journal of her mind—barely admitted to but always kept—she is doing this in the imaginary journal of her mind.

Now. Now she's face-to-face with her own willed subdominance. This yearning posture that flows under all household service; she recognizes it. As if she's doing a domestic service for him. Relieving him, tribally—as nursing mothers gave their extra milk to their men, or to dogs. How good to bend the forehead blindly, in the humble posture excused. All doctrine disappears in the doing. Blessed to bend the neck, the last vertebral resistance gone crack. I am understanding—obedience. Which is the other rhythmic of giving birth. This is the other side of birth, of giving it. I'm swallowing what comes of human intercourse. I'm in the humility of the task.

And at the same time, an ancient childself, once hung for nine months on its own mother, is suckling. So it goes, from fleshgiver to fleshgiver, like the needle sewing, over and back. This man-mother—mother him. Her mouth is filled with nacre. as so often her lower body has been. Once. Now. Before.

Afterwards peace, without fire. Honor is not involved. The mouth, like the anus or the nose, can be wiped with grass. Ah grass, kind polygraph, writing voluminous.

Standing above her, he's shrunken. He's bending to her; they bend too. Pearled with her sweat. Touching her sleepy hair.

Going, he says. Driving back.

"Naked?" Her mouth. Strange to speak with it.

No, all's quiet over there. Past three o'clock. He'll pick up his clothes, and drive back. Is she all right? Will she be? Can he leave?

He is all travel-sounds.

There's satisfaction. In being the one left.

Yes, leave me here. On home ground.

In that nest of whispers, maybe. "Naked?" was all she said.

In her state of sexual grace, she lies comfortable. Savoring the nakedness for a spell.

Going down; that's the name of it. Into the hairy glade.

Where, belly up, the enemy lies, mothering.

Now lie here, waiting to be discovered. In the name of all those who must drive home clothed.

Lying there, she drowns in her own life, upward. Discovers it.

$\mathcal{S}$o the body on the riverbank slips its moorings—*Cargo coming in!*—and heads for its past. Nobody knows how long these interior journeys really take. Under the eternal starlight of the self-fixed eye.

Meanwhile outside, other facts will be authenticating. Some still buried deep in that travel-log of tickets to nowhere, excursions unwilled and letters unmailed but finally received—which all families keep without knowing it: Others already scattering broadside among the village coroners.

Who's to record them, who's to pay for them? Haunted messages flying like terns over the body of this narcissist. Attaching silently as banners, to guide her barge. Out toward those shoals where the catering is never over. Where the smashing never stops.

F or shortly before, Arthur the butler, glass in hand, has come out to the Kellihy gate. The goblet holds Bajan rum—sugar-cane rum of a double strength you usually get only in his native islands, plus a sweetening called Falernum, and the proper dab of lemon-sugar rubbed against the peel, and ice. Last drink of the day, and his only one; the rest of the time he secretly drinks fizzy water, and carries on the responsibilities of the house.

He's still in a state of beatitude caused by the pageantry of the party and how well he looked there, which at his age is all the extra he asks of physical life. The loveliest time of a party—especially at Master Bob's—is when it's satisfactorily over, and you can watch yourself memorably backwards in its mirroring eye. He's still wearing the orange loincloth which exactly complements his nutmeg skin; his platinum dye-job is the best he's ever had; at sixty-nine and a half, he remains a caution to stare at—as even Violet, who has a tongue like an adder, admits—and most important, he's not yet ugly to himself.

What he likes, all he wants is to have his comforts artistically arranged, down days which promise some sort of freakiness, in a hightone way—and can do it steadily. For much of his life the Kellihys have given him that wish, and he reveres them for it. Nightclub work—which he'd tried for a short, fearful term after finishing rearing his surrogate family—isn't in it for kicks; plus the hours are wrong—and he's a domestic man. Up here, when the country palls, he can take himself into the city for a marvelously tripartite day. First selling his silverware in the Village, with enough gay overtones to keep his hand in on that gossip, he then visits old friends in Harlem, some on Sugar Hill, some not so well-placed, and some in hospital—where his silver-money makes him a generous giftgiver. By the time the Harlem horrors had about got to him—and the envy—he'd be safely having tea with Mr. Bob's mother, on Park. "You're my real crony, Arthur." Though by nightfall she'll be drunk enough to have to be helped to bed, they're both pleased he no longer has the job of doing it. By day, she keeps herself up as well as anybody in *Town & Country*, where her picture appears often, in the crisp clothes and hairdos which enchant them both. For him, the tea is always tea. "What you wear to that sodality thing, Miss Lorna—your blue? Just right. And that new man has got the real tone of your hair." She'd never blued it—too snappy a dish for that, thank God.

"Mr. Bob seeing to your rum, and what's that other stuff?" she answers. For thirty-five years she's seen to Arthur's tipple, and can never recall its name. Certain of his other comforts over the years she properly ignored. But has always remembered the sacred anniversary of his mother's death as well as he does, though the two had never met. And always has a mass said, at St. Pat's. What she won't do is put money in his pocket—or on his future. "Burns a hole there, Arthur Manderville—how's that nephew of yours, by the way?" Back at the University of the West Indies again, and not so hearty, as she knows well. And is always glad to hear. "Money *sent*, Miss Lorna—it's no good to them. He's as bad as Mr. Bob."

They confab over it. Yes, he'd see to the new baby's christening—neither wanted Sister to put her nose in—and he since had. Though naming the baby for him outraged him even more than it did Miss Lorna; over the wire, she'd had to calm *him* down. "After all, you *are* Church of Rome." And yes, he'd smootched Miss Bet's way with the priests here, who really want none of her. Both he and the old lady—who is two months younger than he— trust no woman except herself. But no, she wouldn't yet "arrange" for the Catholic home in which he hopes to spend a classy old age—which meant pay for it. "No sirree. You're not ugly enough yet. I can still look at you. And I've been thinking, Arthur—maybe you should start depending on Mr. Bob for that. It would be good for him." And good for you too, Arthur. Steadying. "Right, Miss Lorna. If I could ever get to him when his pockets are full." Next time she sent Bob money, she said, she'd let Arthur know well ahead. She'd promised it. "Then you can get your innings in, Arthur. Before Bets."

A wicked woman, on money matters. And when she sticks to tea. His only chance with her is if she falls ugly, as they both call it, before he does. "Then I'll want you to see to me." In which case she has it all set for him to come along early, to the same home she's going to. "It's all at my lawyer's, Arthur. A co-ed home too, don't you fear. Priests we can get. Company's what we'll crave." And when he pays his hospital visits—as friend after friend fell ugly from all the diseases which could take pieces out of you or hang gadgets on you—he has to agree with her. "So *that's* settled. Now tell me, Arthur, is it true that a colored man is head of the government of Barbados?" Just reminding him—in case he has any private thoughts of going back there instead. "Yes, the Governor, Arthur. I'm sure that's what Monsignor said." She knows he cannot approve of it. "And you can bet that British daddy of yours Arthur, I don't either." She's the best company, not barring Violet. He and she have the same tone.

Which tells him he isn't really to credit her on that lawyer. So he'll have to depend on Bob. He has a plan for it.

"Tone, tone—" Arthur says aloud. Like to have that moon, on a silver salver. Take my picture carrying it.

Tomorrow's going to be the kind of day he and Violet, long-term fellow Kellihy-addict and straw-boss, will spend happily. Plenty leftover booze for her, enough cozy little tasks-in-solitary for him. Straightening up the spare-room allotted him for his silver-work—where Miss Bets also sometimes struggles with a gentleman on the couch, but according to Violet never quite gives in to them. Or tidying up, from every bush and vine within yards of the pool, pleasant reminders of the party, and of how he'd looked there. He's already made the baby's formula, enough for two days; what Miss Betsy will do with her own milk is for her to say—he's weaned her babies before. A batch of his work-tools is already sloshing toward a fine clean-up in the huge dishwasher the caterers have left, not even saying they'll be back for it. Crocked worse than the guests, they'd ended up leaving the high-slide as well—and the boy. Violet already has her old phonograph crackling—she won't have radio—and is this minute frying up crab she'd made little Roddy seine for all day yesterday, saying to the poor kid "You drown, I'll kill you. And set fire to you first, with your own matches. Lay off those from now on, by the way. One garage a year is all we can handle. Try the school."

Violet is the only real anarchist he knows; in her daily life she hews to it. Women ought to be expert liars, cheats, thieves, she says—whatever they could get away with. "And Miss Betsy could be as good as me at all of it. But she won't only swap." After breakfast, he'd get Roddy and Dodo off to the day-camp, which was so important an activity to all adults in the house that he and Violet often chipped in to pay the bill for it. After that a nap, then some poker maybe, he and she playing for baby Arthur's Greek coins from his Uncle Sean, divvied between them, or Violet's subway slugs, that big Arthur always made for her. And when those ran out—maybe for the caterer's boy.

Lose or win, after that he'd dry out his tools and get to work on Mr. Bob's telephones, on which he and Miss Lorna have an arrangement. She can't head off all the brokerage-houses; Bob always finds one where the Kellihy credit—even when it's his—is unfortunately enough. Telephones are even harder. It takes finesse to know when his smart Bob is just drunk enough to ignore a tape-recorder going. Or else so far gone that you can cut off altogether the wire he's talking on. Especially when the boy himself is wise to the deal, and for Arthur's sake sometimes even cooperates. "Whyn't you let the boy run, Miss Lorna?

And pick up the tab later?" But she'd rather give Bob the money on an apronstring. Can't stand to see him play with it. "Now if you want a free hand with your investments, Mr. Bob," is what he'll say. "We could come to an arrangement." And Bob would gleefully cooperate. "For your sake, Arthur. For your sake." When the market-mess that Bob will make is brought to her attention, he, Arthur will say "I couldn't help it, Miss Lorna. I *feel* ugly, before my time."

But no hurry. After this party, no money will roll in for a long while.

At this point in his ceremonial drink, the mother of the idiot-boy opposite comes out of their porch pushing him before her, settles him with his lap-toys, spreads her arms in a slavey gesture to the air, and goes in again. By then the early silence is already nibbled by the tiny drumming of the cars coming cross-river from the Thruway, a mile north.

In it, he stands on the edge of the rainforest, on the moss-terrace where Crooty, his first white lover, raised tree-orchids, which he called his "ladies," sending far abroad for their tender, mad illuminations. While wild plateaus of rain sweep the garden, he and Arthur watch from behind the knobbled Georgian urn in the drawing-room, and sip Darjeeling with rum in it.

Finished with his drink—his dream-chaser, as Violet calls it—Arthur always walks briskly back inside to his family, to what they still call his butlering. This morning, holding off, he'll stand and hark.

Back home in the Islands is a grave he's been paying for.

Somebody's walking on it.

No, the grave itself is walking.

It walks up-island, on the Atlantic side, in the jagged, creaming water where nobody swims, and up past the old white inn of his first job, where the British came to eat the breadfruit pie. It walks the ocean all the way here, stiff as a waterspout.

Hoo. I know what you come to tell me. Arthur, don't you let yourself fall ugly up *here*.

Git, I tell you. You not my grave any more.

It's gone.

The inch of chaser in his goblet is teetering like an ocean. He swallows it.

Over the road, some yards south, a tall shape parts the low scrub that hides the doctor's old dock. A man. Balls naked. Not the doctor for sure. Who's away anyway. Maybe the older boy. Who won't set foot over here, but met in the village always greets him most politely. A chilly white couple, that boy's parents, cold white fish of the suburbs, like a lot of them along here. And with scarcely a sign of any kinfolk. Zombies, that mate themselves up out of the marshes. But he likes the boy.

"Hoo," Arthur says aloud, arching a wrist.

Not the boy. Moon's sinking, but he can see a pair of those tiger-shorts. Big blond buck, only one Bob could get to wear them. Piss-drunk by the stare of him. Oughtn't to drive. But he ambles to the lone car left parked under their embankment, drags out a shirt from it but slam-bangs into the front seat still bare. Off he goes.

Hoo.

Telephone ringing, ringing, inside the house. Where's that sot, Violet?

But thank the Lord for modern sound.

Time to take the dye-job in anyway, Arthur. Sun won't be good for it.

Stately as all get-out, bowing to the mirror inside the band still on his wrist, he obeys.

The boy on the porch opposite, who is a man of thirty-three, says nothing.

The Kellihys are meanwhile having an affair.

Five miles inland from the river, the old coachroad to Tappan divides formally around the scabbed and poulticed bole of a tree left over from Revolutionary days—and then flows on again. The village fathers want to cut the tree, but the state won't let them. Or perhaps it's the other way round. The caretaker of the De Windt house, a shabby landmark which sits well back in the unshaven meadow left of the tree, can never remember which of the two pays him. He sleeps where George Washington once did, and that's enough for him. Or would be, except for the nights when an old MG two-seater, kept for honeymoon sentiment, cracks by him on its way to the Seventy-Six House inn only a mile away, but doing eighty, every time. Yes, he knows the car. Knows them. The Seventy-Six has long since closed for the night, but for those two, his friend Walter—the waiter who sleeps *there*—will always open up again.

Betsy is singing "There is a street called Pearl," in the fullthroated tenor which friends will know took her only when she was high. Bob is driving straight for the commodity markets of the world.

He dangles there bloody-mouthed, with a shaft through a chest that was always delicate. Bets' handbag—containing the pics of five children, the address of a doctor on East Seventy-third Street, four unpaid parking tickets, a calendar-diary with redprinted exhortations, and the Lord's Prayer written on a purse-sized atomizer—is thrown clean. Her eyes are wide, but no more affrighted in the next world than they were in this one. She is dented forever, but clean. The robins will stop their singing but after a moment begin again. The air has that classic cool of before dawn, any summer morning. How they have connected, the Kellihys, in the end!

Light as a second crop of summer grass, their legend will be. The best man at their wedding—Sean, the philosophy brother—who will come first to identify them, will remember forever how the bride's dress, overflowing the MG like a sundae its saucer, had had to be tucked back in, and how wittily he did so. "Vanilla Coupe!"

THE
DOCTOR'S
PRESCRIPTION

Meanwhile a man is walking home from Spain. Up the dark River Road, to the future of his house. He's thinking of home—a church he no longer believes in—and of how to desanctify it. Where a church is groined of flesh, and gemmed at odd altars, with children's eyes—that's not easy. There must be a ritual. None he knows of doesn't scatter dung.

A car soughs by from side to side of the road. Doesn't kill him. Though the driver, jerking a shirt on, has both hands off the wheel. Nothing will kill him; he walks like the hardy skeleton of himself, feels it. Slightly nervous, though, in this blotchy close landscape with its tame quicksilver river, after the burnt-in encaustic of alp and high rivulet he's had from his balcony, and from the window above his bed before that, all of it a black-and-tan anodyne for a doctor changed into a patient. With the night wind scratching its single bow on sand, and a gray smell of mountain lichen. He'd grown to like best the days of imaginary sun. When off in the distance or ozone, a hole in the shape of a speculum tapped an orifice in the

· 185 ·

sky. Imaginary Spain tapped him. Between the stern alluvial plains offered his eye, and the alto lisping of the nursing sisters, he began to think of it as a land of public
prayer.

It surprised him that the accidie common to his disease hadn't affected him. Otherwise, a clinical case, strin-
gently clear—as proper to one diagnosed by the patient
himself. Collapsing in a circle of colleagues all merrily lifting the white drinks that meant gin-at-last and the end of
their tour, he had heard their bow-tie voices stop. From his
plague-ship already lifting anchor he'd called out from his
faint, up to that rim of wellwishers already halfway to the
American shore. "Hepatitis. You'll see." By James's later
report, none of them had got it. Only him, the least adven-
turous. Who, once released from the round of museums
and Plazas, and drinking only bottled water, had played
cards the whole time, even on the excursion-bus, whose
mountain-driver's technique had been fully described to
Charles, in a last letter from health. The trip had been
routed them by way of return, or else he'd never have
found himself in any country's provinces. Once, playing
twohanded with his seatmate Dr. Bill Caldwell, lifting his
eyes from a no-trump bid as the bus lurched over the
land-rim, he'd seen into an abyss three thousand feet
down. And once, a passenger chicken squawking free
from the rear in a moult of dirty feathers, had defecated
on him. But more likely the germ had been in the greasy
deck of cards, already opened, that Caldwell had got from
the roomclerk in Barcelona. Paid for, of course. Had he
brought his own backgammon set, he mightn't have been
walking here, four months too late for this American vege-
tation of shadows. Effete, dainty almost, after Avila. None
of it standing clear. But he'd known there'd be two or
three sets in the crowd, and so there had been; he'd played
all the way over, in the jet. On the bus, all three sets had
been bespoke. So it must have been the cards—which,
clever as it was of him to note even in illness, he hadn't

mentioned to Lexie, as one of the household details a husband might. In Montevideo—that fight they'd had about her slumming—she'd cried out "You always travel light. At other people's expense."

At first, he'd intended to write all this to James. Since their internship, James had written scores of letters to him from his travels; half-way on, Ray had found out they were not only to be shared with Lex and the kids, but to be kept. Now at last he could have returned the compliment. With an import James's letters had never had. The real key to James was in those wives, and other women. In the way James liked to sleep with strangers, and the pace of it, he was almost a foreigner. Not like himself, brought up to a hygienic distaste for any flesh but the family's. Which Lexie had almost been, by the time James brought him home. And normality takes over hard enough. Four children, no expense—or love—spared. Short of being analyzed he was as clinically aware of himself as most. Perhaps his own family had had a certain distaste even for its own flesh. His maternal grandmother after leaving instructions for the undertaker to pluck the hairs that grew on her toes, had arisen just before the end to manage this herself. That incident had helped send him into medicine. Before he understood that only vanity had caused it, or else that obsession with mortality which sent women into self-pity before their time.

"Mortality's more like it," Lexie had offered. "At ninety-six." She had a head on her shoulders, not always set square. But women, she said, were in charge of the basic facts. Which kept them as normal as they had to be. "Oh I'm fascinated with docs," she'd said the night he met her. "Have to be, I work for them. But *seriously*—they show up our civilization, don't you think? Plugging ahead like mad in the midst of it. And never giving it a thought." At the time he'd counted this in as one of his attractions for her. Her talk since had made it clearer. He was to be her lead-in to the world. And must expect to be beaten for it.

Except for an anxiety on James's part now and then over Lexie, they didn't speak of wives. No reason for her to see his letter to James; she'd know the conclusions in it soon enough. But he'd taken a precautionary measure. "In any case, don't show this to Lex. I write her separately. But these are the facts." Which are that work, not a wife, is the key to him. Twisted now out of its lock.

In the end he'd mailed only that one of all the letters written on his balcony. Using the Hermes typewriter he'd had since college—just the toy a mother would give—he's managed to handle all the personal notation of the years since; yes, it's traveled light. Until the Spanish hospital. There, in its own weakened state, it seemed to be learning a newly liverish language caught from his own inflammation. The minute he finished that first letter, his eyes watering with the effort of feeling, he saw suspended above that dwarf keyboard, in blue, hepatic print *Don't trust James.* When he asked himself why, the old machine, which was himself in a way, imprinted on the keys, without his touching them: *Sunday afternoons.*

They'd been feeding him so much liquid, and such unfamiliar ones, and of course no alcohol or other dehydrants; under such treatment perhaps the brain is forced to make its own wine. Or in that alkali climate where the bones dry so serviceably into age, a compensating fleshy edema of the spirit occurs. Down below his balcony, when he first gets to it, the wind-abraded passersby distort like El Grecos. So that's all it was three centuries ago then—good cloth.

"They have marvelous cloth," he writes Lexie on a Sunday afternoon. "I'll bring you some." On the following Sunday, she'll read it over, sitting on the porch with James. Behind them, his spirit walks as it always has—behind them. The children too are trained not to break in on him. Next door is the smashing that attracts. "No depression," he writes to her carefully, and to James looking over her shoulder. "As I often tell patients, in hospital one's accessory education has a chance to come out. No renal symptoms in the eyes; if this typing's off, blame the old Hermes. Have Charles cut the bamboo before it gets out of hand. Has the appointment at Joint Diseases been made for Royal? Ask Chessie—does the river still speak Swedish, saying ø, ø (he'd inked that in), near the dock? There's a young nurse here, student, reminds me of Maureen."

It had been a terrific strain, to put himself in touch. He'd almost forgot to mention Maureen. Actually it was the woman who swept out the wards who reminded him of her—the same irritating patience. A dirt-swallower, our Maureen—of other people's dirt. And so am I, he'd thought. He'd hailed Sister Isaac then, and had her put the typewriter under the bed.

Was it depression, when the inner monologue brimmed out of the pores like sweat, when the blood-count seemed to attest to the patient himself the rate at which white lies could breed like corpuscles?

In the night he woke out of hand, on a raft of bed-sheets criss-crossed with bamboo thoughts.

Poling the raft for a time was Borden Wheeley, a Miami internist who'd been the self-styled barker of their trip. Born a cracker ("The mind is as red as the neck," Caldwell had whispered) Wheeley'd come to medicine from the ministry, and found himself giving so much free advice that he'd taken a degree in psychology "so's he could ask patients to pay for it." Now he had "every other worry-wort in the Sarasota Ayreach in my lap," plus two farms "to invite you-all to, or a marina; take your pick"— and a Rolls-Royce. After dinner his eyes tended to water over how "Muh pappy never got to ride in it"—which effectively prevented him from seeing the check. "These here Spanish are more in touch with their feelings," he said at every pause in the itinerary. (And now again, poling—with the bargepole he maybe knows deepdown you wouldn't want to touch *him* with.) "Europeans are. And it ain't all flamenco—look how they put themselves in touch. 'Cept for us crackers and a few Texans, you people all so tight-assed—." He finished most sentences with a drink. "Like lab hamsters?" Caldwell had said. "Open the trap-door, and trot-trot out come the feelings? Which have tripled overnight? God help Sarasota? Borden sashayed out of his chair to shake a leg with the widowlady he's picked up in Lisbon. "He'ps itself."

His "only enemy in the world" was DeBakey, the Texas heart-transplanter—"Ought to be in a Mexican jail."

"Transplantin' pussy—why don't he try that?" he'd said, attaching himself to Lexie in the Miami hotel dining-room two years ago. Sweeping an emphatic arm, he'd upset her drink, just served—and had gone on talking to the other men. She'd waited—not too long—for him to order her another. Then she'd taken Borden's own drink, a Bloody Mary, and poured it carefully on the sleeve of his maroon-velvet blazer. "Now why'd you do that?—" Borden yelled, and quickly clowning "—this here come from the Via Venito." When Lexie was truly angered the space between her eyes and brows, double most persons, flushed, along with the cheekbones, making a sudden harlequin mask of red. Once he himself had taken a mirror to it, to show her. It scared him. For *her*. Perhaps he'd never made that clear. Her voice though, grew softer. "Why did I do that, Borden? To keep you in touch."

In the nightmare, he'd called again and again for the Hermes, and when they brought it, their nuns' eyes askance ("Ah, ah, poor man" he saw them exchange "it is his family")—began a letter addressed to Charles: the first of a series whose changing addressees never get them— since they are never sent. "I am scared for your mother," he wrote Charles. In the end he'd written all the children (though not this). Even writing to others, not necessarily family or even intimates—each night picking a different auditor.

He has the letters with him now. Is he waiting for someone to collate all of this? If it could be taken out of painful med-school annotation, perhaps someone should? As an account of a journey, a disease, and perhaps, an American. He has them all now in his bag.

Perhaps every family ought to have a central clearing bureau, such as hospitals shared with other social-service organisms. Where a member could apply for knowledge of himself to others, and in turn lay it on them. With an annual meeting, complete with sky-charts, where all might assess the family course through the cloudbanks. Or where a boardmember may rise to show his charred fingertips, crying "Wake up! This is Hell!"

Would he have said that. At any time?

At a paling which borders a strip of uninhabited land leading out direct to the river, he stops and leans. People who owned land they never built on used to awe him. He would always have had to make use of it, or else sell. Now contrarily, he feels he'd like to acquire just such a piece of ground, to be saved out like those patches of the original prairie which one saw in the West. To be kept, raw and spendthrift, somewhere in the mind.

Behind him, in a small square redbrick house across the road on the terrace side, a front window goes up. In it lives a skinny, agile spinster he'd once treated for erysipelas. Ever since, whenever his car met her bike, she smiled crumpledly from the deformed side of her face and lifted an arm in salute. Now he raises his left arm, holds it there in the dark, not turning round, and lets it fall again to his side. A streetlamp is near. After a minute, the window goes down.

Well, he's home again. And she'll tell the road; she sells cosmetics door to door. Or perhaps he himself should knock on all those doors which line the road, the upper hill-road above it, and the cross-streets between— meanwhile naming each according to their diseases, which so often are entangled with their hopes. Not that this weighs on him, any more or less than it used to; it's simply that he's a patient now, and no longer wishes to treat their privacy, from a similar state. Privacy—is that the name of the feeling? Then he's a carrier of it. He doesn't wish to treat it, face to face. Let James do it. Who feels safe only when traveling.

On the other side of the paling, in the rivermist, there's James, in a silky English raincoat and flightbag marked with a large Red Cross, competently walking the waters of his ideal job. An anatomist born, James had trembled through his whole internship at the sight of live bodies being incontinently raw-sick, their blood pouring secrets he didn't want to know. Cool as a saint otherwise, early as a student he'd linked up with Ray, whom he'd heard retching away into the gray sink off the dissecting-room. To Ray, who'd often treated dogs under his veterinarian father, his own reaction there was unaccountable. Humans were merely larger than dogs in most cases and not mute; indeed now and then in the ward, where he was quite comfortable, he saw all the hierarchies of dog among them—street-bitches who veiled their eyes, whimperless, and men who had the houndsmell of the ultimate stray.

Together, he and James had done better at med school than if apart. Later, interning in the same hospital, where there'd been more than one pair of what James had called "joined lacks." And like temperaments? James had thought so. "I anger patients, with my psychological bent." When James was following it, he could look villainous, the long nose flaring, the eyes Scotch-shrewd. "You're as a cold as I am in the consultingroom, Ray, but in you it comes out shy." And not as bright, was implied. And no, he hadn't been, surely. "What you need, Ray, is to bury yourself in life. A family." And there was Lexie, wanting to bury herself the way girls do, and not sexually shy, like him. Smarter even, in James's way, but dead-dumb about it, and without villainy. Still, her sexual aggression had come at him like intelligence; did she know that? Or the intelligence, buried, came on like sex? It had excited him, and frightened him too.

"*Chessie's* intelligent," his daughter's doctor said, probing him. While Lexie, who'd been there before, waited in the anteroom. He'd felt abashed—already in the examination-box. Yet the man wouldn't look him in the eye. "Your hands, Doctor—" the man said. "—Why they're just like your daughter's." He supposed they were. The long hands of a long frame, inherited. Piano hands, some said, admiringly—though he couldn't. Chessie played well. "Ectomorph," he'd said. And the man had suddenly met his eye. "Your daughter's hands repel her. Any reason why?"

He'd been almost relieved. What tiny games they played here! In contrast to what he'd been called in to see just that morning—a great liver-mass, crawling with cause and effect. "In her childhood you mean?" he answered. "Isn't that what *you* should be telling *us*?" A smile from her doctor. That kind takes a lot from people. And should. "Dramatics, I think you'll find it" Ray added. "On both sides." Sure of course, man, Ray meant his wife—who else? That colorless silence they used, the touted therapeutic holding-back; let them treat a myeloma with it. "But I did have a grandmother. Who was that way." Telling that story, he'd relaxed. Letting the man worm it out of him. "Yes, I sometimes despair over Lexie—same as I do over Chess." And had had no thanks for it." "Ah—" the man said. End of the fifty minutes.

Meeting Lexie in the vestibule, he'd found her stunned, remote. She took Chess so hard. But was incapable of holding back. For four blocks, to the parking-garage, she managed it. He had chattered, for him. "I told him about Grandmother. Sort of thing you tell psychiatrists. But you know—I don't think the guy believed me. I think he thought I made it up." Waiting for the attendant

to bring down the car, he said "They're just inter-
mediaries. Half of them are in it because surgery gave
them the shakes. I won't take shit from them. Don't you."
She said nothing, walking whitefaced to the car. Spent. He
felt exhausted with her. "Anyway, I told him I'd do anything for Chess. *Anything.*" Inside the car, she turned
heavy, priestess eyes on him. "So did I, so did I. In those
exact words . . . But, Ray, Ray? Do *we* believe *us*?"

Had he answered that finally? In the letter he
shouldn't have mailed? Sitting on his balcony, days later,
tapping away at the Hermes, he'd heard it all from below,
like from the prompter at the opera:

James will tell Lex whatever I tell him. Always had.

And all this had come about because—as he'd accidentally discovered years later, when conducting the
spellbound Charles through the endless lab-displays of a
classmate of his own who was now a pathologist—he was
markedly allergic to formaldehyde.

Charles had come about because of it. His other favor-
ite, after Chess. And Maureen, the forgettable. And little
Lord Fauntleroy, as Ray's own mother—a Daughter of the
American Revolution who was suspiciously fond of the
British side—liked to call the boy. And Royal's foot.

As a father, he knows himself to be in his own mind
the same patched-together yet luminous figure that he is
to others—and that this has affected him as a man. For
knowledge of himself he has always depended on the reports of others to others, and on their final authority.
They seem to expect this of him, and that he will be remote. Nor can one expect him to report himself with the
exactitude that his wife reports herself. Women have a
bee-like concentration on their own roles, forever bum-
bling into those pollens. And raging afterwards, when the
group-smell, the hover and fever of the hive, follows after
them. To repollinate.

As a man, the punctilio with which they can phrase
him can make him abject. They can even understand—or

she can—that fatherdom doesn't dog his consciousness at every step. But neither can fatherhood realize him to himself, in the way she's always claimed her maternal bonds do her. The niche he'd always thought he had has slipped from him, slowly up-ending, rigid, burred, slaked, to show itself—only a shell.

What's dogging him is that he can't tell her or them or even himself—what he's bringing back to all of them. It would help to know whether he's been not only the stilted, responsible but powerfully absent father here (as he's often been told, or pridefully suspected) but whether he's also been absentee-landlord to his whole life. If so, they won't tell him; they can't. He hasn't given them enough to go on. She's said it, time and again, and he begins to believe her. "Women are all adjective," his lifelong friend James once said. "It's not the best language." All the while James's first wife, that lambent little pouncer, sat muffled to the nose in her black, against her hard black walls, slowly divorcing him. James and he, going up to James's roof to survey the city, had felt themselves to be its powerfully swimming verbs. *Fools,* his own wife had said, coming up after them, to stare. *She's all funeral, that one. But not for herself.*

For four months now, he himself's been cut loose on a sea of adjective—set adrift on the tinge and flush of things, rocking on the warble of emotions at bedsides after doctors have left them, smelling the cookery of his own muscles, hearing the backstairs crockery of the universe, at its slap and bang. Watching the whole stealth of the qualitative creep Joseph-coated over the sundial, and swallow it. Turmoil. But organized as any logic.

Zut alors, hein-hein, jawohl, the hospital's internationale of nuns said to him, along with the smooth Spanish he couldn't hang onto, until the first one, who spoke English also, said, pushing under his chin one of the kidney-shaped zinc pans which must circle the cosmos, "Ah yes, Doctor. In sickness we carnify." Sister Isaac Jogues' plastic sunglasses perch like a spider on the hot globe of her face; in a moment will they crackle into flame—sputter, pop—and burn off? Her English was French-sprigged, but clear. "We grow into our flesh." At night, her cooler face leaned over him, cameo. As it flitted the dark of the one electric bulb, art-nouveau spirals of words came from it. Smoke-rings he couldn't decipher. The electricity seemed worn here. Possibly she was really asking him to *spiritize?* When he came to his senses, idling between blessed stations of bouillon, he was shocked to find that the smoke was real. The whole damned ward had been full of it. Each bed almost had had its cigarette. A disturbing rescue-hut, toxic and lifegiving in the same heave. Like his trip.

He lets go the paling now, and walks on, avoiding a look at which houses he passes. As their medical server, he knows the story of each—but tonight means to obtrude his own. His yellow shoes go in front of him like another man's; in fact don't belong to him, though new. During his whole time, he'd worn ward-clothing; either he was still half in bed, or after hospital-gowns, his own one suit was too heavy, or the sportsjacket shouted "American!" The gray-cotton orderly's pants-and-jacket they gave him was a comfortable uniform, like convalescence itself. Sister Isaac Jogues, named for a French missionary martyr—"In the New World, M. le Docteur"—and trained in France, had taken away his excuses with the real reason for them. "*Tcht*, you're a type wants to delay a little, *non?* 'T'sokay weetha me."

The last day, when his own clothes were brought, the shoes were missing; the retarded woman who had charge of enough backstairs items and tasks to tax a genius was still searching when he left. Thievery was not to be suspected. But Hector Ibañez, the small hospital's director, who spoke good English, felt responsible, as if Ray might think himself forced to pay with his shoes for the long, quasi-medical conversations they'd had of an evening, after Ibañez' duties were done.

"I can go home in these," Ray'd said, pushing forward a foot in one of the soft foldover slippers he'd had in his bag. "Or maybe—what's the Spanish word for sneakers?—happen to have an extra pair?" A josh, of the simple sort they'd been having. Hector had an ancient American tennis-racket brought him by an elder brother, the hospital's owner and director before him, who'd served an internship at the Flower Hospital in New York, as he said: "Five hundred and fifty years ago." Hector'd stuck out a foot. And on the last night, think of it, it was discovered they wore the same size.

"Between friends—" Ibañez insisted, stern tears in his eyes. He'd been a monk, writing ecclesiastical reference-books, until that same doctor-brother died, and duty had called Hector to this lazier work; now the hair in his former tonsure flourished, purple-black and frayed as the unlit cigar he entered with each evening—a token of status maybe like an epaulet, or a housekey to the laic life—for after a time Ray suspected it to be always the same cigar. Like Ibañez' flowery self-introduction and adieu every evening. Through the day, the formalities that even the least of people here clicked at like rosaries cast him a supportive perfume. It was the conversation of people who also danced communally; the words were like knee-dips and bows-from-the-waist, not of themselves to be saved. He couldn't ever remember much of what Hector said, but the man's attitudes, stiff yet flowery as the sheaves on a coin, would stay with him for life. He would like to bundle up just such a sheaf of them, he told Sister Isaac—who was also Hector's sister—in Hector's presence. "To send to my son Charles." Hector'd wrinkled his nose over his moustachios. "Like the bundle of rods on the Fascist medals, you mean—? Pfui—he wouldn't want those." It was his only political remark. "Why to the son?" Sister said. "Why to him?" And then, with a covetous glance at the Hermes "Ahh—because he also writes?" They waited. Sister always spoke in threes. Her second thoughts were worth waiting for, Hector joked, but her thirds had been kept in a special family album ever since her girlhood. "Why—" she'd said "—do the Americans always want *us*?" He thought about that, in the long grave thoughts which were possible there, a stream always at his side. Every time she spoke, she took a little more of his skin away with her.

Charles' weekly letter was read to the ward in three parts: First, a portion to other patients in return for their own extracts. Then, certain passages which Hector would relish, having as he said "known your country through my brother." And sometimes, only to Sister, the parts that troubled him. She never commented, as if she knew that he was merely trying to hang onto the family images that shift in an invalid's absence—or doing it for extra surety that he wasn't going to slip out and away from them. Into a future life that meant more to him even than they.

The tiny hospital, which had no front or back door of its own, occupied the two middle floors of the building, once its own in entirety, which now also housed a government warehouse above, and some sort of agricultural department down below—all of them connected by the same elevator. A rickety outer staircase had been attached to the ward's rear door, like a chute for all wastes. The warehouse floor, which had no personnel except rats, was given over to the storage of framed military portraits from the Franco side of the last war, all ranged with respect to rank, the towering gesso frames of the generals accompanied by those of their aides-de-camp, done in oil also, but the frames narrower. The walls, of what once had been the Ibañez' apartment, were velvet-covered—which was perhaps what had inspired the government. One far wall was hung with tinted photographs, not quite so large, of official couples. "Colonels," Hector said, pronouncing all the syllables. The women, all handsome enough except for the crimped space between the eyes, had an endearing, almost homebody look lurking soft behind their haughty corals and formidable hair—or perhaps it was the innocence which came to all the dead of only forty, fifty years back. Yet one could imagine them lowering their eyes. He'd touched the bodice of one of them—a young girl almost, with a high comb like a red canna-flower on her head, and seeing eyes. "Colonels and their wives," Hector said. "I assure you, wives, all of them. But if you like that one, it can be arranged." Hector had with him a black rosette of ribbon. Walking over to one of the aides-de-camps he attached it. "It pleases me to keep the necrology. Especially in my own house." All the generals already had their death-ribbons. Some were a dust-covered red. "What are those?" Hector drew a long fingernail across his throat. "Shall we say—*Sold*."

In the ward proper, the atmosphere was that of some homely pension—with its own stewpots, waiting lists and profits and losses—which happened to serve medical guests. Two doctors consulted and operated, neither of them residents. Under Sister Isaac, four other sisters nursed, assisted the one male cook, and waited "on table." The retarded slavey's husband was both orderly and marketer, washing his hands, it was to be hoped, in between. The operating-room, which Hector showed proudly, was reasonably modern and included a dentist's-chair from which came the loudest howls in the hospital. Twice a year medical students arrived, allotted—as happened during Ray's third week—from some civic bureau above. The excitement over what provinces these neophytes would be from was far larger than he'd seen during any emergency. One of the half-dozen chronic patients, a man who'd worked in London, said to him seriously "Senor, a fellow from Saragossa slips in that thing there"—a catheter—"bitching different than a fellow from Almeria."

Clearly there were also hierarchies in how one got to be a patient at all in this tiny facility, where a man's town-entity loomed larger than money, or even suffering. What happened in the unseen female ward he assumed went the same way. The hospital itself, founded by the Ibañez pair's father, now submitted to the government publicly, and adjusted in private, gleefully. The cook, stalking into the ward from the kitchen—which Ray, when ambulatory, learned was next to the operating room itself because of a matter of pipes and electrical lines—was now and then pacified from Hector's own pocket, though not before signing a receipt. "Wine custard can't be made without good wine," Hector said. "In summer, we abstract many little gaieties from the fund for bedsocks." At first he and his sister seemed to be in the ward neglectfully often for a director and his nursing supervisor; whenever they were, the hospital's innards were unrolled to Ray. "You make too much of me," he'd even said, hoping to relieve them of professional courtesy. Then, after one peculiarly circuitous chat with both brother and sister, the English-speaking chronic looked up from his equally chronic game of piquet and said offhand to his other neighbor, first in English and then Spanish "The Director and Sister are studying for their *alternitiva* with the Doctor here." On inquiry, he was told this was the license issued by the Royal School of Bullfighting—and laughed uncertainly, at what must be a dig at all medicos. But at last, routing himself through their protocol of innuendo combined with franknesses quite opposite to his own (a local process which he was learning faster than the language) he understood that the pair were hoping to learn everything they could scrape from him. If he went back over their chats of the last few days, he could even hazard that their new cases had numbered a pneumonia, a diabetic amputation, and a Hodgkinson's. But for dignity's sake, neither would ever ask him a question direct.

Let Sister Isaac walk on one side of him now—she'd want the river side—and Hector on the other, the two gray radishes of his moustache pointed at the houses of his friend's medical domain. Both of them ready for consultation on a case. And all three of us watching the progress of the yellow shoes.

Let us consult. We all three know who the case is.

The case of a man who isn't in touch? This would never occur to either of those two. Never does, to people who are.

How can it occur to the case itself? Think of Borden Wheeley, who barrels through the world and its widows on the cheap phrases he thinks will unlock him and them—only succeeding in making himself untouchable.

"Yet you say his practice is the largest in the Miami area, Doctor Ray?" Hector says. "Surely you make mistake about him. And yourself." They walk on. "You have big practice here, Doctor Ray? How many souls?"

Souls? I think of them as houses.

Sister's more practical. "It's not the same as just touching people, Hector. On the nose or the neck. Or anywhere." She doesn't blush. "Doctor here, he's done plenty of that. Just like me. Look at his buttons."

He's still wearing the tie-pin and cufflinks engraved "Dr.", which Lexie gave him when he began. When they began. When he put them on at leaving, Sister Isaac had thought them official insignia. "Ahh—the Señora," she'd said, nodding when he explained. He'd formed the habit of reading her Lexie's curt letters, watching her. She in turn tested them, glancing as curiously at the English, the typing, as if, in spite of all her languages, she couldn't quite have read it herself. She had her own names for the pictures of his children: Tall Son, Tall Daughter, Middle Daughter and Little Lame. Was he wrong, or had she pressed him to talk of them—therapeutically? She'd never call it that.

"It comes from his job then, Isabela?" Hector says. "*You* do not suffer."

"Fool, I am a nun," she says, sotto voce. *Have the kindness to remember it,* she always sighed, when Hector chose to forget. She takes Ray's hand now. "Doctor. We are not what you think. *You* are not what you think. It is the disease."

· 201 ·

Is it? Then name it, Ray. Spanish hepatitis? Liver perspective? Distance dialysis? One should always listen carefully to the patient's description of his disease. Hospital depression—or its opposite? Am I merely suffering from mountain viewing, or a balcony complex? "Are ward conversations always so frugal?" he'd written James. "We doctors should remember that. I'm coming back with a headful." A doctor should never be sick, James had replied—it broke down the immunities. As for a job in the public health, my dear Ray, it's clear you're one who should never travel. Know what's wrong with you? Middle age. The disease of the first inner monologue.

"Where does it hurt him?" Hector's not a man whose attitudes keep him from walking, but now he stops, to look south through the downriver mist.

"Where does it hurt you, Doctor?" Sister Isaac pummels him in the liver region, competently delicate. "In the wife? In the children?" She exhales sympathy through her teeth. "Ahh—ssssiuuu. Here. In the li-ife. . . . Ha! I have made a poem . . . *The wife makes poems, Hector, but does not send him them.*"

"In the father, maybe" Hector says gloomily. He sleeps with women now as part of his new status, but fearing monkhood may have made him infertile, can't bring himself to marry one until she conceives. "And in the Holy Ghost—does he suffer there?"

"Silencio . . . Look at this river, how it prays."

It was Lexie who said that. When he met her walking on the road here once, and caught a shocked glimpse of her as she must be when alone. More accurately, she'd said "Ray, the river prays for us."

But against that one-time revelation, cutting across the family day like a squall of light from the river itself, is that other caution she's always cornering him with. "Why do you impute your mother's thoughts to me—I'm not her. Nor any other woman, necessarily. I am not any of them." And now I'm a nun to him, she'd say harum-scarum to the air, her silent witness. So much a part of their lives, invoked so often, that auditor in the air, that in the event of divorce it ought to be named as correspondent. And now a nun he links me to, she said to it. Tell me somebody, why? Why he'll never look me in the face and say merely: This is she.

He'd been brought up to think of family women as the bitter herbal essence in a man's life, that was why. As the seat of judgments which could change the taste of food on your tongue—unless ignored. And even then.

"Which way issa the-e-Flower Horspital?" Hector was fading but still upright, a column of emphatic accent in the mist. "*Effa* I could introduce you my brother, *khee* would help you. But *khee* is dead."

"And so are we," Sister Isaac said, washing her hands at the ward tap, shaking them high over her coif while she looked out the window at the mountains, as if those too were patients in her charge. "Dead to him. And he to us." They wouldn't forget him. But he was only a patient. As a doctor himself, he knew that the patient was always less to them than they to him. But he and they were also officially and mutually dead to each other the minute he'd handed them the envelope. Even though they were happy for it, had expected it, and had beamed at their apt pupil for learning their ways—while he, feeling like a graduate, had beamed back. All along of course he'd paid his weekly pittance via a ticketed bill of particulars from the municipality, but this was from him. For having changed him. For having looked him in the face. On the envelope which held his check for a thousand, he'd written in a Spanish carefully checked beforehand with the chronic cardsman: "For the bedsocks." At the last minute, he'd left them the old Hermes too.

Over there, Sister Isaac, waking now in that leaky old room, papered with newsprint, which was everybody's office and only nocturnally her cell—is still admiring it. It was trained in France.

"So he is in America by now," Hector is saying over their coffee-cups. Adding his witticism of yesterday. "Now he has only to suffer from my shoes."

He's nearing the house now. In his bag, besides the unmailed letters, are the presents he chose, refusing all escort, in the town's stripped bazaar. Where he did well. He happens to be one of those buyers who always astound others with his silent knowledge of them. This comes from being a solitary among them. If other fathers are not so adept it must mean they aren't solitary. Only with Lexie do his choices falter. "I'm wearing them—" he heard her say to Chess once, hearing the glint between them even through the bathroom door "Everywoman's pearls." For Chess he has a pair of ear-dangles; he can already hear her "Oh wild. Absolutely wild." Then it'll be a contest of wills—between her two—as to whether she'll wear them. Or fling them to her mother, saying, "They really belong to you." For Maureen a trusty leather purse, large enough for all her tasks. For Royal, after some doubts, an intricately dovetailed diary-wallet which can only increase his hoarding—in money, surgical appointments and secret jottings—of the statistical world he believes to be the only one. For Charles—for whom, in spite of himself, he always finds the best—a fine old astrolabe, which he yearns to have Charles instruct him on.

Charles is the only one he's not had to be in competition for. This is an old secret, rusty as a garden-lock on a gate swinging into the few assignments with himself that his chosen livelihood allows. Chosen for that reason, his wife, that interpreter-after-the-fact, would say; has said . . . "James chose a profession which would keep him approvedly from people; you, Ray, use it to keep you from yourself. Abetted by your mother, who saw having a doctor in the family as the one social vaccine which would cure a vet's family—of the odor of manure" . . . When Lex got excited she fell into rhyme, which disconcerted her brother, who saw it as merely one more aberration. Ray, brought home to meet Lexie the sweet kid sister, had fallen in love with what they thought they'd hid from him: Lexie the rhymer, the dark repository, the symbolist. Yes. he did identify her with his mother—but not carnally, never. Rather, because his mother, otherwise totally unlike Lexie, occupied the same dark tribal niche in the family, there did cling to Lexie a votive tinge—of that tabu. What it killed Lex to acknowledge was the other resemblance— the circumstantial one. (Or whisper it—the artistic one.) Between her and this older woman of limited mind and even mean character. Whose orderly New England basement made her "feel dirt." Whose painted milk-cans she hated with a Picasso's loathing, or a radical's: "Eagles! Why does she aspire so low!"

Why were women so hard on women? "Weakness rejoices in the sight of weakness," she'd said—though over the years he was less and less sure of the tones in her voice. "Men rush to the defense of other men when the chips are down," he said. "And are larger beings for it you mean?" she countered. "Yes, that happens. Or they have more chips." From the back of the porch, that day, James, who was playing chess with Royal, said "Our little sister suffering from nervous injustice? A venereal complaint." And she laughed. James could be as unkind as he pleased, if she liked the phrasing of it. She and her brother shared a language; also they knew how language itself shut Ray out. It was what he was shy with, now. On the porch a minute later, James had lost to Royal. Who'd said with the smugness he couldn't be smacked for "James likes losing to me. I'm his favorite."

"In a family," James says "the same spoken lines come in over and over. Intimacy exhausts. Don't tell me Ray that you still thrive on it."

Yet over the years, even James has grudgingly reversed his position—on her position. No, she's not off her head or out of it—my sister-your-wife. She's incontinently, stubbornly on edge—on the swerving edge that's inside all of us. But this James will only privately admit. And never to her.

"Most family women are like her," he'll say, porch-lolling. "You call us 'family women'—" she interrupts through the window "—the way cows are called ruminants.'" He ignores her. "Mentally, they're much more obviously creatures of their environment, than their men." For them, he said, life was—whatever happened. And in any argument of mind—even if they had mind—most shared one great position. They were all wavering on top—"Streamers to any wind"—and immutably fixed, down below. Like birds who followed the migration patterns, shrilly criticizing all the way. "Lexie makes emotional argument of it. And longs for an intellectual one." She philosophized as she flew, almost as if she knew where. "Driving us mad, though, in the process. Because everything they do is outsize." James's cheeks have taken to reddening when he talks so. She came out on the porch that day, and linked arms with him. "Yes, James. Inside us, all inmates are."

At times he sides with both of them.

"Women'll do anything to make themselves memorable," James said gloomily last time they saw him, opening his hall closet on his last wife's wallpaper, which bared its orchid fangs at him. "Anything. From their execrably floral house-keeping—to poetry." Grinning, he'd handed Lexie the poncho she'd worn into town straight from her class, reaching around her to tap the notebook protruding from its pocket. "Yah, they'll hang their damp psyches out to dry anywhere. They'll do anything, Ray, to stick in our hearts."

"Men write poetry," she'd answered, clutching the notebook to her.

"Right," her brother said, "but for a man, Lexie—poetry's a deed."

He himself's bringing her the town leather-worker's triumph, a portfolio polished to the tortoiseshell glint she loves; surely this time he's hit it right. Maybe the gold tooling's too much. But it's on the inside, a discreetness he can point out. When he says, with careful malice, "Only your poems will see it." Saying it—as her flickering eye will tell him at once—almost in her style.

It hurts him, that she's so aware. It puts the burden of being the denser, colder person always on him. It bores him. Like having in the house an aquatic plant which must be forever fed, so that the rest of the family may see the dark waters swirling this sea-anemone that lives with them. It kills him. Like the air around a mushroom that may or may not be malignant, which keeps casting its spores. But her awareness doesn't fright him for *her*, as it does James. No, he admires the cellar-strength of her, hanging onto her own being as if it's a kind of tool-kit. Or will turn into one. Keeping her little miseries for a rainy day. But flashing out in an evening tarantella, with a Carmen smile, if you will just take her somewhere. It touches him.

Why does he have to get away from it? Grinding in Hector's left shoe, he stares up Ricer Street, only a hill-path meandering down to meet this road and mark the townline. Why? Because she can always tell him—why.

She keeps their story. Ever rehearsing and improving it, like one of those caretakers who live in the basements of famous-family houses which are now museums on view. Had she really suffered from less opportunity, or from wider expectations than his—right from the start? Had the chicken come before the egg there?—no one will ever know for sure. But why had she crossed the road to him? When she came under his wing she was frightened stiff of her own demon demands, glad enough to huddle there, and grow, Sure, they pushed her to. Pushed him. Who hadn't a story—he'd been reared to think—but merely a road. Both of us—we pushed ourselves. If couples were born with premonitory heraldic mottoes on them—branded in like genes (instead of acquired, like his college-plates, like her initialed ring from her father) then what would their escutcheon be? It's under the skin, maybe, and comes out in the marriage, to twine above their heads like a garland slowly sinking with the years to thorn their linked necks: Frightened Young.

Some marriages along the road here were homeopathic cures; a little of the same disease on each side permitted the couple to jog comfortably, as in a Siamese-twin truss—or to drown like Hero and Leander, in company. Others were allopathic unions; the mutual sight of a partner's diseased acts induced a sharp refraction into health—sometimes on both sides. At which point the cure for all diseases of coupling—to separate—came as a surprise.

He walked slower as he neared his house. One more bend now and he'll see the old tower he'd had so many plans for, until the wasps and the children took over. With Lexie ever-ready with her romantic poultice, saying loud for the neighbors, and to everyone's applause except his, "Plans are what a tower is for." Maybe so, if you can remember daily, with the same incisive pain, what the plans were. She'd had her inner monologue from the beginning. With women, as he knows from his practice, it doesn't wait for middle-age. "It's how I live!" she flashed once at James. "It's my way of—getting in." To what he only wanted to get out of. His whole life with her had been a conversation, it seemed to him. In which he knew she thought he never said anything.

In a way she preferred that. Having him—the provider who couldn't provide the life she must get for herself—to thrash against, meanwhile. Alongside James, their interlocutor. Between the two of them, she was honing herself to a finepoint of readiness. She had the blunt, weaving strength of an animal on its way to a gene-imprinted task, or niche or mate; she herself didn't know which, yet. But against that, he and James showed up as the weaker ones, who'd "found" themselves too early.

Does she know by now that she's going to leave him?

He won't say even to himself how long he's known. To Charles, once in a Chinese restaurant, in Boston where they'd gone college-hunting, he'd said, after their day and a half together, "When you three older ones leave . . . your mother and I—." Bear witness that I've told you, he wanted to add, couldn't. The restaurant had a violently painted almost bas-relief ceiling—a great wheel of the Chinese zodiac, intertwined with dragons in parrot-green and carmine, and mandarins with fleshy porcelain faces. Charles handled chopsticks well. Small expertises came easily to his son's long, intent frame; he was a craftsman. Of people as well, Lexie said. Like any mother, she felt she had her children's personalities on rein—if lightly. As if created for her interpretation. All mothers felt that, or most. Yet the world had misunderstood women's possessiveness, she said. They didn't so much want to own their children, as to interpret the world to them.

But their own long, sibylline days worked against them, giving them certain powers they oughtn't to have had. They ended up understanding the non-domestic world, the "worldly" one, with the finicky patience of onlookers who didn't function there. Because Lexie hadn't, she took on the job of understanding him instead; if no children had come, that might have been her life. He'd had childless men patients, husbands who were strangled by that, and some who were supported by it. But children take your place there.

"If you do—" Charles had said, nipping a sliver of black mushroom between his sticks, and not waiting for his father to say "Do what?" "—will *you* keep on the house?" The boy was trembling, for all his show of control. "For us?"

Such a jolt. All these years that he'd thought himself behind her, there. All that time, their allegiance had been to him.

Aha, that lioness of understanding, your mother—we've passed her by. But what do I dare say to you?

"That ceiling," he'd answered. "Put together in some crummy factory gets joblots from Hong Kong." And yet it looks so wise. "It'll work out," he says, craven. And sees in Charles' face that he's lost him. Because, as Charles' mother often tells him, his father won't confront.

She wants him to confront what confronts her—that's it. How dependent she is—even yet! A little melt of tenderness is still in him though, for the lovely gawk she was at Chessie's age. Or a year or two beyond; he always loses track of Chessie's age. Those two have the same deep scowl, almost malevolent. On Lexie's plump, rainwashed skin at that age, looking almost humorous. Chess is a rod, unbendable. With the sallow skin of a Spanish heroine.

He put his bag down on the road. That's who the girl in the military portrait reminded him of. The thought of Chess weighs. "I carry her around in my mind like iron," Lexie says. "And she knows that, Ray. When *I* don't—this house takes over. The old house cooperates with us all—with me, God knows, but especially with Chess. It's her dungeon, which is safe. And the other kids, they cope—Charles the most. When I see them at it, Ray, I die—for I don't know what. Not for pity, not even for love; no, it's beyond that. For youth and its terrors, maybe—seen once again. Ray?—do you ever see your youth and its terror any more? No, you don't; I can see you don't—do males escape it young?"

She walks back and forth when she goes on like that, but always homing back to him. And always finally forgetting Chess. *Sensibility,* she'll say—lovely word, isn't it? Such a fluttering—we think too much, and go on about it after. Our teacher at the college says we're all suffering from it. God knows, I want to get rid of mine—I think. And then (she's looking at him, dreamily)—*And then, Ray—I think not.* She'll walk over to him, on the lapsing rhythm of that. He always knows the rhythm; maybe that's *his* sensibility: Knowing what to expect. And getting ready to pay for it. She's smiling by now, seductively. *Ray, you don't know whether I'm raving, do you—or whether I damwell know what I'm about. Maybe it's both, hmmm? Ray*—she says in that beautiful gut-voice of hers, the one that knows it's making conscious echoes but would slam you for remarking it: *Ray, when I rave like this, what, what am I dying of?*

A car of teenagers jumbles past him. *Damned old fool.* He's in the center of the road. I hear you. I hear her. Always have. I hear you, Lex—but you won't admit it. To yourself. Because you're speaking, growling—praying—to more than yourself. Or us. The family's the only stage you have, that's all. But we're not your true audience. "My rages?" you said, when I scolded you for the children's sake. "They're my dowry, Ray. The girls'll inherit them. And the boys will marry them. Even that little faker, Lord Fauntleroy. I already see it coming, in Charles." *Think back, Ray,* she said, in that diagnostic voice they all hated for its smug roundup of their privacies—and for which she often begs their forgiveness, afterward. "Think back, Ray. Didn't you marry it yourself?"

She was wearing a puffed gown with long dripping sleeves that last night, looking as she had for the last year or so of their bedroom crisscrossings, no longer a wife domesticated to flannels or silk gone unmended, but newly lithe and bodily composed—though not for him. Newly imaged in self-respect (due to diet, she said)—but not because of him. She took hold of his coat, that last night. He was just in from a late hospital-call; no time in his schedule for loungerobes, if that's what she wanted. He can still hear her. "Forgive me, Ray. I'm still such a goddam amateur."

At what?—he could have asked. Your days or your nights? But didn't dare, and had gone on to the study, where he then slept. The formal nightgown, too elaborate for her, not her crazy-pretty style of daffiness, had been a replica of one Betsy wore incessantly. Did she know it? Or not? Or know without knowing in that way she had, which he could attest was not put on, but inborn.

This time, for once, she's answered him. In a postscript to the last letter he'd had from her before leaving for here. By now there may have been another. Since he wants no waiting fiesta, he'd sent no notice ahead. Even though lately her letters have warmed a little. Not into love, but as if she's posting him her half of a dialogue. Which they must now agree to agree—does exist.

"On that nightgown. Women in my—setup—have their closet cruelties. We do unto one another what we would do unto ourselves. But I'm learning." She no longer said "Forgive." As for the house-news—she's having the tower shored up, on her own initiative. "Chess's taken to going up there. When I asked if she wanted it for a studio to draw in, she wouldn't say. It was after she got the job in town. She really did you know; she looked wonderful. But when she came home, she went up there and didn't come down. The kids went after her, made a game of it, and finally got her to come down. But she didn't take the job." The warmest parts of her letters are often about Chess. Or the arrangements for Royal's foot.

Whenever he handed Sister Isaac one of Lexie's letters, she immediately sat, laid it in her lap, patted her coif and clasped her hands over it before she began—exactly as she had come to do for one of their medical conferences. While Sister read, she bowed rhythmically to the privilege. He imagined each sentence as deposited in her store of them—kept for him. For though she never commented on the letters themselves, it became her custom at this time to render him her opinion on the progress of his own health—as if the whole procedure was in fact a medical rite. After this last letter, only six days ago, she'd folded her hands. "You are really ready now, *non M'sieu* le *Doc-*

teur? To leave." Then blushed dark, as over a breach of hospitality. *"Cha, Isabela!"* Hector muttered. But they must have talked. The mountains ever at the window had a way of moving into the room at these moments, active participants. As a river might be.

From over their peaks, his own people speak to him, without benefit of telephone, in the nightsmoke. She in particular never stops. Over here he measures them all incessantly with the invalid's egg-cup eye—reversible to large or small serving, soft-boiled or hard. To know people, they say, you have to know yourself. To know yourself—know them. A paradox blowing in the window from a mountain-top. But not dispelling the smoke.

Hector's cigar, a stub by then, revolved in his mouth.

He himself said suddenly "Tell me what you think about this." Tapping the letter in her lap. "About all of them."

Sister nods formally. She'd expected this. Palms pressed against her spread knees, she stared into the folds of her habit, into some pocket where her secular wisdom was stored. "There are *types,* Doctor—*pardon,* women— who are like nuns without Jesus." Adding, with a shoulder-squaring intake (of pride? he thought afterwards) "And sometimes, they are not nuns." But when she was about to issue her third comment, and he'd said, urgently "Yes, yes," Hector'd made a sign to her, and she didn't reply.

So here he is, the occasional streetlight glancing on him as he walks, showing him just as the brighter lamp at the townline had revealed him to the local busdriver: a tall daddylonglegs of a man, with the shouldering pathos of the recently ill. Nodding his bags and his "See you" down and off the high step with the reserve of a man deep between journeypoints and harboring himself. Dealing himself to himself close to the vest. Horrie, the night busman on the New York run for eight years now, knows him well. Saying a sharp *"Hi"* when he got on. But only "Right, Doc" when he asks to be let off more than a mile from his place. Yet a warmth had passed between them, as of men dealing to each other. On the plane just left, his silent seatmate, a man of middle-age with a resolute visor of hair, had smoothed his shaven chin continuously; now and then a forefinger painted an invisible moustache. In chat it developed he had never had facial hair. "Nor missed it."

What's he missed about himself? Not wanting to live as she does, in a swirl of rhetoric. Is he a smaller man than he thinks, and merely yearning over the barrier-reef of his limitations? Or is he still the man of his younger hopes?—a vast, shady customer.

He has to have more of himself to go on with. Before he decamps. So he's come home.

Nobody need write any more letters now. The unmailed ones in his bag will go into his study, and into the locked medical files; to wait there like the record of a dangerous journey not yet over. On which a man's fidelity to his profession, to his very children is being questioned, and drawn by some magnetic needle to an as yet unidentified pole. So that the customary passions of his life—or what passed for these—are seen to be automata—not parts of a soul, but of a neighborhood. "Same thing might happen to a Spaniard from one cup of American water, I'm aware of that," he'd told James in that one letter. "The colon prefers its own bacteria. Would he suffer from our freedoms, you think? I'm like that just now, in this oasis of nuns, and unfrocked monks. When you're away from yourself you see your lacks."

The trip home has been the hardest; no wonder he's walked the last part of it. A closet-cruelty to himself? Christ. Will he be able to undergo again all the illuminations she's always scattering in front of him? Can he continue to fend off, to say to her—always silently—"I do not choose your lighted path"? He'll keep the letters, but maybe never consult them. They exist, they have to be kept. They are his disease. A souvenir, from Jerusalem.

And here's the house. It shocks him. It has his name on it, even if well off to the office-side. Low-roofed there, and open to any bell. Tall on the house-side, and full of complicitous corners. Through this four o'clock world of brainy shadow, he can see that the tower has indeed been shored. The lawn is passable. He can be sure that the bamboo's been cut, and that it's growing again. Beyond his own trees, Kellihys' shows a lone attic-light on high, and a moving feverglow in the basement—nothing between. Not a bad score, for the Kellihys. But making his own dark house ride more steadfast. For one flash he sees each as a house among other houses, on a road. What makes people think that a man and a woman—whose lives are in perpetuity so *other*—can ever navigate a mutual destiny by means of such a house, of any house? That lamp over his door is a vampire lamp, bleeding out life and blanking all souls; it will burn, and lure, and come to nothing. A house is a game of pick-up-sticks, whose hoarded straws will outlast him, his family—and still fall. He must warn Charles.

Then his eyes shift up. His mouth closes. The hour changes. He's home.

Upstairs, out there in the prow of the house, is its figurehead. Does it see him? The angle at which it sits—due north—suggests not. Perhaps it does, but refuses that side of its knowledge. Does he, down below there, see her as a blot-head drawing back into her own wallpaper—or as a real girl? Or even as elder daughter, as in the family casebook? They'll never know which. On his part he would help if he could—and has tried.

But it must be clear by now that, in so far as a man can be, he is a man built up of other people's notations, even in his own mind. In the main, family references. Which may have been what he—instinctive as any of us—embarked on a family for. And on a profession too, though there he was pushed. He's pushable. But as those who live with him have learned to accept—with an unusual twist to it. He's pushable on the big things; there's he's like water. Or seems so. Maybe sliding back on himself on the end? There's not been time enough for them to judge. But they all know that on the small, cranky issues he is a rod, adamant. Or his routine is. He will not be budged. On reflection, one can see what might make him as he is, in both instances. Since his character must wait on its expression by other persons—he waits too. And in turn, this of itself builds up to a kind of character—canny if not mean, residual. In addition, all fathers of our time, our place, are of course a kind of collaborative—even more than the mothers, if you look close. And in this—he collaborates.

We must follow him now, up the steps. What happened—happens. So far, our notations, drawn from persons related to him, are almost inexcusably exact. And would be apologized for, except for that question always moot: Can those who aren't aware of themselves really expect privacy? Isn't privacy for those who know they have secrets, who know themselves at least in part?

For those who do, the worst emotional mystery is a man or a woman, lived with—who doesn't. Or who draws a blank. We must govern that—the family of such a person keeps saying to itself—or else tremble forever on the crater of the unperceived. Even to perceive him or her as that—is a gain.

So Ray, has always been researched—chill word. And since his recent leaving—along every route possible. Charles is a route. The son as written to, and all that haunted library of a summer writing as a son, a brother, a man—to himself. Maureen when approached, is at first a burst of tears, no help—and then a surprising store, spontaneous. "Father wants to be very conventional. He's like me." Tears still dropping. "We can't be freaky." Though being compared to the Spanish maid-of-all-work—as a father's sole greeting—does hurt. Royal says, walking alongside James on one of their city days together, "Daddy's got no tact; he can't lie." Says Royal, a former expert. His foot-operations are refining him; he's practicing truth and is turning out as good at it as he is at anything. Presently, he wants to be a psychoanalyst. "But Daddy's witty too—you all never see it. He's so sly. Remember what he said to you about his accountant? 'Mr. Rooney has very touchy prerogatives.' And what Mummy always quotes he said to her when he first met her? That he liked to play with his mental blocks, he had so many of them?"

While Lexie, reported this last, looks guilty, remembering those stray aphorisms so cherished by her, polished up even, so that after years neither Ray nor she is sure whom they stemmed from, she even wondering if perhaps they aren't fabricated out of her own need to be with a sentient man. Or later, out of wifely shame. "Ah, Lexie—" James will write, in response to her questioning later "—our recording angel-ess. Who believes that not to be aware is against the human covenant. You know I doubt that angels ever were female. Certainly not archangels. Research that for me, won't you; I may be marrying a Japanese girl. . . . And am far too busy, at my age, to write any sort of memoir." From Honshu, still single, he'll write "Our little dickey-bird, my nephew, tells me that my friend, your husband, has done just that, journal-style. (As you must know, your son Royal has skeleton-keys to all of us.) Extraordinary of Ray—if true. And yet oddly like him. He got the idea from you, of course—to examine himself. And us. For your sake. A triumph of a sort. On both sides, as should be. No doubt they're simple enough observations, Ray being Ray. But you being you, will interpret them. And call it poetry. I've no doubt you'll be grindingly fair. Naturally however, I remain on Ray's side."

Up the steps now, up the steps. In Hector's yellow shoes. There are two sets of front steps to most of these houses on the river's terrace-side, this first set lifting you to the lawn level. Here, for this house, two huge horse-chestnuts border the flagstone path to its porch. Overhead, their tops combine. In the very center of the second story is a small sewing-room, now a bath, used mostly by Lexie and the girls. Though everybody uses it at one time or another, because of the tub's great size. In spring, the bower of tree-tops presses its white cones inward to the bather. Through a pointed window, with a small ledge.

Delay no longer. Now, up the porch-steps, firmed three years ago. He has his keyring, as well as his nocturnal habit, sharpened like a crackman's over the years, of reentering his house noiselessly. For a while, when the two elder were babies, and Lexie by nine P.M. was exhausted—by that peculiar post-partum weariness which engulfs so many young wives in his district—he even wore sneakers for her sake.

His tendernesses are strange, awkward. This is important. Do they come from love, or duty? Or other obediences? That sheepish gawk before a kiss. That side-long calculation, to sneak . . . Is this why poetry can't be made of him?—or Lexie, shivering, won't try? Photo-enlarge him wall-high—Charles did it for his birthday once—and

· 218 ·

here's a man at a desk, prescribing in everybody's best interest. The original, passing it daily, averted his eyes.

"Ray doesn't like to be made much of" his mother said, smugly premarital. "But don't ever let him *delay*, mind you; that would be the worst thing for a medical man" she says, mealy. "A word to the wise—" she whispered, almost human, "—my son does like to scuttle along." *Ray?* young James said, betraying him, a quickly reassuring arm around his sister, "Why—at the hospital, he's fine."

While that younger Ray hung his head between them all, sidelong. Did he already know what each of his family will learn early—that he can never quite make his emotional appointments? He'll never refuse obligation, only delay it until it disappears or turns into another—chain on chain. Stubbornly scuttling along the bottom of things, he avoids all crimes—murder, sodomy, even adultery maybe—what do we really know of him and Betsy?—and gauchely, almost gently—love. Saying to others mutely, with a halting smile: You'll not make anything classical out of me. Even Lexie will never be able to.

Yet in ten minutes—he's inside the door now, has eased it silently behind him and must be looking up the central stair—life is going to monster him. So that he'll loom forever over his kin as a certain kind of ogre. Even when he's in their presence they're going to have to imagine him. Life's caught up with him. This ogre of the inarticulate.

The best way to imagine him is Hoppe's. As provincial newspaperman used to these items, a homestyle Jean-Jacques. Born in the town—imagine that he's come for his daily inheritance. He usually knows the house.

The doc's house is interesting, he reports, because it's a layering, as all the older river-houses are. New England had its coach-roads which predicted the houses; York State has its rivers. In spite of the tower, this house isn't American Gothic at all, but a bastard form of Hudson River-bracketed, and like any interim architectural style, marks a whole civilization gone by the boards. Note the pointed church-window, gone to bathroom, but still very important to the house. The downstairs rooms—the usual ones—are not our concern. Except to remark that the entire structure has horsehair-and-plaster-filled walls, now a regrettably lost art. Central staircase, revolutionary-straight.

The doc is going to walk up it. At the top of the stairs, standing at the center stairwell, he'll see down the wide hall to the back of the house, whose second story is built out onto the hill. Direct center to his gaze—and ours—are two bathrooms that look out back, added later and built side-by-side for late-nineteenth-century thrift: sturdy old pipes, copper of course, wooden dadoes that Lexie and the girls papered above, marble sinks. On the south rear corner, next to one bath, is the second girl's room—Maureen's. They tend to treat her as if she's deaf; she partly acts it. She's the one resembles Doc most, temperamentally. T'other side of the other bath is the little lame one's room—a smart cricket he is—I'd trust what he tells me, nothing soppy about that little master; how did Lexie ever breed him?

As Doc stands up there—let him get this far—the front wings of the house, left and right, jut to either side in back of him, jutting forward. There's no stair-rail, never been one—he'll have to balance himself. As usual. To his left and in back of him, facing the river, is his and Lexie's room, amply made of two knocked together, the front half low and bayed, being older, the rear half high and square, to admit that old bed they picked up somewhere. Behind Doc's right elbow is the girl Chessie's room, front and north, also a bay, and a fireplace, the only upstairs one. Best is none too good for that poor girl; the mother treats her like a second wife. Between the girl and little Royal at the back on that side is the oldest boy's room—Charles. He's as much like his mother as a reasonably normal boy can be. Doesn't know that; nor does she. Duty-bound personalities, both of them. A natural sympathy exists— transferred. His to his father. Hers?—not that simple. Not easy, to have a husband who looks to his son for moral guidance. And who maybe should. Note particularly that when Charles, at twelve or so, was allotted his own room, Doc said "Should he be so near Chess?"—and she couldn't get him to explain.

The innocence of such a woman is unfathomable; believe J. J. Hoppe, it goes beyond the good. Bypasses it. But not in the style of a lady upstaging a peasant—there you'd be wrong. It's the innocence of intelligence isolated—I told her once. And she replied, her heart pink on her cheeks, and in the holy voice kept for such subjects "The three i's." She'll never get past language, that one. It's at some such trading-post that women like her generally stop for good, I told her. *Halfway*—I said. "Skirting the steppes *you* scouted at thirteen?" she answered. "Leaning into the waterfall with my collapsible cup?" . . . There you have it. And them. They waken in full flesh, those women—to their digressed lives. It sensitizes them—she saw mine. But the windings of *his* mind were closed to her. Couldn't bear to read it because she's married it?—who said that, back there? Could be you're right—little voice-in-the-crowd. Great readers, women are—but read right past the premonitory brute, always. Won't see the cheapness of circumstance. *Doc?* He's an item.

Did he first creep pitty-pat into the his-her bedroom

and see she wasn't there? Down in her city, maybe, stretching those afternoons into nights. And no one hears him. And he's home. He's never gone for the river-dom of this house like she has; the office-wing is where he's at. His profession is what keeps this strange guy mucked in reality—or did. But now he's home. In the house-by-the-river that's kept Lexie with him so long. She don't know that, yet. The house hid it from her. Just as to the very last it hid from both her and him that—nestled in its ample corners and other-century opportunities—a band of four children can and does lead a totally separate life.

Here he is though. We've followed him. Up onto the broad landing, where he stands in the not-quite dark. Suits him. Some of Doc's patients—I, Hoppe, was among them—complain he's too glad of another opinion. I like to have a man—I won't have a woman at me medically—who's definite about your disease, and about its afterlife too. Its prospects, and yours. If I'm sterile, say—should I let Lilian have the artificial impregnation she's always nagging for? Yes or no? What I want is to be recognized for the item I am. But Doc—know that niggling little catch-in-the-throat he has, always saying "what-what?" I'd say that the man himself, when it came to do this or that, was always waiting for the specialist. Well—here I am.

Here we all are, the whole town, watching. All except me prepared to pity him. Watch the door of the little center bath, I say. The daughter, Chessie, is going to come out of it.

She'll be in one of those crazy-pretty gowns of hers, and through that thin stuff it's as clear as Darwin and Krafft-Ebing both, that her long bone-structure is a ditto for Doc's. His bones are his imprint. Striking girl. After her mother worked for us, I cased the girl, looking for Lexie-spots. All in the head only, I found. Lexie's brain, the farthest-out nerves of it, in that body—and making a terrible outcry. Happens. The child in question has to make the best of it. Doc's legs look like a deer's on that girl.

And his long hands like the long hands of the Lady of Shalott—or a monk's. Going to be a swinger, that girl. Who hates men. But will sink her teeth into herself.

Go on, whisper, Grand River. *Did* the gown belong to Lex. Did the girl borrow it, like she often did with Lex. Or did Lex wear it once—and then give it to her.

And now the main whisper. Does Doc think it *is* Lex?

Really think you're going to reach an answer, folks? Agghh—townfolk.

Now then—we do know something real. What Doc said to her. From the other children? Maybe. Who knows who told who? In the end, they always tell a lot. In that kind of young circumstance. The child-guerrilla life can't last. We always get to it.

"Brought you a present," he said, in Doc's formal, even way. He has a standard voice. Can't make much of it. Something doggy about it maybe; his father was a vet. But at this point, I'd say, is when the ogre begins to form on him. Some put it further back, to the disease. Some put it even further back. Either way—Doc's going to kiss his daughter. Hear it, that little snigger?

Done. On the mouth. But *before* he recognizes her? Or—and here it comes, the little item, out of its rustproof existential file—or *then*?

Well, folks. We're a village aren't we. Of unnatural acts.

She knees him, by God. We have that on oath. Or the nearest those specialists like the one who treated her ever come to it.

("Mrs. . . . er—" they say he had the gall to ask poor Lexie, "is it true that Chessie's father made a point of teaching both her and her sister the . . . er . . . art of self-defense? Eye-thumbing, and so forth? Made them practice it? With him?" And poor Lexie, by now numb with the life of her children, those Christian guerrillas, as they have now been revealed to be, will say sardonically—with that stricken, Aesop-smile growing on her—the narrator's smile, ever in her mirror—she tells the friends who mark it, "It's *all* true.")

The town gossip, here in the hall too now, is salacious. Did Doc erect—they want to ask—wouldn't he of? Long time away, long disease. In a dirty foreign place full of dirty ideas. Give *us* an idea, Hoppe.

Fuck off. Everybody tighten your bootstraps, belt and brain, and think of your own children. Or your sacred lacks. For here comes young Charles.

And my stint's over. J. J.'s had enough. Ask *them* for the rest of it. All of them. Even him, Doc.

Will I meanwhile print my little item, as is, or otherwise? Do I ever? Unless it goes to court? I've got the story; that's enough. That's what attracted *her* to *me*, that I had them. But we're not two of a kind. She'll want to hang her story on the line, somewhere. It's hers of course. And she's not the gal to remain an item. That's what attracted *me* to her. I like metaphysical cunt. Never have any luck with it. Oh, language is acts, yes. But leave that to Wittgenstein. Between a woman and a man—it's dangerous.

So hop to it, staff. What'll I do with that item? What we always do. Bury it.

GUERRILLA
GAMES

Charles is dead asleep on Royal's bed. After nights of not having enough of it. Reading philosophy downstairs, with his ears pricked. Or lying with the door to his own room ajar, until Chess noticed. She never saying. Each time just shutting it in passing, with those airy, deft fingers of hers, never making a sound. Whenever he comes to the miniature parts of a machine he's making—a watchpin-size camshaft to be slid in, the frailest wire to be hooked—he's always asked Chess. She moves between noises—his sister. Loudness is pain to her; nobody's whisper escapes her. She always heard Dad come in, no matter how late. Lying stiff on her bed, eyes fixed on the wall. But she only began to hear voices when he left. It took Charles a long while to see why.

Meanwhile, on nights when he and Maureen and Royal find it's necessary—no need to take a vote—he shuts his own door ostentatiously and steals in to bunk with Roy. Whose nightlight insomnia is a part of the household. Roy's door can be left ajar. Roy and Chess are the poles, the constants of their team of four. For different reasons, those two have to get what they personally want. Maureen and he, Charles—the subteam—are maneuverable that way. Still, it's agreed that what he and she want for all four of them—not adult standards, never, but a cautious compliance—is now the only thing to do. Against those standards—which loom ahead of them like furniture they don't want—they're all four a united front. With an aim which for the past months has fused them even against their one-time squabbles. Which seem to him now like the cast-off mittens of four other children entirely.

Yet it's a game they're playing too, or else the three of them couldn't stand it. Or maintain it as they have. A game in which the deer is real, but he and his brother and Maureen don't hunt to kill, but to preserve. We're conservationists, he tells them: Chess can stand anything, in one way—and nothing, in another. And this house is her only preserve.

How can this be, when both their parents frighten her?

"I'm their mix," she said once, in one of those sleepwalker lulls which can come over her midsentence—when the voice takes over and meanwhile those same delicate fingers of hers, unnoticed by Chess, shred anything in them. Last week slipping her own gold watch-bracelet off and twisting it apart link by link, until he noticed. Maureen sneaked it off to the jeweler, blaming the dog. Royal, their front man, carping "He knows we don't have a dog." They'll put the repaired watchband back on Chess' dresser, and she'll say nothing. But never do that again. Whatever does this in her never tries the same thing twice. It shifts objects, and catastrophes. That's why half the time people never notice—even their mother. That's why Chess is so hard to protect. Maybe only a team like theirs, nearer to groundlevel, to childhood offenses still in the blood, and to fairy-tale belief in their own powers—could manage it as they so far have. For on the subject of those damages that inflame adults—to possessions first, and then to

· 228 ·

principles—they've all had a short but bitter lifetime of training. On how to dim back such offenses in and among the other already broken adult toys and rules of the household—or else hide them utterly.

Chess will never have to explain to him or Reeny or Royal why such a house can still be her preserve. It's theirs too.

When Dad left, she bloomed for a week. Then it got to her. What had already got to him, Charles. Finally, and with the kind help of Uncle James, it got to all of them. That Dad, if he was leaving for good, would be taking the house along with him. In similar cases along the road here, the house-as-was had never survived.

So Charles has marshaled his summer militia, from basement to attic, and now the tower, too. They're holding the fort at least until autumn, when Chess goes away to school. A freeish one, chosen by Lexie—where to be erratic is almost okay. Though there have been rumbles. Chess is never really with the others, the school reports. "Take a look at her on the playing field—she's always in back of the others. Behind. Wandering." And yes, she did those marvelous stage-sets, does those weirdly original drawings. But her school's like any school really; brilliance is never enough for them. So—off with her, to the doctor they recommend. Who tells them, and tells Lexie, who whispers it to him, Charles (in one of her frequent intra-child breaches of confidence, which all of them in turn are used to receiving): "'Get her out of that house,' the man says. But do you believe that Charles?—that the house is bad for her. This house is her refuge ... *isn't* it?" He says yes. Aggh, those doctors, Lexie says venomously—practical suggestion is not their line—and the school of course is closed. No skin off their backs. And we all know what it took in the first place, to get Chess to go there. How last summer, her first year away, healthy as she seemed when she came home, they all saw her deep relief as the house closed over her. Closed. Charles understood that, though in him it is only a tendency. The call of the place where you are ultimately known. In a way, every other place to come will involve pretense.

So, in summer, Chess' strangeness—which Reeny hates and fears, Royal dissects and Charles himself half-deifies and groans for—belongs to them. Their team is Royal the medic, Maureen the nurse if ever to be needed, himself the manager—and Chess. Chess is the quarry, and the goal. She has to outwit them—and the part of her that's on their side—as she can. She's under a spell she can't stop. They understand that. Even Reeny's "Why *can't* she—" is no longer sighed. At the same time, they're compelled to help her stop—and to pick up after her, repairing what can't be helped. And to keep the whole proceedings—a parade that starts up again, like a millwheel, every morning—from the powers above. The team-members understand each other completely. Including Chess.

But he's exhausted. So is Maureen, who has never given her full approval. Concealment of any kind assails her own timid hope to be an ordinary adult, which to her is now the apex. Royal is not emotional, maybe too young for it. He himself is at the breaking point of energy and fidelity. Both. He can feel the long muscles of maturity forming in his arms and in his thoughts; he's eighteen. He's got to break with this cops-and-robbers posturing of childhood, and yet he yearns to keep it on; it belongs to the soul, to a purity he doesn't want to leave behind. It's what Chess has, at her worst and at her best, undivided—but kept together as one by her madness. It's what he admires her for. But why does such purity of intent, of vision, create only mayhem and despair around it?

To have no one to ask is what's breaking him. No one to share Chess with. Her energy is endless. She's possessed; he knows that. Her demon, which may destroy her, never tires. When under its dominion, wandering the house dressed in shorts maybe, in dead of a winter night

· 230 ·

when the furnaces are banked—she's not even cold. He marvels that the adults haven't noticed this among all her other oddities.

Royal's noting all of these down, for his future medical purposes. How for instance, at the very times when she's her old humorous, cynic self—funny as hell, sharp as any customer and saner than anybody—her tall frame locomotes badly. As if it has to be kept shyer than her brain. She has the best legs of any girl in town, but shuffles them. Yet when Chess is in trouble—a phrase they took from Lexie—she moves like a starved beauty, a power thinning to its own wraith. Hormones, we bet, Roy says primly. "I discuss it with James." Swearing that he's not told James what's going on. True or not, Charles envies him. Royal's done what he hasn't yet but knows he's going to; he can't yet face how, or when. Royal's deserting, to the other side.

Lexie's going to be hardest to convince. Their whole technique of hiding Chess, of alternately not noticing and over-noticing, comes from his mother; teamwork has only extended it. Nowadays to beyond where it should sanely go; he knows that. "Chess is exactly like me when I was young," their mother's always said. But he and Maureen and Royal are *not* like Chess. Though young. It hurts them, that she won't let herself see that. "Chess is in trouble," Lexie'll whisper to him at some town affair where they're all together as a family—the PTA auction at Royal's grammar-school, the Democrats' bazaar. "Go cope, please, will you? Bring her over to your friends." Or in reverse, she'll even make use of Royal's limp. "Chess, *dance* with him."

They're coping. When, early one morning, one of Lexie's treasured pair of Sandwich lamps was there on the livingroom floor, laid oddly prominent on the rug, the glass-bowl part unbroken but wrenched away from its brass stem, who sneaked it up to his workroom and fixed it before "anybody" came in?—while Reeny half-closed the sliding doors and watched, and in the kitchen Royal kept his mother occupied. They've each and all become masters of the sudden fit of bawled song, or of clomping like troglodytes—while the unmissed third of their trio spirits away father's desk-obelisk, lying on the mat outside his shut office, or the piano-score scrawled all over with pencil. Or while the two others slip away to stand worriedly outside Chess' door. "Teeen-age weirdos!" their mother says fondly, a gold shine in her eye, in her alto-happy voice. "You're *all* nuts."

They've given up counting how many poltergeist events there have been since the lamp—or must have been before. That incident's now merely the one marking when they first knew it must be Chess. He's since read up on poltergeists. "Fleers against the family," one Scottish account said. Hers aren't always committed at night. And the train of them—or what you'd have to call the theme of them—changes. Often in tune with outside incident. When Kellihys' burned, for instance, the breakages stopped. The little fires began. Always—as if carefully—when they and their mother were in the house. Never when Lexie and Chess were alone there, or when everybody was going to be out. A little pile of shavings in a corner, once. A pile of clothes—an apron of Lexie's, an old hat of Ray's—smoking, not too negligently, in Chessie's own fireplace. While she sat, downstairs.

"Ah c'mon Chess," he said to her direct—she'll take it, from him—"gonna burn the old folks, do it outside." She'd let him clean it up. Listening mocking, but satisfied. Now nothing may happen for a day or two, but no longer is there a week or two between episodes. Getting shorter between; that scares him. Conversely, he's finding he can say anything to her, and does, kidding from a tight chest. "Stop this jazz, will you Sis; it's wearing us out." Or brashly "No look, *stop* it with the knives. Gives Reeny the creeps. And what are we going to do for steak?" For kitchen knives are being displayed on hearths and bathroom-floors, across a desk. And putting things back is beginning not to be the answer. Unless they can turn the house right side up, as fast as she can turn it inside out. As he's learning with a sinking heart, the rate at which order can be restored after riot is never proportionate.

And sinking him ever lower is the slow, oncoming knowledge that she is grateful when charged. That she wants desperately, yes, to have her trouble recognized. That though she can be actressy through all of this, in some last trapped corner she's not acting. That most of all she wants to be *coached*—on what she's done. Above those long, thickly lashed brown eyes, the wing-shaped double space below the brow pinkens, with thanks. Behind the full, rebel mouth is a tremor, of a girl shaking violently in her effort to be—with others. While back of those cold cheeks, somewhere behind those features, though he can never place where, is the emanation she wants wrested from her. Love. It's why he's sure she will never hurt anybody, any of them.

"Chess, don't threaten us," he says desperately, once. Picking up the largest of the knives yet, on a landing. "Do something nice." And openmouthed, hears, distanced in her throat, a ventriloquist *Thanks*. And she does do it, cooking breakfast like a chef from a far heaven for three days running—lingonberry pancakes, French toast flavored with kirsch, stuffed omelets, until they have to beg her to let down and she says, trembling "No, I better not."

Even her cooking—inspired, Lexie calls it—is on the edge. Who stuffs omelets with cream, like gratitude melting? Or puts buttered mushrooms, like love-tokens, in the oatmeal? "Cook away," he said, giving her a peck—he was the only one who could—"but spare me the honey on the radishes"—a conceit of his own—and she smiled.

When she's like that, it's hard to remember her as ever any other way. It's then she'll write the parody of *Pamela* on which her English teacher will mark "A clear, clean prose, almost as eighteenth-century as the original, yet yours. And publishable, gal." It's then that Chess, showing this to him scornfully, will march to her desk, twine herself there, scratching her hair into a haystick tumble, all of her gone soft and ordinary as any dormitory girl, and write two cool paragraphs that sends them both into stitches—a parody of the English teacher, signed "Gal." At these blessed times he'll bring his own term-papers to her for grammatical correction, which she will do thoughtfully— an artisan, without pride.

When the bad times come on her, he thinks "How could I ever forget? How could she?"

For even then, she never loses rationale. Rather, it's as if the icy grip of the consecutive holds her in thrall; she's remembering the black logic that other people forget.

It's then he begins to surmise that the logic of the technically sane, even of the greatest, must have some little human stumble in it to keep them so. Each of the rigorous philosophers he sinks into for their mollifying ache of wonder, must have had it—exactly like the flaw which appears in each one of his own machines, work well though they do. So that, from Hobbes to Hume to Kant, and all those before and after, the universal spaces can be passed on for study—even to a lowly student-reader like him. Otherwise, without such a stumble, each one of those superheads could have turned the universe inside out— leaving only a circled black hole for those afterward. In mechanics, call the flaw simply a lack of perpetual motion. A machine has pathos, he often feels, watching one— because it's only the sum of all its parts; even if each of these be perfect, the total fact of them will one day do it in.

Among these men, whose great heads range his own prospects like the severed stone heads bordering a picture he has of the Bodleian Library at Oxford (where he secretly wants to go)—what would be the common flaw, always transferable? Even to Schopenhauer (on whom he, Charles, is doing a thesis for the scholarship competition which might get him there), passed on even to that anti-philosopher, who tried do the whole works in—one small hitch which made his try impossible. He still had enough self-compassion to live.

She doesn't have it. He should write his thesis on her.

If he could only give her some. Of that most ordinary life-stuff. Which any clod has, but she doesn't. What appears to be her monstrous ego, dominating him and the others, is only the shadow of a vacuum, on the edge of which she's pedaling for dear life, in order to stay with them. And she's twice as vulnerable to suggestion as other people. Or magnetically so, in a complete radius. Sooner or later, at some hint from outside her, the dark needle within her—points.

The voices she hears have been the worst for them. Because they themselves at first believe in them. Even now they never doubt that she hears. In the main it is Lucy, a girl from her school, who calls and calls. "She keeps calling me." On the telephone, they think—as who wouldn't—though they're never there when it rings for her. The legend of Lucy that she tells them is vivid and elusive at the same time. Lucy wants something; she comes to their house for it, but never while they're there. She's immured at home—an apartment in New York—and yet on the loose. She's here, in the house. "Where?" they said, and went to find her. They even had an image of her—a rich girl, who had to cadge carfare. That day, they had all been in the house since the day before. They'd marked off the house, in territories. Rambling as it was, could it hide a stranger from them, with their years of hide-and-seek here? "The summer kitchen!" Royal said—he's covered twice as much ground as anybody. But of course she wasn't there. The only place she can be is in Chess' room, with Chess.

"Gone," said Chess. "She got scared." She shrugs. "Let her spend the night somewhere. Maybe behind my fireplace." And just in time, she grins. But they've caught her. In her own room.

Charles looks at the scrawling on the wallpaper—or as drawn, behind it.

Only Royal has the heart to be indignant. "Just yesterday I asked Roddy Kellihy. Whether he'd seen her go in or out of our house. A girl with short blond hair."

Charles himself is ashamed, abased. As they get ever closer to Chess, is it better for her, or worse? Does she still feel safe in the house? Or should she be wrested out of it? If she were to be . . . He sees her—the big, serene doll she can be in her calm moments—packaged somehow like that forever, off in some other place. She was always the quietest, most beautiful baby of them all, Lexie always said; should she get away from Lex? From both of them? With each parent, the getting away would have to be different. Or would it be no use? In any case, would the black needle, swinging slowly—point?

She never feels the need of redress though. To them, the parents. As when he leaves here, will surely happen to him. Chess thanks no one, for being born.

College will rescue him. He feels guilty for being glad. But how he wishes he belonged to one of those families— loving enough, far as he can see, or even fatly quarrelsome—who tentacle more healthily to outside life than to themselves and their own language. He has two friends like that, whom he admires but is mum with—and one like himself, with whom he has long talks.

Rocky's family are devout Catholics, but at Charles' age Rocky is already out of there, into a commune and living with a Jewish girl. "Roz's family's the same tight bunch as mine though; they take communion together night and morning—the rest of the world can talk to them later. *You* know, Chuck." It's a relief to nod. "Used to think that was all to the good," Rocky says. "We-uns against the world. Or before the rest of it." Rocky's father and the girl's are both lawyers, which Rocky is studying to be, though working in her father's office because his own mother won't let his own father do that for him now, or let Rocky back in the house.

"Mariolatry is what it is," Rocky said this afternoon, waggling his beard at him, over a beer. The commune's livingroom, in a cupolaed old house up the hill that eight couples have rented together, is neat as a pin. "Mary-what?" he asks. The girls who stay home—at least half the group's—are in their own confab. They all know he has to get away from his own house, though not why. How sweet and open they are, moving like reeds in their own rhythm. "Cult of Mary, to you Charles. You Protestants mightn't know it but you're living under it, just the same. Your mother's thin, and goes to college. Mine's fat, and goes to church. Roslyn's mother is a member of the League of Women Voters of Great Neck—and is fat or thin, depending. But they all three of them set the moral tone of their house." Across the room the girls are now stretching a quilt or a canvas across some kind of loom. Two of them are in granny-skirts. Two are in halters and shorts. Roz, Rock's girl, is instructing them. "I'm kicked out of our house because of it," Rocky grins, proud. "And into Roz's Dad's office because *her* mother thinks I'll marry her. Right, Roz? And you, Chuck. You not careful, you gonna stay on to be head of your house, because of it." They know about his father. Not about Chess. Half the commune says he can come live there, if he wants to get out and can get a job; half says he can't come unless he brings a girl—a single would change the atmosphere.

"Mariolatry" he says, savoring it. He likes the longer words; they reach for him like pairs of hands, out of the mists of the philosophical systems he's been reading in, all these stretched, prickling nights. It's the universes which are stretching themselves before his very eyes, drawing him into the superspaces. *Logical positivism. Categorical imperative. Epistemological*—anything. He rarely looks the words up. His sense of the world is under his skin and only

· 237 ·

hunting its embodiment—let the surrounding text bear up the meaning and bring it to him. He feels like a trial-meet swimmer, training beforehand in the backstroke, the freestyle, the butterfly, not only to qualify but to find his stroke.

"The moral tone of a—" he says. In the kitchen at home, Lexie, cleaning the sink, telling Maureen once again how many teaspoonsful for the cocoa, says "Royal! Take those steps one at a time." Tiptoes past him—you can get away with anything with her, if you're reading a book; sighs after his father's retreating back, "All right, Raymond. Only *tell* me," slaps his own face for the dirty word on it, moons out at the river like a hunger-marcher looking for an imperial palace, and leans back in to the ping-pong table, saying "All right, Charles. Now teach me to slam!"

He's finished his beer. "I know how they do it, sure. But why?" Across the room, the girls shriek at him. "Because you men wouldn't let us do *more*! . . . Because that's all there *is*." Roz, natty in a pair of the leather jeans she stitches for herself and Rock, looks up from her canvas. "Was, girls. *Was*." Rocky puts up a ducking elbow. "Right, right. But save it, will you girls. Look, there's only two of us."

When the three men who work at night come sleepily down the stairs, craving supper, he and Rock and they go out to the garage, where Rocky's stashed a bottle his father gave him. "Dad comes over here all the time." They pass the bottle. "The girls won't drink whiskey anyway. Say it destroys the braincells. They won't even get stoned any more. Say it's bad for the genes." Through the kitchen window they can see the girls' heads, bent now over supper, dreamy and reserved. Sweethearts, all of them. If Chess were like them, if only. His throat aches, guiltily. For himself. "Your Dad not back yet, huh," Rock says. "Look maybe you could start out here, as a single. We'll work on it. Maybe we can swing the girls."

On the way home, he half yearns for it, heavy with what's coming at him. Then thinks, no—not with that group, great as they are. Roz or no Roz, they're too Catholic. Or call it that. Driving into his own driveway, he starts to laugh. At how Catholic those little darlings still are. Two hours out of here and he gets back his own jokes. Unfair, Immanuel Kant, yes, unfair. Since his own house is what gave him his jokes. He can hear his mother saying it to him after one of his schoolfights, or a sister-fight, or even one with her. "All right, Charles? Got back your jokes?"

Lexie's not in the kitchen, but waiting for him on the porch, in that soiled purple wrapper they all hate. For demeaning her. For her clinging to it. Rather let her drive to New York even, looking like somebody's girlfriend. As one day Chess at her most sensible slyly had said. Waving his mother good-bye that day, he saw she'd learned how to corner the Volvo. Oh, let her return looking even the way she did for a while, as Royal said with a leer to him, "Cherry ripe." Just let her not look as low and bedraggled as these days. Or as hard. Back then, at least Dad was here. Nowadays Royal has even curlier theories. Sitting at the top of his bed the other night, he'd said thoughtfully to Charles, who'd wound himself in a ball at the bottom, "I figured Chess would be better though. Now that Mom isn't getting any."

It took Charles a minute to catch on; then he said as venomously as whispering allowed, "If it wasn't I needed you for guard, I'd knock you back where that came from." No, Royal said testily in his regular voice. "It wasn't James. Nobody gives *me* credit." Then froze and grabbed up his side of the blackjack deal, ready on the bedspread in case Chess came round the door. No—nothing. Not that night. But Royal's the best guard of any of them.

"That you Charles?" his mother says from the porch when he comes in from Rocky's. "Ah. You're back. The girls are getting ready for the Village Hall. Or Maureen is

. . . Look—Charles—?" She doesn't even hear the desperation in her voice.

He straightens to it. "Okay, *okay,* I'll handle it. You going to the Kellihys'?" He hates even to say their name. "Me?" she says. "No." And tightens the wrapper. He wants to give her a joke. "Why don't you get out of that thing," he hears himself say. "Know what Rocky says? He says you set the moral tone of this household." Her mouth falls open, aghast. His too.

So, tonight, he's coped. Twice. First, at the Hall, among all the old biddies smirking at Chess—then afterwards. When, after their midnight cocoa, Royal sneaks to him. "*Lucy* is back."

Chess is in the library, sitting formally in her crushed brown hat, which tilts past the angle of chic. Reeny's wail when they left—"That's cra-zee!" hasn't changed it, nor the biddies either. The strange, peaked antique dress, with its mournful bandings, hangs on her, irretrievably smart. So that, either way, she'd caught the attention she can never quite bear.

The three of them surround her. We aren't cornering her—any more than she corners herself, he thinks. Any truth that they tell her, she knows already, better than they do. But we have to tell her. For our own sake. She puts *our* world in jeopardy. Our system. We have to speak. We don't hear Lucy. But we too have the right. Not to.

"Chess—" he says, stepping forward as the elder. "We-re—giving up."

At his voice, Maureen steps to his side. She teeters there, on the edge of his confidence. "I can't take it any more either. You're treating us like we don't count. Me. Like we're dirt." She falls back.

He's amazed. Maureen's never spoken up for her life before. Chess has forced it.

And here comes Royal, always slickly mum, stepping forward too. On him it looks threatening. On his little brother Roy.

"Giving up?" Chess says. In her lap, the thin, blueish fingertips which finesse machines for him are turned up, yes, like a doll's. Immobility is what she can't shake. "On me?" He can see it's a relief. And then she trembles.

"Never on you, Sis." Only on the chase. "Ohhhh, Sis." Maureen, the fountain.

But even Chess knows her sister's tears are never for herself. "It's Royal, don't you see? Don't trust him. He wants to put me in a hospital." She slants at him, contemptuous. "Like him."

"But you're healthy." Maureen turns. "Do you, Roy? She's stronger than any of us."

"Not in his kind of hospital. I told you." Chess is white. "The kind Lexie worked in. Royal fools all of you. He'll be the kind of doctor wants everybody sick. And none of you see why."

"I will not." He's still a little guy. They tend to forget that. His lower lip is even fluttering. "Why would I?"

"To pay for your foot." She tosses it casually. Beyond rancor—what nobody's ever dared to say. Her sanity is awesome. There's too much of it. Nobody can stand that much, Charles thinks.

She turns to him. She always knows what he thinks. "Charles . . . Charles?"

"I *have* to. If it goes on." He squeezes his eyes shut, hard. "I'm going to have to . . . welsh. *Chess.*"

She sits there. Then puts out a hand to him, soothing. "Don't worry. They're leaving, you know . . . You'll *all* leave. But first—Lexie." She has a bitter way with Lexie's name, behind Lexie's back. Like a magic formula, being tested. "L-Lexie," she says now, As if their mother's standing there. She hunches. Casting about, side to side, to each of them. Asking *them.* He can't close his eyes. She makes a humble little mmm—aaa of pain, never heard before. "Maybe—could I stay—on?"

Not even babyish. The real voice from the womb? Calling, beyond all jokes.

"We two could get jobs and live together. In town. We'd make them let us," Maureen says, stalwart. "Even in the fall. If you could've only kept that job. I know I could get one." Maureen reminds him of those girls in the commune. He's seeing them all through a long, dark telescope. All of what's happening. It could only happen in a family as close as them.

"What would she do about Lucy?" Royal says. His eyes screw cleverly.

And what will we do, about him? Our little brother, who isn't a traitor really, or a liar per se. But was born a little cheap. As if the foot itself had shriveled because the makings gave out.

Chess stands up, tall. But not moving an inch toward him. Whichever her state of being, she has the breadth. Of a terrible openness maybe. But almost significant. "She went. For good."

"Yah, she was at the Village Hall. You said you saw her. Minute you got inside the door."

"*Stop* it, Roy," his brother says.

"No one confronts it," Royal's high, mimic voice says. "Only me."

The two others gape at the cheek of him.

He's right. But why does it have to be him?

Nobody stops him from nearing Chess. Or sneering up at her. "How's she come and go, huh, and none of us sees her. Or hears. On a UFO maybe? What kind of voice does she have anyway, this Lucy?"

"Soft. But *I* hear her." She shrinks from him. To Charles. "I *hear* her." Is he flagging?—she's mutely asking. People's energies flag after they've been with her for awhile—she knows that. Lowering her eyes, she dwindles. Sits down again in the chair. Her hat and dress follow her, loyally.

"Chess. What does she want? What's she *saying*?"

She sits there bowed. A little croak comes out, human though. "*'Help.'*"

He almost understands how it is. Must be. To be all metaphor, inside one's self. So much so that all the masked meanings scramble one another, in the radio sense. Not via one powerful beam in the brain—like Russia turning Radio Free Europe's broadcast into anti-sense. No, his sister's body is all metaphor *physically*, every sensation maybe received doubly, triply, or in itself phantomized. Her own body's the vacuum—full of electronic, electrochemical cries. So that the struggle in her brain—to keep to the simple meanings which other persons level at her in their modest unsick way—may be one of the most valiant in life. So that at times, trembling in one's resonant flesh, one can only immobilize. Or report one's body from that distance where the brain recoils from the symphonic horrors offered it.

So that Chess sits there, two feet from him, entowered in her Babeled flesh. Doomed—by her power of reason—to carry on. And by *them*.

His mouth awry at the suffering, he kneels to her. He will force the halved metaphor together.

She knows. She's ready. Reaching up, her tapered fingers shaking, she straightens her hat.

"Lucy?" he says.

$\mathbb{A}$ nd now little Lord Royal, awake and collating at the head of the long brass bed, twice his own length, at whose feet Charles lies drugged—hears something. Like any good doctor, he doesn't want to wake an exhausted sleeper unnecessarily. And he understands the quality of Charles' sleep. His city visits to James—those peeps into James's office and the international parliament of medicine, or into the carefully unreeled documentary of James's own experience—are to him an introductory internship. These nights here, out and abroad on the plains of a family chase, are his laboratory. In which he alone isn't terrorized. Even when he's in hospital for himself, observation is his power-reserve. Which the mushy nurses applaud as bravery. Mean as his sister Chess can be, she understands him better than anybody. For study, what good are the healthy? Sick people are his health. As long as he can have a light on at night.

And of course he's a better guard than Charles. One must not *care,* James says—it spoils the vision. One must observe. Royal agrees. But Charles is wrong to worry that he would ever give James valuable information. Which might someday contribute to a thesis of his own. On how it can be that a person with Chess' trouble—he'll have to say "disease," naturally—understands him, them all, better than anyone.

Yes—there's somebody down by the road. Although this room's in the rear, the long central hall acts like a sounding-board, bringing in every river-enlarged trespass, to be enlarged by the hill at the back. If you hold quiet, you can hear the river lap. Yes, somebody's on the porch. Not Lexie's step. A man's. With his mother probably, who'll be barefoot in her usual way. Which she has no idea embarrasses them—Maureen especially. It's a wonder she wears shoes to the city. Or would be, if he didn't know what she goes there for. Which Chess took pains to tell them all. She watches her mother like a jealous twin, whom nothing escapes.

"Your sister Chess wants to get back inside her mother," James has told him. "They say we all do—but this is different." James has told him a lot. "Chess is frightened of her too," Royal told him. "Ah, all we family members lie heavily on each other," James said, pushing him past an usher's glare at the Academy of Medicine, where James was going to speak. "That's because we know each other's sicky secrets. Like I know for how long you wet the bed. But that needn't matter now we're friends, eh? Eh?" James's face up there, like a hawk in a dinnerjacket, did give him the jumps. "No," he'd said coolly. "Now that I've stopped." Adding to himself: And once I get something on *you*.

Very delicately, he'd reported some of this to his mother. "Family?" she said. "They accuse you. And only they can soothe." But she bypassed him, on any dirt about James. He'll have to wait until he gets to live in James's house.

He can see why Chess admires his mother, and hates her too—for being the healthier twin. And if what James says is true—as a kind of castle where you want to hide and they can't let you. "Oh, Chessie does want to get away, deep down," he told James jauntily. "Everybody sees it—except Lex." Who James says keeps all knowledge of Chess underground. "As her all-but-mirror-image, which she cannot accept. Can you understand that, nephew?" Roy isn't sure. "Well if you were my son, say—" James says, bearing so hard on Royal's shoulder that he slipped going up the city morgue's steps. "Sorry. If you were my firstborn boy, say. And *I* had a foot."

After a bit, Royal said he did understand. Inside the morgue, he kept unusually quiet. It was certainly the place for it. He didn't blanch at the sights, not even the pickled ones. James was proud. "Not like your Dad."

Outside, James picked up on Your Mother, again. It was almost his favorite subject. "They're disturbingly alike, Royal. Both powerhouses. But Lexie's going to make it. Chessie's a powerhouse blocked. You must prepare yourself, Royal. I fear your mother *is* going to make it—out of there."

Roy almost giggles. It's fine training for a psychoanalyst. *I fear,* his uncle said.

Nodding now at the chrome nightlamp whose shade refers back his image, he's serious. Chess *is* prepared. How *she'll* leave, is what he has to watch.

Careful not to wake Charles, he eases his good foot to the floor, then his other, and goes to his desk for one of the notebooks he never bothers to hide. They think him too young to be investigated, or to be interesting; he counts on it. Since he has few resources as yet, the house being his lab, nothing in the natural funk of a household is ordinary to him. Opening a folder of data on the secondary body secretions—on ear-wax, which is suspected of some correlation with breast-cancer in women, and on what the British call toe-jam, whose possible harmony with the environment nobody seems to have followed—he turns to some recent notes on the menstrual cycles of his women. An overheard remark of his mother to Chessie—that they're so alike they even menstruate at the same time—has put him onto it. Maureen's not in on that cycle far as he can tell. But since she's too neat to leave things lying about, and her general gush conceals her emotions, she's a norm he won't much bother with. The other two are what fascinate him.

It's been easy. Chess is so careless in the bathroom. And his mother so frank, about everything. Since Lexie sleeps like the drained dead at these times, and his father used to give her otherwise inexplicable iron shots, they were all told early about the functions of women—which openness his father pretended to approve. Though his mother's unconcern about her nudity drives his father wild. She twits him with it; has a thing for it. Still flitting naked across the hall to the bathroom—except at those times. His father hates it when his mother comes to dinner in bare feet. If you ask Royal, it's not natural of either of them.

But Chess, during her and Lexie's joint periods—which according to his record have synchronized four times out of the past seven—is much calmed. Except when Lexie goes to the city. To have lovers, Chess repeated, moral and hating. She plans to find out who Lexie meets, and call them up. And someday, she says, she'll do the same as Lex. Maureen wouldn't believe any of it. "You just came on *early.*" Reeny said.

"Does father know?" he'd asked. He was a year younger then. *"Him?"* Chess said. And Reeny shut her up.

Charles thinks father does know. Though Charles never will discuss it. Who Charles hates is Bets Kellihy. And what he calls the whole bog-rotten clan over there. Though he has a soft spot for Arthur, who makes him laugh. Arthur has a harder time than any poor butler should, Charles says. "But you go over there once more though, to bathe Dodo, I'll beat the hell out of you." That kid from the Missionary Institute, older than most paper-boys, and a little odd from religion maybe; Charles was sent to pay him once. "Pay him for the Kellihys' too—" Lexie said "—the boy looks so miserable." Charles came back saying "The sods. The stinking sods." Not to worry, his mother said. "We'll get it back, from Bets."

Does Charles know about his father and Bets? There's an innocence about his brother which awes Royal. Or a willingness to believe the best. When he asked Chess she snapped, "Look in your notebooks." She knows Royal's worth investigating. She knows everything.

"Lexie'll go to the party," she said tonight. "You'll see. She'll even wear shoes to it." Why else were they being packed off?—she said. Not just for them to be like other kids—hand it to Ma, she never did that to them. Chess, before going to the Hall, finally convinced to, is haughty, mocking. And in her own far-out eye marvelously dressed. Siding with Reeny, he isn't so sure. "The lunks won't get it," Chess says airily. "But somebody will." And one older boy had. But by that time, Lucy had arrived. And came all the way home with her.

When Charles knelt to her, saying what he said, he and Reeny held their breath. Would Chessie rage, stalk off, or retreat? In their span she's done all of these. But never what they expect.

She said nothing. But her lips formed an Oh. She put out her hands, slowly, across something. Charles grasped them. The two of them held on. Like lightning, then, she broke away, leaping. Calling out, "'Love and Friendship'!" They ran to the piano together and played it—as they had in their earlier teens. A Schubert duet with much crossing-over of hands. Higher and higher. Round and round. Loud. "Louder than the party!" she called. The music from the party wasn't much yet—only a fever-clink sound of people, that stole in from next door and ripped off their silence, giving them nothing in return.

Afterwards, she had a lovely, sleepy sanity they'd never glimpsed before. And was easily urged to bed. Usually nobody ever succeeded in urging Chess. "Yes, sleepy," she said, closing her door on them. But she left on her light. From the library window below her bedroom, the three of them saw the light falling on the grass, a shaft from the baywindow. Was she sitting there again? Charles on other nights has sneaked out the back way and out to the front; but one couldn't see from the lawn. Out on the road, any passerby, walking either north or south, must see her. And be seen. So they'd have to take her on trust. For the night.

But when the three of them leaned in from the library window, it came Royal's time. "I can tell you where Lucy lives."

Charles haggardly stared at him. "Don't you be fancy. I'm walking on my eyelids. Where?"

Royal led them there.

The tower is bare. No drawing materials, even no chair. The deep-ledged window looks out into the treetops like a pulpit in the air, with no sense of the house below. By day one can see north to the Kellihys' rolling lawn, to the east, the wavering river and its far shore. Between it and them across the road, and directly in front of them, and some yards south of the white cottage opposite Kellihys' where the retarded boy is sat every morning—is the high, dipping-off bank they call the dock. The tower walls are newly white and clean, left so by the last workman. In the middle of the floor are the roll of masking-tape he asked for, the handled blade he chipped the panes clear with, a dried-up paintbucket and a flyswatter—all of which belong to them. The bucket is upended. Why would she sit up there though? Chess hates heights.

"Shhh, she'll hear us. We're right over her head."

They aren't; they're off side. But it gave him kind of a thrill to say so.

"She said she'd sleep," Charles says. "We have to trust her. Not just act as if we do. It's the only way, with Chess." He stares out the dark window. "With them."

So he's admitting it. What Royal's been telling him. Suddenly he stepped back from the window and turned off the light. The long chain hanging down from the oldfashioned ceiling-bulb swayed between them in the dark.

"Somebody out there, Charlie? . . . Is it her?" Once, at the beginning of her trouble, her first night home from school she did that, raging out into the winter road and away from Dad. Standing out there, refusing to come in. Charles had finally persuaded her to.

"No. Come on, let's go down."

"Who was it?"

"Some man. And some woman. Going down to the dock."

"Lemme see." But the ledge is too high and deep. He can't see over it. He lifts his hod-foot; he can't get up there alone. And Charles, staring him down, won't help.

They tiptoed down the stairs, passing Chess' door, which was still closed, and on down the hall to his own room.

Charles is certainly white-looking. He collapses on the bottom of the bed. "Shut-eye. I've got to." But it seems he can't.

"You going to snitch on Chess, then," Royal says, warily, "or aren't you?"

"To who?" Charles grinds. "Who's there to snitch to? To James?" And after a while, he does sleep.

You can't really depend on anybody except yourself. And your notebook. Which now advises Royal—in between some notes he took at James's lecture and a dainty drawing of Dodo Kellihy's privates—that yes, according to his mother's dates, she is in a proper physical state to receive a man if she finds one. So it was Lexie out there. With some man from the party. He can always read Charles.

And now, listen man. That couple. They're coming into the house. The guy is, for sure. And he wouldn't be here without Lex. His mother's as lightfooted as Chess. Some mothers in a room are like mountains to climb over, but his mother lets them forget her presence. When other kids are in the house, she sinks back even; she is the mother-wraith. A light sorrow presses his chest. All his friends compliment him, on her good taste.

He knows the quality of Charles' sleep. His brother's forehead is already lined like a thirty-year-old's. How must it feel, to care like that; to have an aristocratic self which won't lie? Which can't?

"Charlie. Wake up."

He's sleeping against his fist. The eyes open, blank.

He wipes the wet from his mouth, smiling. "The in . . . tense inane."

"What?"

"I was walking up it. Up a pure stair." He doesn't move.

"Listen." He whispers it. "Somebody's out on the porch. They're coming in."

When the front door is shut down below, however quietly, a shock of air travels up the stair, all the way to the back, to warn. The old house cooperates.

Charles can't wake. He turns his head from side to side, to show he can't.

"*I* can't go," Royal hisses, raising his foot. "I make too much noise. And we have to. We have to know everything."

"Chess?" his brother says drunkenly. "Oh Chrise."

He put his mouth to his brother's ear. "Lexie and a guy, I think. It was them outside before, wasn't it. She's bringing him in . . . Chess'll go off her rocker . . . Go on out. We got to."

Charles is on his feet.

"Here," Roy breathes, holding out his brother's glasses. But his brother's already out there.

Roy waits, his eyes bright. He has to know. Everything.

At the back of the long hallway a minute later Charles stands, swaying a little. The long dark passage is like the universe he's been climbing in sleep, the same faint parallels converging on the ever-receding illusion nipped between them—a logical space draining toward an end conceivable.

Is that it—a man and a woman—or a girl—clasped, and musically grunting? The image at the top of the stair?

Inconceivable. Don't look at it. Turn back.

In Royal's room, he fell on the bed again.

"Who was it?" Royal whispers in his ear. "Was it them?" At no reply he mouths inaudibly, "*Lexie* and a guy? I only *heard* a guy." He is watching himself in his chrome lamp.

"Gimme my glasses." Charles put them on.

That's the way to look at it. Lexie, made young by midnight grace. And the anonymous man he saw from the tower, going down to the dock with her. Now brought into the house.

Not his own father. With Chess.

Parallel lines. Which way will he have it?

He's awake. He stands up, gripping the brass knob of the bed until fingers smart. He grips harder. It *was* Chess. And his father is home.

Choose, Charlie. In the lamp surface, Roy's warped face is waiting.

"Must have been. Them."

Downstairs, the door hushed closed. A man, going down the porch steps. With familiar tread. A guy, his father. Gone.

Royal hasn't moved. A beetlewatcher, his arm slows wavily now in front of his mouth. His lower jaw drops, a mandible. At the same time, he grasps his left ankle with the other hand, laying himself along the bad leg in the exercise which both eases and stretches its shortened tendon. The angle of the foot is such that he can touch his chin to its arch. He rests there, goggling. "Well—now we know."

The doctor is sitting on his own steps. Behind him, at the head of the flagged path, a second flight of five broad wooden ones leads to the wide porch that encircles the house. At the path's bottom where he is, four high, narrow stone steps, early ones, lead sharply up from the road to the rise of land where the house is. All the old houses here have them. He is sitting on the top one, between two stone pillars. Added by some pretentious turn-of-the-century owner, he's never thought of them as his own, or as belonging to the real house. Tonight he leans against the nearer pillar, his head between his knees, his wrists crossed over his genitals, trying not to retch. Don't keep touching where it hurts, a doctor has to say, day after day. Tongue away from that sore; stop picking that scab. Hands off your eyes; stop rubbing them. Don't keep trying to press it, that lump you didn't know you had.

The pain in his groin is ebbing; he misses it, wishing he'd retched. Where does it hurt, still hurt? Where's his injury? In the fatherhood? In the familyhood. *Where, oh where*—goes the song his mother sang—*has my little girl gone?* His own mother never had a little girl, except herself. What is a father? What is a family? He grasps the round stone ball on the righthand pillar, pushing his head against it. And again. The other stone ball waits for him. Everything's touching him. Everything wants an answer, at once.

All he'd wanted was to give her the same kiss he always had, since her beginning. The kiss on the two-year-old top of her head where the single curl used to be. The hugged one for the mitten searching in what she herself had named his "candy-pocket." The absentminded evening kisses, the graduation one—where had they gone? When?

"Brought you a present?" He knows he said that. But which present had he had in mind? The earrings? Or the portfolio?

Or was it the fault of the damn nightgown?

When did he know it was Chess? How long after did the kiss go on? *When* did his arms tighten, his mouth bruise down?

He groans. That sound he made. Just before he knew it was Chessie? Or just after he knew it wasn't Lex? He can still hear it. He's never made a sound like that one before. Or has he? Who's he asking, pleading with?

Borden Wheeley would know. "Wey-*ull* . . . Lookit ole candy-pocket. Transplantin' pussy, right in his own house."

And then she kneed him. A pure action, straight from the adrenalin. As taught.

It was a kiss from Spain, polymorphous for all of them.

Whatever. Whichever. Chess will know.

As her doctor explained to him, that kind of straddle is *what* she does know, the very crux of her mental life. She sees the doubling alternative too clear—and everywhere. "It's why she can never decide, never choose a path. We have to bring them together for her. If we can."

"What a god-damn statement," he'd said to Lexie that night, reporting, their arms linked. The psychiatrist linked them, every time, in a glossy hatred they could share. "If you see anything clear, oughtn't you hang *onto* it?" she'd answered. In what James called her on-the-barricades voice. "If you see *anything.*"

It's all coming back to him. Home. A place where it never stays as dark any more, or as light, as it once did, Lexie said not long ago. Much of what she says has either no meaning to him, or an inaccessible one, but still sheds an aura that clings. Any room where his wife is seems always messy with her shadow—along with those shadowy women she ranges always beside her, related or not. Energy streams from her, centerless—one day a bilge-stench, the next a sporadic perfume. When she does chop logic—and she can, God knows—she's as hardened as one of the swart old nurses who dogged his training with servile malice, handing him a roll of gauze or a specific, or even a diagnosis he should have been quicker with. "Yes, so it was trachoma," Lexie said in the cool chippy-voice she quarreled in, striding the hotel-room after her slum-spree in Montevideo. "Women *can't* travel light. We're in charge of the basic facts."

The block of dark he's staring into is whitening, lifting

with a stirring freshness which should engage the heart. In another minute he'd be able to see the opposite riverline, two and a half miles out—the view people say they stay here for. And in its foreground, right across the road, the little promontory he owns. A bit of land that seemed always to be moving forward. Owning it soothes, like owning a wave. A private thought. Nothing that she dragged him to, in the way she does—caw-caw to every pebble on their common beach. In another minute (Dawn! she'd say) he'd have to hunker onto his feet and walk back into his history. The bag of presents is still upstairs, where he let it fall. A bag of farewells. Of noise, dropped inside his silent house. In a minute the cleansing sloth of invalidism will desert him. The power-web of his disease, that precious invigoration, will melt. He'll be back in the crushing cell-drudgery of health. No, stay. Stay. I know where it hurts. I sight my injury. I want to be alone, with what I am.

The hand he's been clasping on the granite ball is raw, wet—bleeding? No, dimly white, birdlime or some insect jelly-mass, rank with living-smell. Something from nature, sticky as semen, seeping from the stone of his house. In the second he's examining it, the light lifts; it's day.

Out there. On his wave.

A speck, a sail. Unmoving. Flotsam, water-wrangled into human color, wood into limbs.

No, he knows that odalisque. Yearly, daily, he's paid for it.

Dead or alive, it tells him what he knows already. For two people, there are two dawns.

Wiping his hand on his pant-leg he runs toward it, in his new yellow shoes.

And one more dawn, for the children. This is the morning the guerrillas will struggle down from the alps of childhood, onto the great divide.

Royal's asleep. It's always a surprise to catch him at it. Charles watched. His younger brother sleeps like a man of affairs. Royal's bad luck came early; now everything else can be arranged. And will be, handily. With all his excuses in the best order of any of us. He'll leave this house the way he slides from Lexie's lap.

It's the father and mother who make the enclosure, anyway. Charles is going to tell Lexie that in the morning. And write his father wherever he's gone off to again. I feel nothing, when you're not here. No obligation. No boundaries. The front door here opens too easy to the riverbank; the back wall has collapsed into Spain. I'll tell her that in the morning. I'll write Ray.

The time-wheel he'd constructed to show his father's travel-zones is still hung down in the kitchen. He's ashamed to have it there, a signal plain, showing the scientific gap between his one-sided romance with his father, and the latitude to which a father can desert. For whether his father is still here or not—or even, impossibly, was not the man in the hall—can make no difference now. He's seen the possible visionary side of his father. Of them both. Thing to do is to desert them first, both of them.

He steals off Royal's bed, and down the curved back stairs. The kitchen door opens on a paved alley directly under the mossy hillside, roofed by the second-story porch. Facing him, built into the hill itself, is an earth-cellar with a blackened, vaulted door, behind which ancient cables, once good for something, subside into the years. He takes from the wall the cardboard contraption, whose precision and calligraphy cost him a week, and slips it into the trashcan. Up above, it's getting faintly light now, but there are stains of diurnal dark here which keep their own earth-clock. Where the old pavestones end is a millwheel which no one can move, has ever moved. Never was a mill here within record, not for miles around. It's a man's whim, or a team's—sunk here. The alley's an unresurrected place, in a house which has had room for many; he loves this one best. Mill-smell itches his nostril like catnip. He stands on the edge, pooling his reflections, unresurrected too.

Absently, he ghost-walked back inside, movie-stalking through the front of the house—Monsieur Hulot on holiday, smartly heel-toe—and bounded up the front stairs. The girls' bath was open, dimly. Early morning, in the half-dark, all the bathrooms here smell like cathedrals, cool with damp thoughts, and time. Is time a thought? Before it intersects with space? Is space infinite duration? Or is it the presence of matter eternally referential to itself—like Dutch Cleanser clinging to the tub where the enamel's chipped? Always been that black tin-spot there. Since his own eyes began. A span which is holy to him in spite of all his efforts. Careful of noise, he lifted up the closed toilet-seat. Suspended in the interior moment of animal muscle communing with its own consciousness, he peed.

Oh Christ. I was happy. On the floor near the toilet, a pad stiff with what must be blood. Damn the girls. He won't pick it up. Quietly he put down the seat again without flushing, closed the lid.

A long whisper, his name, from the back of the hall. In the mirror, shadowy over the sink, he summons his captaincy.

"Charlie."

It's only Maureen. He steals close enough to confab.

"Our toilet's stopped up."

"Jesus. Can't it wait until morning?"

She doesn't know whether. A retriever only, these days she brings him and Royal all facts with the same tentative woe. He understands why the Greeks killed messengers.

"I'll get the plunger."

"Thanks, Charlie. It's only that I get—you know."

"Sure."

"Scared. When anything."

A roundcheeked comic girl in her long nightie, too comfy to be in the middle of this. But a blessing to him because of that. His mother, always casting Reeny as the spinster-to-be, is dead wrong. Lexie's always casting all of them, in her mind. In the good times, before things went bad, where she put Maureen used to anger him. And Chess. "Don't worry, Reeny," Chess herself used to say, tickling her sister's woe away. "Know what? You're going to marry hard and fast, red and early. The missionary boy is already stuck on you."

"I'll get the plunger," he said.

"Uh-huh. Gee thanks. You try. I already used it."

And she put it back, of course.

They retrieve it from the utility closet over the back stairs. He cuffs her, patting her back down the hall. Her habits are as circular as her outlines. Some guy will love her for it.

In the girls' bath the horse-chestnut trees were clumbering inward a greengold light.

"Gee, you're not kidding." The toilet's chugging up pink-stained pads. "What the hell—"

"I didn't."

"I know." And the same guy will fall out of love with her. But maybe not in time. "I'll have to get a wrench." The toolbox is downstairs. On such an errand, there and back, the house seemed endless.

Why does she do it?—he thinks, working at the old trap, working back to Chess. In the commune, they'd had to group-censure a girl for doing the same—or nearly. Using their john he himself had seen the withered purplish rag tossed near the can it had purposefully missed. The other girls had complained, Rocky told him, grinning. "When they themselves leave a line of pill-bottles on the shelf stretches from here to Christmas, just to keep in our minds what they go through."

Digging in the old U-pipe, he whistled; the commune always cheered him. Last time there, the girls had been spouting Teilhard de Chardin. Which was not—they said haughtily—religion. Stirring the polenta, they were. Pretty as polenta-machines, all of them. He was just in, fresh and hardy, from his books. "No, more like intellectual perfume," he'd said. "You can dab it behind your ears." They'd squawked at him. Little tape-recorders, their soft arms covered with flesh pink as bubble-gum. If they all hated their families, why were they living in what they prated as an "extended" one? He could see them around the same table three years from now, with all the babies— one was already sneaking from behind the pills—reading Emerson.

He laughed out loud and dropped the wrench.

Royal comes out and down the hall, on his hod foot. That rhythm is enough to impress quiet on them. He never has to waste words. He'll have some competence Charles and Maureen don't. Or analysis.

Older than he, they wait, silent. He has to have it.

He leans over the toilet. "How long those been in there?" He picks, delicately.

"Ick." Maureen.

"Must you?" Charles stands up. "She was tired when she went to bed, that's all. Depressed."

"That kind of blood. Menstrual blood. I've never seen it."

"Bide your time then. Or ask James." Charles picked up the wrench. "Stick to earwax. And shut your mouth."

"What do you bet it's not that kind of blood." Roy's eyes are bright. "Fools."

All three heads swivel. As if on the same neck. Their mother's often commented on it.

Chessie's door was still closed. It breathed closure. The two boys turned to Maureen.

"Oh Lordy." But she knows her duty. As more than sister. As female guardian of the secretions of the house. Cautiously she opened Chess' door.

Empty. Not slept in? Who knows? Chess' bed is never made. On the bed is a large leather folder, shining new. Charles draws nearer, to the other object.

"What is it?" Maureen whispers. "Where'd she get it?"

"An astrolabe." Yearning, he picks it up.

Underneath, scattered on the sheet, some bright metal bits.

"Oh," Reeny says. "Oh what a shame . . . Earrings . . . Oh—they were beautiful."

Royal's their leader. Though Charles forges ahead of him. Up the tower steps.

The tower's full of light now, straining through the high fracture of the trees. Chess is sitting madonna-still, on the up-ended bucket. She's wearing a tee shirt with the sleeves pushed up, and khaki shorts. Her long showgirl legs are twined. Her hands are palm-down in her lap, clasped tight. When Royal pries them open the handled razorblade falls to the floor. The bloodsoaked pad in her lap remains. The wrists haven't been slashed, but hairline-sliced. What oozing there was has stopped. A few drops are on some paperscraps near the blade.

She must have stroked so delicately. Teasing the blood out from the skin. Daring the vein. Waiting for them to find her? Or not?

"It's already healing," Royal says. "Quick, get my kit."

Maureen's already running for it.

The kit is Royal's pride. "No time to prep. But the glove-pak is sterile." He works nimbly, taught by Ray, and such practice as he himself can find. "Oh, let *me*" he's said to their kneescabs since he was five. When Ray services the Little League's injuries for free, he goes along. And more than once in hard-pressed emergency rooms—as he'd gleefully reported—a little lame patient wandering in from the wards hadn't been noticed until too late. *Don't look,* they said to him.

No one here to say that.

The wound in Chess' wrist is already a jellying seam, puckering fast against the enemy. Royal, finished with it, turns up the other wrist, to show a seam identical.

A mewl comes from Reeny. Charles' throat is grateful to hers. While Royal repeats his routine on the other wrist, Chess herself doesn't make a sound. Doesn't move, or look at them. Yet Charles can never quite believe she's tranced. Not that she's sly, or pretending. Somewhere he can feel consciousness, maybe bleeding too.

She's bandaged. White handcuffs. Royal fingers them, longer than a doctor would. "She'll have to have a tetanus-shot," he says, proud. "But it's okay."

"We can take her to Doc Bly—can't we? She can wear her longsleeved blouse. We can say she stepped on a nail. Can't we?" Maureen is testing. Not only them. She leans toward Chess. "Later on, I can lend you my copper bracelets. She'll be healed enough for them to cover, won't she, Roy?" She almost touches her sister, her arm, just in time drawing back. "I'll *give* them to you, Chess."

Who does Maureen remind him of? Their mother. Lexie, pleading with normalcy behind Chess' back, forever tidying up behind her. Trembling, at what she sees other-wise. Casting Chess loudly for all to hear, as that scruffy early heroine, herself. Challenging fate to contradict her, beating it by a hair.

Until now.

Out there on the riverbank somewhere, is his mother, moving her legs to a man's. Soon she'll be walking them back in here. He pities her.

And admires her. Both of which she knows. Some-times flaunting it—casting *him*. "Fight me," she'd said, stunned, after she'd slapped him. "*Be* me. Don't back off, like your father. And don't be sorry for it."

But Chess, who hasn't moved, has them all in the palm of her hand. Between those wrists.

Except for Royal.

He's repacking his kit tenderly, each bottle and tube,

keeping out only the probe and scissors which will have to be sterilized again, and the used gloves and roll of gauze. "No way," he says, looking up. Clasping his kit to his belly like a skilled workman called in, and now dismissing them. "No way." Maureen won't look at him. Will brother Charles grant him that satisfaction? Yes, he can always count on Charles. On all of them really. "Give up. She has to go."

The air in the tower creaks like glass wiped. It's the trees, scratching. Not wanting in here surely. But it's morning.

Royal screws up his eyes. "I could tell Ma for you, if you want. When she comes in."

Maureen's bending to Chess. "Sis. Say you'll be all right. Say it." Her hands accidentally graze the wrists. Head hanging, she stands up. Her eyes are streaming. "Where Lexie worked that time, they stamp their clothes. All the kids' clothes, underwear, even. And when they go home for a week-end, they're still wearing them."

Royal is walking over to Chess. When he walks slowly, that compensating hip takes one's eye. He stands in front of her, staring. "Like my rabbit. Remember? Just like him. It's fright, James says. But there's another name for it. See?" Before they comprehend, he's passing the probe back and forth, back and forth in front of Chess. Her gaze is unflickering.

Charles knocks him back.

They are all three amazed.

"They *do* that to them," Royal says, his jaw trembling. "It's an *experiment*."

"She's not them. She's us."

Roy shrugs.

"You don't own her," his brother says. "Just because you patched her up." But in hospital, they will, he thinks. They own them after a while—Lexie'd said. "Professionally, of course." But they really do, you know. They own them. I wasn't up to it. It takes such arrogance, Charles, to think you know what's good for them. I flunked.

"You all play Chess' game," Royal says sullenly.

"*You've* been playing it too, Roy."

Half-smiling, Royal looks up at him. Exactly as he did when he was in the hospital—looking up from his hamster, which was running in dizzy circles in the maze Charles had built for it. For little Roy.

Remember, your little brother's only six, only eight, only ten, his parents say in Charles' ear. Never speaking of the foot.

"Roy? I'm beginning to think we play yours."

"Charlie—" Reeny says. "Charlie . . . Listen. We could all work in the hospital maybe. You and I could get jobs there. And stick around her, maybe."

He could, almost. Not quite. No, he can't. Reeny would try, bless her, but be persuaded against it. Or be turned away. He knows who would do it, could. And be considered crazy for doing it, if need be. His mother would do it. And stand up to it. She would qualify.

James—he heard her say once—*what am I overqualified for?*

Chess is shivering. Unseeing. Like a statue coming to life.

No. She sees Maureen. Direct.

"I know I promised. I know." But Reeny is stepping back, back.

"What, Reeny? What did you promise." She can promise, Charles thinks. Why can't I?

"We were going to live together. And have boyfriends. She says Ma puts me down. She said I could." Reeny's curly hair frizzes at him. "And I promised." She whispers. "Never to let her go to a hospital . . . We swore it, Charlie. She's afraid they'll give her shock. She says it won't help. She says she's not insane enough . . . And that's true; you know it is. She never says anything wrong. Crazy, I mean. Even about Lucy. Never. She only . . . well, you know." A whisper: *Acts it.*

Chess has stopped shivering. Her face is sad but not judgmental. Not of them. As if the world is listening over her shoulder but will never dream of answering. Her mouth is almost humorous.

Reeny kneels to her among the paper scraps. "Chess—I'm so tired . . . I'm so tired, Chess."

But for once Maureen's not going to cry. When you welsh, you don't.

Royal limps to her. "You're all crazy." He dumps the kit down beside her. "Here. You're gonna need it." He turns on Charles, staring up. Defiance turns his fair skin to boiled milk; his feathery eyebrows crinkle in knots. He knows what they think of him. That only Ma is fooled. "Well—what did they swear it in—blood?"

Ohhhhh, Cha-arles. Reeny, from far off.

From the floor, Royal gawps up at him. When, hit, he falls lightly. The heavens don't fall with him. Who'd have thought? When someone hits Roy. "You might have broken me." His voice is holy. "You might have *broken* me."

Nobody moves to pick him up.

He feels over himself, largely. Scuffles to his feet, paper bits scattering. Bends suddenly, spry little cricket in his jointed way. "Hey. Hey. Lookit this. It's from Dad's typewriter. His *records*. Hoo-oo. Father's *medical* records. She's been tearing them up. Now will you listen to me?"

The scraps are on a familiar thin foreign paper, bluelined. Closely written though, unlike those sparse sheets to his mother. Letters to someone. He sifts the scraps, yearning. One says "—ear Cha—." He can find only one fully legible. "What the Spanish" it says, in the old Hermes type. Yet there's an identity to these bits of paper, a haze through the word-tatters, recalling instructions at times almost given him. An osmosis, between the ruled blue half-syllables, of feelings that almost spoke. "They're from letters. To *me*. From Dad."

"And she tore them up."

Royal has his uses. Charles himself can't say that to her. She can't know how it must be for him. Those connections. They're what she's incapable of.

It's brought her back, though. He knows that desperate smile. Its satire unites the two of them. "Now you don't have to worry." The voice comes stifled but clear. "You can welsh."

He shakes his head, gathering up the scraps. "I'll put them together again. Rocky's mother does jigsaws with three hundred pieces in them."

"Humpty-Dumpty?" Chess shrugs.

She sees round all corners, he thinks. Except one. Except whether or not she wants to die. He's putting the scraps into a long envelope luckily found in one of his jeans-pockets. The envelope says Harvard University on it. Even there, will he find anybody as capable of certain connections as her?

"It was Father in the hall. Wasn't it." The tissue-thin scraps cling to his rough fingertips. Several fall. He retrieves them. "When I came out in the hall." He folds away the envelope. "He's home."

She won't answer him. Why should she? Why should she be answerable to any of us?

"Father?" Reeny says it joyfully, but in the middle of a yawn.

"Then it was him we heard after, wasn't it? Coming in, then going out again? Going down to the dock . . . Charlie." Royal's voice compels. "Charlie, then he'll catch them, won't he. Those two."

"What two?" Reeny, on the floor, leans against Chess' bucket. She's tired, but back to what she was, tired in her own way. A sleep drunk. Since babyhood, found cuddled under stairs or bushes, in cellars, all sorts of places, some dangerous.

"You know. Those two we saw go down there before." Royal mouths it to him. That man and woman.

"Why you whispering?"

"What's it you two know I don't?" Reeny's arms huddle her knees. Her head sinks to them.

Chess lowers her eyes.

"Boost me on the ledge," Royal says.

Nobody does. Evil would come of it. Reeny who might have, is asleep.

The sun is up.

Charles is standing with his back pressed against the far wall.

A beautiful morning. People who live along the river often bother to say it. Paradise, the outsiders say to them. For your kids. They already know. Maybe it's smug not to say it, maybe only shy. As it is with him, Charles. To voice even in the soft, tamed river-voice that people acquire here, what these trees, that river-sky, this shadow-mellowed road means to him. Will mean, wherever he goes. It's a place of light, a place of dark. He closes his eyes to it.

In the window, dead-center, will be the dock. Or what once was; we call it that. Only a wave of green land now, with some rotten pilings to swim against, below. To be warned against—each child. Himself at three, happily plashing. "They must swim," his father says, bending a long young face like his own now, and in a tone still cherished. One of Ray's last firm statements. His father's statements are few enough; he'll cherish them. In the commune, he'll lay out the pocketed scraps on the table; eight heads will be better than one. All there will understand what he's after. Having riddles of their own.

It seems to him that yes, his mother's the one responsible for having caged the family in a globe more personal than it should ever have been. His father was after all doing something wider in the world—even if he never seemed to know why. "Personal?—" she'd say, if taxed with it "—well, the world sure handed me a lot of it." He knows her every reaction; her thousandfold words dimple his flesh like water-torture, knead his brain like dough. She knows the why of things; she's been handed enough time to. He hears her sigh, as young Ray, his father, leaves the dock, to go back up. Treading water, she grasps him strong against herself. She taught him how to swim.

More savage now, but each year openly tenderer too—she'll get her way. Whatever it's to be, he admires her for it. And means to shun all women like her. But not as James does. What he wants is—not a chick, but not a discoverer either. Some girl younger than him maybe. Who he can help.

Not like Chess. People who say that—Rocky, good concerned pal, has said it—will lie.

He opens his eyes.

Chess is quiet on her stool, but not tranced anymore. Her nose is running; she licks her upper lip. Her skin has lost the fishlike elegance it had when they entered; she's slipped her bandaged wrists down between her thighs. She's sane. Is she meditating? Like him, she must know that the interpretation of her life to others—has begun. It'll go on all her life now—that required interpretation. If she grants herself a life.

Grubby as she is now, her aura dazzles him. Dilemma is her halo, shining from her. An impossible anti-saint, unable to be ordinary. So ugly-lovely it's hard even for love to look at her.

Royal's watching him, sullenly. Let him. Shrewd as Royal is, what marks him as still a child is the way time slips by him. Maureen too. Restful to be with them, half in their sluggish cycle—but now it's over. He can't stay.

"Charlie. What are you doing?" Royal sounds scared.

Charlie is walking heel-toe, heel-toe, around the room's periphery. Charlie is practicing his Hulot-walk, for the last time. Daringly, eyes closed. Old movies, black-and-white ones, how he loves them; they are childhood. They unfold like coffin-shaped newspapers, tombs of the forgettable, where all the corpses are live.

Eyes open, he stops in front of Roy.

"Boost me." Royal whispers it. *I want to look.*

They're brothers. Do it. Even if evil will come of it.

Done. Brother to brother at the window, Charles circles Royal's waist with his arms. Comforting; comforted.

There's the dock. On it, two figures facing the sun.

There they are. On the green ripple of riverbank which belongs to this house. Two naked figures with their backs to it.

Whoever went down to the dock with Lexie hours ago has gone. These are his parents. No other man. No other woman. One's standing. One is lying full length. From up here, the changing river seems to flow through them, making their dais tremble. The sun, not yet rayed, more a warm sweat from the east, tinctures both outlines to a glow, anatomizing each body with its yellow stencil. The tactile, green arching of summer frames them, naked but separate.

Must be a painting like that, he thinks. Done in that near-far perspective which always extends just over the road which one can never cross. Sometimes it'll be a perspective empty of humans. Sometimes, off-center in what is called the middle distance, will be just such a pair. Arrested in sleep or thought, in radiance. Or trudging the solemn colorings. Or running frantic before a furling cloud. Not a mother or a father—or not yet. Or not any more. Just such a pair, in the posture that is theirs. I have a picture of it in my mind.

Maureen, waking from her doze, sees the two boys at the ledge, steals to their side. Makes a small sound, looking out.

Royal watches, greedily.

Charles is receiving the picture as he might a gift— naming it. It hangs in the middle distance between recognition and shock. Between his own picture of the universe—and the world. It hangs there uncertainly, not yet philosophy, yet not merely flesh. And with the faintest flow—not critique, but not unreasonable—from the landscape of Immanuel Kant. But he can take it with him now, into those modest nights in the garden of satire, with his machines. It will follow him. Even onto those ranges where he hears the epistemological namings, the haunted messages. Which command him too to receive, to record.

No, he can't say yet. What the sight of those two figures—strict, bare, washed with meditation—may mean to him. Because it is in itself a naming. It is a picture of his world. Which he may hang in his universe.

What are they doing there, naked but separate?

"If they're going to skinny dip—I wish they'd get in." Maureen is angry, resonant. For Maureen.

"If they're going to make love—should we watch?" Royal's voice is skiddy. For Roy.

All three turn.

Chessie is unfolding. Her long, nervous, beautiful legs look pale and cold, even in the hot, attic morning. Her lips move, frostily. "Can—they—see us?"

She's come to herself. She sees it in their faces.

"Not if we stand *back*," her sister says, so reasonably.

"They're not *looking* at us." Her porky little brother is scared.

Charles is silent. There's always more to it than that. More, to us. More than one person, one reason. For why it happens. For why they're out there. And how did Chess know? That they were.

Chess is studying her wrists.

Maureen reaches out to her, pulling the T-shirt's long sleeves down over the bandages. "There, darling. There."

Taking her by the waist, Charles and Maureen draw her to the window. Or she draws them. The three stand there, her tall brother and chubby sister flanking her, each with one of her hands clasped between theirs, and held to their breasts.

She stares for a long time, before she answers.

Cassandra must have been something like her, Charles thinks, holding onto her. Like one of these. A spasm of guilt tightens his hold.

She turns a cold smile on him. "They're waiting for the bus. To see *them*."

Maureen with a harsh cluck drops her sister's hand. It deals in poisoned revelations.

Charles holds on, chilled. She's right. It's a signal, out there. Oh she's right, and that's why we want to put her in hospital. People like her—they pull the signals from our breasts.

From above, Royal, forgotten on his ledge, whispers "Boost me down." It's the one thing he can't do by himself—let down his own weight.

No one attends him.

"Charlie?" Lightly she draws her wrist from his grasp. "Let's run away."

"You and me?"

She looks at him, deep. So he's thought of it. "No."

"All of us?"

She nods.

"Together?"

She makes the same impatient "Tchk!" their mother does. At their father. Shaking her head at him. "Alone."

Maureen says "Away?" Slowly. They can see it dawn on her. Away from you, Chess. From Royal. From you, Charles. From each of you, differently.

"And from them," her sister says at her. "Ha, see Charles? Look at her . . . Listen, Reen. Where would you go? If you did."

A low grin. Reeny has her secrets. "To Grandpa Charlie's. His wife; she says she'll do me over. Just me, she says. And I love Florida."

"See. And *you* could go to Rocky's. You're there half the time already. Or until Harvard comes through. Or Oxford. You know you could . . . And Royal." She shrugs. "We all know where little Roy."

"Yah. And where *she* will." He's white. "Let . . . me . . . *down*."

Chessie bars them. Holding up her arms, crossed at

· 270 ·

the bound wrists. "The minute you do—he'll phone James."

They know he will. Without looking at him.

"Chess. Where will you go? Where can you?"

She trembles. She's never heard that stern, despairing tone from him before. "You won't like it, Charlie."

"Try me."

"Yah, tell us." If Royal can't get down, or up, he can sneer.

Her head lifts on its long neck, the nostril opening black. "Yah to you." She tosses it. Turns to him. "Charlie?" She can go in and out of beauty, like some old movie-star you're watching, from either end of her life. "Charlie, I'm a swinger. Imagine. Me. I am, though. In town. And it wasn't only the job—I got it, but I knew I wouldn't keep it. I went to a bar. Every day for a week . . . They like me, Charlie." She sees his face. "Listen, keed. All I did was sell a drawing. The one of Ma."

She's so proud. Though people have bought her drawings before, they were only neighbors. "The one you said to show the doctor." She'd titled the ink-drawing The Fat Bourgeois. Though in it Lexie looked thin and desperate. "Even he said it was good." She frowns, and for a minute he's afraid she is lost again. She sees that too. "Uh-uh, brother." She smiles. Then flings over her shoulder "And it's an okay bar, little brother. James goes to it . . . Charlie? The owner doesn't pay me anything. But he says that I can go there any night and draw the—guests." She's shy. "I mean, you know . . . what is the right word?"

"Customers."

"And I am a swinger. I mean—I already know I can be."

Chess with a man. He can only nod.

"Don't glom that way. And don't be a simp. I'll stay in a hostel. I've got money to."

"From where?" Royal can't help being interested.

"From Gram. Real Gram. Renata. She wrote—and

sent it." She's shuddering now, but from excitement, and the vitality which sheds from her almost tangibly, like sparks from a frayed wire. "She says I can be all right, if I want to. I can. I can." She says it like a rune. "I can be all right, if I really want to. Away from them."

And it's all true. Or could be. He can go to Rocky's and find a girl there, or somewhere. Maybe at Harvard. He visualizes her without actually seeing her. Some girl in trouble, maybe. Whom he'll help. And Royal can leave, surely. Even Maureen, probably—what a surprise.

And Chess. He doesn't want to see that film. But he sees it. The swinger, drawing her diagnostic pics. Going in and out of madness, on her own. Innocence seeping from her, rank and powerful as filth. Smelling like anarchy to all customers—guests.

Yet it would be—what they three could do for her.

But not only for her. For us too—Maureen, Charles, and even little Lord Roy.

And even—for them. For those two out there.

"Let's. We can all start off together. Reeny has the farthest to go. I'll help." When Chess is strong, she's Lexie distilled—falling apart only within sight of the original. "Eh, Reeny?" She gives her an encouraging tickle. "I'll even wear a proper dress. To see you off."

"Oh, *la.*" Maureen is a custardy rose. "What would *I* wear?"

"Nothing special. She wants to do you over, re-member? And you won't even telegraph. You'll just arrive. They're always there. With Grampa on the dock, talking travel—you know how they are." She even has their mother's ironical smirk. She can inhabit one after the other of Lexie's moods, adopting each like a costume. Or do they inhabit her—issuing from her mouth? Only the saliva of the ordinary, to join them all, is missing. "We'll have to take Roysie here with us. Or else leave him, on his ledge. How about it, Royal? Ready for export? Or not?"

He won't be left out, our Royal. Chess knows how to

handle him. He's afraid of her. Aren't we all—a little afraid of her? She goes too far. Is that why we want her out of our sight?

Geniuses—his mother said to James once—and to his father, sitting offside, the way he did—*they always go too far.* Mocking herself. But pleading too, for what's in her that's also in Chess. Sometimes he thinks Chess is his mother's very vengeance, for what Lexie knew her own powers had been kept from, by the time she bore Chess. As the first son and child, he'd escaped. "When I bore you, I knew nothing; you were all Ray's." But by the time I bore Chess—it was never said. Only implied—by her guilt over what Chess is or does—alternated with her blind, angry pride in it. "Our *two* heroines" James calls them. While his father, silent, never defends. Charles fingers the scraps in his pocket. Who's ever known what Ray thinks? Lexie's vengeance is bent on Ray—and on James. But nature's vengeance— is on her. Her own power, wildness and capability, submerged and souring, wandering chemically afloat in her own girl.

But it's not genius, His great men; yes they go far, far, but knowingly, a compass at the core of their wandering. Not like Chess. And not with those wrists.

"Eh, Charlie." She's been watching his very thoughts. "You'll—go along with it?"

"Run to the city you mean? That's not far. Or even Florida."

"Doesn't have to be. Far enough." She lays the words down like knives. But not from corners now, or waiting to be caught. The certitude is on her now—the same force that allows their mother to say to him "*Be* me"—and perhaps, in the womb, said it to her. "Listen, Chucky-chuck." Diminutives rain from Chess like love, when she's like this. Softening a force which maybe she knows has to be humanized.

He always falls for it. He wants it to be love.

"All four of us?" He sees the four of them running,

with clothes, books, saved old toys and secret collections, the whole impedimenta of childhood flying in clouds after them. "At once? With all our junk?"

"Listen. It'll be like the night of the fire, don't you see?" The look she hands him is strong, gleeful, almost coarse. "We'll each take—the one thing that matters. Just that—and money." She stretches, lazy but sure, to pat Maureen. "Not Gabriel, baby. Cats have to be left. They go with the house."

"What, then." Reeny's immured at once in the choice. So is he.

And Chess is laughing at them both. "We'd all *be* taking it with us. Already. Wouldn't we, Charlie." She stares at him, feeding him it.

The one thing that matters. To *them*.

Yes—she dazzles him.

"What? What is it?" Reeny gets naggy when she sees the two of them like this. "Tell *me*."

He pats her too, making light of it. But it isn't light. "Us."

Everybody's quiet.

"Abracadabra," Chess says then. "Let's be off." She's her old theme-correcting self. Grammar-hard on excess. Biting off what counts. "And *we* won't wait for the bus, my hearties. Will we, Charles."

Everybody's waiting on him.

So he's caught. Since he was fourteen, he's been their illegal transportation, sub rosa, in his friends' cars. And since he was sixteen, in his Volks. Which because of the lack of much garage space near these hill-houses, is parked way up the hill behind them, on the upper road. Often these days, he has to prime the little bugger. When it does start it makes a sweet little racket. The family joke is that the Kellihys will object. Once it goes, it does what you tell it to.

They could all sneak out by the alley-way. Up and over the hill. And out. They wouldn't even have to use the front door.

"You can phone them later where we are, you want to," Chess is saying. "From Rocky's." She's rueful; she knows what this means to him. But stern. He can see her, the figurehead, flying the snub bowsprit of the Volks.

It can't last; it can't last. But she dazzles him.

"And if we don't like it—" Maureen's saying, "—we can all come back here. Couldn't we?"

Royal is drumming his feet on the window-ledge. First the hod-foot, then the good one, *bump* drum, *bump* drum. Then the good one. Then the hod. He has his shadow-tune, which follows him. He likes them to remember that. "Lookit out there. Something's wrong. Why don't they move?"

Their mother's body is sungilded now. She lies at full length, one arm flung back. Father, sitting beside her, has his back to them. His neck is bent.

"Can't we go out there? Can't we speak to them?" Reeny moans it. "It'll soon be time for the bus."

"Sure, go down on your knees. Maybe he's done her in, you shits. Let me down."

Chess, the expert, is peering out. "No, they're alive." Her voice mocks.

"We could go out *there*," Maureen whispers. "Oh please, couldn't we? We could stand in front of them. We're dressed."

Maybe everyone in the family should kneel in turn to the others.

In silence, Charles lifts his small brother down, hugs him for fraternity, gathers them all close.

The sun is rising. The picture is lit. In all darkrooms there must be a millionth of a second like this. When the negative takes. Oh, the wind is blowing, ruffling hair dead or alive. Hold *still*, everybody. Green fronds high above, wave your last. Going to be a perfect picture.

Up in the tower, the four faces straining. Down on the bank there, the naked two who made them. Yes, a perfect picture. A good take.

And in the distance, telegraphed far ahead by the alert water, the mumble of the bus.

Far down in the lefthand corner though, a movement. Below the terrace, out on the road there, just beyond the frame. Somebody moving. It's the paperboy on his cycle, coming down from Kellihys'. Kneeling over his wheel, in fury. They know that posture; he's not been paid again. They will him to go on, fairly or not. Ride on, missionary boy. Ride on without seeing. Ride past.

He stops. Dead center. The front wheel spins, idles, rests. He's seeing them, the two out on the green bank. A strange boy. Or only another boy, in his own tight world. On one knuckle he wears a pewter ring with his Savior on it. The sun catches it. Openmouthed, arm raised, he's shaking his fist at their father and mother. The sun fires his nether lip. A long halloo comes from it. Stops. Comes again. And again. Stops.

What's he shouting, that prints itself on the wind like a banner?

"i-in-nn, an a-aamem—aaa-tion."

"—S——iiin, nnn daa——n-na-aa-tion!"

Charles, walking again, still hears the strange, clotted syllables. Each of us four hears it for himself, herself, he thinks. After a while, the full meaning will come to us. No window's that thick, no tower that high. We guerrillas are trained to hear well.

After a while, the sense of it will come to us. And of the signal too.

There's the bus. Nearing. Almost upon us, unless you know this cove well. It'll be twenty minutes before the bus appears, jammed with heads, after coughing like a schoolmaster at every gate. Which the river and the hill can bounce between them to sound like nemesis.

The missionary boy is gone. The bus'll pass, and be gone, leaving its thin stream of gas. After it goes, maybe we'll feel something. Whether or not it's what those two down there want us to. Maybe they've forgotten us—and are telling us this is possible.

Shall I lead us out of here? Down the stairs, out the front door and across the road, the four of us. To confront.

Or? The possible dazzles him. He sees the team of four, a tall boy, a tall girl, a middling girl and a gimp, stealing out the alley, each with his or her single loot, scrambling the hill to the Upper Road, running, running from a dead fire—in the Volks. The Great Movie-Eye of the sky follows them. From the commune, eight pairs of eyes will audience. Underneath the frame, like the last sub-title the old silents float you off with, is Rocky's whisper at the door each time Charles leaves there— "You're not so different."

He checks his forces. Maureen's not dozing. Royal has his kit again, clutched to his chest. His other sister is for the moment herself—or the one he knows. That chase is over—at least in this house. All three of them have their faces pressed to the glass.

He joins them there. On his way palming the tower-wall a farewell caress.

Their mother is standing now, facing downriver. So is his father, though not hand-in-hand. The sun's lost its gilding fire, or gone up past the house. Their bodies look ordinary. Ready to skinny-dip. Have they any loot? Only the night knows what guerrillas they are.

It's day.

So they too straggle in, he thinks. Each from a little alp, onto the great divide.

At some point while these shore-facts were accumulating, the figure on the river-bank had begun to wake. Her barge is moored again, but still faintly moving. Nobody knows how long these interior journeys take. She can feel the span of warmth that must be flushing over the horizon. It's going to be a hot day in the temperate zone.

So it's possible, she thinks, surfacing, eyes still shut. To dream through all the conscious past, in the I-she admixture that you are. Refracting wave-like to the repartee of memory. In the stern, lyrical, humble agony that consciousness is. Attended by the comic valet-service of your own wit.

Sure, it's possible; everybody does it, every day. We're such slow porcupines of idea, each weighted down at each moment with the whole of a sensuous history. Now and then, in one unbearable earthquake clap—we total it.

But this time, before you open your eyes get as much of it clear as you can, before it all disappears down that grotto which isn't dream, or sleep or even mind, but existence-as-record. Which if you persist there will link you honorably to the lives of others. Not merely as one more mortal born to die . . . In a marriage of record with the world—while you both so do live.

And this moment before opening the eyelids, when the whole grotto is for one life-spark still with you, is the true clarity, the best time.

Am I also, dear valet, in one of my slightly dishonorable sulks?

She can feel herself, at age four or so, stealing out from a teasing kitchen to the quiet, soothing parlor, waiting there to be come after, to be recognized as in the posture of hurt—only to hear an auntie neighbor saying after her "Ah, she's in one of her sulks. No, Renata, don't go after her. What you start will never end."

Sometimes her mother did come after her, sometimes not. Shouting instead "You're not to *start out* as a heroine. Not yet." Her mother read romantic novels, good ones—furred elopers on Russian trains, innocent arrivers in evil English or American cities—and despised herself for it. Later on Lexie herself stretched the distance between them, retreating huffed as far as the apartments or houses they lived in would permit, to an upstairs bedroom, the back one which was usually hers. Finally, as girlhood went on, she parlayed the time too—into hours, half a day, overnight—before she could be persuaded to "come out," smile sheepishly and resume a relationship with others, as well as with her scorned self. The day of her twelfth birthday—whose anniversary the whole family, not one for calendar specifics, had forgot—she spent outside the house altogether, on the Morton Street dock—a princess towering her neglect, tearlessly in control of unspecified disaster, but meditating too, on the mockeries of life. These sorties fuse into habit. One week after her marriage, and after a first quarrel, Ray, returning from a late call, searches for her and finally finds her, after her five-hour vigil in the night-garden, as she'd hoped to be found—pathetically asleep, in the purple dressing-gown.

The oddity is that afterward she could never recall the actual slights which had started her off on these sulks, at first so mild in themselves. Later, in her own private language—her great sulks. Saying the private phrase to herself, she sometimes almost initiates one, circling around some hurt that is constant. This too, she's known for some time. Scorn of self is at the bottom of it. This must be why she is always ashamed—afterward. Once her alternating self-esteem has been a little repaired, or else has risen to the humiliate's counterpart—arrogance. But there's more to her story than that. Could it be that the great sulk, surfacing from her own cells like a cloud of black nucleoles—was in answer to some great injury? Done her intangibly, impersonally. Not in itself (she came to conclude) inflicted by any one person. And—one last, last thunderbolt—she herself can be party to it.

How odd above all, that conclusion should come upon her—in the exact sensation, is *offered* her—during these same involuted, self-arranged martyrdoms. For these become the times also of her most sustained meditation. Almost as if her sense of injustice, based on the indefinable, bore her up in her right to sustain it. In these publicly stolen moments in chairs, gardens, parks and porches, in beds and on window-ledges, hoarding her offended self, coddling it, she had increasingly forgotten the actual offense after a minute, all the blame siphoning out in a healing flood, in the stately divertimento of her progress to a wider self. So that without professors, short on books, and under only this one peculiar authority, she has been teaching herself to think.

What have these last months been but the greatest of her sullen times? Prison thoughts—yes, I began with those. Tainted ones. But in the thinking, the prison has disappeared. Glorious thought-careers have surged from behind bars—and oh sages: O Socrates, O Monte Cristo, and who's that female flamenco-politico—O La Pasionaria—I understand how.

They sprout from the black, barring stripes, in the bright air-float between. Martyrs at their martyrdom have only being—a noose, a fire, a gallows, a blade. Saints at the height of sainthood have only grace. But prison-thought is mortal—boiling headily with all the bloody flux.

Socrates is a man. All men are mortal. And all women are mortal too. As syllogisms go. But a woman is not a man. Was that the injury?

Lexie, take it as offered. Keep your eyes sealed.

In the baby days of her strange woe, her father would come to her, at first in his own jaunty pose as daddy-of-all-treats, but later appeasingly to her sulkhood, as if he knew the source of it. James followed too, abashed in those days, almost respectful then, of the force behind her veiled, vestal eyes. Did he and his father already think of it as her female principle? Perhaps her father already knew of it from his mother? Smartly soon enough, jealously guarding her close, it was Renata, her mother, who had informed them of it.

From her own motherhood, she now knew why. For, Socrates—as you know well, a man, however vain or ego-blinded, cannot carry himself about as if he is his own foetus. Or confuse himself with the foetus once carried, now gone. Even the most doting of fathers cannot, does not, do that. But a woman, starkly pitying both parties, easily transliterates from self to child. I see my mother's face, at these times. I see the process. Call it—womb-punishing.

"Stay away from her," her own mother said, punishing her early for what she herself had acceded to. Inuring her to it. "Women do this." So, by the time of that twelfth birthday, her father and James—gliding around her and away from her at these times as if she was already veiled and in howdah, and rocking toward her wedding-hour—were trained to understand her better than she would herself, for years yet. "It's only the puberty-sulk," their averted glances said. "This is what women do. Forget it. We have public chores."

So that during all the raging marvels of her teens, when she might have been advancing as coolly as any with her bucket of poetry, energy and ambition, an acolyte ready as any to scrub the face of the world, or rub her own, ah, ah, in its musky bottom, meanwhile advancing at her own leisure, in her own spirit, toward tragedy or foolishness—hysteria had instead been granted her at once. Drop by drop, a little salutary water-torture, turning the rage into steam. So that, rocking on her nightly bed instead of on elephant, at last she was tamed, turned inward. So that she might be housed.

Where all the localized embroideries were waiting. And this being the modern world—the telephones.

And I loved it, love it. I love the amah-bliss of holding the child. It's my *office.* As with a priest. Snuggling into that cloister, I retreat. Language becomes linenfold. No need to talk. A faith-in-white-curtains is fair exchange at any font. For faith.

But, God—I've been lucky. I'm turning it all, all into meditation. And I shall manage to turn *that* into something—you'll see. God of gender, I'm not your simple bifurcate. I'm your globed one. Behold me, your transliterate.

Now may I wake?

Not yet. Not until you swear.

Swear what? Let me wake.

Swear never to swear by the cross of sexual injury.

How not? *Why* not?

That way you keep to the prison-club of what women do.

Who are you?

I am the voice of the true clarity. In saecula, saeculorum. Where you too have a place.

I won't swear *against* only. I want to swear *for.*

Then say simply "This is what I did. What I do."

But that voice is genderless.

Human.

Ah, that old word, Define it.

To keep holy. But remain in the world.

· 282 ·

But what if I have only my monologue?
Then mount it on an elephant.
But will I talk this language when I'm awake?
You are awake.

And so she was, almost. Sore, and paisleyed all over
with weed-and-grass pattern. Holding onto the melting
keys of freedom, which turn into burdock with dew on it.
But I remember. I only dreamed at the last. (A likely
epitaph, if you're going in for them.) On the riverbank is
where I am. Set to sail. Ninety degrees still, and the sky just
whitening—August in the temperate zone.

It might be that all over the sloping lawns and terraces
here now, there were other people, other bodies lying in
similar circumstance, pink on green, pink on green, all at
the same slant. Like a good fabric design—one just a shade
too literal. There had been a man lying nude on their own
lawn one morning after a party next door, with his arms
and legs spread, his face to the sky. When she and Ray
crept out in the ebbing starlight to see if it was alive, it had
smiled up at them with calm, castaway eyes. "Beached,"
he'd said. Rolling over, a lion couchant, he'd looked at the
world. And still smiling, had picked himself up and walked
off.

I'll roll over onto my hands and knees. A lioness
couchant.

But she can't seem to.

Help, help, she screamed in her nightmare. I can't
open my eyes. I can't enter the world. And I know I'm not
screaming.

You're delivering silently. Women do that. When
they've been carrying themselves.

Who said that? Cold-soft as gooseflesh. Are you the
same voice?

All of them. *I am the record.* Sleep now. Cry a bit. I'll
scream hard enough for you. When it comes time.

ON
KEEPING ON

As he ran toward her she lay in the half-light like a woman with her throat cut—body arched, knees blasted apart, splayed toes digging the ground. The patch between her legs reared at him, black and creased pink, a bearded mouth rolled sideways. When men were hanged they erected. When women were hatcheted, what went on down below? No morgue had ever instructed him.

Alive. Grossly alive. The neck's whole. Her smile is what gapes, the way he saw it in labor once, stretched like a smaller vagina, the lips rose-wet and muscular. Her eyes were wide. Their substance seeps from them.

Bending, he saw his self-portrait in them.

She's awake. Leaning over her is the forgotten face. But her feet aren't in the birth-stirrups anymore. She moved them experimentally. Grass. A good place. Her legs slide down. Arms fanning winglike, she caressed the ground, head lolling. He had nothing to do with it. Not this time.

· 287 ·

She sat up, feeling her mouth. Her jaws ached with health. "Did I scream?"

What a look on him.

"No. You didn't."

What a look on her. She's measuring him.

The way he's holding himself down there. Crotch-sprung. Like a man who's—been to more than Monte Carlo. Her lip twitched. "Somebody kick you?"

His hands left off their nursing; his head hung. Not too soon for her to note that its features had always been too neat for her.

"Excuse me." He turned and ran down the riverbank.

She could hear him down there, hawking. She tore off grass and wiped her mouth with it. He's still sick, then. Maybe that's for the best. Allowing the two of us to just slouch off from each other, in grunt and slur. Like trained apes out to spoil the documentary set up for them. Too smart to talk.

Down on the beach he was coughing it all up. So it was her up there in the hall, behind him and Chess. When he'd caved in, the air knocked out of him. Out of the corner of his eye, a white figure, merging at once back into a doorway. Whom he took to be Charles, in his old white ducks. Always falling asleep in them. Roused him a hundred times.

But could it have been her? Sleeping raw the way she did, even into November. In the hot nights stealing out of bed, down the hall onto the upstairs porch, and onto the black hill. Coming back in to tell him "It's like swimming in the dark." Or to butt her head against him, a bitch with her pup, nosing him. Whispering into his chest "Her light's still on."

Down the backstairs and out again that way, she could have gone. If she saw them. Out one of the doors of that ever-accommodating house—always so proud she is, that we've never kept them locked. Out to show the world her nakedness.

He moved downstream, as if the river might pool his vomit, and slapped water on his face. The Hudson flowed upstream here and was salt. What's that on the mudscarp? A shoe, a woman's. A pair of them draining with tide, filling with it. Twitting their pointy toes at him: All that goes on here silts away—no other answer, dearie. Maybe it was her; maybe it wasn't. It's all of them you're mourning, isn't it—even Maureen. All of them standing blindly aware, one to a doorway. In the silting house.

He went up the bankside almost lightly. So much has been lost.

She sat up at once. To show him how it was with her. This is the way it is, Ray—without pearls. But it sticks in her throat. "So you're back."

She stared up at him as of old, from under eyelids sulked to the purple of her old dressing-gown. The exact division of her body always amazes him. As if some polymath, richer in anatomical lore than he could ever be, had scored her in three parts and each time deeper—once at the girdle-of-Venus line at the neck, twice at the under-arc of the breasts, and last at the pale, visibly powerful slope of the stomachline. What is there about her nudity that's almost painful to him? That he must protect *her* from? "Do stand away from that window," he'd snapped on their honeymoon—and knows she's never forgiven him. Despising him forever, as a puller-down of shades.

My sister equates nudity with honesty—James once said. It isn't *her* self-display. It wasn't our mother's either.

Agreed—Lexie replied to the air. But what really bugged you, James, and Daddy too—what bugs all of you—is when we reject our nudity as household art.

"Yes, I'm back," he said. "But not for long."

His eyes are sunken, but in a younger face. It's now plainly a face which always hurt somewhere, but could never say. She can see more clearly now that those cells which speak must have been left out of it, or have been crushed. How she used to plead with it, quite pitifully. How it used to anger her, always to have to be the one to break down their life-tensions into speech.

Now she's grateful. For whatever will make him unlovable. The way a Sabine woman might feel, when rescued. Looking back at the abductor she'd lived with for years, not unhappily enough.

"Pair of women's shoes down there."

"Not mine."

"I know." In spite of himself—as she could well see—he took his jacket off and held it down to her. "Here."

"No thanks."

It was still very hot of course.

In spite of herself, she reached out to touch one of his new yellow shoes. "Spanish?"

"A gift."

The jacket dropped to the ground in front of her. He gripped his shirtcollar, easing it. Is he too going to divest himself, at last? To stand here naked also, in silent explanation?

There flashes over her what she always wanted of him. To understand her nakedness—beyond the sexual. To say to her, by those silent means which are allpowerful: I am thy nakedness, too. To have him capable of lying here, her replica. And not for love.

"How long have you been down here like that?" It burst from him.

She shivered. Ah—in that case. An idyll—she mourns it. "Since you left."

The truth. She wanted to tell him the whole truth. She stared at it.

He's covered that face of his.

"Ray—." No, she won't have this. Old feelers, old mutuals pushing up.

He kneels beside her.

She kneels beside him.

"Look at you."

"Look at *you*."

They rise on knee, hands upraised and spread before each other's faces. A prison couple, pawing glass. Which one of us is the visitor?

How she'd blossomed. And yet fallen away. He doesn't dare touch her.

How he'd fallen away. And yet—bloomed. She drew a finger down his gaunt cheek.

"Its from the disease," he says. Proudly.

When they cling, the rucked-up jacket slides between them.

I am thy nakedness, she whispers in his arms. But not to him.

"Don't—."

"—explain."

Both have said it. The nearest they've ever come, to equal speech.

"Not—anything?" she said.

"Anything."

"You mean that?"

"You do?" he said.

"I do."

He nodded. "I mean that."

They're in a rhythm. Call it the dawn-rhythm. When two people begin to know they are two.

"Only what we'll—have to say." She glanced behind them, in the direction of the house. "Like what we'll do now. And how."

"And—where."

They were quiet for the same minute.

"But no whys and wherefores." She hesitated. "Unless we—want to."

He considered. Nodded.

"And no excuses."

He hesitated. "None."

They were silent. Would it be the triumph of their life together, if they could hold to that?

"Agreed—" he said. "Then—I've just this minute gotten off the bus."

"Agreed. And I've been—lying here. Waiting for it."

His eyes widen, but hold. This man, long ago rejected in the flesh, is by circumstance her one sharer. From long association able to stalk the underbrush of her mind in all its yallery-greenery of serio-comic reference. Where, as they both know, one minute she's in vestal command of all the mysteries, but the next is wandering uncommissioned in the semigloom of her kind—as a family professional whose personality, by reason of a work-history only loosely corroborated by others, has to operate at some loss.

His glance slid down her, reinforcing her nudity. In the warm, viscid air, she'd forgotten about it, as real nudists must.

"I see," he said. "Of course."

He must think she's waiting for someone. Stripped, to him she's erotic only. Fair enough. When that's how she came to be here. "No," she should say, "there was someone. But he's gone." I heard the car go by.

She resists. In their minds, did all naked women wait merely for them? Not for—other connection.

What did a naked man wait for in the eyes of women? Not for them alone, that's certain.

She'd equip him. That's it; she herself always equipped them. Lying in bed beneath or above any one of them, with his throat and sex bare to her hand, she herself complicitly armed them—even before they did it themselves. Respectfully she hung the powerbag between their legs like a codpiece, and cocked on her pillow their judge's-hat.

For in her mind they already lie twice as open as she

to life's accounts. Lying in her bed, they waited to rejoin the world. Or in the piercing contemplation of arrows already received. They wait in such busy dignity. In her own mind.

It's why she can never wholly love or murder them.

"I didn't mean to ask," he's saying.

Granted. But I mean to tell you.

"We were taught only to connect with each other," she said gruffly.

And we couldn't. No need to say.

She's touching his arm. "There's something more, I'm not sure what. But we chose the village instead. I want to live by my own—." Her mouth went wry, muting the rest of it. "And I want them to know."

How many patients had touched him on the arm like that—woman or man. Nobody must know, Doc. Doc, I can't wait to let it out. The village always chose the village, one way or other—is she just discovering it?

I want to live by my own images. That's what she said. They all said. And I want the whole village to know.

On a bush behind her's an opulently striped beachtowel unlike any of their own faded ones. In hospital he'd already warned himself of how the house and all in it would have acquired new objects, new facts and new people, a tide which would have swelled over the lump of him. There's an underground of waterfront sex here. Does she now belong to it?

"You'll go on as you must." He said that to all of them. Except himself. He made himself look at her—personally. She deserved it. "You have the right."

But if she's going to do what he has a hunch she is, then he'll have to stand by.

He's looking at her body, her face too. She's forced him to. If he could have done that on his own—seen her true and whole in the altogether—how her body too would

· 293 ·

have smiled for him. Her face trembled, ready to be radiant. The long hysteria's ending. Even he's admitting it. She stood up, breasts forward. It was how she stood on her ledge. Would stand, if the children came down here.

But they haven't come. After adult parties, children sleep late.

"This is the way——." But it stuck in her throat. The children stick in her throat.

"It's growing light." How different the light was here, complicated, offering him back his native life.

What's this? She's reaching down for his jacket, drawing it toward her, bent over from the waist straight-knee'd, like a woman digging with a hoe too short for her. She's slung the jacket over her shoulders, shrugging it close. The most humble gesture he's ever had from her. Now we can talk, she'll say though. Now—can't we talk.

She's touching his shoe.

Those gift shoes of his. So heavily perforated at the narrow wingtip. At the heel's a flange reminding where spurs were, once. Not a father's shoe.

"Oh, they walked me here," he said down to her. "They'll—walk me back."

Her gaze traveled up him. "To the nuns?"

She can feel his shock, vibrating all the way to his shoe. "How come—what makes you say that?"

That's it, then. What came spuming between the lines of every letter. He's not a father any more. He's receded from it.

She's careful. "Oh—Bob Kellihy said it. 'Don't leave him too long with the nuns.' Ah well, you know. Catholics. They always think that everyone."

He was breathing fast enough to remind him how sick he'd been. "Ah, ah, such women—" Sister Isaac said, raising her head from that last letter "—they have time to

· 294 ·

brood." On what can take a man four months and three thousand miles to arrive at. With a whole hospital to help.

Where, ward to ward, bed to bed, is as Catholic as he'd ever need to be. Faced with a piece of the public health so simple that even he can manage it. Yes—he's going back.

The light's still lifting. The grass is still grass. "Oh yes, the Kellihys" he said from halfway across the world "—how are they?"

"They're having an affair." Her voice floated up dryly. "With each other."

She'd hauled the jacket over her head, so that she had to peer up at him sideways. The nursing nuns, excused from wimples, still tilted their heads on this same slant. Did all woman have nun in them—as Sister said? As all men have monk. Nothing to do with celibacy. Or the red tawn of the penis, or the hanging, clitoral heat. Or even with parenthood. Something not to do with any of it.

Even in that teaser, Bets?

Struggling with her on the Kellihys' spare-room couch, he'd knocked down some of Arthur's silverwork; this happened every time. Shhh—she said at once. Below him her broad Cupid's-bow mouth pouted for its kiss, her long corals swung between breasts—oddly enticing in their flatness—which had dropped. Four kids, was it? Or five? "No, Bob and I have an agreement. I only pet." A word from his own mother's archive. It had been the night of the christening party. He'd picked up a silver cup just finished for it, and handed it to her. "Your chaper-one."

"That Bets," he said now. "The whole teaser apparatus. But she can't."

"Really?" Down in the grass she's plaiting is Betsy, besatined and beery, signing books of photographs she's not in, tagging after the priests. Saying—as she did say once, and was brushed off for—Lexie—may I attend your class. "It's all for Bob, you mean."

"Oh they're fond—enough. Alcoholics like him can be very adroit sexually. That's known."

Yes, it is.

"But behind that front she puts up—oh the senior K's know by now what they're buying."

"What's that?"

"A mother. Bets is to the mother born. All she really likes is slipping them out."

"She tell you that? Evenings?"

"Evenings and drunk. When she has a baby, she said. Then she feels her worth."

Ah poor Bets. Join the class.

"But when she's had the baby *and* is drunk. Then it's the best."

"Ah—poor Bets."

Their eyes meet.

He's half-smiling. "Oh I went for it. The teaser part. I need to be encouraged. As you may recall."

"I recall." The shame—cast on her own aggressiveness—that a woman—a girl—doggedly accepts. For the sake of the man. And the sex. Mother-reluctant, that's what you were, Ray. And yes, I went for you—as young men went for jobs.

He turned to look at the house. He's a tall man; his legs are much the longest part of him. Seventeenth-century legs she called them during their courtship, awarding his bones the elegance she wanted from life. Looking up them, they're a tower yet. Until you arrive at the eyes.

"I won't go in the house. Better just to leave again."

It's true then. He wants to hide.

"Put it on the market," he's saying. "You never really liked it."

What can I say? It was where I hid.

"Some people think it already is," she said. "Some—are still rooting for us."

"For the practice," he said. "They get used to the same ear."

"Oh?" she said. "Oh. Of course."

"But I want out."

So he's said it. This man of few words. While she who has so many is mum. Mother-mum. We don't leave. We take cars to the bridge. Or tear the shopping-lists apart, face by face.

She got to her feet. "Ray. I thought maybe—. Charlie'll be on his own by fall. And Royal in hospital. I thought maybe that you and the girls—might like to stay on here for a while."

"No!"

"Why not?"

"It's not—safe."

She stared. Did they become mothers that quick, from a distance? "You can always lock the doors."

His hands were making that tic-like routine again. The heel of one, swiped hard on the palm of the other. The other hand reversed it. No, that's not so great for a doctor. But would James still do as he'd warned her he might? A custody ruling against her? For her own good?

"James will arrange them all right," she said in fury. "I'll insist on it." In exchange for Royal. I know my own force. "But there's no reason to *trust* him." And you haven't even seen what I'm telling you. That I'm the one leaving. "Ray. I said you could have them. The girls."

In the dissecting-room nausea used to heave him like this. So that he used to rock, James said, like an old woman in church.

"She knee'd me." His head flung toward the house. "The way I taught her to." His teeth scored a thumb. "And because I'm back."

On the upper road came the yearning siren of an ambulance. She glanced up, counting on her fingers as always. No, all are safe. Were safe. "You were in there?"

Heaving, he nodded. Clasping himself, he dropped to

his haunches. The dying siren is still faintly traceable. Like the scream she can never make.

What's he told her? In the somber precincts which she imagines his mind to inhabit, his automaton patrolled, trained not to observe itself. Or to take clues from others. When these pressed, when she did—it fled. But where?

She dropped to the ground beside him. Arms around him she rocked with him, exchanging the same spongy, adolescent gulps. She's no better at it than he is. Behind them the tin-voiced psychiatrist, forefinger on lips, stole away with high, exaggerated sickroom steps.

Ray's jacket, rooted in, turned up a handkerchief, big and European, a red darn in one corner. Tearing from the darn, he took the smaller strip, handing her the other. "I smell. I'm sorry."

His bedside manner. As cool and distant to himself as to any patient. If he revolts himself, if it's sometimes human to, he will never realize it. This will always terrify her.

"So do I." But I can handle it.

Standing up again, she blew her nose with a strong tweak, crumpled the strip into a ball and threw it, far.

He watched it disappear. For a moment it floated; it was linen. He crumpled the darned half in his pocket. "Look—I'm going to ship out now. I'll write." First to Charles. To all of them in time—I'm no fiend. Charles was the only one he'd miss, but this a father must never say. Let her keep her own illusions about loving all of them.

He's never looked so canny to her. "And the kids, Ray?"

"Handle it."

Aie. Relief—like a stomach-blow. Then power, bathing her. They were always mine.

He's getting up to go. He was never a father.

Then she's scrambling after him. But I was going to be the one. To leave.

The trilling of the birds began again. Observing them had been his passion once; she never seemed to notice them. He watched her with interest, just as when a boy, eye to the grass, he used to watch the underleaf life. Conscientiously, as if in domestic habit, she seized his jacket from the ground; will she put it on again? No, she's walking with it, absently whipping it in the wind. Still unseeing, she drapes it on a bush. The night before giving birth, women and dormice houseclean. Always foreshadowing, women are. Dooming themselves. Yet the fluid lines and swells of her have an easeful devotion to the ground and to their own rhythm which stings him with the same envy animals incite; if she were to pad off on all fours he wouldn't be surprised.

Facing the river, head bent—can she be smiling? Taken by vagary, she reminds him of the way indoor birds, perched in an aviary or hung in a cage at the vets, shift irrationally to the climate, or the visitors or their own innards—with exactly the same innerfixed eye.

Now she's standing in front of him, her feet planted apart. From going barefoot, her feet have broadened but acquired personae. The right one can pick up sticks; the left one's still lady-delicate. "So—we're both leaving. So this is the logical life." Her breasts jut at him aggressively. "We-ll, will you look at them?" she said, eyeing down at them. "My two jokes."

The sun is up. Or its forward artillery, gilding her, the hillside, the house, in readiness. She stands tall, triumphant. a column of sunshine, blinding him.

From beyond the hill, again the mad toularou-rourou of the ambulance. He tensed. "Where's it coming from?"

"Tappan. Coming back."

And over the hill to the hospital. He tracked it. Fading

north, to where if he stayed on here he might be meeting it. A gray soothe of abdication closed over it.

"So—both of us," he said. "Yes, what a surprise. I thought it would only be you."

She's speechless. She dropped back on her green hummock. A pillar, collapsed inward from its middle. Speech is her pride. It flashes over her—why. She equates it with getting there first.

"For me to make the break—" he's saying at her elbow. "At first I thought it was only the disease. You know me. But it was in me to do. All this time." His face drooped at her in the ultimate shyness. Of self-understanding. "I was never sure you'd be ready to, tell the truth. Maybe I banked on it. James and I both." His expression is sad, generous. "So I'll be off soon, eh? I'll go up the hill and borrow Charlie's Volks. I know where he keeps the key." He swallows. "Kept it."

The grass she was plucking turned to hay as she tore it. But I banked on you. From the beginning so help me, I must have banked on you. To stay. "Well, go on then, why don't you." From the bottomless sulk it came, fretful, spiteful—and yet humorous? "Go on, yes." She looked down at her breasts. "We don't want you—on our bus."

"Our?" When he was in his "surgery" his face still refocussed like this. Tightening his best feature, a marked triangularity of the upper lids. In a tender scrutiny not of her or any patient, but of his own inner fund of competence. Early on, this look had roused her like an aphrodisiac; she'd had spells of putting a hand on him at eleven o'clock in the morning in his own waiting-room, or luring him into the trumped-up partitions behind it, where in his first years he'd done his own biologicals. He'd thought her jealous of his trade. What she'd wanted was to sleep with that competence. Blending her envy of it in him, with him. By the time he came to bed, he'd always lost it. Or in the last years even by merely crossing the little limbo passage which connected office with house. He'd never had the power to diagnose *her*.

Ah but it was always muddling—the images she had. When that happens—accuse. "That's what you thought, didn't you. A man coming for me on it. Who I'm waiting for?"

He shook his head. "No. Or not exactly. What are you? Waiting for."

So thin a vision. She gripped the ground. "What I said. To be seen."

"Guess I've been alone too much." He stared away from her. "With the religious. Who're often very matter-of-fact."

She heard her own flat laugh. "On the subject of adultery?"

No. On the subject of real thorns, in real flesh. And absolute desert-wanderings. "I thought you meant to board the bus. Or try."

"*Board* it." Her glance swept down over herself. Clearly it had never crossed her mind.

"We'd a case once." On his balcony he'd sometimes thought of it. "Horrie let her on with the morning crowd without seeing her. Rest were too stunned to say. Bly saw her at the police station later. Said she was perfectly rational." Just call me a streaker, she'd said. And let my children know.

The sky is pink behind her, silhouetting her dark. "I never heard. You never said."

Nights you came home from town—from the hairdresser, with your hair electric from bed—how should you hear? Asking me to shake hands with my own sons. No, I never said.

"They hushed it up."

"Who was she?"

"Those two women I made a call on once? The younger one. The soft blonde. With the puzzled face." She thinks he never notices.

She didn't move. "She left her children behind."

Over at the Kellihys a deep whimpf-whimpf began vibrating through the trees. The largest dishwasher in the world, it sounded like. The Kellihys are cleaning up.

"Party?"

She doesn't answer. The lawn between her and him, them and the Kellihys, the river and all of them, stretches astrally, giving up the last of the dark.

"Remember that young guy we found on the lawn once?" he said eagerly. "Remember?" Gave him coffee in my office, and offered him a paper examining-robe. No thanks doc, I'm fine, he said. "Been sleeping on a rainbow, for a fact. My belly still feels the arch," he'd said. And strode off free as air.

He saw she was shivering. Elbow on knee, chin in hand, like Rodin's The Thinker—though she'll never in this life resemble it. "I wanted witnesses." Her voice is hoarse. "When I should want—deeds." She flung her arms up, to that audience of hers. And rolled over, face flat to the grass.

Should he go now? She always left it to him. To be irresolute.

Spain has made his ears sharp. Beyond the morning sounds thrusting the day up he hears a familiar ping-ping. The paper-boy here is earlier than most; the road's accepted his zeal. Or the river has. What he himself will remember of this place forever is the barcarolle-ing splash of children in its water, the clickclack pingpong tracery of Charles and himself on the porch, even the muffled thump, impartially muted, of Royal's foot.

The paperboy's as slow as he's early; can't see him yet through the trees. Or he's stopping at Kellihys', though it's long past the first of the month. Short shrift he'll get there if they've been giving parties. He himself has never sent them a bill. The Kellihys give our parties; they streak for us. But like all true partygivers, never on principle. So it doesn't help.

She's still lying there as if she'll knit herself to the grass. In a cleansing energy.

He'll remember her as a voice. Always a voice.

The boys? They need no tallying, never have. Unlike as they are, they're his body natural. Which remembers them.

Add Maureen, dutifully—as the one he always forgets.

And the other one. Don't name her.

He checks that window. Not there.

A witness is not what he needs. He rubs his face, his hands. Yes brother-in-law, I need to hide. But that's for later. Before that—a deed.

Done. Such a small deed. He stands watching her.

Eyes closed, lips pressed into weeds, she's boarding the bus. Mounting its steps in her own skin, that last disguise. What's the reason for this charade?—ah, she'll tell them. How it is that women who meant to assert the personal confused it with the female.

Passengers may include a few women who work the early shift at the next town's paperbox factory, but by and large the aisles would be crammed with commuting men, cleanshaven and breakfasted. She'd stand just past the driver. Schedule-freak that he is, he won't be stopping. But it wouldn't help him to keep his head down.

What she wants to tell him and them is what goes on below all the talk-talk, below even the silent screaming—to give them a psychograph of her own dark interior, and what deeply murmurs there. Of how it is to be a Lexie-on-the-hill, waiting for a Ray to find her. In the ultimate sulk—as if she's always expected the synopsis of her life to be played by some winsome but unimportant movie-star. Of how all her life she has felt the humiliation of having small aims.

Naked on a bus; can't explain, can't say a word. Of how in all the exercises of her life—meals to be made, children to be made—she's dealt only in small patterns concluded. Of how, each morning, a woman had to project her own poem on the populace. A hopeless situation. Yet daily it was done—with a nylon soup-net. Compounding the absurdity, the ego and the humiliation all at once. And the soup. So that while the men before her can go ragged with inconclusiveness—in tragic asymmetry—she's been allowed the minimal satisfaction of small ambitions quenched. While the men keep for themselves the tors unscaled, the grinding treks which come to nothing—the great, souring inconclusiveness of life.

She raises her head to see who she's been telling this to. Maybe only one woman, dozing behind her babuska. But all the men are looking back at her, eyes bloodshot with the experience of keeping women like her. They include: A redheaded man—who goes in early, in order to keep two of them. One Robert Kellihy, Jr., whose four cars are out of gas, whose pocket is out of money but has turned up a one-way ticket—and whose presence in the city is that morning required by his mother, at nine o'clock sharp. And there in the back seat—with his felonious masher's hands showily on top of his raincoat—is the village molester, gazing outraged on her nakedness.

What did the streaker say, bravura—"I am your Representative"?

And what would she herself say? "This is the way it is, it is. And it has nothing to do with sex"?

Hadn't she heard the bike? That boy would see her. And him. He stands stooping but tall, his deed done.

Up on the road overlooking their riverbank, the bike stopped. He could feel the boy standing there, in depth-charge quiet. Then the shouted syllables rolled over him, over her, motionless there.

The bike moved on. The boy's second shout skimmed back through the trees.

She rolled over, luxuriously flat to the sky. Lazily an arm lifted in backward salute, flopped again. "What'd he say?"

"Sin. Sin and damnation."

"He doesn't count," she muttered, stretching sensuously, and sat up. *"Ray!"*

He felt foolish. Country-suburban devilish—and without a party's excuse. His naked buttocks are dudes to this air. A good enough frame, and well-hung, but in younger locker-rooms these days his shoulders look rounded. He has left on the shoes.

"Ah he counts with me," he said, eyes glinting.

A man's body—husband, father or lover—shouldn't it look more resolute? All the bodies that had been on hers have been admirable ones. Yet, all male bodies seem to her to be still hunting their armor. Even that chub gladiator the caterer's boy, shedding his jeans in slit-eyed arrogance, or standing naked in his ten-gallon hat, would be belied somewhere—maybe by a rib slender as glass, or the target hip-plate above the angry sex, or the mutely hollowed clavicle. They're caves of bone, in which deeds must, *must* generate.

He's moving off.

"Where you going?"

"Where'd you think?"

"You going to walk down the road like that."

He stood still. "No, I'm like you. I never thought of it."

Some yards further on he was climbing down the bank. "Going in," she heard him call. "Clean myself off."

"Take off your watch," she heard herself call back.

So now were they that suburban couple who merely got up a little sooner than the rest? And lay out in the non-wild, hoping for kicks?

Over the bank the watch came flying at her, landing with a thud.

So we're not the stuff of legends. Or not yet.

He hates river swimming. But borrowing another person's gestures—or hers—is useless. He'd tried before this to say silently "I side with you"; he never gets it right. This time, at least she hadn't laughed. That startled "Ray!" even warms him.

From out here he had a seal's view of the strip of town. The gently antediluvian houses straggled the waterside and hill in placements which often seemed to follow some conformation or purpose long gone. He could see clearer from here how life-in-general pushed its hollows through the earth, and through people. He could safely regard how he and she came to live in one of those houses. How he'd made them come. Because the city was his rival; he could never have hung onto her there. Bright as she is, she'd never suspected it. People always came to the suburbs because of something. It was travel parodied.

Down in the underwater the Hudson was briny dark. Eel on bottom, shad still to be netted in May, and crab returning, but on the surface utterly trafficless. A summer morning without inflection, holding the land in pause. In the river the great teeming pause which was life. Riverbottom thoughts, one got here. Does she know yet what he does? That men at their best don't swim in couples but for the planet only?

Carefully he stroked back from the central channel, which was timbreless and very deep. Eyes open to the oily Pleiades ahead, nosing through the brown alluvial shorewater, he was swimming for the planet and with it, like everything else down here. And up above. His fingers grasped land; he vaulted onto its shelf. Not bad—he'd have years yet. Not to live in the future only, always denying it.

Halfway up the bank he turned back again. Hector's shoes—he'd left them down below; better get them. Airports were prosy about bare feet. For his flight back he'd as soon be thermally protected only, in some friar-stuff of brown or white. It had always half surprised him, that for flights into what just might be forty thousand feet that much nearer God, the air-services didn't provide even temporary migrants with some such stripped-down uniform. After he'd made clear his intention to work in the ward, maybe Hector, now reduced to his dead brother's medical black serge, would dig up for him one of the old monk-tunics the Sisters surely had saved.

Up on the roadside again his own clothes are where he'd dropped them. "Conservatively" pinstriped and dotted, they seem to him now a clown's. But on the undershirt is one of the ward-woman's crazy red darns, with which half the hospital-gowns were spotted. He put the shirt back on, for affection. Plus his undershorts, against allergy. Poison-oak sprouted here every spring. Chess, who'd inherited his bones, his tender skin— and it might be, the hoarded soma of a lifetime of dreams unrecollected—once swelled to dropsy from it. Lexie, toughskinned as a gypsy, is immune.

Approaching, he saw she'd arranged herself on elbow—and on circumstance. This nonproducing ripple of land he's provided her with has just enough rise. For much of the day its cranky, offshoot road remains hermetically empty. But shortly a few persons traveling of necessity south will have a champion view—for one camera moment longer than life—of a woman with a river behind her. And he can see how for her to set herself up as signal is appropriate. The bodies of women lurch beyond anatomy. Toward what may be obscure—but artists have spent paint on it.

She's been disposing of her two extra men, which through all the movie-colored infatuation has been how she'd thought of them and had treated them. One, in spite of his pose of hunting only sex in her, had helped her respect her mind. The other, hungering for other people's talents as the rich sometimes starved for protein, had given her a candidate's hopes. Both had shown her that she's had four kids by a man who, in the pure matters of the body—which run on carnally to the heart—is bitterly and maybe hopelessly shy.

When he sits down beside her the fertile river is shining from him. For a moment she's almost sure he's going to cover her with himself; then it passes, in her, and maybe in him. The air's tingeing peach, pearly acrid as a baby's sweat.

She sneaked a look at him. Never coarse enough for her? But surely the rape was mutual? Thinking back on how it was with her, she isn't sure. Youth-sex, hot for immersion, and a young mind already in extremis, in its urge not to be eunuchoid. A matter of the spirit—with the sexual self conniving. Against her abiding fear that all her relationships would be with herself.

But the man beside her is still the mystery she raped. She could slice his throat to raw meat with her armed tongue, before he could tell her what he thinks.

Where's she walking to? To the high edge of this riverbank, which here falls away in raw fissures and mesas for ants, down to the soggy pebbleline below. No one could build here; what's he been saving it for?

Her ankles have swollen with the night's heat; her buttocks are redprinted with weed. The pattern of my wife's backside changes with the season and the sofa; I must assume a similar swell in her brain. Women and the moon were both oedematous—part of their charm. Stark naked—she's gone behind a bush to pee.

He recalled how after Charles was born the contour of her back became as he could glimpse it now through the scrawny bush—fatally thickened from the outline of girl. And how this had frightened him, repelled him almost. For as he now knew, this was the most subtle sign of maternity; a woman could become nearly skeletal and still keep that contour. While by the time a faint prolapse in his own belly had occurred, it was age, not fatherhood.

Yet Charles has been accepted at Harvard and Oxford both—and hasn't yet told her. Instead writing him—in the formal misery which keeps his son untouchable yet keeps them kin—that he can't decide. "Of course Boston's conveniently near Chessie's school." Then a paragraph down: "Would you mind if I went into medicine too, the mental side of it?" And finally the postscript stopper. "I think I understand what you might be hassling with, Dad. I'm reading William James' *Varieties of Religious Experience.*"

To be understood like that. Lightly, without moral suasion, by one's own child. He felt the grace of fatherhood. His son's heart, firmly transplanted on the pocket-ruin of his own.

Tears haggled for his face.

Relieving herself, she said goodbye to this beloved promontory, its nile weeds and crystal sky. A lookout, a lighthouse even, but conservationist to the end. Up here it all went into the chlorophyll, women like her included. Downriver her city tumbles heavenward, a Chartres of waste. But within it are all the trampoline hills, multileoparded. A language-thrill went through her— nonsexual. I never wanted to be ideal—only alive. Joy alone was never my thesis. She saw the winter city as she used to, its darkly scarlet innards—of people, sunsets, chickens—scattered on the stonegray streets. In those iceberg evenings which harshened down on many lines of troubled roof, could her life pursue some thesis, unfinished maybe, but always emancipating from the too pure arch of self? There will they let her be that— objective? Not a gender but a human animal rising?

She stared down at the clump of weed she'd wetted. "Called dock in the vernacular" the children's flowerbook said. "Otherwise *snakewort*, or *adder's root.*" Once it was rumored here that someone had managed to grow a dafora, a plant from a warmer clime and poisonous; when it bloomed was why the woods smelled of shit and sirocco— threatening. Others said it was only a native mulberry dropping its tassels and pulp in some secret acre not yet built upon. There were no real crops here. Yet these mysteries are what she hopes to remember, hopes the children will, when they're grown. Though from now on with them she must keep to the vernacular. They'll have enough to bear without her language forcing them to bloom before their time.

She can smell herself steaming up from the shiny leaves. Dogs stunt a path that way. Afterwards turning their backs on their mess, their hindlegs scuffing. Trembling, she tore at a sparrowgrass bush, dropping fronds on the spot where she'd been. She knew the mess her language had made. All she'd meant to do was to carry her family with her, rung by rung, as the pulse of the world flooded her, lifting them along with her, bootstrap insight by insight—but always domestically—as was happening to her. All she'd meant to do was to characterize the world for them. She'd been forging it—her language. But once empowered, there's no hiding it. At times the woods behind her house must fill with the smell of female dissenter, rank as a new menses. And with the odor of childbloom forced.

Peering through the bushes she saw he wasn't watching her but the river. How Buddha-quiet he'd grown; that old tee-shirt might already be a monk's singlet. With one holy darn. Ever-suggestible he is, yet hard. In all their children there's some of that. Of him.

Be off then, Ray. Will I be the one to go back to the house?—I always am. Yes leave me. To the self-pity I can never master.

She stole a look at her house. It's always our house, whether we choose it or not. There you are, nanny-house. Still guarding those loving banditti, my children. Who'll suck us dry if they have to, because they have to. Because they too are in thrall. To the flesh we've given them.

Stay, nanny. Hang on just a little while yet; I'm coming. One village to pass; then I'll cross the road to you. And what'll I do then?

She drew a long breath, lifting her. I'll organize.

Her body's wealed, scratched, swollen feverish and

ever vulnerable. Its bare soles never harden sufficiently. Abusing it helps.

Let him dare laugh, she thought, emerging. He's clothed.

She's grinning down on him, half superior, half abject. But with the quick self-ridicule which always rescued her, she shrugged, sweeping a glance over herself—an actress throwing a line away. "This is the way it is, Ray. Without pearls."

Without his pearls. Cheap hurts she can always inflict. But she can never steel herself to the big ones. Will that still do her in?

He can see her in that city flat he'll do his best to pay for—maybe one near Royal's hospital, and also convenient enough to her brother's so that she can leave in nightly charge Maureen. Who's suitable to leave, and in the daytime will sweep. In time will her mother find a job—in one of the talking disciplines? In order to become one of those women at her brother's parties—those evening Statues of Liberty, with their hair in braids instead of spikes? Who more often than not, he'd observed, had a child at home to sweep.

And a string of pearls from the past, now and then wearable. For a couple of James's black girls, lazily stretching their zebra necks and flower-toed feet in a party-corner, to laugh at.

"No, never trust your brother," he said. "But I suppose you'll go on seeing him."

"My brother?" She smiled, flopping down beside him. Her hazel smile, big-eyed. She can't help her innocent coloring. "He and I have a mutual friend. Who's finally made me see what James is to me. Has always been. James is the way I know my own force." She snapped her fingers, an odd gesture in a naked woman. But that appeared to be the end of James. It would take some odd gestures, that's for sure—to be rid of him.

"The city's deep, Lexie. Deep." He studied the tangling shoreline of the river; he should have known that sooner or later it would lead her there. The river was her lifeline, while she was here.

"Deep?" She flung her exalted, alto laugh at him. "I'm out of my depth—and I mean to stay there."

He retreated. He knows her depth.

She sneaked a look at his watch, still there on the ground. Soon men will be standing at every river streetcorner, with their watches strapped to their wrists. Not a one of them on this road was born here. Ah how good it was to know an environment—any—but in your very grain, dusting your brain dark forever, searing your heart in tannic light. The city's not deep, only multiple. It might look like a clutch of verticals aiming at God but its history was always horizontalizing, all connection and disconnection going on at once. There I can travel out from what I am, and no one the wiser—except everyone. Maybe to be what I am, without benefit of where? No—that's poetry.

She wondered what sex Tom Plaut's baby had been. And Mrs. Plaut's. Women don't live by images alone, Tom; perhaps by now he knows. But Plaut's language was the public one the minute he was born. In the eyes of the world he and it have a continuity of scrutiny, on an altogether different scale. Painful to him at times maybe, but marvelous—to all those who have only voice.

I know that to some I'm all voice; maybe that's why.

Here's Ray, who has almost none. And married her for it. "The coloratura's husband," James said scathing, behind Ray's back once. And Charles rushed at him.

Listen, all of you. Even Dad, whom I haven't much thought of in a long time. All of you with whom I've had argument. That was Girlbud. This is Lexie speaking. To herself:

Lexie. If a language is so private it makes people stare—then make it public. Make it a deed.

Could I do that, she thought, awed. In some small station of life—which might get to be an outpost—could I be workhorse to an idea? Not a proclamation. Or even a treatise. A little manual of my own. On how it keeps with us. One person's manifest—on keeping on.

Awareness—yes, she lives for it. But not like Charlie's philosophers, under world-mandate. Because she has to. Hers being a special case of it, which the world finds ungraspable. She'd have to define it herself—and still not fall in love with it. Only to end up circling that tunnel-of-selflove which the world called "sensibility," and was particularly happy to attach to the awakenings of her kind.

She wonders humbly whether she will have to be an intellectual.

He's been watching her. Hunched there—the way rebels are? No—though she may think so. In the way of those patients who, after long cures, are signed out. He's seen it often in those discharged by rule in wheelchairs even if they can walk—this sudden adoration at the door. There's one scratch on her breast should be seen to.

"Lexie." His hand touched hers, pressed on its own privates. "Lexie—there's still time." To go back across the road and be normal again. Back into the house, both of us.

"Oh, there's time, *time*—and thank God for it. Thank you for reminding me. Ray—thank you for many things." Her face shone. Out that door. He could tell from her voice. "So wait with me, if you want to." Her eye flicked once-over him. A wife with her spouse, entering some fete of an importance both are unaccustomed to. "Anyway you want to."

So they wait, each trailing generosities which fade and return.

There's a barge on the river now, traveling as they always did, south.

"Look at it." He pointed angrily. "Piled high with slag. What can the city want with it?"

"They put out to sea." Her hand clasped her mouth. "All that charnel. That I used to know about. I know none of it anymore. Nothing."

"Out to sea. To burn it. Or to dump."

She showed her teeth. "I may want to know damnation too. It's my right."

The trilling of the birds began again, that sound which always seemed to her to speak the one road, the true path, when all it meant was that summer—or winter—was done. The house-of-cloud is gone. Gone in like a moon. All the while, it was her house.

Shuddering, she bowed her head. Whatever she is has come about because she sees herself as the irrationally mute half of things. As they see her. So that when she does speak, she screams.

And still she waited, for him or one of them or all of them, every cell in her screaming to be found—to be found tragic, equal, necessary. In equal part.

What's he whispering?

"It's like being in the stocks, out here. Isn't it. Like being put in the stocks." With each urging word his hands find a purchase on her, clenching her thigh, buttock, abdomen as if she's cold putty he's molding. Her neck—in iron hands she'd never felt before. Her hair. "That why you were lying here?" The whisper tongued her ear. Sank by an undisclosed channel into her breast. "Look up there then, Lex. Look."

No. She knew what he wanted her to see. Ancient wooden stocks, once in the village square, were now preserved in the vestry of the Dutch Reformed Church. Where eight-year-old Chess, malingering after Sunday School, once got herself caught in them. After everyone had gone. No, don't look up there. Bury your head deep.

Nowhere to put it, except her own fundament. This was why women wore skirts.

Up there. In the bay-window. The figure that's always

· 314 ·

there. The girl who's always cold, and never feels it. The blot-head. Looking down at them.

Feel cold, Mother? Stupidly bare? In the world of those who aren't you and me, who pull the wool over themselves? What you harbor against little Roy, Mother—that cool tinkle of self-confessed guilt—that's nothing. Against this other monstrous tenderness which dooms me. To be wombed again with you. Your other monster child.

Dig your fingers into the ground, Lexie. As night beyond night you've dug them into pillow, bed, Ray's breast—against the undertow urge to rush in and put your arms around the girl up there for keeps—to be as murderously sick. To say: Eat me—for putting you into the world with your angry hunger for me. Eat. My nipple is still in your mouth. My brain is your brain. That double counterpart. If we could, we would bed with it. Like sister children, running away. To each other's wombs.

The figure was gone.

Yes, the stocks. Male and female used to be paired there together. As if their sins could ever be the same, or their damnations either.

His hands worked against themselves, kneading. Water'd done nothing for the slick on them. He held them out to her mutely. Hers were strong with housecraft. Clasping them over his she held their joined hands quiet. "What, what—?" she crooned, absently gentle, as to a child. "Something on them, eh? What, what?"

He bent over that fourhanded fist. Mutual blame. It must be what we yearn to rest from in the afterlife. Or in foreign wards, or vacantly public tasks.

"Parental slime."

He saw that her body had aged overnight; it had already begun to hoard up their guilt for them. What overpowered a woman in herself, what finally overpowered the men who loved them, was so curiously the same. They interpose their bodies between themselves and all events.

He pities her, this lost cohabitant of his planet. With the pity one has for foreigners, in one's native place. It's what Hector and Isaac will feel toward him.

She's thinking that their story was deformed from the beginning; there was no way of telling it classically. Or is there. Two people so unaware, yet they have come to the riverbank in the end.

Or is it the awareness, when it comes—mine—that deforms, since it speaks. The old legends, maybe they were better. Two bowed down and wending their way, as in a paradise lost—but still paradise?

She sat back on her heels, an open palm attentive on each thigh. It's her condition. Perhaps their story would be only as deformed as human stories are.

"It's the same, isn't it," he said suddenly, loudly. "In any walk of life."

What can he mean? Is he awarding her one? His face has assembled itself. Where's the trembler of a minute ago, the father? Sloughed.

Ah, she'd know him anywhere—this other one. This tribe.

"The same," she breathed, softly mocking. And now indeed, they are separate.

He too sits on his heels, thumbs linked behind him.

How we've traveled.

Did she say that aloud? Or not?

Dreaming there, he doesn't answer.

There was something she had to tell the children about him at once. She can't remember it.

It seems to him that they have had their heart-to-heart. Life has prepared them. Out of their differences awarding them the silence other people found in love.

Is it so strange then that he's reaching for her with the same engrafting movements those other people find?

As he smoothes that wild hair and scraped breast and

mounts what melts toward him, it seems that he and she are rehearsing what would have been their middle age together, even their old age. Who hasn't seen such couples?—he's had more scope than most. Two musing at the edge of a bed or across a table, nodding absently at each other's totems—at the totem the other now is. Each conceding at last the vital process of the other—now that there's not much of it left.

It's not that her zones are up, submerging her; physically she's long since a professional. Or that she doesn't know—even on the open ground she once craved—that he can never be her nakedness. It's that what first raped her in him has grown strong on him again.

He climbs on her. The foreigner.

The bus, lumbering out of the cove a mile north to backfire the shot that set off the early-morning race here, hove itself out onto the shore road.

In the same plunged second that he reminded himself where he was, where they were—and held on as he could anyway, she rolled him off.

They sat up, slow-motion, in the bruised, unfinished way one did. In the confusion of not being animal enough.

He picked up his watch, strapping it on, winding it intently. Ashamed—that he can never brutalize.

"Sorry, Lex."

"Don't be. Nothing would have changed."

He saw it square. To him their children have always been the real interruption of the sexual fugue. To her—would it still be the telephone—that unremitting hole which drained his services from her?

She sat on her haunches, airing the rawness between.

How maiden he looks—they look—when this happens. When that long muscle of theirs falls short. Once, at

317 ·

one of these times, she'd rushed to a mirror, to catch the moment of coition still on her face, and was shock-pleased to see that white vacuity. To see her rational self—a self which so often pained her because it so often had to go begging—beaten into dazement.

"Nothing," he said. "And afterwards anyway—all animals are sad."

"They are?" How could one know? "Are you?" She waited, for his slow nod. "I'm not. Or not really. It's not exact enough. For what I feel."

"An old saw," he said. He was still winding his watch. "What do you feel. Afterwards."

How ignorant she is. Many must have recorded that non-personal afterglow—has any of her sex ever tried?

She'll have to get it right, or else no use to it. Holy ardor toward the act itself—is that what she feels? And toward the natural world that allows it.

"I feel loyal," she said. "To the situation."

In her language. Exactly.

But other people stare.

Let them.

She's folded her arms in the cradle position. A palm under each elbow, like a plinth. As if he's in there. All his shrunken baby-parts exposed.

"And to the man, if you want the bloody truth." Her mouth wrinkled, folded into her teeth, opened wide for a taut, oval cry that never came, and fell back smooth as a bud, young. "Loyal to every one of them."

He saw that he'd broken the watch. But it had been accurate. Bus is on time. Old engine still had the same miss in it, projected far ahead by the wet river air. Quiet now and again. Then it grunted on, in a lurch of gas. Hard-breathing at each corner, it's picking up a life at every stop. Set lives, as his own had been. But I wasn't a patient yet. I was only practicing.

The gassy smell was energizing.him. What he needs now isn't blood but the smell of motion. Oh I needed blood though. In sickness we carnify. One haunted message maybe—to a life. To be worn in secret on a sacred thong. All the rest an iridescent fever of the cells—then the dark green mold of the bones going back to the energy scum? She's still squatting there. Hearing what?
"Bus is on time," he said.

"I hear it." Yammering brassy for each customer. Stuttering on.

This is the brink moment, Lexie, just before the image you nurture is broached to the world. All private images of any intensity are lunatic, until externalized. After that it's up to you. And the world. Whichever one you choose. Or are chosen by. When enough people chose a same world, then there might be a religion, or the art of piano-playing—neither of which is her icon. Or the fine art of loitering in the Hotel de Ville and letting music in as many registers as known pass through you—which is.

Here it comes down the road, all her village. Gossip binding those in the bus mouth-to-mouth with those there was no room for. Will you stand up in salute, Lexie? Or lie down as you began. With your ear to the ground.

She begins to count off by streetcorners and house-numbers. Every straggle of path and wall is engraved on her it seems, each house by shape and catalogue—wood of white or brown, or black-shuttered, stucco stained with damp the way old linen does, and the earliest houses here—of clapboard above and undershot jaws of rose-geranium brick. She can stroll the whole prospect, to re-arrange a leaf. In allegiance. It's not leaving her as it should be. This eccentric inlet whose gloss already twangs bit-tersweet in her ear: Landing Way, Ricer Street, Bitker Terrace, Route Nine—a faraway eddy of a river road I once lived on. What are the streetnames in Tierra del Fuego; what would she find there? Waves of rearing anthracite foaming rabid at all newcomers—but when once lived near, revisiting the beach like native mind?

And I forgot the Village Hall—were any children still sleeping there? Cottage by cottage, by new-plastered bargain and august house with five porches, all rotten, the parents are returned, fast or loose in their beds. But here and there now, one by one a man pops out a door, not stopping for history; everybody knows what commuters do. Why do they keep following her, the fathers, each on his time-wheel, each in his slot?

Except at the Kellihys.

Was that the bus halting; who could it be picking up there? Red spurts of music, white honeysuckle of a breeze in the throat, always the caterers thumping their dogsbody rhythms—when did it stop? Don't stop the music, Bets. Or the babies either. Take in the paper, Bob. Good neighbors helped pay for it.

What's the bus waiting so long for at Kellihys'? A caterer's boy?

Yards away, it can't have seen her yet. In her bower visible only direct in from the crown of the road. Or from her house. Where, rubbing his black furry arch against one of the stone pillars which mark the path to his doorway, is her cat.

She could go back in there for good. Back alone, to resume her valuable reflections. Or could she persuade him, Ray, that enough has happened in the red-dark of themselves; it need never be externalized? Yes—bright, crude but competently drawn as a lithograph, she can see the two of them sauntering out of the bushes, hands joined in the approving sight of all. What's she doing here, except holding herself up to view more literally than most?

Ah no, an education has begun here; she won't fault it. She's one of the lucky ones, who wake in time to see the arrow sticking in the morning cereal: Rehearse for Age. A circumscribed life can be useful. Boiling down the evening alcohols, the herbal rages, until you have enough brown stock for dynamite. Even the landscape here has helped, lifting her high on its silver salver, so that she might see moral hints even in a downpour of rain. And images, in their season.

It's not that the force with which she sees herself is fading. Only that her wretched body is thrashing itself into as many angles and simperings as a woman trying on a hat, a bridal gown, and a pair of blood-proof rubber-pants, all in the same mirror. She sees her vision of herself as she ought to be now. Not this trembling body which has lost its confidence. A Niké, a winged victory—modest class. A woman damaged enough to be classical. Would she have arms—or should these be stumps? May she have a head?

Release me, body. Not from life. Just enough—to slump easy. To be able to just—lurch on through. Release me—body which acts like mind.

She rose on hands and knees, to any eye a whole woman, looking back at her house. Never to be turned to stone by the sight—though she might pray to be. The house recedes, a gothic moth only hovering. Ready still, at a word from her, to hold them all on its wings yet awhile? No, it knew her better than herself, had always known. That she was the face in the pool, terrified but rising steadily. To set fire to her own house.

A yearning pang struck her, straight from the birth-couch. Then it was gone. Prepare to be ashamed now—of being ashamed.

Poor old bus, he thought, getting to his feet, craning to see. On the blink again? In front of Kellihys'. Where Horrie must be having to climb over half of tonight's story before they'll let him phone the garage.

Poor Lexie here, behind him. What frail hopes she always floats her images on. On a bus. On me.

There comes Horrie. Bouncing out of Kellihys' and into the bus again, for one more try. Or to consult. Good old Horrie, the bus'll be saying; he stays the route. Meaning that we all do.

For, poor Lexie, how we switch bargains on you. How

we use you, to fox yourself in the end. That bus, your village—you're not merely waiting for it. It's following you, always following you. To watch how the nude bargain comes out.

What's that other familiar revving, up the hillside? Between them and Kellihys'.

In Spain, at eleven A.M. every day except Sunday, in the public square under his balcony the same little hunched bug of a car starting up the time-wheel in his head.

Breakfast-time in Grand River, and his son the all-night reader going out for it. Or some of that legion he lends his car to.

No wonder it won't move, the way they load it.

Smiling to himself though he'll have to find other transport, he urges on the old rattletrap. Get going, youngsters. Up this early, to wherever you're off to. There—they've got it running. Smooth. There it goes.

Fading. Gone.

"Somebody's taken out the Volks."

Did a spasm of maternity plump her cheeks? "Charlie. Going for buns."

Holy are the meals prepared by children's hands.

In one of those purses which were her attaché-cases—tucked well down in a bunch of those hieroglyphs of her life which when dumped on a table could be ridiculed both for their insignificance and their inclusiveness—was the flyer the troupe of Chasids once thrust at her on that last solitary city outing; she'd never been able to throw it away. It contained instructions on the mission of women, and girls. Which was—to light the dark world, from the family distance. All its admonitions, crowding Chasidic, were those same ones more commonly directed, without regard for race or religion toward all her kind. But the flyer was more practical. It gave the candle-lighting times for all major American cities. And the procedure by which, in whichever one she found herself, she might cast her holy light to illumine the world—without entering it:

First light the candles . . .

I do it. A candle as high as a house.

. . . then cover your eyes with your hands to hide the flame.

I do. Look here.

At this point you may recite the blessing.

I do. I do. I do. In the double language *under* language, which they never hear:

Airt. Moil. Bast. And Belding's Corticelli—which is not Betelgeuse. To be a compass, a guide. To toil, to drudge. To be flexible, as bark. And to hang like a star—by a thread.

I recite the blessing, for all my tribe. Which until yours hears it, will infiltrate the children, and hallucinate the world.

But how to say it in a language they understand? The common one.

She lays her ear to the ground, where she can hear the voice of the Thruway, a religion of onward swaying her dais and passing through her, the voice of the many calling to the single without sex or need of translation. We are not alone. We are never alone. Here is the apparatus. This is the contract.

Hurry. Answer. Recite the blessing. The bus must be moving again. Ray had his back to her, and was craning up the road.

It's what a blessing might be when it's half banner, half prayer. So that any invoker might stand in a kitchen, or thousands might converge on the Stock Exchange or run to the Champs de Mar to sew it on the air:

KEEP US IN VIEW

And now, let's be silent. Let's none of us speak. Let him speak, at the end.

Turning, he saw she'd stopped her thrashing. But he knows the force of that meditation. She's a woman in a bell-glass, breaking out.

Christ. No—don't lean on Him. Sister Isaac! Attend! What's breaking out of there? An image of his own, long nurtured? The enormous hip rising, the breasts that spout, the mouth a babble of rivers, the Maja, blinding the landscape in her slow assemblage of herself—a rotted widow-leg not burned on the Ganges and now whole again, a tenth finger from a small all-female unit in the first factory of Du Pont de Nemours, a marble foot, never compromised, from Greece?

Plus a head. In the bloody trunk of the neck, the arteries, clamped, are now waiting. Surpliced arms reach for the head—his. Sister Isaac, Sister Judas, attaches it.

He's grinning. Or appears to be. Because she's on all fours, crawling toward events? Not waiting for them to come upon her?

She stands erect. A dinosaur, in the act of extinction, looking round itself for the last time. The homely lines of river, road and hill are already a landscape printed on the page, untouchable.

So this was Eden. And that is why I am here on the riverbank. I am the rib, leaving it. Be aware—and beware. For a rib may magic itself into anything, to while away the long hours of being a rib.

These are her jokes. Will they wheedle her away from that ultimate seriousness in which she's the full half of humankind? She'll have to chance it. What she'll be up against is the sweet-simple scripture hardening in Everyman's arteries from the beginning. The exquisite satire embodied in all Edens will always be at her expense.

And here's the bus, bearing down on them.

Ah Eden, my village. She stretches luxuriously for it, showing the full dimple of herself. Ruined, yes ruined. But only for the suburbs.

He's not grinning. What he wants to do, he hasn't been given the face for.

Lexie. Scream for us.

Ah. Ahhhhhhhhh. I give birth to them. The women. Him. All. Awareness—it's the unnatural, natural act.

And now—I biggen. I recover, from confinement.

But—how to tell the story? Of how people stammer in and out of the dark. In the fiery glades of the families. Into the hairy Everglades of nights that pass into history— knowingly. How to tell the story that's always about to begin?

In the end, Ray took off his shirt. But left on his shorts. So that those who passed would know this was not Eden.

So we sat. The world was all before us.

Then the green latch opens.

Faces yearn in on us.

Time was. Time is.

And the bus passes.

But what has she baubling her ears, hung twinkling in the septum of her nose, indented gemdeep in the forehead—and rubying the warm navel, and sparkling onyx between the legs, in the cleft blur of hair?

It is her body that shines, an illuminated story—in every pore, hanging in cell-song, that sad jewel, Joy.